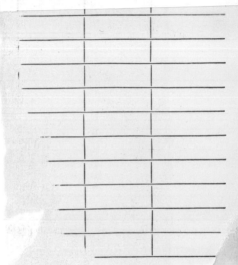

KAYWANA STOCK

*Also by Edgar Mittelholzer and
available in the NEL series:*

CHILDREN OF KAYWANA
KAYWANA BLOOD

Kaywana Stock

Edgar Mittelholzer

151048249

NEW ENGLISH LIBRARY
TIMES MIRROR

© 1954, 1959 by Edgar Mittelholzer

First published in Great Britain by Secker and Warburg Ltd., under the title
The Harrowing of Hubertus, in 1954

❋

Published as an Ace Books edition 1959
Reprinted five times
Published as a Four Square edition 1965

Reissued in a NEL edition January 1968
Reprinted February 1968
New edition February 1969
Reissued in this new edition April 1972
Reprinted January 1974

❋

NEL Books are published by
New English Library Limited from Barnard's Inn, Holborn, London E.C.1.
Made and printed in Great Britain by Hunt Barnard Printing Ltd., Aylesbury, Bucks.

450010465

PART ONE

1

ONE morning in the middle of March, 1763, a terrible rumour came down the Demerary River.

Hubertus van Groenwegel and his family were at prayers when it came.

'Oh, Lord,' prayed Hubertus, 'send down Thy blessings upon this household.' He always prayed in English, which he spoke with fluency, though with a marked Dutch accent. His wife, Rosalind, a Maybury — the Mayburys owned Plantation Signal, ten miles up-river — was English and it was chiefly through her and her family that he had learnt the language. He was very proud of his English — and proud, too, that his four daughters could speak both English and Dutch. About a third of the plantations under private ownership belonged to Englishmen, and Hubertus, because of his knowledge of English, was equally as popular with the English families in Demerary as with the Dutch.

'Oh, Father Almighty, have mercy upon us and protect us from the dangers of the coming day. Assist us in our many tasks and undertakings, and guide us in our decisions that we may mainfully carry out — '

'Manfully,' interrupted Rosalind, softly but clearly, her face quite serious. The faces of the four girls remained serious, too, for this was nothing out of the ordinary. It was an agreed-upon thing between Rosalind and Hubertus that she must correct him whenever he made a slip in his English, no matter what the occasion or the company.

'Manfully,' amended Hubertus, 'carry out our labours on this plantation. We strive to please Thee always, oh, Lord God. Help us to do Thy will, and help us . . . ' Here Hubertus paused. For it was at this point that the loud knocking on the kitchen door sounded.

Rosalind and the four girls opened their eyes, but Hubertus kept his shut. He had an air of stubborn patience. His face did not show any obvious annoyance, but there could be no doubt that he was determined not to let even so unusual an event as a knock on the door at seven in the morning ruin this the first ritual of the day. He was in all things, piety unexcepted, a man of rigid resolve. People sometimes laughed at him, for there was much about him that was absurd, but they never failed to admit that he was a man of character.

Bible held before him between clasped hands, fully dressed for the day, he stood near the sideboard, a shortish, thick-set fellow of thirty-six with a massive head, his face almost mathematically square, his chin strong, his mouth thin-lipped and determined but not markedly cruel. He had black, dead-straight hair – the hair of his mother, a Spanish-Indian half-caste – but his eyes were greyish-green like his Dutch father's. His complexion was a healthy Nordic pink. His whole being exuded a vitality, a magnetism, that was personal and spiritual as well as animal. This vitality added immeasurably to his dignity and force of personality. Indeed, it arrested the laughter of many a would-be-mocker.

Rosalind, an inch or two taller than he, made, by contrast, a by no means inferior figure. Slim – though she had lost her girlish shape – and with a narrow but pretty English type of face, she still possessed, at thirty-four, a fresh, youthful charm. Her blue eyes were steady, and contained a light of courage and integrity. Separated from her husband by the large dining-table, she stood with her back to a window, on the other side of the room, attired in a morning robe, the four girls, in their nightgowns, arranged two on either side of her.

Once again came the knocking on the kitchen door. And now the bare feet of a house-slave could be heard. The bolts of the kitchen door grated, and the sound of the door being opened followed. Then voices in crude Dutch. A slave addressing a slave.

Hubertus continued his prayer. There was a frown on his face. His annoyance at the interruption, however, in no way affected the flow of entreaty addressed to the Almighty. For he knew that no slave would dare enter the dining-room until Prayers were over.

'Our Father . . .' And Rosalind and the girls joined in the Lord's Prayer. When it was over, Hubertus' manner relaxed. He smiled, and whenever he smiled he appeared quite a mild, uneccentric man. Placing on the sideboard the Bible from which, earlier, he had read a chapter of Isaiah, he wagged his

8

head and said, 'It is that father of yours, my dear. The sugar-mill has broken down again.'

'I'm certain you're wrong,' said Rosalind. 'Father wouldn't send and knock us up at this hour because of the sugar-mill, Hubertus. Wilfred has probably taken ill. He was complaining last week.'

'It's Grandfather,' said Jacqueline. 'He had a headache last week.' She was the eldest, and twelve.

Mary, who was ten, thought it must be old Mr Harker. 'He's dead. Pemba told me he gets dizzy feelings every morning. He's seventy-three.'

'More likely Mrs Harker,' said Rosalind. 'I believe she's going down with the Sickness.' A mysterious epidemic, not unlike typhus, called – for lack of a better name – the Sickness, had been raging in Demerary, and in the neighbouring colonies of Berbice and Essequibo, for more than two years. Slaves and whites were going down with it, many fatally.

Luise and Susan, nine and seven, respectively, were unanimous in their conjecture that the brig from Barbados with Mr Clackson and his wife and daughter had arrived, and their mother suddenly exclaimed and agreed. 'Yes, that is more likely what it is, Hubertus. The brig has been sighted from the Brandwagt, and somebody has sent up a message to the Harkers.' The Harkers, of Plantation Sapphire, lived eight miles down-river.

They stood in a group, waiting for the slave to come in with the message. To have gone out to the kitchen would have constituted a gross breach of dignity. One must never go to a slave; a slave must come to one.

It was not long before the thud of bare feet sounded and a slave appeared at the door: Katey in her brown linen smock. All the female house-slaves in Hubertus' home wore brown linen smocks, and all the field slaves were supplied with brown linen to cover their middles. Most planters supplied brown and blue linen indiscriminately, but Hubertus preferred uniformity. There were many things in which he preferred uniformity; it stemmed from his desire to be constant, consistent, in outlook.

Katey peered very cautiously into the room to make sure that Prayers were over, then she entered. Her manner was excited. She had evidently been disturbed at her morning toilet, for her woolly hair stood out stiffly all round her head. This emphasised her excited manner as she said: 'Massa! Missy! Slave just come from up-river, from Massa Maybury.' She spoke in Dutch. The slaves all spoke in Dutch; even those on the plantations owned by the English spoke more Dutch than English. 'Bad message Massa. Ow, Missy! Massa Maybury send to say news come from up-river last night. Big trouble break out in Berbice Colony. All slaves gone bad and burning houses and murdering Christian massas. And Massa Maybury say news come saying some of the bad-men crossing over to Demerary Colony. Yes, Massa. Massa Maybury say you and the Missy must pack up and prepare to go to Borsselen Island with your children and your people. Take all your people, for safety, and before the bad-men try to talk them into joining with them.'

Katey was blowing, as though she had been running. She glanced from her master to her mistress, obviously anticipating loud exclamations of alarm. Rosalind, however, merely said: 'Well!' softly. Hubertus smiled and nodded briefly at his wife, then glanced at Katey and waved his hand.

'Tell the slave to tell Massa Maybury we thank him for his message. I shall come and see Massa Maybury this morning. Go.'

Katey went, deeply disappointed at not having created a sensation.

Hubertus shut the dining-room door, his manner and movements calm. 'I believe there is truth in what Father has sent to tell us. For some time I have been expecting trouble in Berbice. The Company in Berbice is too lenient towards the slaves. It is a mistake to be lenient to slaves. A man is either master or slave. If he is a slave, then he must be treated as such – with firmness, with severity.'

'Yes, but not with brutality, Hubertus. I've heard the private planters in Berbice are terrible brutes. They're even worse than the Dutch in this colony.'

Hubertus raised a forefinger of admonition – gentle admonition. 'You are still one-sided, Rosalind. Why single out the Dutch, my dear? The English are no less cruel. They pretend they are humane, but that is purely their hypocrisy. The English are cruel in private, but we Dutch are cruel so that all may see. That is the only difference.'

10

'Hubertus, what are we going to do? Father says we should pack up and go to Borsselen.'

'Your father was always precipitate. No, we shall stay where we are. I am sure there will be no necessity to go to Borsselen. As a fort, Borsselen could not defend us against an attack of moths, much less slaves. Furthermore, you must not forget our family motto, my dear, "The Van Groenwegels never run".'

'Poor Grandma Hendrickje. I wonder if they're all safe on the Canje.'

'And Cousin Jacques and Cousin Faustina,' said Jacqueline. 'They're right on the Berbice. Great-aunt Flora, too.'

Her father winced and lowered his gaze. Mention of his family in Berbice generally affected him in this manner. He had great doubts about his relatives in Berbice, especially those on the upper Canje River. In more than one letter to him his Aunt Flora Teuffer — she lived with her family on the Berbice River — had hinted that the Canje members of the family were notorious not only for brutality but also for immorality. And his aunt had made no exception even for Grandma Hendrickje (she was his great-aunt but he had always called her Grandma). Years and years ago, as a boy, he had heard vague rumours about his own mother — that she was a profligate who had abandoned him as an infant so that his father had had to send him to Essequibo to be cared for by his grandfather. She and his father had lived with the Van Groenwegels on the upper Canje; he knew that for certain: his grandfather had told him so. His father had died when he was an infant; the rumour was that he had committed suicide. He had never been able to get a clear picture of what had happened. His grandfather and grandmother had always avoided discussing the affair, but the impression had been left on Hubertus that very dark deeds had been committed on the upper Canje when he was an infant and a boy. Hubertus had grown up with the conviction that his relatives on the Canje were people to be regarded with suspicion and uncertainty.

'When last have you written Grandma, Hubertus?'

'Not since the death of Grandfather Aert last September. I asked her to try to persuade David or Laurens to go and manage the Essequibo plantation, but she replied saying they were not eager to take on such a task. You read her letter, didn't you?'

'Yes, I remember it. Such a pity we had to sell the Essequibo plantation. Grandfather Aert always wanted it to remain in the family.' She spoke with affection and genuine regret, for she had been very fond of old Aert. When the other proud Dutch families of Essequibo had tried to persuade old Aert to forbid Hubertus from marrying her – 'an English outsider' – old Aert had brushed aside their prejudices and taken her part. He had come to Demerary to meet her family, and he had assumed no lofty airs. At that time, in 1748, the Mayburys were humble cotton-growers. In the planting heirarchy, cotton was rated lowest, with coffee next. The aristocrats were the sugar-planters, and the Van Groenwegels were not only sugar-planters but an old and highly respected Essequibo family. They were descendants of Commandeur Adriansen van Groenwegel, one of the early governors of Essequibo – a governor of the days when the seat of government in Essequibo was Kyk-over-al, the tiny island at the confluence of the Essequibo, Mazaruni and Cuyuni Rivers. Old Aert, before his death in September last, had been a good friend of the present Directeur-General, Laurens Storm van's Gravesande, who governed from Fort Island in the Essequibo River. Indeed, he would have had every right to assume lofty airs with her family. But he had been courteous and friendly and sympathetic, and had given his consent to the marriage. Her parents had taken a liking to him on the spot, and they, too, had been grieved at his death, having during the years following the marriage of herself and Hubertus become very close to the old man; he had had them to spend time with him on the Essequibo, and had given them help in their planting affairs.

Hubertus opened the door and clapped his hands, and in less than ten seconds Pemba, the children's nurse, had appeared. A tall, stout, imposing Negress. There was character on her face, and the children respected her. 'You call, Massa?'

'Yes, Pemba. Go and tell Barkum to call Manaibo. I want Manaibo to do something for me. It is very urgent.'

'Very well, Massa.'

Hubertus shut the door.

'Are you going to send Manaibo up the river to investigate?'
'Yes.'

Manaibo was the leader of a group of free Arawak Indians

12

who lived on the plantation. Free Indians were encouraged to settle on most plantations in the three colonies, and especially in Essequibo and Demerary. In return, these Indians who were adept at hunting and fishing supplied the planters with fish and game, and rendered valuable services when slaves escaped into the bush. It was a poor plantation which did not support its free Indians. And the planter who had Indian blood in him was held in high esteem in the society of the colony, for such a planter commanded greater respect from the Indians, and had greater influence over them. Manaibo and his group were trust-worthy fellows, but they would not have been so trustworthy had Hubertus been unable to claim that his mother was half Indian.

'Father, what shall we do if we're attacked?' asked Mary.

Hubertus, without turning his head, glanced down at her. It was a mannerism of his, and it made him seem to be examining some speck of dust on his high cheekbones – his Indian cheek-bones. Imperturbably he told Mary: 'We shall pray to the Lord God for guidance – and load our muskets.' He gave a sly smile, stretched out and tweaked her chin. Suddenly he looked at Rosalind and said: 'I must eat now, my dear. I want to go and see your father the instant I have sent off Manaibo. There is no time to be loss.'

'Lost.'

'Lost,' amended Hubertus.

Rosalind clapped her hands thrice – slowly. It was the signal to the kitchen slaves to bring in coffee.

The compound that surrounded Hubertus' house was a wide one, and it was fringed with fruit-trees – mangoes and sapo-dillas and avocadoes. Beyond these were visible the slaves' pro-vision patches and the slaves' logies, wooden shacks roofed with dried *troolie* palm leaf, a thatching extremely effective against the weather though it harboured insects. Hubertus' home was a two-storied one with a slated roof. A veranda went right round the lower storey, and the building stood on five-foot brick pillars. It was a mere box, four-square, with brown-shingled walls, similar in appearance to most other plantation houses. In the compound stood one or two out-buildings – a tool-shed,

13

a kitchen and a stable. In the rainy season the compound was muddy, in the dry season dusty.

This was the short dry season, and the compound looked dry and hard, for Hubertus always insisted on its being well swept every morning. It was the first place he inspected when setting out on his tour of inspection round the plantation. Other planters would, as a rule, give their attention to the fields first, and, on their return, inspect the house-compound, but Hubertus had his own methods of doing everything. To his overseers and his fellow-planters he was an unpredictable quantity.

After coffee, Hubertus walked round the compound with Overgaar, his head-overseer, a short, red-haired fellow, taciturn at all times except when addressed by his master. Overgaar lived solely to please Hubertus.

The inspection was almost at an end when Hubertus broke the silence by saying: 'Have you heard any rumours, Overgaar?'

'Rumours, Mynheer? About what, Mynheer?'

'Disturbances among our people.' Planters referred to their slaves as their 'people'; it was a term of possession, not of affection.

'No. No, Mynheer. None at all. The usual grumbles, of course. All slaves grumble. But nothing serious or I should have reported it to you at once. You know how careful I am to see –

'I know, Overgaar.' Hubertus put up a silencing forefinger. 'I ask merely to be reassured, because a very disturbing rumour has come from up-river.' He told him about the message his father-in-law had sent, and Overgaar exclaimed loudly. 'Good God in heaven! Can it be true, Mynheer? But it would be terrible. I have always heard that the planters in Berbice were unable to control their people. In July last they ran amuck on two plantations owned by a Mynheer Kunckler, a Councillor of the Berbice Court of Justice. It was terrible. You did hear of that, Mynheer, didn't you? It took several days to quell them. Governor van Hoogenheim and a party of soldiers from Fort Nassau had to take a hand in putting down the rebellion. I hope there is no truth in their having crossed over into Demerary. They are so numerous, and we are so few.'

Hubertus, who had listened to this with a patient, blank face, nodded and said: 'I want you to keep a sharp eye out, Overgaar

14

Report immediately any instance of disaffection.'

'Most assuredly, Mynheer. I shall be most vigilant.'

'Good. And now go and inspect the fields. I won't be coming this morning. I am expecting Manaibo, and I am going up to Signal to see Mr Maybury the instant I have sent off Manaibo.'

'Very well, Mynheer. I shall attend to everything.'

'Overgaar.'

'Yes, Mynheer?'

'Mr Harker gave me some fine tobacco yesterday. Come in this evening and I shall let you have some.'

'Thank you, Mynheer! Oh, thank you! It is very kind of you.'

Overgaar had hardly mounted his mule and ridden off when Manaibo and two of his men appeared from a westerly direction; their camp was near the river bank which was about two hundred yards distant from the house. There was a driveway that led from the house to the river – a driveway lined on either hand with fruit trees and palms.

For an Indian, Manaibo was rather tall. He was about five feet eight. And he had greyish-brown eyes not very common among Indians. Like most of his kind, however, his manner was sheepish and inscrutable.

Hubertus stood by the kitchen stairs and watched the three men approach. They wore lap-clothes only, and their hairless bodies bore tattoo markings. Manaibo carried a crude wooden spear. He was never without it: it distinguished him as the leader of his men.

'You send for me, Mynheer?' Manaibo spoke in crude Dutch, but unlike the Negro slaves, he never addressed Hubertus as master. He was too conscious of his status as a free man.

'Yes, Manaibo. I have something I would like you to do for me.'

Hubertus explained, and Manaibo and his companions listened with expressionless faces. 'Say nothing to anyone about your going, and whenever you return, if it is in the middle of the night, come to the house here and knock and ask to see me.'

'It is a simple task, Mynheer. I shall be pleased to do it.'

Hubertus, his face as impassive as Manaibo's, looked past the men at the fruit-trees. The sun glittered in their foliage, and

15

sackies and kiskadees twittered amidst the branches. The mangoes were in blossom, and very faintly on the air drifted a turpentine aroma that of a sudden grew stronger as a breeze, audible a moment ago as a hissing far away, now came sizzling through the foliage of the trees.

In Hubertus there was a great love of trees. Of trees and of all things that grew from the soil.

It was not this love, however, that caused him now to stare at the trees. His staring was merely his way of indicating to Manaibo that he would be glad to hear any report that Manaibo might have to make. In Demerary, and in Essequibo and Berbice, there were no newspapers, and one had to depend upon one's overseers, on ships' captains and travellers, on the Indians, and on any odd person, for news.

Manaibo, who understood Hubertus perfectly, shook his head and said: 'Not much to tell you, Mynheer. Two slaves on Vlieborg tried to get away, and Mynheer Copps, the overseer, had big quarrel with Mynheer Dubois. But they catch the slaves and Mynheer Dubois order them to have twenty lashes each and their ears cut off. And Mynheer Dubois fined Mynheer Copps thirty guilders for carelessness.'

Hubertus nodded and smiled, and embarked upon another silence of waiting. This time it was not for news he waited.

Manaibo, gaze lowered, spoke after what he must have considered a proper interval of silence. 'Mynheer, the *kiltum* you gave us last month is nearly all finished. My men would be pleased to have some more.'

Hubertus clasped his hands over his stomach and said: 'Overseer Hubst complained that your men got drunk and disturbed him in his cottage, Manaibo. *Kiltum* is not good for Indians. It is not good even for white men. I wish you would try to persuade your men to keep away from it.'

Manaibo said nothing, gaze still lowered. His companions also kept their gazes on the ground. Hubertus knew that they were not alarmed, nor in any way dismayed at what he had said. They knew he would give them more *kiltum*. It was against his principles to give rum to Indians. Drunkenness, he was convinced, was impious. And that white Christians should encourage these unspoilt people of the jungles to drink rum was doubly blameworthy. Such action must certainly be displeasing

16

to the Almighty. Yet unless one gave *kiltum* to the Indians one could not secure their services. To have adhered to his principles and refused to supply them with *kiltum* would have meant that his family would have had to do without game and fish, and, of greater importance, his slaves would have been more difficult to control. The presence of Indians on a plantation acted as a restraining influence on the negro slaves. The slaves knew that the Indians would frustrate any attempt to escape into the bush, and would side with the plantation master in any riot. Hubertus could not afford to let his Indians desert him, therefore he had decided that whether it was displeasing to the Almighty or not, he would have to let the Indians have their periodic gift of *kiltum* that went along with the other gifts of axes and beads and cheap brass jewellery he made them from time to time. In his prayers at night, he acknowledged it as a sin and asked the Almighty to forgive him. And he felt convinced that the Almighty readily forgave him. God, argued Hubertus, was a reasonable Being; he would not express this to anyone, but he felt within himself that in assessing the worth of a mortal, God never failed to take into consideration the circumstances of each man's individual situation.

'Manaibo, suppose I didn't give *kiltum* to your men. Suppose I said I did not want drunken Indians on my plantation.'

Manaibo and his companions lost their impassivity. Their eyes came up. They were amazed – and puzzled. No less than Hubertus, though he did not show it. He had not intended to say what he had, but he had said it. A tiny white spot had glowed in his head and the words had issued from him. There were times when Hubertus believed that he possessed another self over which he had no control. It caused him to do and say things he would normally have hesitated to do and say. It sprang surprises on him. Yet he knew that he approved of this self; he did not regret its presence.

'Would you desert me if I didn't give your men *kiltum* Manaibo?'

'No, Mynheer,' Manaibo mumbled. His companions shook their heads and mumbled: 'No, Mynheer.'

'Why shouldn't you desert me?' asked Hubertus, his voice cold. A slow, powerful rage was brewing within him.

There was a silence, then Manaibo lowered his gaze and

17

said: 'You have my blood in you, Mynheer. Indians do not desert their own.'

Stolidly Hubertus stood before them, eyelids lowered; he might have been examining the speck of dust on his cheekbones. His hands clasped on his stomach abruptly broke apart. He flung them briskly outward and said: 'Go. Go and do what I ask. Tomorrow you shall have some *kiltum*.'

He turned and walked away toward the stable. Clapped his hands. And when Barkum, his head household slave, appeared Hubertus asked him if the yacht was ready. Barkum, as short as his master, about forty, thickset and greying, one ear missing – it had been cut off, when he was a young man, for a misdemeanour – replied that everything was ready. The master could leave now if he wished.

2

WHEN Hubertus arrived at the little *stelling* where his yacht was moored in readiness to take him up-river, a small boat with a slave was drawing alongside. The man had already been hailed by the eight slaves who manned the yacht, and as Hubertus stepped aboard, Harram, the leading member of the crew, told him: 'Massa Harker send slave with message to say the young missies not coming for lessons this morning, Massa. Bad news come from up-river, and Massa Harker think it best to keep home the missies today.'

Why, thought Hubertus, should everyone take fright at a mere rumour of trouble in Berbice? I am not afraid. Am I different from them?

'Tell him to go up to the house and inform the missy.'

'Yes, Massa.'

The two Harker girls and the four Lieker children from the neighbouring down-river plantation came thrice a week to Hubertus' home to be schooled along with his own children. Hubertus employed a tutor, a minor government official whose salary was less than half that of Hubertus' assistant overseer and who had snapped at the opportunity of earning a few extra guilders. The Harkers and the Liekers contributed to the salary paid to Mynheer Anton Ruys. Twice a week Hubertus' girls went to the Harker home for lessons in English with the English tutor, an Englishman who worked as part-time overseer on their plantation.

'Harram, when does the tide turn?'

'Two hours' time, Massa.'

Hubertus clapped his hands, and the Harker slave, on the point of leaving the wharf to go to the house, turned and approached.

'What is the news from down-river, my man? Is your massa preparing to go to Borsselen with his family and his people?'

'No, Massa. But Massa Harker call in all people from the fields and talk to them and tell them they must behave themselves good. He tell them if they behave good they will get their full rations but if they behave like the bad-men in Berbice he will stop their rations.'

Hubertus pondered a moment, then asked; 'Has the brig from Barbados with Massa Clackson and his family been sighted yet?'

'Not yet, Massa. No world from the Brandwagt up to last night. I hear Massa say to Missy he hope brig come in by to-night.'

'Very well. Go to the house and deliver your message to Missy.'

Hubertus waved to Harram and the yacht moved off at once, the oars cleaving the black water. Harram urged the men to exert themselves, for the ten miles to Plantation Signal would occupy the better part of the next two hours. All journeys in Demerary depended upon the tide, for there were no roads. The river was the highway, and a journey against the tide took three or four times what it would have when the tide was in favour. No one ever journeyed against tide.

Like the linen worn by his slaves, the colour of Hubertus' tentboat was dark-brown. A gloomy craft, even the small win-dowed cabin astern for passengers was decorated in the key of brown. The hull of the boat was painted a pale brown. Uni-formity in one's appearance and in one's attitude toward one's fellow-men, felt Hubertus, gave one distinction, and gained the respect of one's acquaintances. That was why it upset him when his other self caused him to act in a manner not in keeping with his laid-down policy. Sitting in the cabin drawing upon his thin,

19

two-foot-long pipe, it was less the rumour about the trouble in Berbice that disturbed him than the memory of what he had said to Manaibo and his companions a short while ago. He was disturbed and yet pleased. Flattered. It was as though he had indulged in a boyish prank of which he ought to be ashamed but was secretly proud.

An eccentric or unconventional action seemed to Hubertus a betrayal of his fellow-men, a contravention of his personal philosophy; a disloyalty deserving of reprimand. But he was an individualist, and his egotism was such that it flattered his vanity when he committed an eccentricity.

Loyalty, felt Hubertus, was what mattered most in life. One must be loyal to God and Christian men and women. The negro slaves and the Indians he considered as beings in an entirely separate category. The negroes came from the jungles of Africa; they were heathens who had been intended by God to be the servants of white Christians. The Indians were primitives, heathens like the negroes, and though they could not be officially enslaved, Hubertus deemed it perfectly just that they should be used whenever possible to perform services for their Christian superiors. One did not have to be loyal to slaves and Indians.

Hubertus did not believe in loyalty to any one sect or group. He believed in loyalty to all men – all God-fearing men. In April, 1741, when the new law permitting settlers of all nationalities to enter Essequibo Colony and stake claims for concessions had come into force, Hubertus, though only a boy of fourteen, had expressed his pleasure. 'Aren't they Christians like us?' he said to his grandfather. His grandfather, like most of the other Dutch planters, had been upset and alarmed. Since fourteen Hubertus had made up his mind that he would be the friend of all Christians, Dutch, English, Swiss, French or German. In the years that followed he had deliberately sought the acquaintance of foreigners. At sixteen he had fallen in love with a Swiss girl who had had a talent for drawing and painting, a talent Hubertus also possessed. Nothing had come of it, however, for the girl's parents had taken her farther down-river to a new and more favourable concession. At that time most planters, in keeping with the policy of a former governor – Governor de Heere – had begun to move nearer to the coast and the richer alluvial soils.

The official notice announcing that the Demerary River was to be settled had no sooner been published in October, 1745, when his grandfather applied for a concession for Hubertus. Early in 1747 Hubertus and thirty slaves had come to Demerary, and within six months he had become friendly with a German, a French and an English family. The English family was called Maybury; they could only afford to plant cotton.

Hubertus smiled reminiscently out at the passing scenery. A pipe never failed to soothe him when his thoughts were troubled, and it generally induced in him a mood of reminiscence.

The frontage of his own plantation had not yet passed out of view. All the land, all the trees and shrubs, that moved within his gaze belonged to him. Plantation Good Heart – owner, Hubertus van Groenwegel. If anyone looked through the official records at Borsselen Island, the seat of Government a few miles down river, that was what they would see. And it would be noted, too, that this Hubertus van Groenwegel was an officer of the Burgher Militia. Every white planter in Demerary, and in Essequibo and Berbice, though no white servant or overseer, was a member of the Burgher Militia, but only a much-respected member could hope to be given a commission.

Plantation Good Heart, on the eastern bank of the River Demerary, had a frontage measuring a thousand rods, and was seven hundred and fifty rods deep – that is to say, from the river bank to a point inland; that was the extent of most of the sugar plantations in Demerary. Plantation Signal, run by the Mayburys, had a frontage of four hundred rods; it was a coffee-plantation, though old Mr Alfred Maybury, Rosalind's father, had recently acquired a sugar-mill and was contemplating the cultivation of sugar canes. Already he had planted several experimental fields, but the sugar-mill was a decrepit one and broke down at least twice a week.

Only here and there cultivated land was visible, for Demerary was a young colony, and the plantations were only partially developed; on most of them the acreage under cultivation represented a mere fraction of the total area. On the river banks, especially, the jungle predominated.

The sun was high in the sky when Hubertus saw the opening in the bush that indicated the boundary between Plantation

Signal and its neighbour. This boundary was a path twenty-four feet wide, and it was reserved by the Dutch West India Company, the proprietors of Demerary and Essequibo; at some future date the Company hoped to build roads between the plantations. Knowing the methods – and the parsimony – of the Directors, however, Hubertus was certain these roads would not become a reality in his own lifetime. He was even doubtful whether his children would see them. Like every planter in Essequibo and Demerary, Hubertus had an extremely poor opinion of the Company. How could anyone respect a company that paid its colonial governors such ridiculous salaries! Commander Laurens Lodewyk van Bercheyck received twenty guilders a month – a salary the private planters paid to their overseers, and with better board and lodging. The salary of Van Bercheyck's secretary was sixteen guilders a month! And accommodation on Borsselen Island, the seat of government, was so poor that Van Bercheyck had to live on his own plantation, Plantation Pearl, on the east bank, nearly opposite to Borsselen Island.

Wilfred Maybury, Rosalind's junior by two years, and an only son, was awaiting Hubertus on the tiny *stelling*. He was a tall, thin fellow with prematurely greying brown hair and a high, rather beaked nose in a face narrow like his sister's. Wilfred was not handsome, however; he had the air of an alert bird, his green eyes seeming to take in everything about him all the time. It was difficult to imagine him asleep.

As always, Wilfred greeted Hubertus in his nervous, jovial manner. He spoke in bursts, and was inclined to stutter. 'In a most fearsome pother, the old man. What with the sugar-mill giving him trouble, and n-n-now this terrible piece of news. He'll be relieved to see you.'

'How are the records?' smiled Hubertus. Wilfred had a mania for keeping records – and a mania for talking about them. He had a statistical brain and a complete lack of diffidence in questioning planters and government officials in his quest for figures relating to slaves and produce and exports and taxes. Hubertus took pains to indulge him, because Hubertus liked him and admired his zealousness.

'Coming along splendidly,' said Wilfred. 'I've just completed the slave figures for the past ten years. M-m-most shocking, the

22

price of slaves, don't you agree? Four hundred to six hundred guilders for a slave is really too much – that's the price we've been paying for the past two or three years. The height of exorbitance. Shameful!'

'It is. The Directeur-Général himself, I understand, is distressed at the state of the slave market, but evidently he can do nothing.'

'I believe he doesn't try hard enough. I hate t-t-to be uncharitable, but it's my strong belief that no government official can be thoroughly efficient if he is at the same time a plantation-owner. When Gravesande has to be occupied with the affairs of his own private plantations, how can he at the same time give proper attention to the affairs of the colonies under his control! And Soesdyk is no easy place to run. Only the other day I secured some interesting figures from there. . . . '

After he had detailed the figures relating to Plantation Soesdyk, the Directeur-Général's private estate, Hubertus, who had listened gravely and not without genuine interest, nodded and said: 'Yes, I can well believe your figures are correct. But tell me, Wilfred, is there any fresh news from Berbice other than what your father sent me?'

'Not that I know of. I hope there won't be any worse. If there is real t-t-truth in the rumour and the rioting is as widespread as feared, I shudder to think of the condition of those poor fellows in Berbice. Do you know what were the census figures last year? Slaves – three thousand, eight hundred and thirty-three. Whites – three hundred and forty-six. You note the odds, Hubert? I do hope this rumour proves false. Your people have shown no signs of disaffection, have they?'

'No. I asked Overgaar this morning. Everything seems to be normal.'

'Ours, too, are behaving themselves very well.' Wilfred glanced about cautiously. They were walking leisurely along the driveway toward the house. He lowered his voice and went on: 'I had another row with Father last week. About the way he t-t-treats our people. Shameful! I detest brutality, Hubert. Detest it. And I've heard Father more than once complaining about you Dutch and your cruel habits.' Wilfred looked agitatedly at Hubertus. His head trembled slightly. 'There it is, he actually had one poor old fellow's hand burnt. In the kitchen –

in the very house where we live. He made Bannister do it. Magrum, I admit, did steal a basket of yams from Bannister, but is that any reason why Father should have sanctioned an act of barbarity? And in our kitchen, Hubert! Why not openly if he wanted to make an example of the man? But, of course, he argues that ne wanted to t-t-teach Magrum a lesson. He – he wasn't concerned with making an example of him before the others. The t-t-truth is Father was ashamed that it should be publicly known he was guilty of such barbarity. Yet he curses the Dutch. I – I – I . . . ' Wilfred was too furious to continue with any coherence. He was flushed, and his head trembled uncontrollably as though he were in the grip of some nervous complaint. Suddenly he burst out: 'I was so annoyed I threw it in his face that he was once a struggling cotton planter! A *cotton* planter! You know how he hates to be reminded that he began with cotton! Ha, ha! That wounded him. I know it did! And I told him what a failure he made even of that! Yes, a failure! One miserable bale! Ha, ha! That was all he produced the first year! Did you know that?' Wilfred's good spirits returned rapidly. He went off into spasms of spluttering laughter. '*One* miserable bale! I have it all recorded. The next year it was one and a half bale!'

'That was cruel of you, Wilfred. Father is very sensitive about his early days of planting.'

'More cruel than what he had Bannister do to Magrum! The poor old fellow's hand is still in bandages.'

'I am against such brutality myself. Neither Hubst nor Overgaar would dare let me discover any such act. I warn them every day – be stern, be firm, use the whip. But no bestial tortures. No barbarity. Yet we must not judge your father, Wilfred.' A sly look came to Hubertus' face. 'The times we live in do not permit of an excess of humaneness. My grandfather always told me that. He said that one of our ancestors stressed that only by hard methods could we hope to conquer the obstacles of this world. He was a very humane man himself, my grandfather, but he was firm, strong and hard. Better it is, I feel, to err somewhat on the side of brutality than on the side of softness. Severity with slaves must not be too harshly reproached.'

'I agree with severity – but I will not tolerate arrant cruelty.

24

If this news is true about Berbice I d-d-doubt if I would feel too much sympathy for the planters there. They are fiends! Fiends, Hubert!'

They had arrived at the plantation house, which was about half the size of Hubertus' home. The roof was thatched with troolie leaf, and the compound was small, the slaves' logies very near to the house.

Mr Maybury was on the veranda – a veranda that extended only along the front of the house – in conversation with Bannister, his overseer. Bannister, a huge, coarse-looking fellow with pale-green eyes and thin lips, towered over the old man who was short, lean and slim with thick white hair. At the approach of Hubertus and Wilfred, Bannister began to edge off along the veranda rail like some gross reptile fearful of being attacked. By the time the two younger men had ascended to the veranda Bannister had gestured a hasty farewell to his master and vanished inside the house and Mr Maybury was advancing to greet Hubertus.

'Good to see you, Hubert, boy! Good to see you! I thought you would have missed the tide.' To judge by the strength of his grip and the sound of his voice, a stranger would have found it difficult to believe that Mr Maybury was seventy-one and that he had survived a bout of the Sickness only four months before. The vitality that exuded from his burnt and leathery face, and particularly from his alert blue eyes, seemed to leave him in bursts that could be felt. It was as though invisible cushions were being hurled at one. The very hair on his head had the look of some boisterous white fire fed by his inexhaustible vitality.

Hubertus was very fond of his father-in-law. Because of his own vitality, he admired vitality in others. Added to this, the old man was naturally a likeable fellow.

'I came expecting to see your baggage stacked in readiness for a trip to Borsselen, Father,' said Hubertus, flicking a sidewise glance over his cheekbones at Wilfred to emphasise the irony in his voice. 'Your man gave me to understand you were on the point of flight.'

'Do you know one damned slave who can take a message correctly! I told the fool to tell you that if the worst came to the worst Borsselen would be the best place for us all to muster. Why the deuce should anyone want to *flee* to Borsselen?'

25

'I agree entirely, Father.'

'Nevertheless I'm very perturbed, my boy. If those niggers strayed across into this colony it would be the end of everything. Our own people would join forces with them in a trice. They don't love us, Hubert, and they aren't fools. They know we're hopelessly outnumbered.'

'And they know what b-b-brutes we are,' mumbled Wilfred, scowling.

'Eh? Eh? What's that, Wilfred? Don't mumble. Speak up.'

Wilfred was silent, frowning and drumming nervously with his fingers on the veranda rail. Hubertus gave him an affectionate smile. Mr Maybury uttered a puffing snort. 'I don't like mumblers. Always speak up. How are my four charming young misses, Hubert?' he said, turning with a swift smile to Hubertus. 'I haven't seen them for nearly a month.'

'As charming as always, sir. They asked me to convey their love to you. Luise, in particular, was most insistent that I should not forget.'

'My special little sweetheart! I envy you, my boy. My ambition was to have six daughters – instead of which I had only two – and this creechy hawk of a son. Stop mumbling, Wilfred. Stop mumbling!'

'Hawks don't mumble, sir. They screech.' Wilfred, in a sniffing pique, strode off inside, leaving his father in hearty guffaws.

'As touchy as a hen with a brood,' said Mr Maybury. 'He hasn't taken after his mother, bless her poor soul!' A sudden gloom came into his manner, for he had not yet recovered from the grief caused by his wife's death a year ago. Mrs Maybury's constitution had not been strong enough to resist an attack of the Sickness.

'There is more goodness in Wilfred than you suspect, Father,' said Hubertus gravely. 'He means well, and you should try to understand him.'

'Goodness! Pouf! Milk and water goodness! He'll never make a good manager for this place when I'm gone along. Too soft. Left to him, the damned niggers would be eating at our table and sleeping in our beds. He believes we should dispense with punishment and pamper them. Born with ants in his brain, that boy! Ants in his brain!'

'Yes, his attitude toward the negroes is somewhat mistaken,

26

but he means well. He has a good heart.'

'Of what use is a good heart toward niggers, Hubert! Treat them kindly and they forget themselves and kick you. That's what I'm always telling him. They don't understand kind treatment. Only lashes. I know of an actual case up-river. There was a fellow who arrived recently from Antigua. Had ideas of kindliness and humane methods. And what happened? He admitted to me himself. He said it didn't succeed. His people grew slack and idle, and when he asked them what more did they wish, one of them replied: "Massa, you don't love us no more. You don't flog us no more".'

Hubertus nodded. 'That is true. Stop punishing them and they fancy you have ceased to love them. That is the mentality of the slave.'

'Most certainly it is. Mind, I don't approve of out-and-out cruelty. You Dutchmen are fiends, Hubert. Fiends of hell! You go too far. I don't mean you yourself. You're moderate. You're Dutch but you have the compassion of an Englishman. But there are others, as you know yourself, who do dastardly things. Tar and feather, cut off ears and hands, plunge feet into boiling oil, brand with red-hot irons. That's taking it too far.'

Wilfred's head suddenly appeared at the door that gave into the sitting-room. 'What happened in our kitchen last week, sir?' What did Bannister do to Magrum? Tell him of that, sir! Tell him if you dare!'

'Fiddlesticks, boy! Fiddlesticks! Bannister was merely trying to frighten the fellow, that was all!' But Mr Maybury grew flushed, and was obviously uncomfortable. He ran his fingers through his tousled white hair. 'Magrum needed a frightening, the damned thief! It was his sixth offence.'

Wilfred sniffed and vanished again.

Hubertus smiled slyly and murmured; 'Wilfred means well.' He was more in sympathy with Mr Maybury but his affection for Wilfred was such that he felt he must be tolerant. In any event, he would not have taken sides. Hubertus never took sides, for he had no belief in perfection. One, argued Hubertus, should only show loyalty to that group or faction which stood for absolute perfection. God was perfection, hence he believed in God and could be loyal to what was divine. Men were imperfect: no individual or group of men could claim to be faultless,

27

hence his loyalty must be to all men and not one man or one group or faction. His own wife and children he loved, but should their faults be pointed out to him by a stranger he would not try to defend them. No man, felt Hubertus, should be praised or damned outright.

'Wilfred means well but Wilfred is a fool,' said Mr Maybury. He gripped Hubertus' arm. 'Come inside and have some wine, my boy. We must relax and discuss this new situation. Breakfast will be ready in about an hour or so.' In Demerary breakfast was never before ten. Very often at eleven.

The old man clapped his hands, and the thump-thump of bare feet sounded inside.

3

THOUGH tension remained in Demerary and Essequibo, during the week that followed, there were no more alarming rumours from up-river. Even the Indians, including Manaibo, after several forays into Berbice territory and along the trail that linked Plantation Loo in Demerary with Plantation Savonette in Berbice, could report no signs of hostile rebel slaves moving toward Demerary.

In the Van Groenwegel home, however, there was cause for another kind of alarm; it was an alarm felt chiefly by Rosalind for the openly amorous manner of the newly arrived Mrs Clackson toward Hubertus.

The brig from Barbados that brought Cranley Clackson and his wife Woglinde and their three-year-old daughter Clara arrived a day later than it was due – on the afternoon of the sixteenth. Cranley Clackson had, through the help of his friends, the Harkers, purchased a small cotton plantation up-river, on the west bank, the former owner of which had taken over a new and large sugar plantation near the mouth of the river.

On Thursday morning, the seventeenth, when Dora and Clarice Harker came to Good Heart for lessons – the fears of their parents had now abated – they brought a letter for Hubertus from their father, and in it James Harker told Hubertus of the arrival of the brig with the Clacksons. 'We want them to meet our friends and for this purpose we shall be at home to

28

you and your family on Saturday. I'm asking your father-in-law and Wilfred, too, and the Liekers. . . . You'll be interested to hear that Cranley's wife was once in the Essequibo and seems to know you.'

'Who can she be, Hubertus?' said Rosalind when Hubertus handed her the note to read. But Hubertus shook his head. 'I cannot tell you, my dear. I knew a great many people in Essequibo. English, French, Swiss, German.'

'If I'm not mistaken, Eunice Harker did mention that she's German.'

'Mrs Clackson?'

'Yes. She married a French Jew and went to St Eustatius in the West Indies, and her husband died there and she went to her uncle in Barbados. Then she met Cranley Clackson and married him.'

Hubertus gave her a comically owlish look. 'You appear to be much more acquainted with the lady's history than I am.'

'Her name is Woglinde,' said Jacqueline. 'Dora told us at lessons.'

Hubertus started and frowned. 'Woglinde? That name is familiar.' He was thoughtful an instant then exclaimed: 'I know! Woglinde Prutt. She was a girl I admired very much. I was eighteen and she seventeen.' A slightly reminiscent, slightly mischievous, light came into his eyes. Leaning against the veranda rail – he and Rosalind and the two elder girls were on the back veranda – he began to nod his head gently, his eyes darting quizzically from side to side as though he were communing secretly with dust specks on his cheekbones.

'She was delightfully shaped,' he said. 'I nearly lost my head.'

Rosalind smiled affectionately, then frowned in disapproval, glancing at the two girls. 'I've told you you shouldn't speak so freely before the girls, dear. Jacqueline and Mary, go inside.'

Her husband looked contrite. 'I always forget,' he smiled, as Jacqueline and Mary obediently went inside. 'Memories sometimes carry me away.' He gave her a swift look. 'I'm a passionate man. You know that, Rosalind. It's in my blood. We are a passionate family.'

'I wouldn't have married you if you weren't. But you know

29

how to control your passion – that was what I liked most about you.'

'Yes. It is the English in you. Always control. Always restraint. I like restraint – that was why I liked the English from the outsat.'

'Outset.'

'Outset. That was why I liked you, too, my dear. Beauty, strength, tenderness and restraint. You had all these – and still have them. It is not often one finds all these qualities in a woman.'

As always, when he indulged in open compliments, she averted her gaze, flattered but uncomfortable. And, as often on such occasions, Hubertus took her hand, lifted it and chastely kissed the tips of her fingers. There were times when, in company, he would indulge in this gesture – to her intense pleasure but embarrassment. It was gestures such as these, added to one or two odd mannerisms, that had given him a reputation of absurdity, even eccentricity, among his acquaintances.

What the community thought of him, however, did not trouble her. She could excuse his absurdities. In her eyes they counted for nothing when contrasted with the obnoxious immoralities practised by the great majority of the planters in the three colonies. Many people, she knew, considered her a prude; many people, even English people, thought her attitude towards morals ridiculous. Who, they argued, in these times did not revel in pleasures of the flesh? Why should she condemn the planters for deriving enjoyment from their women slaves? What were slaves for but to serve and to augment the pleasure of their masters? It was always with pride that she retorted: 'My husband, I'm glad to say, feels as I feel. He at least retains his self-respect and keeps away from our female slaves.' Yes, for this she loved and respected Hubertus. Let him appear absurd and eccentric to others; what did it matter so long as, in her eyes, he was clean, strong, pious and upright!

She had faith in Hubertus. Sometimes she believed that her faith in him was even stronger than in God. Her devotion to him was no ordinary devotion; she honestly felt that he was superior to every other man in the community, not excepting Directeur-General van's Gravesande himself! Indeed, her devotion was so strong, so encompassing, so absolute, that she often experienced a frightened feeling. It was not right to put so much trust in a human being.

'I wonder,' mused Hubertus, 'if she has lost her shape.'

'To discover that,' smiled Rosalind, 'you have only to contain yourself for forty-eight hours.'

Plantation Sapphire, the Harkers' coffee plantation, was less than three-quarters of an hour's journey down-river.

The Liekers, who made a very early start, were always about fifty yards ahead of Hubertus. Every time the van Groenwegel yacht rounded a bend the blue pennant of the Liekers came into view, fluttering lazily in the breezeless air. Mary commented once that it was getting a bit frayed. 'So is ours,' said Jacqueline, with a glance astern, out of the window. The Van Groenwegel pennant was of a bright red, with the letter K embroidered on it. For generations it had been like this, and Hubertus, despite his mania for uniformity, had refrained from changing it to brown. The letter K stood for the name of a remote ancestress – a name Hubertus had forgotten. She was supposed to have been very brave, and had died fighting.

The Harkers' house, like that of the Mayburys', had a thatched roof, though the veranda went right round. The compound was fairly spacious, and the trees that ringed it were mainly sapodillas.

James Harker, tall, balding, blue-eyed, with a red-brown moustache and side-whiskers, came forward with his bending gait to greet them as they ascended to the front veranda. 'My dear Hubert! My dear Rosalind! How delightful it is to see you! And these four vagabonds! Come in, all of you! Come in!'

They would hear the deep baying laughter of Gert Lieker in the sitting-room. And suddenly a splash of contralto merriment that caused Hubertus to tilt his head and frown.

'Who is that?'

His question went unanswered. And at that instant Hubertus saw Wilfred emerge from the sitting-room. 'What a great relief to s-s-see you, my dear Hubert!' he cried. 'Have you heard about the special sitting of the Council of Justice? Have you seen the new orders? But you would have!' He burst into titters. 'How foolish of me to forget you're a B-b-burgher Officer!

Tell me, what do you think of them, Hubert?'

'Very sensible,' murmured Hubertus.

Wilfred gave him an affectionate pat on the shoulder. 'Just the comment I should have expected you to make. Very s-s-sensible! Yes, I suppose they are s-s-sensible. What else could Van's Gravesande do!'

What are these orders, Vilfred? I do not read de paper gut.'

It was Gert Lieker who had joined them. His English was rather poor, though he never gave up trying to speak it when in the company of English people. He was a tallish, bulky fellow with a pleasant face, always shiny with perspiration. He frequently mopped his forehead with a coloured handkerchief, the sourish, sweaty smell of which created a sort of aura around him, for the handkerchief was always in evidence, either clutched loosely in his hand or hanging out of his pocket.

'Hubert calls them sensible. And I agree. Very s-s-sensible. I've memorised them, so I can tell you them. "If a manager shall find any of the rebels on his plantation he shall be bound to give an alarm by firing two shots shortly after each other, and the same five minutes afterwards, to be repeated from plantation to plantation until Fort Zeelandia in Essequibo shall take it up. Those who have no cannon to fire with muskets."

'That,' continued Wilfred, his head derisively tilted, 'is Section One. Section Two reads: "For the present everyone is forbidden to fire any other shots, even with an ordinary musket, on pain of severe correction." N-n-note that! Severe correction. No definite fine stated. But l-l-listen to Section Three: "In regard to the Burghers, everyone is bound to carry out the orders of their respective captains, and at the f-f-first alarm to assemble at the houses of their officers, properly armed, and – " '

'Hubertus! Oh, my Hubertus! How overjoyed I am to see you!'

Hubertus recognised her at once. She had grown a trifle plumper, and she stood in an odd, ungainly way as she regarded him, but there could be no doubt that it was Woglinde Prutt – now Clackson. Mrs Cranley Clackson. He smiled and held out his hand. He said in Dutch, for it was in that language she had addressed her greeting to him: 'It's good to meet you again, Woglinde.'

She ignored his hand, and taking a limping pace forward, threw her arms about him. 'I will not shake your hand, Hubertus! Oh, it would be an insult to the memory of all we have seen together when we were younger. Did you forget me, Hubertus?'

Wilfred and Gert Lieker began to shift their feet about in discomfort, amazed looks on their faces. Near the veranda rail, James Harker and Rosalind and Johanna Lieker were also startled.

Hubertus seemed the least surprised. He smiled, returned the embrace casually, and firmly, very gently, gripped the plump arms and put the lady aside. 'I have always told you to control yourself, my dear Woglinde. I can see you have learnt no lessons since last I saw you.'

She had light-brown eyes, and a slow moisture began to appear in them. Two wisps of her red-gold hair hung loose over her forehead, and after blinking once or twice she brushed them toward her temple. Cranley Clackson had appeared at the living-room door, and was smiling out upon the scene. Hubertus was certain it was he. A medium-sized fellow with sparse greying fair hair and very green, steady eyes, saddish and soft. A man of evident refinement. A man with a sense of humour, thought Hubertus. He probably understood his wife, and was not jealous or offended at this unusual display.

'You still have that cold way of speaking, Hubertus,' said Woglinde, her manner chastened but not remarkably discouraged. She began to laugh softly, all the plumpness of her going through a vague, delicate, trembling dance. It was very enticing, and the uneven, gauche attitude in which she stood enhanced rather than decreased the animal quality of her individual feminine charm. Hubertus wanted to touch her; it was as though he could feel his hands being dragged in her direction, activated by some terribly powerful, delicious force. His hands trembled, and he had to exert his will to keep them steady and at his sides. Outwardly his calm remained.

'You will perhaps be so good as to introduce me to your husband,' said Hubertus, smiling past her at Cranley Clackson, who immediately returned the smile and advanced toward them hand extended. He spoke in English, and Cranley replied: 'I'm most delighted to meet you, Mr van Groenwegel. I trust

33

you will forgive my wife for having caused you this rather unnecessary embarrassment.'

'Don't apologise for me, Cranley! I won't have it!' She was laughing. 'Hubertus, my beloved, you understand me much better than he does. Oh, but where is your wife?' She began to look around, and her gaze settled on Rosalind. 'So it is you he made de marriage wit!' She spoke in English, her pronunciation extremely imperfect. She hobbled across to Rosalind and smiled: 'I am very glad to meet you, Mrs van Groenwegel. Your husband, he tell you he meet me ven ve are de young people in Essequibo?'

'Yes. Yes, yes, he did mention it,' smiled Rosalind, red-cheeked, half-amused, half-astonished. 'I'm delighted to meet you.'

'Me! No. Oh, no! You must not be delighted to meet me. I not very good. You see how I limp, limp ven I walk? My badness, that make me so.'

'Your badness?'

'Yes. One night I climb out de vindow to go meet a luffer, and I fall and hurt my foot very bad. I married to Jacob ven dat happen. Good man more dan me, my Jacob. Jew-man but he good. My people, they say: "You marry Jew-man! Shame!" I say: "To hell! Jacob good man!" Jacob's fadder, he say: "You marry Gentile-girl! Shame!" Jacob say "I luff her. I marry her." And Jacob marry me. Ve run off to St Eustatius, and ve happy. But I have my luffers just de same. I say to Jacob: "My sweet, I luff you, but I luff my luffers too. I like de plenty of men." Jacob, he sad about me, he grieve. He not like dat, but he luff me and I luff him, so ve agree I must haff my luffers ven I vant dem. Only vat happen is one night I climb out de vindow soft not to vake Jacob, and I fall and hurt my foot. After dat – no more luffers for me. I live good vit Jacob until he died five years ago. I cry and cry and cry ven he died. Den Cranley come and meet me – '

'Woglinde!' Cranley approached, and laid a hand on her shoulder. He might have been her father. 'Will you please not annoy Mrs van Groenwegel any longer, my dear? Some people are quite respectable, and are not fond of hearing such tales as you take a delight in retailing.'

'You see that!' she cried in Dutch. 'Always scolding me!

Cranley, if you scold me once more I'll run off with Hubertus and you'll never see me again in this life. Hubertus my love! Will you run away with me?'

'It's a matter I would have to consider carefully,' smiled Hubertus.

Everyone tittered, and Mrs Harker called from the sitting-room door: 'Breakfast is nearly ready. Will you all please come into the dining-room? Emily my girl, will you come at once and see after something for me?' Mrs Harker was a quiet, small, over-polite woman, blue-eyed.

Emily, the eldest Harker girl, twenty-three, obediently went in as her mother turned and vanished. She kept glancing back and tittering.

There was whispering and tittering all through breakfast. Woglinde insisted on sitting next to Hubertus, and engaged him in continuous conversation. She employed the most intimate endearments in addressing him. She squeezed his arm, patted his cheek, ogled him, and her laughter, raw and sensual, tantalising, kept splashing over the room at frequent intervals. Hubertus, perfectly at ease, entertained, attracted, enjoyed himself immensely. Now and then he would glance at Rosalind, who sat next to him on his left, and smile. And occasionally he would slyly pat her knee as though to intimate to her that he was in complete control of the situation and that she had no need whatever to be fearful.

Breakfast lasted well over two hours, for the table was laden. It was a large table capable of seating twenty people, and there was venison; and fish and chicken and roast pig lay stacked up on platters on the sideboard; and dishes of fruit and vegetables and sweetmeats kept being brought in at intervals by the slaves and offered around – yams, cassavas, plantains, sweet potatoes, tannias, and mangoes, sapodillas, avocadoes, golden apples. And preserved shaddock rind, guava jellies and stews. On the table stood a jungle of jugs and bottles so that the guests could help themselves as they pleased to *mum* or gin or rum or wine or brandy.

There were moments throughout the meal when Hubertus experienced sudden grey qualms of doubt. As he listened to Woglinde a feeling of revulsion would take possession of him, and more than once he thought: Perhaps this is how my mother behaved. She was rumoured to be a dissolute woman, Rosaria van Groenwegel. She lured men in a shameless, barefaced manner. I can remember overhearing Aunt Mathilde say that. . . . A shudder would go through him, and he would feel as though he could rise and put as much distance as he could between Woglinde and himself. In his fancy he saw her actually as his mother ogling his father or some other man.

Despite her vulgar unrestraint, she was far from unperceptive, and he knew that she sensed these unexpected moods of his. Once she said to him softly: 'Hubertus, you not listen to me. You hating me, not so?'

He told her: 'I think it would be wiser if you spoke in Dutch. You sound very ridiculous when you attempt to speak English.'

'I thought it was polite to speak English,' she retorted, in Dutch, 'as I am in the company of English people who cannot speak Dutch very well.'

'They can understand it fairly well – as well as your husband can, I am sure.' He frowned and stirred in his chair, for without warning, her hurt manner affected him. He found himself shuddering now with desire instead of revulsion. He said: 'How did you injure your leg?'

'It was just as I told your wife. I tried to climb out of a window quietly so as not to disturb Jacob, and I missed my foothold and fell.'

'You were going out to meet a lover?'

'Yes. I had several lovers in St Eustatius. In Barbados, too.'

'You seem to have no shame. Does Cranley permit you to do as you please with other men?'

'What can he do? I've told him that if he tries to stop me I will leave him, and he loves me too much to dream of our being separated.'

'You mean he prefers to share you with other men rather than to be parted from you?'

'Yes, I mean that. It's only you who treat me like dirt. Other men eat the dust I walk on. I only have to look at them and they want to hold me and devour me. Why are you so cold to me, Hubertus dear?'

'Was I cold when we were young on the Essequibo?'

'You took my virginity, but you did it coldly. You didn't

love me.' She stared at him as though challenging him to deny it.

He smiled and nodded. 'You're right. I didn't love you – in spirit.'

'You loved my body?'

'Yes. Is there any man who could resist doing that?'

'You can have my body any time you wish. Tonight.'

'We're not on the Essequibo now. I have a wife and family, and I hope you'll remember that, Woglinde, and conduct yourself accordingly.'

'That cold voice of yours. But I mean to have you. I was so glad when Cranley bought this plantation, because I knew I would see you when we came here. You're the one man I have never conquered. Before long I shall make you say you love me. I shall make you unfaithful to your wife.'

'You have always been lacking in scruples, and I think you underestimate my character.' His manner was icy, his eyes almost glassily cruel. 'I have no use for unscrupulous people, Woglinde. You will learn that. I do not countenance immorality. We have enough of it in this colony, and in Essequibo and Berbice, too, for that matter. I advise you to adopt a different manner if you wish to be friendly with me and my family.'

She began to laugh deep in her throat, a crooning, contralto, tremulous sound. 'You will stop speaking like that when I get you alone in the bush. Remember on the Essequibo? You used to speak to me in that way, too. You were always a good boy, Hubertus. But I made you take me.'

He was silent, knowing that she was right; there was fleshly power in her. Even as he sat here beside her admonishing her, he knew that it would have been no easy matter to resist her if they had been alone. . . . I believe, he thought, my mother was like this. I'm convinced of it. There is evil here, and evil must be fought. I will fight it.

Suddenly, however, a feeling of absurdity came upon him. Why should he make such an issue of this? Perhaps he would not see her for weeks or months after today. And in any case, why should he be such a prig? One should be generous toward dissolute people. Tolerant and forgiving.

Across the table, Wilfred was telling James Harker about a

37

planter who had escaped from Berbice with some of his slaves. Hubertus listened and caught snatches of what Wilfred was saying . . . 'Cornelius Anderson . . . brought with him a hundred and twenty-six slaves. I t-t-took care to ascertain the precise number . . . Said his neighbours were butchered – tortured and butchered in a horrible manner . . . What? No, no. I d-d-did ask him about the Van Groenwegels, but he knows nothing. N-n-nothing at all. B-b-barely managed to escape with his life. He had no time to enquire about other families . . . Inevitable that this should have occurred. The barbarities practised by Christian colonists in these parts are shameful . . . I s-s-sometimes shudder to think that I am a white man . . .'

'That's your brother-in-law, I've heard. Such a queer man. I can't understand a word he says. Is he married?'

'No. He's a good fellow. Full of ideals, but a good fellow.'

'Jacob had ideals, too. He was a good man. Too good for me, I was born with badness in me. My father told me that when I was fourteen, and he was right. I shall die a bad death, Hubertus.'

'Everyone has it in him to be good. You are no exception. If you are bad it is because you choose to be so.'

'You think so?' She laughed. 'I know better. I have badness in my bones. I shall go to hell when I die.' He glanced at her and saw that there was moisture in her eyes: she was pitying herself despite her carefree tone. 'But while I'm alive I shall enjoy every moment. Every single moment. You're listening to me?' A quavering gurgle came from her, and her amber eyes seemed to spurt tiny flames as she glanced at him and gave his thigh a quick squeeze under the table.

4

It was several weeks before Hubertus met her again, and the encounter was as unexpected as it was disturbing. In the meantime, Rosalind's alarm abated, especially as events at large provided much diversion.

A sloop with men and ammunition, sent by a Mr Gedney Clarke from Barbados, arrived, and proceeded up-river to

Plantation Loo. Mr Clarke owned four plantations in Demerary. Wilfred, as to be expected, carried out investigations on his own and came down expressly to tell Hubertus exactly how many men and how many rounds of ammunition and how many muskets were stationed at Plantation Loo in readiness for an attack from the Berbice insurgents. Wilfred spent a few days with them, and was present when the circular arrived from the Council of Justice for Hubertus to sign and pass on to the Burghers of his district. It was a circular that had resulted from a special meeting of the Council on the twelfth of April, two days before; it told that the Council had resolved that 'every manager finding a rebel should give information on pain of a fine of 1,000 florins,' and also that every slave should have his free Sunday and proper rations on pain of the same fine. Again it stated that the Council would frown upon anyone who gave *kiltum* or spirits of any kind to any of the soldiers or, particularly, the slaves; 'on pain of a fine of 600 guilders,' the circular added.

A rumour came down the river that the slaves on Plantation Dalgin, owned by Mr Edward Birmingham, had rebelled, but this proved to be exaggeration. Later, however, Hubertus heard that there had been some trouble. Commandeur van Bercheyck sent up orders that Mr Birmingham must have the troublemakers immediately arrested and taken before the Council of Justice for trial, but Mr Birmingham laughed at these orders and refused to take any action. The Council, without any doubt, would have sentenced the men to be tortured and burnt at the stake, or broken on the wheel, and Mr Birmingham valued his slaves and could not be sure that he would be adequately compensated for their loss. Even though the Commandeur threatened to arrest him, Mr Birmingham persisted in refusing to obey, and eventually the matter was allowed to rest there, though the Commandeur sent in a strong report to the Council and some weeks after Mr Birmingham was asked to apologise, which he did.

One day, toward the end of April, a letter arrived from Berbice for Hubertus, brought by the captain of a small brig. It bore the signature of Faustina, a first cousin of Hubertus and the wife of Jacques van Groenwegel of the Canje branch of the family. The letter read:

'My Dear Hubertus, – It is such a long time since we have seen each other, and since we have corresponded, but you probably will not be surprised to get this, as by now you must have heard of the terrible trouble that has come upon us here and you must surely be waiting to receive some word from us. To describe in detail everything that has happened during the past month or so would be impossible in this letter.

'Aboard this ship with me are Aunt Flora Teuffer and your cousins, her children, Paula, Sarah, Marcus and Vincent. Vincent, you may remember, married our Cousin Juliana of the Canje family. Mother Teuffer, Aunt Flora's mother-in-law, is with us, too, but you will be grieved to hear that Juliana has either been drowned or captured by the rebel slaves. She was in a *corial* with some Indians who were helping us to escape, but the rebels began to fire at us from the bank and Juliana's *corial* overturned. She has never been a good swimmer, and we can only conjecture at what must have happened. Her baby was with her, and we're certain it must have been drowned. If she succeeded in reaching the shore she must have fallen into the hands of the rebels. Jacques, my husband, our cousin, I know for certain, was captured. I received a letter from him by a Mervrouw Schriender, who was sent by Cuffy, the rebel leader, to Fort Nassau with a message to the Governor. She was a prisoner at Plantation Hollandia, the rebels' headquarters, where Jacques is still held prisoner.

'Four days ago I gave birth to twins, both boys – yes, in the midst of this confusion it happened. But everyone is being very kind to me, and I have not much to complain of. We have none of us made any plans, and with the situation as confused as it is we cannot even speculate what will happen to us tomorrow. Whenever it is possible, however, I should like to come to Demerary with the children; besides the twins just born there is Raphael who is a year old – he was born in February last year, 1762. Mother Teuffer speaks of going to Suriname as soon as a ship is available, but I don't think I should like leaving this part of the country, and in any event I can make no decision about going anywhere until Jacques is released and is able to rejoin us. I feel sure he will agree to going to Demerary, as our plantation on the Berbice here is in ruins and there can be no telling when these slaves will be subdued.

'News of our relatives on the Canje is sparse. In his letter to me Jacques said that he heard the rebels say that Grandma Hendrickje and Pedro and the others put up a terrible fight when attacked and were undefeated. It would seem that they are still holding out up there. Grandma Hendrickje is a most remarkable woman. She's over ninety but is still as obsessed as ever with the family traditions. What a pity the other planters could not have had a quarter of her courage. Oh, Hubertus, the cowardice shown by the planters was shameful. I really became annoyed and disgusted when I remember the behaviour of our menfolk at Fort Nassau. They simply refused to put up any sort of fight. They crowded aboard the ships with the women and children, and the Governor van Hoogenheim was compelled to order them ashore again, but even when very reluctantly they returned, they still clamoured to be allowed to go back aboard. They sent in two petitions to the Governor. Petitions! Instead of organising themselves into a fighting body, they sent in petitions to be allowed to flee! And the captains of the four vessels were not much better. Captain Kock of the *Adriana Petronella* was ordered to go up the river and relieve the people who were besieged at Peereboom – in the churchhouse – but he never went more than a mile or so and anchored off Plantations Fortuyn and Zublies Lust. He was afraid to go any further. Jacques was among the people besieged at Peereboom. He could have been safe with me now had Captain Kock only shown a little more courage. Instead there was a terrible massacre at Peereboom. The Negroes treacherously opened fire after giving their word to a truce. Jacques was fortunate to have escaped alive, though as I've said before, he was captured and is now a prisoner at the rebel headquarters at Hollandia.

'I shall keep in touch with you from time to time to let you know what our situation is like here. The Governor and his men are on their way back to Dageraad where we first stopped on our way down the river. He hopes to launch an attack on the rebels, and we are all hoping it will be successful. Please give my love to Rosalind and the children, and accept the same for yourself.

'Your cousin,
'FAUSTINA.'

41

'The Standvastigheid,'
Fort St Andries,
23rd March, 1763

Hubertus was deeply affected by this letter. He was very fond of Faustina, who, a year younger than he, had gone to Berbice four years ago to marry cousin Jacques with whom she had corresponded for many years. They had carried on a courtship by post, and it was by post that Jacques had proposed. As boys in their teens, Hubertus and Jacques had also corresponded; Hendrickje had insisted that the two branches of the family should keep in constant touch.

Faustina was the illegitimate daughter of Mathilde, the youngest of old Aert's children. Hubertus had heard it whispered that his mother had tried to make overtures to Captain Hubertus Lodewiecjk, Mathilde's lover. Mathilde had caught her ogling him and exposing herself in a lascivious manner – at that time Rosaria had still been a slave, not yet having married his father, Jabez – and Mathilde had had her severely flogged and put in the stocks for a day and a night. Hubertus had been named after Captain Lodewiecjk, who had been a much-respected visitor until he sailed unexpectedly on his ship without even so much as proposing marriage to Mathilde. He was never again seen in Essequibo. Mathilde had died of the Sickness in Berbice, shortly after arriving in that colony. Because of her death, Jacques and Faustina were not married until February of the following year, 1760.

Hubertus remembered Faustina as a young woman of fine qualities. He had always admired her. For her he had a deep affection; he had grown up with her on the Essequibo as a brother, and between him and her there had always been a close bond. He had generally taken his problems to her – he had told her about his escapades with women – and she showed him the letters Jacques wrote her, and confided in him whenever the need arose. Her mother, a soured woman after her disappointment at the hands of Captain Lodewiecjk, had never shown her much affection; indeed, Mathilde had always treated Faustina as though the child were the cause of all her unhappiness. Often Hubertus himself had taken his aunt to task for this unreasonable attitude.

42

It was a great relief to learn that she had, at least, escaped capture and was safe aboard this ship. He said to Rosalind: 'I shall write to her and tell her she will be welcome here with her family whenever they can secure a passage.'

'Most certainly. Their plight must be terrible – and with twins to take care of! They can have the guest room, and Luise and Susan can give up their room and let them have that one too'.

'We must remember them in our prayers this evening,' said Hubertus.

It was Sunday, and on Sunday Hubertus held prayers in the evening as well as in the morning. He held them on the back veranda, after dinner which, a very light meal on Sunday, was taken at five o'clock.

The routine this Sunday did not vary, and prayers over, the girls went inside to prepare their lessons for the following day, and Hubertus and Rosalind remained on the veranda to pass the time until the dusk had gathered and Hubertus had smoked his pipe and was ready to make his evening tour of inspection of the compound and the slaves' logies.

Rain had fallen during the morning half of the day – the long rain season was about to begin – but the afternooon had been fine and sunny, and the air now was cool with the scent of leaves and fruit blossoms and the vague aroma of damp earth. A vine of bluebells ran entangled amidst the balusters of the veranda rail, and a cricket among the leaves kept cheeping on and off, heralding the night. Over the tops of the mango and sapodilla trees on the edge of the compound the sky was wispy with remote pink clouds, some of them like frayed tails and some like showers of rain frozen miraculously in space. Some dissolved after a minute or two, but some spread and developed into great orange fans.

The thump of an odd tom-tom and the wail of slave-voices in mournful song drifted now and then toward them. They were Sunday sounds. Sunday was the one free day allowed to the slaves. On this day they tended the provision patches allotted to them, and sang and beat their tom-toms. It did not matter to them that they were desecrating the sabbath, heathens that they were. Heathens, thought Hubertus, watching the cirrus, were not accountable to the Almighty for their actions. God

43

pardoned them from the outset, for they knew no better. For them there existed no harrowing problems of right and wrong.

The cricket cheeped more insistently, and the pink had faded from the clouds. The mango trees looked pathetic in the quickly deepening twilight, their leaves long and drooping; flat, flaccid fingers forever beckoning downward. Under the sapodillas Hubertus saw the first fire-fly. It glowed palely and vanished. Glowed again – under a mango tree. . . .

He rose, put down his pipe, patted Rosalind's shoulder and, without a word, moved down the stairs and into the compound. His Sunday evening inspection was always conducted alone. Overgaar and Hubst, his overseers, did not work on Sundays.

It was the duty of the household slaves to sweep the compound on Sundays. They had done their task well, as he could see at a glance. A dark object lay on the smoothly swept ground, and as he approached it it rose swiftly and flew off with a soft flutter of wings and a cry of 'Hoo-yoo!' Hubertus smiled. Goatsuckers reminded him of youthful escapades on the Essequibo. Evening jaunts in the bush or on the banks of the creeks; as a boy in the company of other boys; as a young man in the company of a young woman or an exceptionally tempting slave wench . . . Woglinde Prutt . . . Luise van Hoorn . . . Rauba . . . Sarkam. . . . There were moments when it gave him a shock to realise that his philandering days were past. It was hard to believe that one was now a mature man who must devote his time solely to his family and his plantation – and his God.

As he approached the logies he experienced a twinge of regret. Only a surface ache. Such regrets never went deep. The resigned calm of responsibility that came with age had long since coalesced within him. Regrets, when they came, seemed borne on a soothing breeze from a satisfying past. He had had his pleasures; the memory of them was enough for his imagination now that he had matured; he could taste them in retrospect and be quietened.

The drumming and the wail of song ceased abruptly. His presence had been discerned. From logie to logie he went, peering in at the human contents huddled in corners or crouched on the floor as though in fear of a blow or a curse, an admonition prelude to punishment.

He did not pause for long at any doorway, though on two

44

casions his interest quickened at the sight of a young, attractively shaped female – such a female as, fifteen years ago, he might have called upon, with an arrogant gesture, to follow him into a nearby clump of bushes, there to be coldbloodedly enjoyed.

This very evening – this very instant – he could have made such a gesture, and the object of his interest, though astounded, would have been rapturously compliant; she would have felt honoured, specially favoured, and she would have been expected of extra rations and gifts of clothing and ornaments, for it was the unwritten law among planters: slave women might be debauched, but they must receive favoured treatment and be rewarded in rations or clothing. Yes, this very evening he could have permitted himself such a luxury; he could feel the stirring of the animal in him – the dull ache in his stomach, the dryness in his mouth, the tremor in his loins.

No. One must grow old gracefully, with discernment and prudence. The lusts of youth must be put behind. God had willed it thus. Only the despicable and depraved sought fleshly pleasures beyond the ardent span of youth. The years . . . oh, the years. . . . Heat dissolved with the years. Everything moved toward a richer maturity with the years.

Now the last logie was inspected. He made his way past a bed of eddoes toward the main track that would take him to the driveway. It was his custom, after an inspection of the logies, never to return the way he had come. To have retraced his steps would have been almost equivalent to a second inspection; it would have meant repassing the whole line of huts; the tom-toms and the singing would have died down again. He preferred to spare them the effort of that renewed discipline.

A mood of pleasant contemplation was upon him as he emerged from the track on to the driveway. He kept remembering the shapely black breasts he had gazed upon, and the knowledge of the pleasure he could have derived from them saturated and heightened the ecstasy of triumph he felt. . . . Triumph over the flesh. Only the years, he thought, taught one how to score such victories. . . . The spirit flourished through the harsh nourishment of the years. . . .

He heard the footsteps behind him, and turned. Halted.

In the dusk the two slaves were barely visible, but the other

45

figure was clad in pink. A female in pink. She advanced wit
a limping gait. He saw her wave, and knew for certain then tha
it was Woglinde.

'The Fates are with me,' she laughed. 'I didn't hope to me
you here, my darling. I'd come prepared to have to brave th
frowns of your wife before I led you off into the bush.' He
laughter went spattering into the foliage of the mango tree
Hubertus could almost feel it like a chill spray upon his fac
Chill but perfumed. Entrancing.

'Did you send us a note? I don't recall it. I . . .'

'Marda! Bukkum! Go back to the boat and stay there unt
I send for you,' she told the two slaves, who immediately wer
off. She smiled at Hubertus. 'No, I sent you no note. I wante
it to be a surprise. I was going to say I was on my way to th
Harkers but the tide turned before I could get there. A litt
miscalculation.' She giggled. 'You think she would have be
lieved that, Hubertus? Of course she wouldn't! But what c
I care! When I want to get my man I can be bold. I don't car
how many lies I tell, good or bad ones.'

He stared at her, steadily, almost brutally, then allowed hin
self to relax. 'I suppose it is what I could have expected of yo
You haven't changed very much. What of Cranley? Did yo
tell him you were going to pay the Harkers a visit?'

'Of course I did – but I feel he suspects I was going to sto
here. Cranley is no fool, my darling. Very educated. He ca
read Latin and Greek, did you know? My uncle in Barbad
thinks highly of him. Did you know I had English relatives i
blood, Hubertus?'

'On your mother's side, I understand. Shall we go to t
house?'

She took his arm. 'All in good time, my love. Let us wa
among the trees for a few minutes first. The Fates have be
so kind we cannot afford to throw away this opportunity.'

He stood where he was, but made no attempt to shake of
her hand. He felt as though he were involved in some kind
miracle. Could this be a deliberate test arranged by the A
mighty! The coincidence of this encounter seemed too startli
to be merely accidental. Or perhaps he was allowing himself
be fanciful.

'We must go to the house, Woglinde,' he said quietly. 'Y

are my guest – unannounced, it is true, but that does not matter. You must be lodged and fed and entertained as would any guest, unexpected or not.'

'You've become exactly what I had thought you would, my love – a most respectable planter. You're very pious, too, I hear. You say prayers every morning, don't you?'

'Yes. And on Sundays morning and evening.' He laughed, put out his hand and patted her cheek gently. A lovely, tempting creature. Unbelievable that after all these years she could still have retained her allurements. Despite a maiming accident, too. He told her so, and she replied: 'I have lived, that is why. But my limp is no disadvantage. Men love it. One leg shorter than the other – it isn't every woman who can boast of that. Don't I limp delightfully, Hubertus? Tell me.'

'You do. Shall we go into the house? It's getting dark.'

'You really won't let us walk, among the trees first?'

He did not reply. He looked at her and debated the question with himself. Tempting, very tempting. He remembered the afternoon when he had taken her on the Essequibo. A June day, in the middle of the long rain season, but that day there had been no rain – only blazing sun, with thunder rumbling in the south, distant but troublous. He had rebuffed her several times, because he had respected her parents, and he had felt it would be a disloyalty to them to deflower her out of wedlock; her parents had always spoken of him as a fine young man – an example to the rakes who debauched their fathers' slaves and every free young woman they could pounce upon. And he had not loved her with his spirit; for him that had always been important. Three or four other young men had been after her, but it was because he kept rebuffing her that the perverse wantonness with which she had been born urged her to concentrate on him. That afternoon she had led him on just a little too far, and he had taken her – almost with disgust but with compulsion. Then she had left him alone.

If he took her this evening there would be no disgust, but he would have betrayed his personal code, he would have offended the Almighty. A double disloyalty. No, a triple. He would have been unfaithful to Rosalind. It could not be done.

'I can see it. You're thinking like a righteous man. It would be wrong to walk amongst the trees with me, you tell yourself, because I shall shed my clothes and pull you down into the grass. Oh, Hubertus! I so like being made love to in thick grass. It rained this morning. The grass should be damp, but I don't care. Come, let us walk.'

He said very well, let them walk, but the decision did not result from weakness. The urge of desire in him was rising, but his reason was still in control. What decided him to walk with her was that he abruptly, as happened occasionally, saw himself as his fellow-planters saw him – a figure of absurdity: a somewhat pompous prig; a soft-voiced eccentric. It made him uncomfortable, this vision of himself, and the only way to banish it was to act in a manner not quite in harmony with the pattern of behaviour he had fashioned for himself.

She kept up a perpetual clatter of conversation as they moved under the trees. Her naïvety was no pose; he knew it only too well. From the instant he had set eyes on her a few weeks ago he had known it; she had not grown up, had not developed in any way: she was just what she had been at twenty. At thirty-five, her body had taken on a little more flesh, but her mind wreathed with the very green urges and whims it had done at nineteen and twenty . . . 'You think she will be jealous, Hubertus?'

'Of our walking like this?'

'Yes.'

'No. A few weeks ago she might have been. Your behaviour at the Harkers, I admit, alarmed her considerably. Such a thing had never happened before. No woman had ever attacked me in the manner you did that day – not since our marriage. But now she has come to assess you for what you are – a flighty, irresponsible wanton who could not possibly be a danger to our marital bliss.'

She gave a thin shriek of delight. 'She thinks that of me! Oh, you say it in such a solemn, respectable manner, darling! Cranley would have laughed. Cranley likes to hear people say things solemnly and with irony. He is like that himself sometimes. He has so much humour.'

'Are you in love with him?'

'In my way I am. But I love you, too. I love all men who can make love. Stop here and kiss me.' She was pressed against him, and the perfume of her began to permeate his senses. He found

48

himself responding, but he only held her arms tight; he would not kiss her. They were in a quiet spot, and could hear ants ticking amidst the leaves of a croton clump near some manicole palms. In the near-distance, around them, goatsuckers uttered their hoo-yoo cry. The dusk had grown very deep, and the fire-flies now glowed bright, swift arcs that oft-times moved right before their faces.

'She thinks me flighty, does she? A mad woman. But you like mad women, Hubertus, don't you? You think you like re-spectable people, but you only fool yourself, my love. It's people like me you really like. Bad, bold women who will not mind shedding their clothes on damp grass.' She moved like a leisurely, patient snake against him, but still his reason held out; his perspective would not be put awry. Coldly he kept asking himself: 'Should I let this happen, or should I not?' It seemed monstrous to repulse her at this stage; inhuman. In-human to her and to himself. Yet . . . wasn't loyalty to God and one's principles above human proclivities?

'If you don't kiss me quickly,' she was saying, 'I will let my clothes drop, and then you won't be able to resist. But that wouldn't be fair to you, would it, Hubertus? Kiss me.'

It was no idle threat. She was practised at shedding her clothes at an instant's notice. She had done it on the Essequibo. He believed he would, indeed, be lost if she shed her clothes now. He knew his limitations. He kissed her, and then put her firmly away from him and said: 'Now we must go to the house, my dear. Come.'

'Yes, we must go to the house.' She reached up and kissed him. 'I'm satisfied. I know now that I can have you whenever I want – I know now it is bound to happen. It may be tomorrow, next week or next month, but it will happen, and you will take me with love – not like a reptile as you did on the Essequibo. Even now you're trembling. Kiss me again.'

He kissed her again, slightly mesmerised, hearing dimly the admonishing voice of a shadow-self, but not lost. Tottering but intact.

Intuitively she seemed to know that she must be silent as they moved back toward the driveway. Within him there was a new humility. Through her – through this flimsy, bare-faced wanton – he had been able to see himself in a clearer light, and assess his strength and his weakness. He was not as invincible as he had thought. In future he would have to be wary. The years built up an armour within the spirit, but even the armour of the years could be flawed.

Arrived at the house, they found Rosalind in conference with Barkum. She was instructing Barkum to go and search for his master.

'It was I who led him into the bush,' laughed Woglinde. 'I did mean to lose him, the stupid man, but I had mercy on him at the last minute. Aren't you glad? Oh, I'm a wicked woman! I warned you!'

'You most assuredly did,' said Rosalind coldly.

Hubertus, as steady again as a spinning top, smiled at his wife and said: 'Take her to the guest room, my dear. We must entertain our guests, no matter who they are or when they come. Among the unwritten laws of us planters, as you are aware, that is the holiest law.'

5

TALES of atrocities continued to come in from Berbice, but, on the whole, fears died down, for it seemed nearly certain now that, with the precautions already taken at Plantation Loo, it would be most unlikely that the Berbice insurgents would try to stage an assault on Demerary.

On the 12th of May, however, the colony, with a shock, heard it announced from Plantation Pearl, on the east bank of the river, obliquely opposite to Borsselen Island, that Commandeur Laurens Lodewyk van Bercheyck was dead. A son-in-law of Van's Gravesande, the Directeur-General of Essequibo and Demerary, Van Bercheyck had always resided on his own plantation, accommodation on Borsselen Island being so poor. His death came as a shock only because he held a position of high authority, for, with the Sickness raging, news of untimely death was a commonplace feature. Virtually every day came a report from somewhere that, after a long or a brief illness, a husband or wife or a brother or sister had died of the Sickness.

Wilfred represented Plantation Signal at the Funeral, and afterwards stayed a few days with Hubertus and his family.

'I have a strong suspicion, Hubert,' he said, 'that fellow Michael Loof will be appointed temporarily in Van Bercheyck's place. Why anyone should aspire to be a Commandeur of this colony b-b-baffles me. Twenty guilders a month! Why, we pay Bannister thirty, and with rations and accommodation, and I'm sure he thinks it t-t-too little. By the way, that reminds me! I was up at Rylands a few days ago advising Clackson on one or two things. He thinks he can make out without an overseer for the time being, but I told him it would be unwise, especially the situation being so disturbed in Berbice.'

'Are his people proving very difficult to handle?'

'Not from what I saw of them. They seemed p-p-pretty docile to me. He has ten of them. Quite a promising number for a start, but he ought to have an overseer.' Wilfred glanced into the living-room where Rosalind and the girls sat sewing; he and Hubertus were on the veranda. 'The truth is,' he went on in a lowered voice, 'I believe Clackson feels an overseer may complicate matters where his wife is c-c-concerned. Extremely loose woman, if I may say so, Hubert.' He sniggered and threw another furtive glance into the living-room. 'She's suffering from some sort of mania – a mania for m-m-men. I'm sure she wouldn't hesitate to seduce the overseer if Clackson secured one.'

'Did she try to seduce you?'

Wilfred turned scarlet and uttered a splutter of laughter. 'B'god! I – well, t-t-to tell the truth, Hubert, she did give me a strange sort of wink. More than once it happened while I was up there. Couldn't mistake it. M-m-most embarrassing, I can tell you. She smiled and winked at me, heaven be my witness!'

Hubertus nodded. 'Yes, it is a mania, but she's a most attractive maniac.' He stirred and sighed. 'I can see nothing but tragedy for her in the future, poor creature. That child of hers is lovely. Clara.'

'Yes, a delightful little thing. She's going to be as pretty as her mother – b-b-but it is to be hoped not as libidinous. Hee, hee! Oh, and that reminds me! B-b-better prepare yourself for another assault. Clackson told me he wants to invite you and your family to a house-gathering probably Saturday after the next. He's asking the Harkers and the Liekers, too, and Father and myself. Very charming fellow, Clackson. I m-m-must say,

I've rather taken a liking to him. Has an excellent wit.'

Two days after Wilfred had returned to Plantation Signal the invitation came, but it came in a form entirely unorthodox and upsetting.

It must have been not far from midnight when a knocking sounded at the front door, and Hubertus, certain that it could only be Overgaar or Hubst come to report trouble somewhere on the plantation, dressed hurriedly and went downstairs.

The knocking sounded again, urgently, and when he opened the door he saw on the veranda a slouching woman, silk shawl about her shoulders, and two male slaves, the bright light of the moon glimmering weirdly on their sweating, muscular black bodies. In the split instant before she rushed forward and spoke he recognised Woglinde.

She was distracted. She said that Cranley was ill. 'I believe it is the Sickness, Hubertus. He keeps vomiting and vomiting, and I can do nothing to stop it. You must come up with me and see what we can do.'

'*I* must come up! I am no surgeon. Are you out of your head?'

'Yes, I feel out of my head. Mad. I don't know what to do, my darling. I know no one up there except Wilfred and his father, and I didn't care to ask them for help. I don't know them well enough, and your father-in-law doesn't like me. I sensed it at the Harkers that day. He thinks me a wicked woman. I will not go to his house. I will not!'

'And so you came all the way down here. Instead of remaining with Cranley you leave him alone up there and come here to me. Yes, you are mad, Woglinde. I'm completely convinced of it.'

'Please! Don't speak so harshly to me, my love. Come back with me and help me to take care of him. You know more about these illnesses than I do. Hubertus, don't look at me like that. You make me afraid.'

His head was trembling slightly, and his hands were clenched.

'The tide will be turning in an hour's time. We will be there by three o'clock. These men are strong. They can row well. Where is Rosalind? She can come with us, too. I haven't come for love, Hubertus. I've come for your help. You must believe me.'

Within the core of his fury a tiny white-hot voice kept buzzing. 'My mother. She must have been like this. Unscrupulous. Unscrupulous in her passions. . . . My mother. She must have been like this . . . ' On and on it buzzed the same message, so that his fury kept spiralling to more fiery heights. He swallowed and moistened his lips, his head moving slowly from side to side.

'We must do something to save him, Hubertus. I hear this illness kills people in two days. I'm sure it is the Sickness he has.'

A light appeared in the sitting-room, and Rosalind, bearing a lamp, approached, exclaiming softly to herself. When the situation was made clear to her – by Woglinde; Hubertus remained tensely silent – she said: 'Why don't you go with her, dear? You can take the medicines we have in the sideboard. It may really be an attack of the Sickness. That vomiting is a bad sign.'

Hubertus, massive, rock-like, seemed to shiver slightly. He said: 'I am not going. Do you hear me? I am not going. This woman – she is unscrupulous. She may be lying. She has no principles.'

The shawl around Woglinde's shoulders began to slip, as though her grip on it had slackened. She clutched it and agitatedly tried to adjust it. With a thin, almost childlike whimper, she turned and called to the two men, then hurried down the steps.

Rosalind said: 'Hubertus, you must go. I think she is telling the truth. Mrs Clackson, wait! Wait! He will come with you!'

Woglinde was limping quickly across the compound toward the driveway. She gave no sign of having heard.

'I will go with her, Hubertus. I'll get dressed. I don't think the tide turns for another hour. They'll have to wait at the *telling*.'

Her husband said nothing. He went inside. Went upstairs back to bed.

So it was Rosalind who responded to this unusual midnight invitation. She travelled up to Plantation Rylands in the boat with Woglinde, and did not return until dusk the following day. She brought with her the Clacksons' little girl, Clara – a round-faced, brown-eyed creature who would obviously be as attrac-

53

tive as her mother when she grew up. Already the sparkle was
there, the tantalising charm.

'Why have you brought her?' asked Hubertus.

'She's not being well cared for up there, my dear. That
woman is helpless. She cannot even see after the needs of her
husband, much less a child. You should have seen the state she
was in – I mean the child. I had to bath her and dress her. I
insisted on bringing her with me, for the time being, at least
– until Mr Clackson is better.'

'Then you do think he will recover?'

'Oh, yes, I'm sure he will. It's a mild attack. Like the one
Father suffered. And he seems to have a hardy constitution.
like him, Hubertus. He's a fine man – and so cultivated.'

During the next two weeks Rosalind paid four visits to Rylands to assit Woglinde in the care of her husband, and Cranley
recovered. Meanwhile Jacqueline and Mary had taken ful
charge of Clara, and were delighted with the child. Luise and
Susan were not as enthusiastic, and seemed vaguely jealous
and suspicious of the always-cheerful, chattering child. 'She
doesn't seem to miss her mother at all,' commented Luise.
'You're right,' nodded Susan. 'I would have missed Mother
if I had been away from home. I would have cried a lot.'

'I think she's very sensible not to cry for her mother,' said
Mary.

'It shows she's intelligent,' agreed Jacqueline. 'Far more
intelligent than you and Luise. I wish she were going to live with
us always.'

'Mother says she's going back home next week. Mr Clackson is getting better. He'll be out of bed next week.'

Hubertus, who overheard this conversation, suddenly experienced a sense of deep foreboding. It was as though a grey hand
in the far-off future had stretched out and caressed his cheek.
He felt himself shuddering, and scolded himself for being fanciful. No doubt it was the child's personality that reminded him
so vividly of her mother.

For the past two or three weeks – since Woglinde's midnight
visit – he had been in a quiet, unusually solemn mood; he had
retired into some corner of himself with which even he was not
very familiar: an alcove of contemplation and self-analysis
rarely frequented. He knew that he had acted brutally in refus-

ing to go to Rylands with Woglinde that night, but he felt no remorse; in some remote section of his mind he knew for a certainty that he had been justified: that in snubbing her he had acted in accordance with an indefinable elemental law of human behaviour. It was right that he should have snubbed her; why he could not explain, and that was what upset him a little. Yet he felt no guilt; in his fancy he still saw himself as a rock, unshaken and unshakable.

Rosalind had admonished him for his attitude, and he had made no attempt to defend himself; he had just accepted her chidings in silence. To have attempted to argue would have been futile, for in words he had no case to put up. Often he would frown around and ask himself whether he could be more beast than human; whether it was that at times he acted out of deep animal instinct, disregardful of human morals. Did God love the animal way of acting, or the human? The animal way was right; deep in him he knew it was right; one could not be wrong if one was loyal to Nature. Yet men had established their own codes, and Christ had taught that God approved of these codes. The Christian codes of conduct.

Long before Christ had come on earth men had known of the qualities of compassion and forgiveness. Christ had merely championed this way of behaving and given it divine grace. But the animal – the animal had existed from the earliest times. God created the animal. . . . At this point Hubertus would think no further. He felt it would be an act of blasphemy to probe deeper into the mysteries. He must stop. Let him pray. Let him ask God to strengthen his faith.

Late one afternoon he was pacing on the front veranda, awaiting Rosalind's return from Rylands and being harrowed by these thoughts and feelings when Cranley Clackson himself appeared from the driveway and approached the house. He was looking pale, but his steady green eyes were full of life and humour, though soft and sad as always – softer and sadder today, thought Hubertus as he went down the steps to greet him.

'I shall never be able to thank your wife enough, my dear fellow,' said Cranley. 'I owe her my life – I'm quite convinced of it.'

'You must come in and have some wine. Come,' said Hubertus, and led the way upstairs, Cranley smiling and returning: 'I shall have to ask you for more than wine, I fear, Van Groenwegel. A little favour.'

'A little favour?'

'It's likely you may consider it a big one. Opinions differ so.' He said it with such an air of banter that Hubertus was completely disarmed. 'My wife again – irrepressible, irresistible. She wants me to take you up to Rylands to see her. That's what I've come for.'

At the top of the stairs Hubertus paused. He turned his head with a deliberation almost comic. 'That is what you have come for?'

Hubertus was silent, examining the speck of dust on his cheekbone. Without moving his head, he glanced at Cranley and asked: 'Is Rosalind not still at your place? I have been expecting her at any moment.'

'Yes, she's still there,' said Cranley, and now Hubertus noticed a tenseness in his manner. Now Hubertus began to realise that his pallor was not the result of his recent illness; something else was the matter; even the man's air of banter could not conceal it.

'You mean : : . has your wife fallen ill, Clackson?'

Cranley nodded. 'Rosalind would have come with me, but she had to remain – to see after her.' After a slight pause he went on: 'It's the Sickness, Van Groenwegel, and Rosalind thinks she won't live out the night!'

The crickets had begun their night-time cheeping, but it was not dark enough for the goatsuckers, nor the fireflies. They heard a soft wind coming from far away. Then it was with them, and the mango and sapodilla trees rustled, and the turpentine smell of mango blossoms came to their nostrils. It was a cloudy, rather chilly afternoon. Rain had fallen heavily during the day.

'Come in and have some wine. We can set out by the turn of the tide,' said Hubertus. He gave the upper part of Cranley's arm a hard squeeze before they went into the living-room.

The tide did not turn until nearly eight o'clock, and it was raining when they set out – raining with the settled persistence of a rain-season night. They arrived at Rylands shortly before midnight, and the rain was still coming down in a steady, hissing curtain. There were only two big logs at the landing place o act as a *stelling* for craft, for Rylands was a poor plantation, hardly developed at all.

Getting ashore was a slippery, precarious business, and, with the prospect of death before them, the night, to Hubertus, seemed doubly cruel, doubly ominous. All this, the dark and the wetness, the mud, might have been deliberately provided by God to be a lesson to him, a warning. But a lesson to teach him what? A warning of what? He still could not feel that he had done anything for which he could be reproached.

Indeed, as they were squelching their way along the rude path toward the house, Hubertus felt a vague resentment rising up here. He had been tricked; he had allowed his feelings to be played upon. Anger, like a boulder, began to roll around within him, and as they came within sight of the low, thatched hut that served as a residence he was scowling in the dark. By mutual agreement he and Cranley had said nothing during the trip, each with his own thoughts.

A weak, reddish eye of light gleamed in the hut, and it was that that wiped the scowl from Hubertus' face. It seemed very pathetic, that light, symbolic of poverty; it touched him when he thought of her having to endure poverty. With a body and personality like hers it was wrong that she should have to suffer want.

They could hear baboons barking gruffly, with a note of rage muffled by the rain and the over-wet density of jungle foliage. I can smell death, thought Hubertus, and a shudder of fear went through him. He could have been some harsh beast, guided by instinct, lumbering through the dark, about to whimper and be overcome by the mystery of living.

His instinct proved right. When they got to the hut Rosalind told them that it was all over. Woglinde was dead. She had died about an hour ago. And again resentment moved in Hubertus. Again he felt that he had been imposed upon. Cheated. He felt baffled, distracted, and stood staring out into the dribbling dark. He had a sense of being alone, deserted. Deserted by wife, friends and God. What was going on in the room behind him had no relation to him, outside the rain and the baboons mocked him. Made him aware of an oddness, a separateness, in his being.

It was decided that Clara should remain in Hubertus's home. Cranley felt very grateful to them for offering to take care of the child.

'We'll keep her for you,' Rosalind told him, 'until you're firmly established up here and can provide proper care for her.'

'Your kindness moves me more deeply than I can express, Mrs van Groenwegel.'

'Jacqueline and Mary will be overjoyed when I tell them. They are very fond of her. We're all fond of her,' she said, glancing at her husband who stood, hands clasped on his chest, gazing out at the white day. The sun shone down from cloud-flecked sky, and a haze of heat rose from the damp ground – moist, sticky heat, stifling, dazing.

Hubertus stirred, turned slightly and smiled: 'Yes. Yes, we're all fond of her. A beautiful little child.' He added this in a murmur, and turned back to watch the hot scene outside. And as had happened not many days ago at his own home, he experienced a sense of deep foreboding. It was as though some remote voice wanted to reach him to whisper a message of warning. A voice from the years to come.

In the tent-boat, on the way to Good Heart, he smoked in silence, and Rosalind knew better than to try to make conversation. It clouded over and rain began to fall, then it cleared and sunshine glittered on the greens of the jungle. Last year, the year before, and the year before, the rain and the sun had done just the same as they were doing today. And next year, and the year after, and the year after, it would be the same with the rain and the sun. And the trees.

The years, thought Hubertus, puffing at his pipe. Oh, the years. . . .

PART TWO

1

By April of the following year, 1764, the Berbice insurrection had been successfully put down, the rebel leaders captured and burnt or tortured to death. But the Sickness continued to pounce viciously on its victims. Old Mr Harker, the father of James Harker of Plantation Sapphire, succumbed in January, and in a letter from Faustina Hubertus read that all the soldiers who had been sent from St Eustatius in March of the previous year, to help crush the rebels, were dead. All the Councillors of Justice, save a Mynheer Abbensetts, had died, too – and so had the whole crew of the *Standvastigheid* and Aunt Flora Teuffer and Marcus and Vincent, Juliana's husband. Paula and Sarah and Mother Teuffer had survived and gone to Suriname.

'As for myself and the three children,' Faustina continued, 'God has seen it fit to spare us, and we shall be with you, I trust, in two or three weeks when I hope to secure passage on a ship sailing from here next week or the following week.

'I write with a heavy heart, for dreadful tidings have come to light since last I wrote to you; too dreadful to be spoken of in a letter, Hubertus. When I come you will hear of them fully from my own lips. The most I will say for the present is that Jacques, my husband, will not be accompanying us on our voyage. He suffered a brave fate, and I am sure his soul is at peace.

                          'My love to you and yours,
                                    'Your cousin,
                                         'Faustina'

Fort St Andries,
22nd April, 1764

When, about a month later – the long rain season had just begun – Faustina and her children arrived, Hubertus had had a wing added to the house. Part of the back veranda had been sacrificed, and two bedrooms now adjoined the dining-room. Faustina, who had never visited Demerary before, noted no difference, and assumed that the rooms had always been there. She felt very touched when Hubertus told her that he had built them expressly for her and the children.

'And furnished them, too,' she said, gazing around. She fel
in no way self-conscious as she stood there in her stained
frayed, weather-worn dress. The events of the past year ha
cured her of such feminine vanity. She knew that Jacquelin
and Mary and the two younger girls were staring curiously a
her and the three infants, but that fact did not discomfit her
either. After months and months of life in a hut at St Andries
and with disease and death around one continuously, who coul
feel sensitive about the clothes one wore! After the many grim
sights of suffering she had endured, after the many hungry day
and the battle for food for the children as well as for herself
how could she be concerned about the trifling circumstance o
her being barefooted, or about her bleached and tangled hai
and the vague, unpleasant odour that surrounded her persor
Within herself she smiled at the memory of Hubertus' face a
she had clambered down the ship's rope-ladder and into th
yacht. He had winced visibly at her smell, and all the way up
river, he had been obviously ill at ease in her company. The
had hardly exchanged more than the barest of polite common
places. But she could understand his attitude. It was natural. H
had seen no hardship; he had always been accustomed to a lif
of ease and comfort. She liked Hubertus. He lacked the sense c
humour that Jacques had possessed but he was solid and de
pendable. She was certain she would be happy in his household
she was certain that she would be as close to him in spirit as sh
had been when they were young and on the Essequibo planta
tion. She had never met Rosalind until now, but from what sh
could see, Rosalind seemed a good, compassionate woman – an
well-bred. As well-bred as the children.

Storm began to fret, and Rosalind, in her halting Dutch, sai
that a bath was ready for them all in the kitchen.

'How very thoughtful of you!' exclaimed Faustina. 'Yes, I'
sure we can all do with a bath. You will help me with tl
children won't you?'

'Certainly,' smiled Rosalind, her manner shy and restraine

Jacqueline and Mary also volunteered to help, and the ba
in the kitchen turned out to be quite a ceremony, all the gir
contributing aid of some kind. Raphael splashed about deligh

edly in the tub, but the twins, Storm and Edward, screamed in shrill panicky gusts.

Faustina found that it was easier to let the girls help her, for their Dutch was much better than their mother's. Indeed, they were fluent and at perfect ease with the language, and understood her without difficulty when she asked for anything.

I can see Faustina thought, that language will prevent me from getting really close to Rosalind.

Later that day, however, snug in bed after a meal, she said to herself: I wonder if it is only language that will prove a barrier. she has a distant manner that seems to me strange. Perhaps it is because she is English.

'Do you think so, Hubertus?' she asked Hubertus that evening when she and her cousin sat alone on the side veranda.

Hubertus nodded. 'It's her restraint, my dear. It was that that attracted me to her before we were married. But I won't say all English people here are like that. Her brother Wilfred and her father are very warm-hearted and forthright people, and very easy to get to know.'

'Isn't she warm-hearted?'

He looked at her and smiled slyly, and she returned his smile. Her deep blue eyes grew a trifle watery, and she turned her head aside quickly and looked out at the gathering dusk. The western sky was very red. There would be rain tomorrow, she was sure. . . . So often he used to smile at me like that on the Essequibo. Hubertus is so quaint. He's pondering what reply he should make. Whenever he smiles like that it means he must think before replying. In some ways he's like Jacques. . . .

'Yes, she's warm-hearted, but one must be very intimate with her before this trait of hers can be discerned.'

They were silent for a long while. The night-time insects had commenced their shrill fluting, and the air seemed to quiver around them as though the several screeching choruses were intricate veils, each interweaving with the other in a delicate, invisible dance – a dance executed against the low, richer background of frog noises; the croaking of big ugly males and the tinkling chirrup of the tiny tree-frogs. The damp, leafy smell of the jungle seeped into their senses, and of a sudden the first questioning cry of a goatsucker sounded far away amidst the trees, a lonely magical call. Time-destroying. This might have been an evening on the Berbice – or on the Essequibo.

'You are crying,' he said.

'Yes.'

After another silence: 'I've asked you nothing because I know that painful things must have happened in Berbice.'

'Yes. Jacques is dead. He was killed on the Canje – at the old house. They were all killed. Grandma Hendrickje, Jacques, Pedro, David, Laurens and Lumea.'

'And Juliana?'

'She, too, was killed. She suffered the most.'

He nodded slowly, rubbing the point of his cheekbone with a forefinger. At length, he said quietly: 'From all reports, they were vile. A vile and depraved lot.'

'Not Jacques and Juliana, Hubertus. No. The others – yes, they were terrible. Yet I still liked them. They were brave. They fought off two attacks and won. In February. It wasn't until October that they were defeated, and they were in a desperate state by then. No food, and all their slaves – the loyal ones – had deserted them or had been killed. Grandma refused to run. She upheld the motto of our family to the last. And Jacques could have rejoined me. He escaped from the rebels. But he thought it his duty to return to the old home and defend it – even against impossible odds. He died fighting.'

Hubertus wagged his head slowly. 'Sometimes I find it hard to think of them as my half-brothers. My cousins, yes.'

'Well, they are both, so it doesn't matter what you think of them as. Cousin Adrian was your father's cousin; that makes them your second cousins.'

'And their mother was my mother. That makes them my half-brothers.' Abruptly he leaned forward toward her, and she heard his breath lisp excitedly. 'Faustina, tell me. Did Jacques tell you anything about my mother? Was she really as dissolute a person as – as Aunt Matilde used to hint she was? I've always wanted to know for certain. Of late it's almost been preying on my mind.'

She stretched out and patted his hand. 'Why trouble yourself about what is past, Hubertus dear? Don't you prefer to leave it all alone?'

'No, I prefer to know. I must know. Tell me about her, Faustina.'

'She was even more dissolute than Mother used to hint. Hubertus, it will hurt you if I told you of the terrible things she did – and of – of what her fate was eventually. Please don't force me to speak of them.'

'It will relieve me if you told me. Nothing can hurt me.'

She looked at him, wondering at his insistence. There could be no doubt that he was in earnest. He took everything so seriously. Since a boy he had done. Perhaps therein lay his chief strength. And because of his seriousness he had made set rules about living. She remembered, one occasion when she had challenged him outright . . . 'Hubertus, I believe you're falling in love with me.' He had looked at her and smiled his sly smile, hesitated, and then said: 'I believe you're right, but I will check myself in time. You're my cousin. I've made it a rule that I must never fall in love with a relative. There has been too much inbreeding in our family.' Serious and yet subtly mocking. That was what she liked about him. He was never serious to the point of being a bore.

'Do you remember those letters I used to get from Jacques?'

'I couldn't possibly forget them,' he smiled. Even in the deep twilight she could note the mockery on his face.

'Do you remember that certain of them I kept from you?'

'Yes. Yes, I remember. The ones that made reference to my mother and her terrible past. Jacques told you a lot about her in those letters.'

'So you guessed that that was why I didn't show them to you?'

'Yes.'

'I thought I had fooled you. I thought you would have believed it was because they contained sentimental passages. Yes, it was because of what he said about your mother that I wouldn't let you see them.'

He said nothing. A fire-fly made an arc over the veranda rail and alighted on the floor, silently rose in another arc and vanished through the balusters. They both watched it. She looked up first.

'You've never suffered any great grief, Hubertus, have you?'

'No. No, I can't say I have.' He stretched out and touched her knee. 'You have. I know, and I understand what you must feel now under your – under your cheerfulness. Forgive me for being selfish.'

She made no comment, thoughtful. The dusk deepened, and they could hardly see each other. A tom-tom thudded now and then, but half-heartedly, as though the man who beat it was sleepy, heavy-headed with fatigue after the day's labours. On the roof they could hear the tip-tip of rain. In the compound it hissed softly. A surge of damp air came in upon them, but she did not shiver, did not even notice it; hut-dwelling had inured her to rain and damp drifts of air. In other ways, too, the life at Fort St Andries had deadened certain of her sensibilities; faced with the suffering of another she could feel compassion but she could not be demonstrative. It was something she would have to be careful about; she could easily leave the impression of being callous.

'We can't account for what our parents do, Hubertus. You shouldn't hate your mother for what she was.'

'I don't hate her, but I don't like being in doubt about what she did and didn't do. Did Jacques ever tell you how my father died?'

'Yes. Grandma Hendrickje told them everything that happened in the past. There is not a detail she spared them. Your father committed suicide. He drank a death-broth made from bitter cassava and other vegetables and herbs. A slave called Hoobak used to brew it. He was an *obeah*-man, and Grandma Hendrickje had to indulge his whims, because he was one of her lieutenants. Your father got hold of it somehow one afternoon and drank it. Why he did it was never really known, but it was shortly after he had sent you back to the Essequibo. You were just a little more than a year old then, I think.'

'I was given into the care of the captain of a ship sailing from Fort Nassau, Grandfather Aert told me that. But he carefully refrained from mentioning what happened to my mother after Father's death. I know she married Cousin Adrian, but she was vile, Faustina. Those remarks your mother used to drop must have had some foundation.'

Faustina watched silhouettes of the fruit-trees.

'He never mentioned *how* she came to marry Cousin Adrian, and why it is she gained such a reputation for being dissolute.

66

There's something about her death that was disgraceful, too. Do you know how she died?'

'Jacques and Pedro – and Lumea – the three of them shot her – when they were children. Jacques believed it was his shot that killed her.'

Hubertus said nothing, but he sat like a statue – a living statue gazing at her. The rain seemed to have thinned off. Only a slow drip could be heard now: the trees dripping. The eaves . . .

'They had good reason to shoot her – so they felt. She locked a slave called Bangara, Grandma's lover, into a logie and set fire to the logie. The man was burnt alive. She ran away with another slave who was her own lover, but later deserted him and became the mistress of a Frenchman called Raoul Laplace, on a neighbouring plantation. She was living at his house when the boys and Lumea shot her. They waited in a tree one evening until she came into view at a window.'

Tum-tum went the tom-tom. The rain had all gone. A star winked blue-white above the mango trees. Cool clouds were threatening it. Slow-moving rags, blue-black in hue.

'It wouldn't be known what tree it was, I suppose.'

'Yes. As it happens, it is. A jamoon tree.' She leant forward to make out his features. Then she laughed softly. 'Oh, Hubertus dear! You reminded me so much of Jacques. It's just the kind of droll question he would have asked!'

'I have my droll moments. Many. Many of them.'

After that they were silent until Rosalind came to tell them that dinner was ready. For Faustina it was a soothing silence. Now, she thought, I feel really at home. Now I'm close to Hubertus, and the pain in me is a little less. God had been good in keeping Hubertus the same.

After dinner, when the children had gone to bed, and in the presence of Rosalind, she told him about Juliana. After her capture by the rebels Juliana had been forced to become the mistress of one of the slave-leaders.

'One night she tried to escape with another woman captive, and they were both shot dead.'

'How did you hear of this?' asked Rosalind.

'Amelia George told me. She was captured at Peereboom,

67

but with Jacques' help managed to escape and reach Fort St Andries. She's a fine, brave woman. Before she was captured she was Jacques' mistress.'

Hubertus gave her a quick glance.

Rosalind leant forward with a slightly puzzled expression; she had not understood. Falteringly she asked Faustina to repeat what she had said.

Slowly and clearly Faustina repeated it, and Rosalind exclaimed: 'Oh! Good heavens!' In English. Her face very red. And then in Dutch: 'You have my sympathy. You must have suffered!'

'I didn't. Jacques could not help being what he was, and women loved him at sight.' She laughed, brushing at her eyes quickly. 'Oh, I didn't suffer because of his infidelities. I think I loved him more because of them. Hubertus, you understand me?'

'Yes,' murmured Hubertus, his face stolid. Only his gaze eloquent.

She brushed again at her eyes, thinking: Yes, he understands. He would. She would never. Good, pure people don't always understand.

2

THREE weeks after her arrival Hubertus and Rosalind arranged a house-gathering for Faustina. It rained heavily from daybreak, and the guests had to be lifted by their slaves from the *stelling* to the house, for the driveway and the compound became laced with little rivers of swiftly running water. The last guest to arrive – he came from the plantation farthest away – was Cranley Clackson. Faustina was on the front veranda with Rosalind and James and Eva Harker when the two slaves with their burden came squelching across the compound. A third was in attendance, holding an improvised palm-leaf umbrella over the person of his master.

'It's Cranley,' said James Harker, and laughter began to pour out of him. Deep, hearty bellowing laughter. 'By heaven! He looks like an agouti with bellyache! As the slaves deposited Cranley on the veranda James broke out into renewed bellows.

'A damned agouti, that's what you look like, man!'

'I can well believe you,' nodded Cranley. 'Though personally I would have likened myself to something a trifle more aquatic.'

Faustina could not understand what he said, but she liked his voice and his droll manner. His sparse greying hair and his saddish green eyes appealed to her. He was a humane man, she felt. She was sure he did not torture his slaves, nor flog them unmercifully. And the sad light in his eyes – could it be the death of his wife that had brought such a light to dwell there? Or could it be that he had been born with sadness in him?

Like Rosalind, his Dutch was halting, but his accent was much better, and, though soft, his voice contained a quality that compelled the attention of the listener.

Despite the palm-leaf umbrella, his hair glistened with blebs of rain, and somehow this gave him a slightly pathetic air. Unlike the others, he did not sympathise with her on her recent misfortunes, but simply said: 'You look very well, Mevrouw. I'm certain you do not take cold very easily in weather such as this.'

'You're quite right, Mynheer Clackson. I'm very hardy.'

She could sense that he liked her – both from the way he looked at her and from the firm squeeze he gave her hand. Also an indefinable spirit of sympathy seemed to come from him to her.

At breakfast, she was put next to him – by design or accident; she did not know but decided that later she would ask. If by design Rosalind had done it then it meant that she must consider Cranley a good match; she had lost her husband, he had lost his wife: what would be more felicitous than that they should mate? And there was the little girl Clara who needed a mother, who had been living at Good Heart since the death of Woglinde Clackson. Yes, perhaps Rosalind planned to marry her off to Cranley so that she and Hubertus and their four children could have the home here to themselves as before.

It was strange, but no matter how she tried she could not think charitable thoughts of Rosalind. It was as though from the very instant she had met her something in her nature had come into conflict with something in the other woman.

'There are moments, Mevrouw,' murmured Cranley, 'when a

cloud seems to descend upon you – a cloud of thought. But it adds to your charm.'

He spoke as though he had thought out the phrases carefully, but it did not detract from the spontaneity of the sentiment.

'Yes, thoughts often get the better of me, I'm afraid,' she smiled.

'Is it of the past you think – or the present?'

'Of both – and of the future sometimes.' She glanced at him. 'You have your thoughtful moments, too, I've noticed.'

He nodded. 'But I think only of the future. The past disturbs me, so I leave it alone. The present is urgent, so I live it, act it. One should never give thought to the present, Mevrouw.'

Outside it was still raining, and in the new wing the twins were crying. Jerrama, their nurse, kept admonishing them in a coaxing voice. Across the table Hubertus watched her surreptitiously; he had been doing that since the meal began, his face inscrutable but mockery in the depths of his greyish-green eyes. In her fancy she saw him as a mountain – a mountain in whose shadow she would always find peace. But for his presence in this room, she would have felt insecure; she would have felt threatened by the rain; instead of soothing her as it did, the hiss of the rain would have seemed filled with venom.

'What have you planned for the future?' she asked Cranley. The question came after a silence, and he gave a slight start.

'Many things. Many things,' he replied. 'My plantation – I hope to see it flourish. I hope to build a home like this. And I hope perhaps even to marry again and have a family. There is time. I'm forty-one, but my youthful urges resist the ravages of the years with a persistence that is quite unbelievable.' He added the last sentence in English, smiling at her with an air of mischief, then added: 'Some things I cannot say in Dutch, so you must excuse me.'

'I understand,' she smiled, and felt a sudden warmth within her. It was a maternal warmth, and she realised that he would never appeal to her as a lover. He lacked that masculine forcefulness that, for her, was essential in a man if she were to submit to him in physical intimacy. Jacques had had it, despite his soft cynical airs, and in Hubertus it existed to a degree almost overpowering – indeed, to a degree that often proved a little disturbing. During the past three weeks she had experienced

70

moments of fear. The knowledge of her own integrity had not been enough to reassure her; what had calmed her eventually was Hubertus himself: the stern, principled man of God. So long as Hubertus was Hubertus there was no need to fear; his very presence would give her courage, would help her to subdue the physical in her.

One afternoon, some months later – in the middle of the long dry season – there occurred just the opportunity she needed to test out the situation between Hubertus and herself. She was accompanying him – at her own request – to a clearing in the bush where the slaves that night would hold a dance. Such occasions of merry-making took place about twice a year on most plantations, and planters, as a rule, allowed a whole-day holiday in order to give their people time to cook and make the necessary preparations. Some planters even shared out extra rations – though these were few. Hubertus was one of the few, but he saw to it that strict rules in respect to the conduct of the festivities were observed. During the day there must be no drum-beating; no dancing or revelry of any sort. And he made it a point, in the late afternoon, to inspect the clearing where the dance would take place.

As the two of them moved leisurely along the winding path, Faustina put her hand on his arm and said: 'Doesn't this remind you of the days on the old Essequibo place, Hubertus? Walking like this, I mean?'

'It does, my dear. The days when we were both young and unattached.'

She watched his face closely, for she was certain he had put emphasis on the word 'unattached'. Could it have been her imagination?

'Not that you always behaved as though you were unattached,' she said. 'There were many times when you were most austere – as you are being now.'

He smiled, and without turning his head gave her a glance over his cheekbones. This mannerism had, as a rule, the effect of heightening his air of absurdity and eccentricity, but on this occasion there was a difference, she noted. His eyes, always actively revealing when the rest of his features were immobile, flickered with a light that counteracted the tendency to absurdity. It was brief but she saw it and knew that within he was not as composed as his exterior seemed to indicate. There was conflict: turmoil of some kind. It touched her. Chilled the mood of banter with which she had set out on this walk.

Also she found herself wanting to think.

Only it was so warm. The heat swirled across her thoughts like purposeful tentacles determined to put doubt upon any attempt at mental activity. It seemed to twine up from the path with the sole intent to entangle, confute, and then strangle whatever came within its sphere of intense endeavour. Each tick and crackle of a dry-leaf under their feet might have been the birth of a new tentacle that in a minute would burn upward to twirl some unknown tension about them.

She suddenly had to say something. It became suffocatingly imperative. 'She's quite happy – Rosalind, I mean?'

'Yes. Yes, she's quite happy. About what particularly?'

'My being with you all. My presence in your home.'

'I knew you would ask me that before long.' His manner relaxed of a sudden. And it was as though the head had retreated, had ceased for the moment to attack them. She could almost feel the cool of the leaves coming down upon her in a shower, friendly, damp with the memory of old rain. 'I'm glad you have, and I'll tell you. She likes you being here, but she's afraid – afraid of herself, and of you and me.'

She waited for him to go on.

'There is no obvious reason why she should feel such fear. It's simply instinctive. We have lived as a family for fifteen years, and now you and your sons have come here. And you and I understand what she cannot always understand. I can't say more than this, but you know what I mean.'

'I know. Of course I know. From the first day I knew.' Her grip on his arm tightened. 'Has she spoken to you about me?'

'No, not in the way you mean. She thinks you a fine person. Her instinct is unfailing where people are concerned. She would have known instantly if you were evil. With Woglinde she knew.'

'Knew that she was evil?'

'Not that she was evil but that she had no scruples.'

'I'm glad you say that. Woglinde was never evil. Wanton but not evil.'

72

'You told me that on the Essequibo, I remember.' After a pause he went on quietly: 'You must not feel uncomfortable in any way. You're very welcome in our home, and I'm pleased that your sons will grow up in our household. It will give the place more – more strength and solidity. And remember our traditions as a family. We must hold together. Loyalty.'

She smiled. 'You sound like Grandma Hendrickje when you say that.'

'Did she stress loyalty to the family?'

'She not only stressed it; she hammered it into them all.'

'I stress not only loyalty to the family but to all men – all God-fearing Christian men. And, above all, to God Almighty.' She could feel a tremor go through him as he uttered the words. The fervour and solemnity of his manner frightened her yet gave her stability. Again she was aware of the rock-like sternness of him, and again she felt safe from the uncertainties and fluctuations of the warm mist that was the physical in her.

Yet the very next instant this safety crumbled. He stopped, turned her to face him, and his hands on her shoulders, looked at her, his eyes wild, mad. 'To you, too – that's what makes it difficult for me. I must be loyal to you and your friendship that means so much to me. Even to myself I want to be true. I feel deep in me that God intended every man to fulfil himself in spirit and in body. Body and spirit are not apart. They should not be apart.' He shut his eyes, shook his head slightly, the whole bulk of him rigid with anguish. Then he released her and said that they must go. 'Come. We mustn't stop here. I shall suffer for this all evening, Faustina. Think about it and suffer. It's my lot.'

She was trembling as they moved on. He smiled: 'Yes, you should be frightened. You have every right to be frightened, my dear. It is the mad beast in me. It defeats my restraint when I least expect it to. I'm sure I have inherited it from my mother, that lost woman, that pit of evil. Yes, evil. *She* was evil. I didn't have to hear her sins enumerated to know. Some mysterious intuition informed me of it – since I was a boy. Evil, evil. That's why I revere my Rosalind. So pure, so restrained. My dear wife. English, a little cold and withdrawn in company and to casual acquaintances, but warm with a pure warmth at her core. No evil, no mad beast in that lovely heart. You and I have

73

strange blood in us, Faustina. We can see evil and understand it, even pardon it, even tolerate it. My mother. Grandma Hedrickje. Pedro. Lumea. David. Laurens. Slime. Slime on them all. You and I know it, yet we don't spit on their memory. But she – she understands only what is pure, what is good. You and I baffle her, disturb her. Our sympathies seem strange to her. She fears us because our heritage puts us apart from her. She can scent the evil beast in us, but she loves me and knows that I have the strength that God has given me to stamp upon the beast. And she fears herself, fears that in some way she might prove inadequate, that her love might fail – that it might turn into hate. Hate. Hatred for me and my kind. For you and me and your sons. Perhaps for her own daughters who have my blood in them. Van Groenwegel blood. Evil blood. Blood of beasts.'

'It is not evil blood. You must not say that!'

He was perspiring. He nodded and passed a hand across his forehead. 'I should not have said it. You're right. It is a disloyalty. To me and to you. To Grandfather Aert. To Grandma Hendrickje. The old blood!'

'The old blood,' she murmured.

He stopped again and held her, looked at her, a fixed smile on his face. He pressed her to him, stroked her hair, her cheek murmuring. His voice might have been issuing from the earth under them. From under the centuries of piled leaves that was the jungle carpet . . . 'The Van Groenwegels never run . . . The old blood.' Murmuring. The heat swirling around them, wrapping them about with tight tapes, real though unseen. Spiritbinders intent upon binding their bodies. But so great was the sympathy between them that when they broke apart it was mutual: a mutual relaxation. A mutual restraint, stern yet soft. A mutual triumph of spirit over aching flesh. An ecstasy shared while their thwarted bodies still trembled.

He began to laugh in relief. Peace on his face. As it was on hers.

'I shall suffer less this evening. Much less than I had thought.'

'I shall be less frightened. My faith in you after this will be unassailable, Hubertus.'

He raised a forefinger. 'Careful, my dear!' And still mocking, stared past her and whispered: 'The beast!' He nodded. 'Yes,

74

the beast.' Then laughed softly, took her arm and said: 'Come.
We shall never reach that clearing at this rate.'

ADMIRATION and respect for each other grew stronger as the
weeks and months went by, though they were both aware that
beneath the firm crust of their restraint a volcano simmered and
that occasion of physical contact could provoke an eruption.
So they took care to avoid being alone – especially in the open
air. The veranda did not matter; Rosalind often sat with them
on the veranda, and Jacqueline and Mary; even when they
happened to be alone there was little cause for fear: some of
their pleasantest moments were spent alone on the veranda.
But the open air – the trees and the paths – carried the danger
of nostalgia: scented memories of the Essequibo days of their
youth.

Cranley Clackson visited Good Heart every Sunday; he came
for morning service and to see his daughter Clara. He made no
secret of his interest in Faustina, and Faustina responded by
being pleasant though always with a certain reserve which he
did not fail to notice, for he was a sensitive man. Yet he persisted, quietly, patiently, discreetly. His habit was to compliment her either on the robust appearance of the three boys – or
on her own appearance. 'You've lost that care-worn look you
had when you first arrived,' he told her on one occasion. And
on another: 'Every time I see you your hair seems to assume
new tints. The last time it was a coppery gold; this time there is
less alloy and more gold.'

Indeed, it was as much on his behalf as on Hubertus' that
she took pains to keep up her appearance, for as a woman she
was not excessively vain, and, in any event, she had never had
to trouble very much about her looks, for nature had given her
handsome features and an attractively shaped body, and
neither circumstances nor the years had aged her much.
Hubertus had commented on this, and she had replied: 'It's in
the family. You should have seen Grandma Hendrickje! At
ninety she was erect and well-shaped. Jacques said even when
she was sixty she didn't look more than forty-five or forty-six.

Great-grandmother Katrina was like that, too, Mother used to say.'

Hubertus liked Cranley, and invited him to all house-gatherings. He asked him to accompany Rosalind and Faustina and himself to Borsselen Island to a house-gathering arranged for Burgher Officers by the new Commandeur. The appointment of Michael Loof, the planter who had succeeded Van Bercheyck temporarily, had not been confirmed by the Directors in Holland, and the new Commandeur, a man called Jan Cornelis van den Heuvel, was sent from Holland, arriving in Demerary in January, 1766. His salary, the planters learnt, was to be thirty guilders a month. 'Ten guilders m-m-more than Van Bercheyck got!' Wilfred stammered. 'Oh, it's really incredible how these f-f-fellows accept these posts!' As though by way of consolation, however, the Directors had sanctioned the building of a proper residence on Borsselen Island. A residence was also built for the Secretary, and even a kitchen, a Company's store and a logie for the soldiers and a good *stelling* went up at the same time.

Wilfred came down at any odd time, generally when they least expected him. He was cheerful company, and Faustina liked him. His interest in statistics grew more and more avid, and there was hardly a moment when he was not reeling off figures relating to the last year's produce or the trade in slaves for some given period. He showed a great deal of fondness for Raphael, Faustina's eldest, and declared that he would take him hunting as soon as he was a year or two older. Wilfred was a keen *labba* hunter. Often he would bring with him the carcase of a *labba*, describing in detail how he had shot it. *Labba*, an agouti-like rodent, made a very tasty dish, and Rosalind's cooks were expert at preparing it.

It was Wilfred who kept them chiefly posted on Cranley's progress in his planting activities, for Cranley himself was modest and said very little. 'An excellent planter, that fellow,' Wilfred said. 'He's going to get far, you take my word for it! Last year he exported three bales of his cotton, and when we consider that the t-t-total exports of the colony in '64, the year before, only amounted to two bales, you can judge how well he's doing. He tells me he hopes to erect a proper residence before the year is over. He – he has the right spirit.'

Cranley's residence was completed in August, the same month in which a predicant was appointed to conduct services in Demerary; formerly only Essequibo and Berbice were fortunate in this respect, Demerary being left to the planters themselves to arrange their own religious devotions. There was no church in Demerary, so the new predicant – his name was Hermanus Lingius – had to be content to hold services at the Commandeur's residence on Borsselen Island and at the residence of any planter who cared to invite him. Hubertus was one of the first to invite him, and on that Sunday planters and their families from the upper and lower reaches of the river gathered at Good Heart.

Cranley then conceived the idea of asking the predicant to Hylands, and so on the second Sunday in September the service took place in the new residence on that plantation.

It was a hot, cloudless dry-weather day, and the attendance was large. The house, a one-storeyed place, had a spacious living-room which, however, proved just too small to hold everyone. The veranda took the overflow, and Cranley was not very much embarrassed, especially as the same thing had occurred not many weeks before at the Commandeur's residence.

According to custom, Cranley provided a lavish breakfast after the service, and so far as this went there was no difficulty about accommodation, for two large tables were laid, one in the living-room and one in the dining-room. Cranley, though without Indians on his plantation to help him fish and hunt, had, through Wilfred and a planter on the opposite bank, secured fish and venison. Also on the tables were roast duck and turkey and stewed pigeons. And *labba* pepper-pot, cooked by one of Wilfred's slaves. Of drink there was plenty, in jug and bottle. Rum and gin and brandy and Barbados rum.

Faustina sat between Gert Lieker and Wilfred, and she had expected to have been entertained by Wilfred whose Dutch was surprisingly good – though, in any case, she had picked up quite a number of English words and phrases – but, to both her disappointment and delight, Wilfred hardly noticed her; his attention was given almost exclusively to a stout girl called Miss Primrose Beckles who sat on his right, and, from his manner, there could be no doubt that his interest in this lady was

77

far from casual. Wilfred who had come to be known as a con firmed bachelor! Could it be that Miss Beckles was going t succeed where so many others had failed!

Gert Lieker, through his aura of perspiration odour, whis pered to Faustina: 'A miracle has happened today, Mevrouw I have never seen him so taken up with a young lady since have known him.'

Faustina nodded. 'And he's not even discussing trade or th prices of slaves. It's all about boating and hunting and fruit trees.'

'A robust young lady. I admire his taste, I must confess.'

Among the last to depart were Hubertus and Rosalind an Faustina. Normally, Wilfred, too, would have lingered, but to day he had gone early. And he had gone with the Beckleses. M Ralph Beckles owned Plantation Hurley on the west bank, few miles down-river, and Wilfred had accepted the offer of lift in their yacht. Old Mr Maybury guffawed a great deal. 'Le me to go back all alone in our boat! Ever seen anything like i The damned girl must have worked some *obeah* on him! El By God!' And all the way down the driveway he kept bellow ing gustily. He even condescended to joke with his head boa man when he was getting aboard the yacht.

Faustina and Cranley walked with him to the *stelling* f Cranley had had a *stelling* built, too. Hubertus and Rosalin were in conversation with Gert Lieker and his wife on th veranda. Faustina saw the Harker's yacht on the point of di appearing round the first bend down-river, their yellow an green pennant blending harmoniously with the greens of th jungle, and as Cranley and herself turned off to return to th house, Cranley said: 'I'm hoping to acquire a yacht by the er of the year.' He spoke so casually that she was completely o guard and started when he went on: 'It would be a real pleasu if you could choose the colours of my pennant for me, Me rouw. Would you consider it a presumption if I asked you?'

'But, Mr Clackson – why, it would be a pleasure, surel But – well, I've always been made to understand that th custom is that such things should be done within one's ow family circle.'

'I had not overlooked that,' he smiled. He gave her a mi chievous glance. 'And I wouldn't dream of insulting yo intelligence by assuming that you hadn't seen through my subterfuge.'

She smiled and blushed, and waited for him to go on. It was nothing that astonished her, for she had foreseen it months and months ago. She had even rehearsed what she would reply.

'Well, what is the answer, Mevrouw? Can I hope that before the end of the year you will have become a member of my family circle?'

The rehearsed reply would not come. She hesitated and said: 'You're asking me to be your wife, Mr Clackson. I like you very much . . . I – I don't know what I'm saying.' She glanced at him, suddenly agitated. 'I've been expecting you to ask me – oh, please don't think me presumptuous in saying that. I mean it. I know you've looked on me with – favour.'

He touched her hand and smiled: 'It's no presumption. That is what gives you your charm, Mevrouw. Your simplicity. Your lack of pretence.' His voice grew husky, and she could see his eyes blinking rapidly.

'It is what has always moved me most deeply about you. Sometimes I cannot credit it. You are the first woman I have met who has proved honest.'

She, too, was moved – moved by his humility and his fervour. She said softly: 'You were unhappy with Woglinde, weren't you?'

He nodded, and they moved slowly up the driveway, a silence coming upon them. The sun of mid-afternoon struck shafts of fire into their backs. She was a trifle taller than he. . . . I'm taller than Hubertus, too.

'Mynheer Clackson, you say I am honest.' Her voice was almost a whisper. 'And I must tell you in perfect honesty that I just don't know what to say to you now. I would like to say yes, and yet. . . .'

He waited. . . . Waiting for me to hurt him. I feel lost.

She came to a halt and put her hand to her face. 'I can say nothing. Nothing at all.'

He took her hand. 'May I say it for you?' He smiled, regarding her almost with indulgence, as though she were one of the children. 'I have known it, too. My good friend Hubertus is fortunate, and I envy him, but I can understand. It's natural that you should be attached to him.'

'But I like you – like you very much. I could readily be your wife. Readily. At moments like this I feel lost. Completely lost, Mynheer.'

Her hand still in his, they stood there in the blaze of sunlight, listening to the tick and twitter of lizards in the dry leaves under the young mango trees. On the river the splash of oars told them that old Mr Maybury's yacht had not rounded the bend.

'We shall speak of this again – next Sunday. Or the Sunday after. It's not something that should be hurried. I, too, know what it is like to feel lost. Time and thought will help you to find yourself.'

She looked up at him and smiled. 'Your Dutch improves from day to day, Mynheer.'

'That is because I have been making a point of studying the language. It is your language, and to speak to you so that you can understand me well it is necessary for me to be practised in it.'

'I'm trying to learn English.'

'But you still speak it very poorly. It would be such a pleasure to assist you in speaking it better. And I feel the day will come when I will have the privilege of teaching you. I feel, Mevrouw, that you will be a good mistress for my house, and that God will be kind to me. We shall have children of our own. No, please don't smile. I'm in earnest. When I'm with you I can be earnest. I have no need to be conventional and polite.'

'You're very good. I recognised it the moment I met you. That is why I shouldn't like to hurt you. I have seen so much suffering, and I can't bear to see people suffer. You must let me think it over, Mynheer. Soon I may know what to do. In the meantime I wish you would be happy but – but I wish you wouldn't put too much hope in having a favourable answer.'

For the next few days she was quiet and withdrawn, and this was so unusual that Rosalind said to her: 'I think it would be wise to take some medicine. It could possibly be the Sickness. I've known of cases where it began with a mild sort of depression.'

'I'll take some if you think so, but I'm not really depressed in the way you mean. It's merely a mood I've fallen into. You must believe me.'

'A mood? Oh. Yes. Yes, of course.' She smiled and added hastily: 'If you ever feel you need the medicine tell me and I'll mix it for you. Phew! Isn't it hot today!' She fanned herself with her hand and hurried away and upstairs. Such a strange, elusive woman! Sometimes she almost seemed to be shy of herself. Yet she was good. Yes, she was good – as Cranley was good. And Wilfred and his father. And Hubertus . . . Hubertus. . . .

It was Thursday. She went out on the side veranda and stood watching the children at play in the compound. There had been a thunderstorm last night, but today the compound was hard and dry, for the sun shone down with all its dry-weather fierceness. A cicada was shrieking amidst the trees, seeming a projection in sound of the hot rays that blazed over the logies in the west. Hubst, the overseer, and Linkt, the carpenter, were inspecting the logies. Hubertus had mentioned that one or two repairs would soon be necessary. Two of the logies were leaking badly. During the storm last night their occupants had had to take refuge in nearby logies.

Raphael and Storm were throwing somersaults near the water-tank, and Edward, not far off, was sitting on the ground, examining some object – a pebble or a palm-seed. A rather quiet boy, Edward; he was not often given to romping; he had eyes like his father's though of a deeper green: lazy, amused eyes. He was curious, and liked peering into corners and examining things. Storm had begun to pronounce a few words, but Edward had not yet bothered. Yes, bothered seemed the exact word; it was as though he felt a little comtemptuous of making intelligent sounds. He spoke with his eyes and his smile. Everyone thought it odd that at three years and five months he should still be speechless, and Rosalind had openly expressed fears that he might be dumb. Yet his hearing was perfect; indeed, acute. Faustina was not worried. Raphael had begun to speak before he was two, but both Storm and Edward had been backward in this respect; it was only a few months ago that Storm had begun to utter words and phrases. Edward would speak in good time, too, she was certain.

As she watched, Clara, Cranley's girl, came into view round

the water-tank carrying an Indian basket filled with what looked like palm-seeds and stones. She made straight for Edward, and seating herself beside him, began to select items from her collection which she handed to him one by one, a concentrated smile on her face. He took them, examined them and put them down in a pile before him, then without warning uttered a crowing sound, rose and gave her a push. She laughed, and he laughed. And Faustina found herself laughing, too. An odd boy! A pain of affection moved within her. Followed by a pain of sadness. If only his father had been here to see him! Jacques . . . There could never be a substitute for Jacques. Even Hubertus . . . A whiff of tobacco smoke came to her nostrils, and turning her head, she saw that Hubertus was standing in the doorway behind her, regarding her in silence, pipe in mouth.

'I didn't hear you approach.'

'Because I approached in silence,' he said. 'It's good to hear you laugh. I haven't heard you laugh since Sunday.'

'You've noticed it, too, have you? Rosalind thinks I may be going down with the Sickness. She wants me to take medicine.'

'I heard her telling you. I was in the dining-room.'

He joined her by the veranda rail, and they watched the children in silence for a few minutes. The smoke from his pipe drifted heavily out into the compound, for there was no wind at all. The afternoon was still. Perhaps tonight there would be another thunderstorm. From far away they heard the cooing of a horn, mellow, cool, yet somehow telling of trouble to come; telling of more than the end of the day's toil for the poor black men. Moaning a portent, spreading a panic . . . Black men coming in from the fields. Black men armed with hangers and cutlasses and axes . . . Death to all Christians! . . . Torture them! Kill them! Shame their women. . . .

'Poor Amelia. I wonder what has become of her.'

'Amelia? Who is that?'

'Amelia George. The girl who escaped from the rebels.'

'Why are you in this mood, my dear? Did something happen on Sunday?'

'Yes. I've been wanting to see you alone. Cranley has asked me to become his wife.'

He took the pipe from his mouth, and it was as though she

could hear every separate muscle in his massive body stiffening. There was a long pause before he asked: 'What answer did you give him?'

Automatically she sidled away slightly from him. His manner was frightening. She had not expected him to react in so intense a fashion. It came upon her that the struggle within him these past months must have been more anguished than she had suspected. Pity began to rise up in her.

'What answer did you give him?'

'I – I told him nothing definite. I said I would think it over.'

In converse manner, she seemed to hear every muscle in his body relaxing. Blood began to well again into the tips of the fingers that gripped the thin-stemmed two-foot-long pipe. She had thought the stem would snap. If it had it would have been symbolical of something snapping in her. She was relieved that it had not. Relieved that he had relaxed.

Raphael was trying to climb one of the mango trees, but Susan, who had appeared, was advancing to stop him, Jerrama, the children's nurse, moving after her with admonitory cries at the boy . . . 'Massa Raphael! Massa Raphael! I tell you not to climb tree! Bad boy! You will fall!' . . . Susan regarded it as a joke and was laughing and not making a serious attempt to lift him down from the lower fork to which he had already climbed.

'You mustn't think I haven't tried,' he said, his head unmoving but his eyes darting swiftly from side to side, distractedly and also with a humility that she had not witnessed before. 'I have tried and tried to rid myself of this – this obsession with you. I have prayed. I pray day and night. I feel injured, bleeding, inside my soul – because of the terrible struggle I have had with myself these two years or more you have been in my home. And now you suggest that you might be going.'

'I haven't suggested that, Hubertus. I've only told you what Cranley asked me on Sunday. Oh, but you are right! I have been thinking of – of going. It seems so fitting that I should marry him and take my children into a home of their own.'

He nodded, and she saw that he was smiling quietly, softly, his eyes wet in the corners. His hands were clasped lightly on his chest, the pipe pressed against him. It had gone out.

'I could never feel for him what I feel for you – though it's wrong I should feel as I do. No, it's not wrong, but I ought to remember that you already have a wife. You understand me, Hubertus?'

He nodded.

'I don't know what to do, my dear. To leave you is almost unimaginable. I feel so one with you in everything – in everything that is of our spirit. It's only our bodies that have never known each other. Besides Jacques there is no other man I could have loved but you. I think I knew that since we were children. You could even have won me from Jacques if you had not been so rigid in your principles. I knew Jacques only through his letters, but I knew you in flesh and blood.'

Raphael had climbed into the next fork, and Jerrama was calling angrily at him, but Susan climbed after him, trying to reassure Jerrama that he would be safe so long as she accompanied him up . . . 'He too young to climb tree, Missy Susan. You mustn't encourage him. He will do it when nobody not looking. Then he fall and break his neck!' . . . Clara had come to watch Raphael climb. Storm had joined Edward, and the two of them were engrossed with the stones and palm-seeds, though Storm seemed interested only in pitching them up into the air.

'You must marry him, Faustina.' His face had grown harsh again. 'I am being selfish. Selfish and sinful. I'm trying to move you into remaining here – near to me. I'm working on your feelings. It is base of me. Base. You must have a home of your own. You must be a respectable wife to a good planting gentleman. For the sake of yourself as well as for the sake of your three sons you must do this. I am a despicable man. I have been trying to soil your womanhood by keeping you beside me so that I may indulge my low creature urges.' His head trembled. 'I'm base, base.'

She gave a soft laugh. 'It's no wonder people think you absurd, dear. Why must you take up such an attitude? You are not base, and you know you are not. And you have not been keeping me here for low purpose. I wish you could be less harsh on yourself, Hubertus. You know you are good but you try to blacken yourself out of sheer perverseness. It almost makes one think you're not right in your mind.'

He began to smile. And nod. 'That may be so. I've often

wondered if there isn't some kind of mad demon in me. No, that is fanciful.' He was frowning now. 'It is simply lack of restraint. I have not yet mastered the art of restraint. That is where my Rosalind is so superb. If you know the torture of spirit I suffer, my dear. And why I suffer I really don't know. I mean, there is so much I have in life to satisfy me, to give me pleasure and pride. This plantation grows more and more prosperous as the months go by. Nearly a half of it is already under cultivation, do you know? Many planters have not levelled one third of the jungle on their concessions. I am rich. Ask Wilfred to tell you how many hogshead of sugar I shipped away last year. I have a hundred and ten slaves. I have a much respected name – the name of an old and powerful family. I have in me Indian blood – also a valuable asset in our society. Yet . . . Yet I am a tortured man. I'm harrowed day and night with problems that seem to wait in ambush for me as I walk. Before you there was Woglinde. Before Woglinde there was my family in Berbice – the rumours of their immorality and depravity. And always there has been the memory of my mother – the doubts surrounding her life. Was she a vile woman or wasn't she? Were the rumours true or false? There were my female slaves – the temptation to cohabit with them – yes, I've been tempted, my dear. Often, often. I have wanted to be like other planters and debauch my women. But I kept myself in hand – yes, I restrained myself – only to suffer torture. Only to be harrowed by nightmare thoughts. Thoughts of depravity. Speculations on my mother's baseness. Was she really base, or could it be that I was misjudging her? Could it be that it had been envy, jealousy, on the part of your mother in throwing out the remarks she had? All these questions have tortured me in the years gone past. And then Woglinde came to test me still further. Then you came, and you have harrowed me as much as you have given me solace. I've never been given such solace since – since I was a young man and had you to confide in. See how inextricably wrapped up you are in my torture! But now you must go. My spirit wants you to stay, but for your sake you must go. That man will make you a good husband. He's kind, and he will be successful, because he is godly and a hard worker.'

They fell silent for a moment, watching the children's antics

without seeing, hearing their laughter and shrieks without hear
ing. At length, she said: 'I have thought it over so much, dea;
and I know it will be good for the boys. And I want mor
children. I'm getting old. I'm thirty-seven. I feel the need for
husband – and for everything else that goes with being a wife
I want to be near you, but I feel guilty more often than you
know, Hubertus. Your wife is a fine woman; it is not her faul
that she and I cannot understand each other as intimately a
you and I can. I'm fond of Cranley, and I can willingly becom
his wife. I could surrender myself to him without any revulsio;
and even be happy with him, even though I don't love him as
should love a man – as I loved Jacques and as I love you. Bu
two things stop me when I think of marrying him.'

He glanced at her puzzledly.

'Yes, two things. One is you – you know that already. Th
other is my name. If I marry Cranley I will no longer b
Mevrouw van Groenwegel.'

He turned upon her an incredulous look. 'You mean . . .'

She stiffened. 'Yes, I mean I'm proud of our name.'

'Our name? Proud of it? Van Groenwegel?' He began t
tremble. His mouth took on a cruel downward curve. 'Afte
what you have told me about those filthy cousins of ours o;
the Canje!'

'Your half-brothers and half-sisters, Hubertus.'

'Don't remind me. Don't remind me!' He spat out the word
in a low, savage voice that might not have been audible fou
feet behind them. 'I don't want to remember how close I am t
them in blood. It makes me feel tainted, too. You hear me
Tainted. It is because of them – and their foul mother – that
have such low urges. It is because of them that I suffer suc
mental torture. It's the bad blood in me, Faustina. The vi;
blood. And now you tell me you're proud of the name. I can
understand that.'

'Yes, you can.' She had not lost her composure for a secon
She stood stiffly, staring out on the compound. In a moment h
would be calm, too. She had no need to fear him. Out of th
corner of her eye she watched him relax. Watched him no
slowly, and heard him say: 'Yes, I can. That's the terrible par
my dear. I can. I'm proud of the name myself, though I spit
you for saying you are.' He began to laugh suddenly, as thoug

t, some secret joke that had just come to him.

'What is it now?'

'You. You I'm laughing at. I've just remembered. You proud of our name. You who are a bastard. Aunt Mathilde's child of in.'

'That does not take from me the blood of the Van Groenvegels which I got from my mother.'

'No. No.' He gripped her arm. 'I have said a filthy thing, my love. I am dirt. You should feel ashamed to step on me.' He uttered a muffled sob, turned and hurried inside.

About an hour later, she was in the living-room when footsteps sounded on the front steps, and there was a knock. Immediately from an upstairs window came a shout. 'Yes, Overgaar! I'm up here!'

'I – oh, yes, of course, Mynheer! I have come to report, Mynheer!'

'Report! I'm listening!'

Overgaar, who was not accustomed to shouting up his report, seemed for an instant completely at a loss, for he was silent.

'Overgaar!'

'Yes, Mynheer!'

'Let me hear your report! I'm waiting!'

'Yes, Mynheer. Immediately. Fields Ten, Twelve and Seventeen were weeded satisfactorily. Gang Number Seven worked on the three newly planted fields as you instructed yesterday, Mynheer, but I was not satisfied with what they did. Jubst says there was too much laughing and fooling. He has promised to see that the drivers are stricter tomorrow . . .'

Faustina smiled as she listened to the man go through his report. She could envisage Hubertus upstairs in the bedroom, solidly posted at the window, his face a harsh block, only the eyes living and tortured. Again pity moved in her. It was doubly terrible to witness the sufferings of a strong man. One expected the weak to suffer . . .

'Men on punishment – three! Habbak disobeyed an order the driver gave him just before the horn sounded for meals at mid-day, Mynheer. He refused to sharpen his cutlass as Barram told him to do, and the work he did suffered. It was just before the horn sounded that Barram ordered him –'

'You said that before! Is that the full extent of his mis
demeanour?'

'Yes, Mynheer! Yes! He disobeyed an order!'

'Give him fifteen lashes!'

Faustina sat forward.

Overgaar uttered a soft gasp. 'Fifteen lashes, Mynheer?'

'I said fifteen lashes! Is your hearing defective?'

'Yes – no Mynheer. No. But – but –'

'But what?'

'Isn't that – a little too harsh a punishment, Mynheer?'

'Are you daring to criticise my judgement!'

'No, no, Mynheer! I apologise. I apologise humbly. Fifteen
lashes it shall be! Mynheer, the next is Pallam. He stole two
plantains and a yam from Rebbama. I searched in his logie
myself and found them.'

'You are in no doubt whatever about his offence, then?'

'No, Mynheer. He did it, there can be no doubt whatever.'

'Very well! Take him behind the carpenter's shed and weigh
his hands and feet and see that he lies for an hour on broken
bottles.'

Faustina rose, deciding that she must act. She must go and
speak to him. It was not the man he was sentencing to this
torture; it was himself: he would writhe on the broken bottles,
not the man.

Yet she stood irresolute, fearful. To approach him now would
be like beckoning to a thunder-cloud and asking to be struck
by a bolt. She heard him sentencing the third man . . . 'Ten
lashes – and cut his salt-fish ration by half a pound!'

She moved out quickly to the veranda and Overgaar on the
point of going paused and looked at her, his expression that of
a man just risen to his feet after a violent collision and fall. She
beckoned him in silence to come into the sitting-room and he
followed her without a word.

'Overgaar,' she murmured, 'please don't carry out those
sentences at once. Wait a while. I think he will change his
mind.'

'Mevrouw, whatever is the matter with the master?' Over
gaar threw a scared glance toward the stairway in the dining
room. 'I have never known him to be so severe. And broken
bottles! It is years we have never done such a thing to a slave –

and it was for a very serious offence then. I know the other planters do it, but Mynheer van Groenwegel! Such a kind and upright gentleman! He has warned us so often to be firm but moderate with our people – and now this! I feel – I feel – I cannot tell you how I feel, Mevrouw. This is beyond me.'

'Something has upset him. Please go now. And do nothing for let us say half an hour. By then I think he will have come to you and reduced the sentences. Go quickly, Overgaar.'

The man went and she waited a moment then hurried into the dining-room meaning to go upstairs to him. But Rosalind appeared from the pantry, and she looked very white and troubled. 'Faustina, did you hear what he told Overgaar to do? Were you listening when he shouted down to him?'

'Yes. Yes, I heard.'

'It's terrible. Whatever can have happened to him?' She bit her lip, flushed and turned away, began to take up things from the sideboard and put them down. Abruptly she glanced at Faustina. 'Can you say what it is that could have upset him during the past hour?'

Before Faustina could reply they heard footsteps on the stairs, and glancing up, they saw Hubertus coming down. His face, blankly stolid as it always was, gave no indication of what thunder might be brewing within him. Even his eyes, usually so easy to read, failed to tell them anything.

'Hubertus,' said Rosalind.

'Yes my dear?' He paused and smiled at her – gently with enquiry.

'Those three men on punishment – I heard – don't you think you have dealt with them a little too severely?'

He nodded – his manner non-committal, though vaguely sad, troubled; his answer, however, was very clear. 'Yes,' he said, 'I think I have.' He spoke quietly, unemotionally, in a tone of bald statement.

The two women stared at him in silence. He rubbed a hand slowly down his cheek. Dusk was gathering, and they all looked grey standing there. Outside the cicada shrieked. Stopped and shrieked again.

'You will tell Overgaar not to carry out the sentences?'

'No. No, Rosalind. I'm truly sorry I lost control of myself,

89

but the sentences must be carried out. It would be bad policy to reverse my decision. A matter of principle.'

4

A LIMBO of several long weeks elapsed.

Hubertus had nothing to say. Nor had Faustina. Cranley asked nothing.

Edward spoke. Without warning he said 'Yes' and 'No', and laughed as though at a joke only he could divine. Within two or three weeks he could utter phrases. He was the especial delight of Jacqueline and Mary and Susan. Luise appeared fonder of Storm and Raphael; some music in Edward, unheard by the others, seemed to strike dissonance in the soul of Luise and set off a tocsin of warning that kept her from him.

Clara was everyone's favourite, but herself she had no favourites. A gay, bubbling child with a laugh shrill like her mother's, she fascinated all, children and adults, but would let herself be fascinated by none.

Gert Leiker's mother died in November, of an ailment brought on by age – she was eighty-one. Not of the Sickness which had passed its peak and was rapidly on the decline.

The goatsuckers cried hoo-yoo! The fire-flies flashed in the dark, and at six o'clock the cicadas shrieked a prelude to the night. And in the still dry-weather gloom, when they were all in bed, they would sometimes hear the roar of a baboon in the bush – a cruel coughing bark that seemed to warn of death crouched in some secret alcove.

The rains of December had just begun when the Beckleses of Hurley announced – and it came like a merry shower from some incredible, unsuspected heaven – that their daughter Primrose was betrothed and would be married in January to Wilfred Maybury! It shook the river. And every planter shook with good-natured laughter.

'Really, I – the truth is, Hubertus, it – it – well, it happened. I mean, I really can't explain it, but from the instant I met her that Sunday at Cranley's place I – I just knew that here was – here was a special person. You follow me?' Wilfred turned red, then white, then red again. 'And to think that she's been living

90

there at Hurley without my even knowing of her existence! Oh, she's a splendid girl. M-m-most endearing in every way. I c-c-consider myself extremely lucky, I can tell you.'

Hubertus patted him slowly, affectionately, on the back, and Faustina saw that there was moisture at the corners of his eyes. 'I'm quite certain, Wilfred, that you are not more happy than I. Now, tell us, how many slaves has her father?'

Wilfred laughed, turned purple, red, white in rapid succession, and gasped: 'You do have a sense of humour, Hubert. Ha, ha! Really, I – well, the truth is, I do know. He has fifty-eight – forty-two males and sixteen females and children. All strong, able-bodied specimens, the men; at least ten of them from Angola. And he's doing well in coffee. Last year he exported, officially, eighteen bags and two barrels of the beans, and in the usual undercover trade with the Islands' – Wilfred lowered his voice as every planter did when broaching this aspect of trade – 'one barrel and eight bags. Oh, he's a good man, old Beckles. From Barbados, though he has a brother and sister in Antigua.'

'Wilfred! Please! That is enough,' laughed Rosalind. 'You haven't told us yet what day is the wedding.'

'By heaven, haven't I? Very thoughtless of me. It's the s-s-second Sunday in January. Oh, I say, I haven't told you! Father is m-m-most enraptured with the idea of my getting married. He – he – you should see him fawning on me! We're the best of friends these days, I can tell you. He's ordered Bentham to repair the house from top to bottom. Says I can't v-v-very well bring a bride into a broken-down old hut like that. He wants to add a new wing, by God! Can you believe it?'

'Of course we can believe it,' said Rosalind. It was the first time Faustina had seen her so emotional. 'Father is very fond of you, if only you knew it! Oh, I'm sure you'll be happy. You must bring her to see us soon. At Christmas. We'll have you all to Christmas breakfast.'

A limbo of long days moving toward Christmas.

And still silence. They would meet on the veranda as they had done before September – sometimes alone, sometimes with Rosalind and the girls. And between them there was still respect

91

and admiration. But besides this there was the silence that had come upon them since September.

It's as if, thought Faustina, we have agreed in our spirits upon a cessation of judgement, a cessation of decision.

Another time she thought: We might be hovering in a void where our reason and our feelings have retreated into some nether place of waiting.

Meanwhile, Edward spoke. Raphael climbed. Clara laughed. The routine, everyday anticlimaxes of the living of people about them continued. With mocking deliberation, it sometimes seemed. Some arch-demon might have been manipulating incidents like the fire-flies' nightly pyrotechnics, and the hoo-yooing of the goatsuckers. The monotonous late-afternoon singing of the cicada. The children's antics and the rippling parade of moment by moment banalities that could not be avoided, that must be tolerated even amid the stress of greater issues.

They saw Cranley every Sunday, but he, too, would make no move to destroy the doldrum quiet. He was polite, cheerful, witty – and mildly sentimental when Clara happened to be present . . . 'Yes, there can be no doubt about it. Her mother over again. I'm convinced her mother looked precisely like this as a child.'

These were the most delicate moments, and the sudden silence that often followed such observations held the lightning of dénouement. There would be a vague fidgeting among them, as though they could feel a phantom wind chilly on their cheeks: the background suspiration of an unseen quartet who, in another dimension, were undergoing these precise tensions.

Two days before Christmas it was raining. Rain came down in a persistent thin-to-coarse drizzle from a sky one sheet of dull greyness. It had been raining all the night before, and the trees, sagging in every branch, every leaf sleekly wet, dripped slow under-foliage showers of their own so that to pass under them was to be subjected to a desultory barrage of drops. But each drop was at least four times the size of a drop falling beyond the shelter of the leaves.

Hubertus had gone for the day to Borsselen to attend a meeting of the Burgher Officers ordered by the Commandeur three days before. The agenda read: 1. The illicit trade in mules with the inhabitants of the Spanish colony of Venezuela. 2.

The illicit barter of produce with the English in the Caribbean Sea, contrary to the ruling of the Directors of the Dutch West India Company.

Hubertus had read aloud the agenda, and on his face Faustina had seen the old sly smile slowly taking shape. Many of the mules that turned the sugar-mill on Good Heart had come from Venezuela, and many a hogshead of sugar had been smuggled to Barbados in barter for plantation supplies – supplies urgently needed and which would have arrived from Holland only after long and crippling delay.

'What can we do, my dear?' Hubertus had smiled, after signing the circular and returning it to the man who had brought it. 'Mules are necessary for the running of the mill. The Mill must be maintained and kept in good running order, and we need parts to repair it. We need tools, implements for the fields, clothing material for ourselves and for our people. If we waited for the occasional ships from Holland for these things we would find ourselves in a desperate state.'

'That's perfectly obvious,' said Faustina, nodding.

'Yes. Yes, I suppose it is,' said Rosalind, nodding, too, but uncertainly, her gaze lowered.

'It's illegal – we all know it's illegal. Gravesande in Essequibo knows it, but he has never taken any action to try to stop it, for he's a reasonable man. Vessels from New England, as you know, are not admitted unless they bring mules or horses, or the salted heads to prove that they sailed with them. But the great majority of vessels arrive with salted heads – the animals die on the way when the vessels are becalmed. We must have live animals, therefore we must do illegal trade with Venezuela. Van den Heuvel, new as he is, knows it, too, but he must make a pretence of discussing the matter and registering disapproval, for the minutes of our meetings are sent to the Directors, and the Directors must be reassured that the colony is being properly governed.'

Rosalind uttered a tentative sound, then said: 'It's just the pretence I don't like. It seems so unprincipled, Hubertus.'

'Unprincipled in men's eyes, my dear – but not in God's. God can see into our hearts, and He knows when we act in a spirit of corruption and when we act because of urgent necessity.'

'Yes. Yes, that is so,' murmured his wife, gaze lowered.

So today Hubertus had gone to Borsselen. A meeting of the Burgher Officers was held every three months – on the first Monday in March, June, September and December. But this month illness and extremely adverse weather conditions had caused a postponement until today. Any officer absent 'without lawful excuse' was liable to a fine of fifty guilders. Hubertus had never been once absent.

At about five o'clock that afternoon it was still raining. Persistently, tirelessly, in a thin-to-coarse drizzle from a sky one sheet of dull greyness turning muddy-grey as the twilight gathered.

The whole day – since Hubertus had departed for Borsselen – Faustina had been hearing in her fancy the echo of two or three sentences uttered a few days ago by the master of Good Heart. It was as though they had remained poised in the sky and now with the rain kept monotonously trailing down and through her consciousness . . . 'God can see into our hearts, and He knows when we act in a spirit of corruption and when we act because of urgent necessity.' All through the morning, all through the early afternoon. A dirge-like accompaniment to the dribble-dribble of the drops on the roof . . . 'God can see into our hearts . . . ' The swish and gurgle of the rivulets in the compound. The hiss and tick of the drops amidst the leaves of the mango and sapodilla trees . . . 'He knows when we act in a spirit of corruption and when we act because of urgent necessity.' Raphael and Clara splashing bare-footed in the compound. Storm and Edward running naked around the house bathing in the water spattering down from a gutter. In the wet warm day. 'God can see into our hearts . . . ' The murmur of voices in the dining-room where Mynheer Anton Ruys was instructing the four girls and the two Harker and the four Lieker children . . . '*Jacta est alea* . . . ' A dissenting cluck . . . '*Alea jacta est* . . . The decision is taken. The die is cast . . . ' She came to a halt in her pacing of the veranda . . . '*Jacta alea est! Much better! Much better! That is it! The die has been cast! The decision has been taken! Correct!* . . . ' She continued to pace.

Now at five o'clock she walked beneath the mango trees, and the foliage dripped their slow big drops upon her, but she did

94

not care, for within her she kept saying: '*Jacta alea est*. The decision is taken. The die has been cast.' And amidst the hiss and click of the drops falling from the leaves whispered the voice that said: 'God can see into our hearts . . .' On and on it whispered, and the dusk deepened.

It was damp but warm and she was tough. Though she was soon wet through and through she did not feel chilled. She paced and waited.

'*Jacta alea est* . . .'

The dusk deepened. But when the sound of squelching steps came from the direction of the river the dusk was not too deep for her to make out the massive, short figure approaching along the driveway. She stepped out into the driveway and awaited his coming . . . 'God can see into our hearts . . .' On and on he came, conquering the mud, a mountain-man of muscle and stern purpose, the rain slashing fruitlessly at his bulk. Behind him came two black men, taller than he, their bare torsos wet with rain. But their height was not enough to destroy the impressive forcefulness of their master as he strode ahead of them.

She saw him raise his head alertly, and knew that he had recognised her. His face was mildly surprised as he came to a stop and said: 'Walking in the rain? I thought you had given up that practice before you left the Essequibo, my dear.'

She waited until the two slaves had passed them before saying: 'I've never stopped liking it. I used to do it sometimes on the Berbice. But this afternoon I did it because I wanted to meet you here.'

'I see.'

'I've come to a decision, and we must talk, Hubertus.'

He nodded, his smile of a moment before going, his face reverting to its customary stolidity. Yet she could detect a kindly light in his eyes. A tenderness. 'Do you mind getting wet in the rain?' she asked.

'No. Do you wish us to walk among the trees?'

'Yes, I was going to suggest that.'

As he took her arm, he said: 'You are very wet. You must have been a long time in the rain.' He spoke almost as he might have done to Jacqueline or Mary and she felt both amused and touched. She reminded him of walks she had taken with him in the rain. 'Always we keep harking back to the Essequibo.

I believe our true spirits were left there.'

'Yes, sometimes I believe that, too. And your presence here makes it seem doubly so. It is as if what I see of you here is the shadow of what still lives on the Essequibo. But shadows can haunt so!' He turned her to him and pressed her to him. 'What is this decision? Is it Cranley? Have you made up your mind to marry him and leave my home?'

She said nothing, her eyes shut. She could feel water trickling down her back – and between her breasts. Down her neck, and down her temples. It could have been tears – a deluge of tears that, unshed, had collected all day and now had been released drenching her whole body. A soothing bath. If only it could continue without stopping for days and weeks . . . No, in a few days she would be betrothed.

'I've decided on that – yes. On Sunday I shall tell him.'

He began to nod slowly, still holding her to him. 'Good. It will be good for you both. You will be happy with him. I should have told you to do it, but I lacked the courage. I'm human, and I could not say something to you which would have meant the loss of your nearness. I have my weak spots despite my principles.' His eyes were half-shut and she could hear the breath like an agonised wind inside him.

'How did the meeting go? Did you resolve to have all offenders severely punished?' She began to laugh, and the vibrations of her merriment penetrated his bulk and were taken up within him and carried on in a lower octave. Deep bass grunting laughter moved through him. They stood clutching each other and quivering. And the drops came down upon them from the sheltering foliage of an avocado pear tree. Large leaves have avocado pear trees, and large drops fell upon them. On their heads. On their shoulders. Then they stopped laughing and she said: 'All day I kept remembering what you said a few days ago.'

'What was that?'

She told him. 'And I thought to myself: "If I ask him to do that it could not be because I am corrupt but because – because of urgent necessity." That's what I kept saying to myself, Hubertus.'

'Why?'

'Because I do have something to ask you, and I do feel it

96

isn't out of a corrupt spirit that I want to.' She hesitated, then said: 'I think I could be happy with Cranley, Hubertus – but only if I could go to him taking with me the memory of you. Have me – just once. Now. I won't mind going to him after. But – but – to go to him without ever having known you – without ever having – no, no! I couldn't face it, my love. I would grow old badly. I would grow old feeling that God had cheated me of the best and most treasured thing I needed. Only once Hubertus. Here – under this tree – let us call back ourselves from Essequibo and let us be happy for – for a few minutes – half an hour – then we can send back ourselves, and we'll be at peace. We'll never rest if we don't, Hubertus. We'll grow old itching and in pain. We'll –'

He put his hand over her mouth and she saw that he was smiling, his eyes still half-shut. It was very dark, and she could barely see.

'You will make yourself breathless if you say more,' he murmured. He was trembling, and she knew that today she had not let herself pace in vain. Lowering her to the soppy carpet of century-piled leaves, he laughed deep inside and said: 'On the Essequibo you did not talk so much. We are there now, so be of few words.'

5

THEY saw the lamp, a mild red eye, in the doorway that gave into the living-room, and knew that Rosalind had placed it there. Its light shone on the veranda and on the steps that led up to the veranda. They went upstairs, and saw her waiting in the living-room. She smiled slightly, sat forward and said to Hubertus: 'You're late.' A pause then: 'I saw the men coming. You were with Overgaar or Hubst?' She spoke like a frightened child, and it was obvious that she knew what had happened.

'No, I was not with Overgaar or Hubst, my dear.' He smiled gently, and Faustina watched him, and felt a deep content spreading within her. It was so good to know that one's estimate of a person had been accurate. 'I was walking with Faustina – in the rain. Among the trees.'

'Oh. Yes. Yes, she said she wished to walk in the rain. A

long while before you arrived. You – she met you on the drive-way.'

'Yes.' He glanced round. 'Where are the children?'

'Mary and Jacqueline are in the dining-room doing their lessons for tomorrow. I've sent the others up to bed.'

'Faustina has come to a decision, Rosalind.'

'Yes?'

'She has decided to marry Cranley Clackson.'

'I'm going to tell him on Sunday when he comes,' said Faustina.

'But he's coming tomorrow. Have you forgotten? Tomorrow is Christmas Eve. He's spending three days with us.'

'Why, so he is. How foolish of me to have forgotten. I've been so distracted all day. Then I shall tell him tomorrow that I accept his offer.'

'You're both wet. I think you should change at once. I – please let me wish you all good fortune, Faustina.'

Faustina nodded. They were all silent, and the lamplight glimmered on the pools of water spreading on the floor. Glimmered and blurred as Faustina looked down. She uttered a soft gasp and moved forward quickly. She bent and kissed her cousin-in-law, touching her knee with the tips of her fingers. The fingers lingered, and she said: 'Thanks. You're so kind, so good. Oh, if only I knew better! If only I could have told you the many things I've wanted to. You're so good.' She rose, turned with a sob, and said to Hubertus: 'Tell her for me, Hubertus. Please. Tell her and make her understand. Oh, I can't!' She hurried out of the room – yet as she went upstairs she was cool and relieved at the core of her feelings. . . . I've done no wrong. I've done what I had to do. If only he could get her to understand! Oh, Hubertus my love! I feel so happy now I could swoon away into death and not mind. I could marry an ogre now and not care. Rainy days will always be happy days for me after today. Tell her that for me. Oh, make her understand how the scent of wet leaves will ever be with us so long as we live, and that it couldn't be wrong. Only evil people could think it wrong. By every rule it was right.

Harriet, her personal slave, came in to help her undress, but she told the girl: 'Go. I shall undress alone. There are leaf-

98

stains on my dress. I want to kiss them, Harriet. I shall never wash this dress.'

The girl stared at her in wonder, but she seemed to grow infected with happiness, too, for she smiled widely, her black eyes alight with the lamplight, before she left the room.

Two days after Christmas Hubertus and Cranley made a trip to Hurley, and on their return Hubertus said: 'They're willing to fall in with our plans, and the girl herself thinks it would be suparb.'

'Superb,' corrected Rosalind.

'Superb,' amended Hubertus.

'I'm certain the idea of a double wedding will delight Wilfred,' smiled Cranley, 'though it does seem an impertinence not to have consulted him first. On my way back I shall drop in and ask him to scold me severely.'

It had been an enjoyable Christmas, with genuine goodwill among them. For Faustina there were many tearful moments, but they were tears for the nobility she saw in human nature. On the afternoon of Christmas Eve Day, not an hour after his arrival, she took Cranley on to the side veranda and told him what had happened between Hubertus and herself the evening before. 'And now,' she had said, 'I can marry you. Do you still wish to?' He had looked at her, his head slightly tilted, and after a pause during which his sad eyes slowly grew amused, he said: 'Had my notions of fidelity been what our Christian society deems they should be, my dear woman, two things would have happened before I arrived in this colony: I should have murdered my dear wife and committed suicide. For the moment, may I have your permission to kiss your hand and again ask you to be my wife?' . . . Tears . . . On behalf of Rosalind, too – tears. It was so obvious that Rosalind felt deeply injured. Indeed, Faustina was sure that a little universe of trust had collapsed in her, for Rosalind's notions of fidelity were very much what Christian society deemed them to be. Yet not once did she show a trace of hatred. A brave woman, thought Faustina. A noble woman. I wonder if I could have shown such fineness of spirit. Oh, I wonder. And I wonder if she has even once tasted with Hubertus such bliss as I have done. I hope she has — once, twice, innumerable times. . . . In a dry, soft bed and on damp leaves under rain-dripping trees. Poor creature. I have robbed you, but I am a thief unrepentant, and to the end of my days I shall be unrepentant. Oh, sweet wet leaves! Lovely damp rain. . . .

PART THREE

1

THE going away to Rylands of Faustina and her children brought gloom for many weeks upon Jacqueline and Mary and Susan. Luise did not seem to mind, though Rosalind could detect in the child a furtive quietude that had not been apparent in her when the three boys were at Good Heart. Questioning her did not help, for Luise only laughed and said that nothing was the matter. Yet the strange background mood remained. Jacqueline and Mary and Susan openly expressed their feelings – Mary and Susan sometimes cried – but Luise refrained from any display of regret. 'I'm certain they must be happy up there,' was the most she would comment. And then, shortly after, as though off guard, she would fall into a dreaming quiet, sometimes starting alert on her own, sometimes upon being addressed by her mother or one of her sisters.

It disturbed Rosalind – but not for long. I'm probably being fanciful, Rosalind assured herself, and put the matter out of her thoughts. She had been born with this capacity to put from her anything that threatened to disturb her seriously. Indeed, had she not possessed this natural form of defence, the weeks and months that followed Faustina's marriage would have been extremely unhappy ones for her, for, in her way of viewing it, she had suffered a great wrong at the hands of Hubertus and Faustina. At Christmas, when Hubertus had told her of his making love to his cousin, she had not been astounded, for her intuition had told her it would have happened like this; she had sensed that the event was inevitable. Nevertheless, hearing her husband confess it, she had felt as injured as though it had come as a shock; she had smiled and nodded and murmured that she forgave him. 'Don't let it trouble you. God has willed it. I forgive you.'

Yes, she felt that there was much to be forgiven. She must be Christian and generous, she must continue to be a loving and devoted wife – but she had been gravely hurt; she had been betrayed. Hubertus, her hero, had shown himself weak, but he was still her hero – perhaps even more fiercely so. Yet in her there stirred a grudge. He would forever be indebted to her. He would have to repent for many a year his weak moment of one evening; he would have to cherish her more than he had ever done if she was to feel that he had wiped out the debt. Perhaps she would never feel that he had.

During the few days Cranley spent with them at Christmas she found herself greatly taxed to keep up a front of good cheer, but she had succeeded. Self-pity had helped her. How sorry she had been for herself at Christmas! And how much she had had to reassure herself that she did not hate Faustina, even while knowing in the muttering tenseness of her inner mood that she detested her, and was jealous of her. Hated her with a hate that had been simmering in her for months. Yet a hate that did not damage her, for she fought it with courage, recognising it for what it was – the animal in her reacting to the presence of a female animal who was a rival. She had suppressed it because she had known it for a thing that was not fine, not noble. She had prayed and she had struggled. And in the process her manner had seemed unnatural.

How could she have got close to me when I was fighting not to let her see I hated her with a brute hate! She is a fine person – Hubertus was not wrong; I know she is fine – but I am human. I want to be Christian, I want to be generous and noble, but I am human. She would never think so. She must think it's the English stiffness in me. Only Hubertus knows, and only that should matter to me. Yet he and I are not the same now in our attitudes. He is kind and good to me, considerate, but the man himself – the animal in him – has strayed from me. It's his cousin he wants to caress. Distance has made no difference to his desire for her. I know that. I shall never tell him, for it would disturb his conscience still more. He and his poor conscience that never leaves him alone. He was born harrowed, and to the end of his days he will be harrowed. I must never do anything to increase the agony he suffers. No matter how much pain he causes me I must never repay him in similar fashion.

By the second Sunday in January, the day of the double wedding at Good Heart, she had found peace within herself. She had put the trouble aside. God, she assured herself, had helped her to do this.

Visits between the two plantations continued to be frequent. One Sunday Cranley and his family came to Good Heart; the next Hubertus and his family went to Rylands. Save the Sundays when they all went to Borsselen or to some other planter's house for service.

As the middle of the year approached – Faustina was big with child – Rosalind discerned that the struggle in her husband was reaching a new height of tension. Sympathetic, she tried to discover the cause, but he, as always, smiled and assured her that he was just being himself. She must not be troubled . . . Is it Faustina?' . . . 'It is all sorts of things, my dear. The fear of being disloyal to my principles.'

In July, he resigned as an officer of the Burgher Militia – to the dismay of his fellow planters, to his wife's great concern. 'It was necessary,' he said to Gert Lieker and James Harker; it was after Sunday Service at Borsselen. 'The affairs of my plantation have become too onerous of late. I cannot conscientiously carry out my duties as a Burgher Officer.'

A few minutes later, Rosalind, watching him covertly, saw him look at Faustina and grow agonised as though with a terrible fear. He revealed it in his eyes, and only she would have noticed it. Openly his manner toward his cousin was impeccable. Restrained and politely affectionate as was becoming. And Faustina, felt Rosalind, was behaving as a good wife should; she was obviously fond of Cranley; obviously happy. Only in brief moments when – so it seemed, her guard weakened, would she betray the deep animal passion that still lurked in her for Hubertus. But Rosalind forgave her.

In August Faustina gave birth to a son, and it was then that Rosalind knew that she would have to be strong as she had ever been strong before. Hubertus pressed his head against her and sobbed. 'Even this,' he said, 'I could not have been spared. Even this.'

'My dear! Oh, my dear, what is the matter? Why should you be upset because she has had a son! We must go and congratulate them, Hubertus. Cranley must be so happy. And she herself. What is the matter, dear?'

They were upstairs in the bedroom, and downstairs the girls' shrill voices could be heard . . . 'Aunt Mary – I shall insist he calls me Aunt Mary. Oh, I wonder what Faustina will call him . . . ' Jacqueline said: 'I wish I were there to see him. I'm sure he must resemble Mr Clackson. . . .'

105

Rosalind saw her husband wince. Hubertus began to smile, only it was not his sly smile. There was agony in his eyes, at his mouth, on his brows. 'I wonder if he resembles Mr Clackson. My child, I wonder, too, if you only knew.' He looked at Rosalind. 'There's no mystery, my love. You must see now why I am upset. I've been dreading this event. Hoping it might have been later. A month later. Had it been next month I should have been relieved – but this month. August.'

'You mean . . . ?'

'Yes, I mean I have been fearing it is my child, and now it seems that my fears have been justified. August the twenty-ninth. December the twenty-third. Think back, my dear. Think back.'

'I see. But, Hubertus, it may be premature. It has happened to several women. It is nothing very uncommon.'

He nodded. 'I've considered that – but there is still the doubt. Why couldn't she have given birth in October. January. October. That would have been normal. I would have believed it was Cranley's child. But now. August. The twenty-ninth. It could be mine, Rosalind love. It could be. Do you think it is? How shall I ever live this down? How shall I ever be assured that I haven't wronged that poor fellow her husband?'

'But even for you it would be premature, dear. December the twenty-third would mean about the end of September. The middle or the end.'

'Or the end of August. How good of you to try to console me!' He pressed his head against her and groaned softly. Raised it and said: 'Come, we must prepare to leave for Rylands. The tide should turn in about an hour. The children must not come. Please don't let them persuade you. I feel lost, my love. I feel on the path down. Down.'

She had never before seen him so shaken. Such hysterics and dramatics were new to him. Or could it be that with her he had always been at pains to be restrained? Did Faustina know this side of him? Perhaps with Faustina he had behaved like this. . . . The old deep hate began to move in her, but she was stern with it, and would not let it get the better of her.

All the way to Rylands he was silent and shamefaced. Once she heard him mutter: 'It's the bad blood. My mother's blood. Van Groenwegel blood.' He spoke in Dutch but she understood

106

'No restraint. Hysteria. Uncontrolled passions. The blood of beasts.'

At Rylands, they found Faustina in bed with the child and the first thing she said as they entered the room was: 'Oh, I'm glad you've come. I thought I would never have seen you again.'

'Why? Did you have such a bad time?' asked Rosalind.

Hubertus stared at the child, his face very white.

'I nearly died,' Faustina smiled. 'It came before time. I had a fall yesterday morning while coming down from the loft. I missed a rung in the ladder. And Cranley was in the fields. Mabella and Gaza brought me into the room here. Hubertus, what is the matter?' She laughed weakly. 'Don't you like my new son?'

He nodded. 'Yes. Yes, I do. Where is Cranley? In the fields?'

'Yes. He left about an hour ago. I'm out of danger now. Everything is coming on as it should. Cranley has been so good to me.'

Rosalind smiled: 'I think he resembles you very much.' She glanced swiftly at her husband as she said this, and she saw that there was relief in his manner. Faustina nodded and agreed. 'Cranley said so, too. He has my nose and brow, but I think he has Cranley's mouth and chin. Oh, but it's so early to tell. He's not even quite a day old.'

'He's premature,' Hubertus muttered. He started and smiled: 'I'm very glad you have come through safely. It was most imprudent of you to climb that ladder in your condition.'

Rosalind's gaze was out of the window on the glaring noon. She was relieved too – relieved because he was relieved. Within, she smiled, for she was certain that Faustina was lying. She had had no fall, and the child was not premature. But she knew her Hubertus, and she was being compassionate; the lie was a worthy one, and Rosalind felt a warmth of love spread throughout her awareness. . . . She knows that I know she is lying, but God will bless her. He will not frown upon her for telling this lie. . . . Suddenly a fear moved in her. Am I becoming unscrupulous myself? Is my love for him forcing me to lower the standard of my morals? . . . She tried to assure herself that this was foolish, but she knew that it was an evasion. She

107

was making herself party to a lying subterfuge in order to spare him mental agony – agony that he deserved to suffer. He had sinned; it was meet that he should suffer. No. No, she must not think that. She must be compassionate, too. The subterfuge was pardonable; anything that would spare a fellow-human pain was pardonable.

Faustina was saying: 'You must go and find Cranley and congratulate him, Hubertus dear. He's so happy. He wanted a son.'

'Yes. Yes, I must go and find him. Immediately.' He bent and kissed her cheek. 'I'm so relieved that – that you are in good health.'

'I'm strong. The old blood! We're a bad family but no one can say we're not tough physical specimens.' She laughed, and Rosalind could detect real happiness in her laughter. 'Look at his face, Rosalind! He hates me to refer to the family. He's just the opposite to what Grandma Hendrickje was. Go and find Cranley, dear. Ask Lakker to saddle a mule for you. He'll show you the way to take.'

After he had left the room, Faustina said, 'Sit by me, Rosalind. You stand there looking so thoughtful. Are you happy for me?'

'Very,' murmured Rosalind. It was strange, but she always felt shy when Faustina looked at her; it seemed that the other woman's eyes probed into places where they ought not to. 'I'm glad it is all over. Where are the children – the other children, I should say? They seem very quiet.'

'Latako has taken them out in his *corial*. They went upstream.'

'Oh. You have Indians here now, have you?'

'Yes, Latako came with a group of others about four months ago. They belong to a Wapsiani tribe, and Cranley was very pleased to let them settle here. They're excellent hunters, and Raphael and Storm are very fond of them. They simply haunt their camp.'

'Don't you think them rather young to wander about the plantation alone? The twins are only four, Faustina.'

'It will do them good. Jacques said Grandma Hendrickje always advocated that boys should be allowed to roam in the

108

en air from an early age. It toughens them. Only Edward is
ot keen. He prefers the house.'

'Yes, there's something really odd about that little fellow.
e has such a thoughtful, yet merry, expression. By the way,
always meant to ask you. How did you come to give him an
nglish name?'

Faustina gave her a swift look, pinkened a trifle and said: 'I
d it as a gesture of affection to Hubertus. I knew Hubertus was
nd of the English and would be pleased if I gave one of my
ildren an English name. I discussed it with Jacques long be-
re the twins were born, and we had decided that if it were a
n we'd call him by an English name – if a girl Hendrickje,
ter Grandma Hendrickje. When twins came along, well – well,
thought I would name one Edward and one after the
irecteur-General.'

There was a silence, and Rosalind knew that Faustina was not
mpletely at ease. From outside came the rattle of a saddle,
e click and clink of its adjustment on the back of an animal.
he day was dry and hot. The heat entered at the window in
fling waves. From where she sat on the bed, Rosalind could
e the still, glittering leaves of a fruit-tree.

'You know that the child is not premature, don't you,
osalind?'

Rosalind started and blushed. 'Oh. Yes. Yes, I suspected.
ut please don't trouble. I think I understand.'

Faustina touched her hand, smiling. 'This is the first time
e heard you say you understand – and say it as though you
lly understand.'

A silence again. A little bush-beetle was buzzing in the
fters.

'Hubertus has been very upset these past few months.'

'I know', Faustina murmured. 'I sensed it. And then he re-
ned as an officer of the Burgher Militia. When I heard that I
ew it was serious.'

'I cannot stand deception of any kind, Faustina, but for his
ke I will say nothing. I will pretend I have suspected nothing.'

'I'm glad. It's the best thing.'

'But doesn't Cranley know?'

Faustina stirred. 'I'm not certain. There is nothing certain
out anything', Rosalind. In any event, I'm early – two or three

weeks early. I mean, assuming it is Hubertus' child, I'm stil
early. I – ' She broke off, confused, then went on suddenly, '
just don't know what Cranley thinks. He's so good at disguisin
his feelings. He seems happy, and yet . . . '

'But isn't it your duty to tell him you believe it may be – i
may not be his child?'

'I know it is, but I can't bring myself to, Rosalind. I can't.
don't want to hurt him, and perhaps he hasn't reckoned th
months. Men are careless about such things. Perhaps he reall
feels it is his child. Well, why should I disappoint him b
announcing that it may be Hubertus'! And I'm so happy t
have borne Hubertus a child. Oh, I shouldn't say it to you, m
dear, but you understand? I love him so much, Rosalind, an
– and I'm proud I've been able to give birth to a Va
Groenwegel by him.'

'But Cranley – your husband!'

'I'm sorry for Cranley. I'm – oh, I never thought I woul
have conceived by Hubertus. Just one occasion. It was such
small chance of it happening. Yet perhaps I should not b
surprised. Hubertus is so virile, and that evening I loved hi
so! In the rain . . . ' Her voice had grown dreamy, almost a
though she had forgotten Rosalind's presence. Her hands wer
slowly clenching and unclenching, and her eyes were narrowed

Rosalind rose, upset. The heat abruptly seemed unbearabl
'Is there – is there anything I can do for you?'

Faustina started, and smiled. 'No. Nothing at all, thank
Please sit down. Don't go.' The child began to make frettin
sounds, wriggling. It was very lightly clothed because of th
heat, and Rosalind could see its shape and length under th
almost diaphanous garment. Faustina gave it the breast, and
it tried to suck, she glanced at Rosalind and said: 'Have yo
noticed the cheekbones? Look.'

'Most new-born infants have high cheekbones.'

'I know, but these are Hubertus' cheekbones. Can't yo
see? Oh, I hope he will resemble Hubertus – and yet I hope
won't. I'm so happy, and yet I feel troubled. No, please don't
yet. Sit with me. I feel so light-headed and foolish. You mu
excuse me.'

Rosalind said nothing, and sat with her, idly watching th
child's inexpert efforts to feed, and hearing the sounds of th

day outside the window. The receding clop-clop of the mule's hoofs came like a dull dirge plucked on slack strings in the puddle of heat that surrounded the house. The bush-beetle must have found its way out, for there was no sound of it in the rafters. Its smell permeated the room for an instant, however – rank, vegetable, musky. Far away a chattering of parrots flared cacophonously and died, all in a few seconds, like a purpose unfulfilled.

After a moment, the leisurely swishing of paddles in water told of some planter going by on the river. The sighing call of the boatmen to the boatmen at the *stelling* fell languidly through the stagnant heat in the room, and the answering call of the boatmen at the *stelling* came after it like a parallel ribbon as limp and warm, as aimless as inevitable.

. . . As inevitable. If only, thought Rosalind, one could be certain that the inevitable would happen. . . . For, then, one could be prepared.

2

DURING the weeks and months that followed Hubertus was tolerably happy. Observing him, Rosalind could see that he honestly believed that the child could very possibly be Cranley's. And as the child grew to look more and more like its mother, Hubertus appeared to grow more certain that he was not the father. Nothing pleased him more than to hear someone crooning and saying: 'Oh, but doesn't he look like Cranley!' And there were many who saw a resemblance to Cranley. Only Rosalind and Faustina smiled and were non-committal. Cranley himself was a sphinx. Try as she would, Rosalind failed to discover from him whether or not he had any doubts about the child's paternity, and once Faustina told her: 'I myself cannot say, my dear. Sometimes I feel he knows, and at other times I'm equally as certain he does not. An odd man in many ways, Cranley.'

On every occasion that Rosalind saw him Cranley seemed as genuinely happy as any man could be. She could not say with truth that she once saw him betray any signs of bitterness or of disappointment in wife or son.

Meanwhile, at Signal, Primrose Maybury suffered an abortion, but again became pregnant, and in February of the following year, 1786, gave birth to a daughter. Easter that year was a very merry occasion for the three families. They gathered on the Sunday at the Rylands house, recently enlarged, and in the afternoon the Liekers brought Predicant Lingius who baptised both Master Graeme Jacques Clackson and Miss Elizabeth Susan Maybury. Rosalind overheard Jacqueline asking Cranley where he had found such an unusual name as Graeme, and Rosalind heard Cranley reply in a lowered voice: 'I admire you for the courage of your curiosity in asking, my girl, but please keep it a secret – and besides my wife only you will be sharing in it: the name belongs to an uncle of mine, Sir Graeme Clackson. Yes, he's a baronet but I prefer not to let it be known that I possess such aristocratic connections. I tell you because you are my special pet.' He chuckled and patted her shoulder lightly. 'My father was a black sheep, you see – that's why the family packed him off to Barbados with my mother and myself. Oh, there's perfidy in other familes besides the Van Groenwegels, believe me.' He put his finger to his mouth, and Rosalind, just around the corner in the dining-room, hastened away silently before she was discovered, her lips pursed in guilt and amusement.

Graeme was just over a year old when Faustina again proved pregnant, a sister for Graeme being born in July, 1769 – the same month in which Hubst, Hubertus' second overseer, was drowned in a boating accident; he had gone hunting with two Indians, and on the way back the *corial*, laden with *labba* carcases, had run into a *tacooba* – a tree-trunk obstruction in the water – and overturned. The Indians, thinking Hubst a good swimmer, had not troubled about him, and the next thing they knew was that he had vanished. Not long after they had reached the shore they saw the water swift with darting ripples and agitated choppy wavelets, and they knew what it meant. *Perai*, the savage swordfish, were active. Hubst's body was never found.

It was not until November that Hubertus succeeded in securing a man to replace Hubst. A pale, but strong, young Scotsman, Robert Guire came from Antigua; he said he had worked as an overseer in St Eustatius, St Kitts and, for a few months, in Surinam. Rosalind liked him at sight, and Hubertus, she could see, had confidence in him. Within the months that followed his arrival he certainly proved himself capable – capable of good work and of consuming large quantities of rum. And there came the day in March, the next year, 1770, when Hubertus went to Borsselen on slave business with the Vendue Master. A day not to be forgotten by Rosalind.

A fine short-dry-weather day, it was pleasant with the cool of March, the sun being obscured every now and then by large masses of fast-moving white clouds. And at frequent intervals the jungle would rustle distantly with an approaching wind that sometimes died away before it could reach the house. When it did it brought with it the rich, turpentine-sweet smell of ripe mangoes, for most of the mango trees were laden with fruit.

Jacqueline had gone to watch the slaves pick mangoes – it was nearly noon – and Mary sat on the veranda assisting her mother with her sewing; they were making clothes for Wilfred's Elizabeth and Faustina's Mathilde. Sewing was Rosalind's chief occupation, and Mary, now that she was considered old enough to give up being tutored, had developed a fondness, too, for the needle. Jacqueline, at nineteen, two years Mary's senior, did not care for sewing, and preferred to roam the plantation.

This was one of the two days of the week when Susan and Luise had to be at Sapphire, the Harkers' plantation, for their English lesson, so only Rosalind and Mary were in the house when the mule bearing Overgaar entered the compound and approached the house.

Mary looked up from her lap and frowned. At seventeen, she was a rather plump girl with the high cheekbones of her father but the blue eyes of her mother. Unlike Jacqueline, she was not pretty, nor did she possess the spirits of her elder sister, and she was far more tractable than any of the other three. 'She is the loyal one,' Hubertus had said once. 'She will be loyal to our way of training.'

'What does Overgaar want here at this hour?' murmured her mother. She and Mary watched the man approach. He dismounted and called up: 'Oh, Mevrouw, could I speak to you for a few minutes? I am embarrassed, and it is very urgent.'

113

'Speak on, Overgaar. What is the matter?'

Rosalind spoke with amused indulgence, for Overgaar was noted for his sensationalism; he became breathless and panicked at the slightest occurrence of an unusual nature, and only Hubertus knew when to take him seriously and when not to.

Overgaar glanced uncertainly at Mary and returned: 'Mevrouw, I should prefer to speak to you alone. Something terrible has happened. It is still happening. Oh, Mevrouw, I am embarrassed. May I speak to you alone?'

'Come up here, then. Come.'

The man fussily tethered his mule to the kitchen stair-post, and as they heard him coming up the stairs Mary rose to go inside, but her mother said: 'No, remain, Mary. He speaks in such a way I can barely understand his Dutch. I'm sure I shall need you to interpret for me.'

So Mary seated herself again, and when Overgaar appeared on the veranda Rosalind explained that it would be perfectly in order for him to speak before Mary. 'She is nearly a grown-up young woman, Overgaar. I think you can say whatever you wish to before her.'

'As you say, Mevrouw, but it is not something for young ears to hear. And yet . . . oh, I'm embarrassed. Mevrouw, I don't know how to begin.'

'Please say whatever you have to say. I'm waiting.'

Overgaar changed from one foot to the other, clasped and unclasped his hands, and then began to tell them what the trouble was about. 'I was in the fields, Mevrouw, in charge of my gangs when I had cause to send a driver to another section where Mynheer Guire was in charge of the work. Some time passed and then the driver returned to me and said that he could not find Mynheer Guire. I spoke to him harshly, telling him he was talking nonsense. I said: "Go back and give my message to Mynheer Guire this instant or you will be fined!" I told him —'

He broke off as Rosalind put up her hand. 'Mary dear, please!'

Mary interpreted, and henceforth Overgaar addressed his explanation to her. 'Oh, my young lady! How astounded I was to learn that Mynheer Guire had deserted his post! It is a serious act! It is a criminal act! Do you know what could have

114

happened in his absence! This is the way that uprisings of our people commence. It is such negligence that causes riots among these black people. When their master turns his back they become idle and talk among themselves, and then they plot mischief. Foul mischief!'

'Yes, Overgaar,' smiled Mary patiently, 'but please go on and tell us what you did. Did you search for him? Did you find him drunk?'

'Ah, you have guessed correctly, my young lady! Correctly! I went to his cottage and found him with a bottle of rum.'

Mary interpreted to her mother who now could not follow the conversation at all. Overgaar spoke in agitated bursts, and to Rosalind he was quite unintelligible. He shook his head and sighed and groaned, and as Mary looked at him and asked him if that was all he shook his head emphatically, shifted from one foot to the other and said in a lowered voice: 'No, my young lady, it is not all. Oh, I'm so embarrassed! Embarrassed! I don't know what to say. I don't know how to tell you what I found.'

'But you say you found him drunk.'

The man clasped his hands; he seemed embarrassed to the point of distraction. Turning slightly, he looked across the compound and stammered: 'I found him drinking, and – and in the cottage with him there was a young lady, my young lady. I – oh, my young lady, it – it was your sister, Miss Jacqueline.' He pressed his hands to his face.

Mary rose, the sewing falling to the floor. Rosalind glanced at her sharply, noting her pallor. 'What is it, Mary? What has he said?'

'Jacqueline, Mother. Jacqueline is in Robert Guire's cottage.'

'What!' She stood up. 'Overgaar, what is this you're saying? My daughter – Miss Jacqueline is with Guire? Did you see them together?'

'Yes, Mevrouw,' muttered Overgaar; he seemed on the point of tears. 'I thought I would surprise him, and crept up silently and peeped into the – into the – oh, it is too embarrassing to say, Mevrouw, but – but I saw them.' He spoke softly in brief sentences, but Rosalind listened carefully and understood. 'Like man and wife, Mevrouw – on a palm-leaf mat on the floor in the living-room. I – I could not believe my eyes! Miss Jac-

115

queline! That pure, innocent young girl – a child I have admired from a tender age. What a foul monster of a man he must be. A bottle of rum on the floor beside them, Mevrouw. He was drunk and muttering into her face as they – they embraced. I – I crept away softly. I – oh, I've never been so embarrassed in all my life. I wish you will forgive me for coming to tell you this, Mevrouw, but I felt it was my duty. Oh, I *know* it was my duty!'

'Yes, you are perfectly right, Overgaar. It was your duty. Will you please go now? I shall attend to the matter myself. Don't go back to the cottage. Go back to the fields at once and see after your work.'

'Very well, Mevrouw – and my deep regrets. My very deep regrets.'

He hurried away, and Rosalind stood frowning out on the compound, undecided what to do. It would be undignified and indecent for her to go to Guire's cottage and surprise them; yet she must do something.

Mary was biting her lip uncomfortably, her cheeks pink. She had sat down again and was pretending to continue with her sewing.

Overgaar's mule had hardly disappeared among the fruit-trees when Rosalind saw Jacqueline appear. She moved at a leisurely pace across the compound, making for the house, and her face seemed as composed as ever. Watching her, Rosalind would not have thought for an instant that she had just come from a love assignation. . . . Is it possible that she could be so deceptive? I can't believe it. Did Overgaar just come here and tell us what he did? This is like being in a dream.

She sat down again, and a few minutes later they heard Jacqueline come up the front stairs and move across the living-room, then enter the dining-room and begin to ascend the stairway. At this point Rosalind called to her to come, making her voice as normal and composed as she could.

Jacqueline answered – also in her usual tone of voice – and came at once. 'Yes, Mother?' She was a trifle flushed, but it could have been from the sunshine. Her clothes showed no signs of being disarranged.

Keeping her gaze on her sewing, Rosalind said: 'How many baskets did they pick? Did you notice?'

'Two or three, Mother. I'm not quite certain.' She laughed, and said: 'I didn't watch them all the time, that's the truth. I went toward the sugar-mill. I was there most of the time looking at them grinding.'

'I see.' A pause, then Rosalind looked up. 'Are you sure you went nowhere near Robert Guire's cottage?'

No, it was no dream. There could be no doubt now that Overgaar had spoken the truth. Jacqueline, pale, simply stared, standing very erect.

Rosalind put down her sewing and rose. 'Come, let us go upstairs.'

Jacqueline followed her, still saying nothing. In the bedroom, however, she spoke. She admitted, very pale, her voice a murmur, that she had been Robert Guire's mistress. This morning was the third time it had happened within the past fortnight. He was unhappy and she was in love with him. They had first become friendly about three months ago when she met him in the fields; she had gone to watch the slaves at work, and he had smiled at her and spoken, and after that she would go about twice or three times a week, and more than once she had met him on one of the dams far aback but on those occasions they had only kissed. She was in no way unrepentant; she seemed defiant and determined to stand up for the man.

'He's had a terrible life, Mother. Terrible. His parents abandoned him as an infant in Glasgow, and he went to sea at the age of eight. Many times he was beaten until his back was raw. He showed me the scars.' She pressed her hands to her face and fought to restrain the sobs.

'But you cannot marry him, child. He's a servant – a man of no education and no breeding. And to have cheapened yourself by becoming his mistress! Haven't your father and I always taught you that it is sinful to cohabit with a man outside of wedlock!'

'I couldn't help it, Mother. I was sorry for him.'

'I wonder if these tales of misfortune really have any foundation in fact. I'm beginning to think that Master Guire is far more of a rogue than we suspected. You will remain in this room until your father returns from Borsselen. I tremble to think what he will do to that Scottish trash when I tell him what has happened.'

117

'If he harms him I'll kill myself. I'll kill myself, Mother.'

'Stop being dramatic. I thought you were more level-headed, Jacqueline. I'm ashamed and disappointed in you. Utterly!'

3

NOWADAYS Hubertus affected a neat goatee beard. At forty-three, he still lacked a single grey hair, and his beard, like his head, was jet black and sleek. He kept stroking his beard gently as he listened to what Rosalind had to say. Not one inch of his massive bulk twitched as he heard about the incident that morning in Guire's cottage, but his eyes gleamed with a slightly mad light.

'Where is she?' he asked, when Rosalind stopped speaking.

'Upstairs in her room. I have compelled her to remain there since this morning.' She put her hand on his arm. 'Hubertus dear, please don't be too rough on her. Promise me you won't beat her.'

He smiled slowly, but there was no mirth in the smile. 'Why should I beat her, my dear? Why should I *want* to beat her. Did I have myself beaten three or four years ago when I yielded to the flesh?'

She gave him a stare, a slow astonishment spreading in her. 'What do you mean, Hubertus? What has that got to do with this?'

'Everything. Everything.' He snapped the words out like musket shots. She saw his head tremble. 'Who am I to despise another mortal for indulging illicitly in the passions of the flesh? Who am I to take her to task? As an officer of the Burgher Militia, yes. As a respectable planter and father, yes. But am any of these things now? Who am I to frown upon her and call her a sinner in the sight of God?'

They stood on the back veranda, and the late afternoon sunshine shone through the tops of the mango trees and made shifty patterns on the wall. The air was cool with the scent of ripe mangoes and wood smoke from the fires of the slaves cooking their evening meal. She watched his shadow on the wall – a short, gross shadow, almost as impressive as the substance that stood before her. A swift pain of love moved within

118

her and she could have embraced him and stammered endearments. It hurt her to be restrained. She felt herself trembling, and the breath seemed about to leave her body.

'Come upstairs with me,' he said. 'I shall speak to her.'

Much of her defiance of the morning had gone, Rosalind noticed. She sat on the bed, head bowed, ashamed and fearful. As they approached her she seemed to tense in evident expectation of a blow from her father. But Hubertus stroked her head gently and said: 'So you have been deceiving us, my girl.' And Jacqueline looked up at him in amazed discomfiture, then bent her head again. He grunted and said: 'That is what is most disconcerting. The way you have succeeded in deceiving us. I would not have credited you with so much guile. Guile and hypocrisy.' He stood there like a rugged stone monument before her, and soon the silence became painful to Rosalind. It became compulsory for her to break it. She said. 'You will have to get rid of him, Hubertus. He cannot remain on this plantation a day longer than is necessary.'

He turned slightly and smiled at her. Patted her arm briefly. To Rosalind, it seemed as though he might be deriving some enjoyment from this situation. This was not how she had expected him to behave; all day she had been fearing that she would have had to protect the girl against him. She had been certain he would have wanted to flog her in a silent, savage rage. Watching his face, she thought it looked ecstatic; he might have been experiencing a drastic torture of delight. Agony that perversely became transmuted into pleasure as it churned around within his scarred core.

'Nineteen in June, aren't you, my girl? Virtually a woman. Stand!'

Jacqueline started at the command, and stumblingly got up. Her father looked at her, grunting. 'Taller than your father.' He spoke in Dutch. 'A woman in body but possibly still a child in mind.' He might have been addressing himself in the course of some private day-dream. 'Our actions spring from the flesh. Why the Almighty has made it so I cannot tell, but it is so. The evil of my mother came out of her flesh. My wife is good because of the yearnings of her flesh.'

'Hubertus!'

'Yes, my dear.' He spoke in English. 'The flesh – not the

119

spirit. You see it for yourself here. Look at this young woman, robust, shapely in her flesh, and she has been deceitful because of the urge of her flesh. She has been disloyal to our training and to the principles we have taught her to hold sacred – all because of the burning in her flesh. How can you deny it? Why God should have made it so I don't know, but it is so.'

'Very well, but please let us not discuss such things now, dear. You haven't even scolded her, Hubertus. You haven't said what is to be done. We cannot let her marry that man. He's her inferior – a servant. A rogue, perhaps. He has deceived her with his tales.'

'Mother, he has not! They are true. He's had a dreadful life.'

'See! Defiance. She does not fear my wrath. The flesh has made her bold. The old weary tale,' he added in Dutch. He began to wag his head, and the great bulk of him seemed to sag slightly. Suddenly the air of defeat vanished, as though it were a skin he had deliberately sloughed off before it could settle in too clinging a hold upon him. He stiffened and said: 'Do not let the matter trouble you, Rosalind. I know how I shall deal with it. I shall cure her of this infatuation in a simple manner.' He glanced at his wife and went on: 'Had you, my dear, found yourself infatuated with a man whom you realised you could never marry what would you have done?'

Rosalind, taken by surprise, was silent, bewildered.

'I ask you, Rosalind, What would you have done?'

'I should – well, I should have tried to control my feelings and put him from my thoughts, Hubertus. What else could I have done?'

'That is precisely the answer I expected you to give me.' He smiled and patted her cheek, and despite his brusque air there was a deep affection in the gesture; it was as though she could feel affection tingling at the tips of his fingers. A quiver of laughter passed through her at the thought of his oddness. He was saying now to Jacqueline: 'And that is what you will do, my child. What your mother would have done. You will be restrained. You shall, within the next few weeks try to control your feelings and put thoughts of that young man from you. You are not restricted to this house. You may wander at will over the plantation as before – yes, it may surprise you to hear me say so, but I give you permission to roam as you please. But

120

ou will restrain yourself and not meet that young man; you
vill neither meet him on the dams aback, nor in his cottage.
shall not have the Indians watch you – no. No one will watch
ou. Only God will do that – and God will tell me if you have
net that man; I will divine it from your manner; deceitful
s you have already been, you will not deceive me, I shall know.'

He left the room, and Rosalind followed him.

For a long while on the veranda she argued with him, but he
vould not alter his decision. Guire must remain on the planta-
ion, and Jacqueline must for her own self cultivate the art of
estraint.

An hour later, when Overgaar came to report, she heard him
elling the man: 'You acted very correctly, Overgaar, and I
ommend you, but I wish you to say nothing to him. I shall tell
im nothing, either. But keep an eye on him. Send every day to
iscover whether he is doing his work, or slacking, and report to
ne. . . . No. No, I shall not dismiss him. He is a good worker.
ou have told me that yourself, and I have proven that for
nyself by watching him at work. He must remain, and I shall
each him to give up his drinking habits and to be a steady
orker.'

Overgaar departed, a very perplexed man.

Vhether Jacqueline would have learnt to be restrained and
iuire have been taught to give up his drinking habits was never
ut to the test. For early the following morning, Overgaar, an
gitated man, came to the house to report. Guire had been found
y his slave lying dead in his cottage. He had blown out his
rains with a pistol.

Overgaar went a happily worried man.

For two days Jacqueline sobbed in her room, refusing to eat.
osalind and Hubertus went up once and found her naked
acing up and down, her hands pressed to her stomach, mutter-
g dementedly: 'I have his child in me. I don't care. Oh, I don't
re what they say.'

'Child, are you mad?' cried Rosalind.

'Yes, I'm mad,' said Jacqueline. 'But I don't care. I have his
ild in me. You can't take it from me. You can't! You can't!'

Hubertus smiled and held Rosalind by the arm and led her

121

out. 'She must be left alone, my dear. This is her first big agony. It will pass.'

Downstairs, Rosalind said 'Hubertus, do you think she is pregnant? What will we do if she bears a child for that man?'

'Accept it as our grandchild. What else could we do?'

She gave him a stare and sighed. 'Sometimes I wonder if you aren't mad yourself. Oh, heavens!'

Jacqueline, however, had not conceived. Before a week had gone she had regained her composure, though her pallor still remained. By the middle of the year her high spirits had returned. In November she married Claas Lieker, Gert Lieker's second son, who had been in love with her for the past two or three years.

4

THERE settled upon Hubertus, during the next few years, a heavy philosophic calm. It had begun, felt Rosalind, with the affair between Jacqueline and Robert Guire. She was certain that since then he had not been the same. He became more and more given to soliloquy, and often she would hear him muttering to himself about the flesh, and the evil and the good that came from the flesh. More and more he took to the reading of books on philosophy – books in Latin, English and Dutch which he ordered specially from abroad; through Cranley and James Harker he obtained several from Barbados: old and rather battered leather-bound volumes, many of them moth-eaten. In his youth he had been fond of reading, but now reading became a passion. Some evenings he would even be impatient with Overgaar for disturbing him when the man came to make his report. The majority of the books he read treated of some aspect of theology, but he did not always sympathise with the writer's views; indeed, there were several occasions on which he disagreed, and almost became angry with the writer.

'I do not subscribe to the view held by St Augustine,' he once told Rosalind, 'that the fleshly in us can only be related to evil. This is foolish! Absurd! It is contrary to all one's

122

instincts. A man who can hold such a view has never experienced any joy in his relations with woman. If the flesh is abused the result is evil, but if the flesh is respected and treated with reverence and restraint only good can come from such an attitude. How do you feel about it, my dear? Tell me.'

'Just as you feel, Hubertus. I'm sure our bodies aren't evil unless we make them so. If we don't abuse our bodies we can attract no evil to ourselves.'

'Good. Good. Very well put. It is my view entirely.' He seemed very pleased with her, and gave her a look that made her feel as though she were a child who had been complimented by her tutor. After a thoughtful pause, his clasped hands resting on the open book in his lap, he remarked: 'Moreover, I feel that we are born with tendencies for good or for evil. It is the blood in us that dictates our allegiance to God or to the Devil.'

One Sunday when they were at Signal, he said that he was coming to believe that sin was less of the Devil's making than of man's. 'It is ourselves who, by our laxity and our failure to observe the word of God, create sin. Sin is evil, and evil is produced by our deliberate abuse of the talents and abilities bestowed by God upon men.'

Faustina, who was present with her children, gave him a teasing smile and said: 'Would you say that I have abused my talents and abilities, Hubertus dear?' And immediately the heavy frown left his face, the sly smile replacing it. He replied: 'You were born with both goodness and evil. I still have not made up my mind which predominates in you.'

'When I'm away from you the goodness predominates; when I'm with you I'm all evil.'

Hubertus joined in the laughter that this sally created, and Rosalind of a sudden experienced a sense of being left out of the company. In some way she knew that she was inadequate. It was always Faustina who succeeded in bringing out the old sly humour in Hubertus. . . . With me, she thought, he is serious and ponderously philosophic; with her he relaxes and can be his easy self – the self that makes him attractive as a man. Could it be that he knows I can never smile on laxity of morals? Yet he himself preaches loyalty to one's principles and one's moral code. . . . In moments like this she felt not only alone but baffled, and it called for a great effort of will not to be despairing.

123

A little later, when they were at breakfast, Wilfred, who sat next to her, told her: 'I can't understand what is happening to g-g-good old Hubert. He's changing. N-n-nowadays he can talk about nothing but theology and philosophy. He won't even take an interest in my records as he did before – not that my records are much good of late, I admit.'

'What is the matter with your records?'

'They're unreliable – that's what's the matter with them. This past year or two it's been a hopeless job trying to secure any accurate figures. Look at the state of the colony. Slackness everywhere. Everybody doing just as he pleases. We're doing trade with the Islands, and n-n-no law intervenes to stop us, so how can our exports be properly c-c-calculated!'

Commandeur van den Heuvel had resigned his post, and his resignation had been accepted on Christmas Eve, 1770, more than a year ago, and since then the colony had been without an administrator, the result being that official business had become extremely slipshod. Ships came and went without observing any of the port regulations, and the planters took advantage of this laxity to do trade with the islands – trade that was strictly illicit. The amount of sugar, coffee and cotton recorded at Borsselen as having been exported to Holland during the past year probably represented less than half what was actually produced by the planters.

'The figures for the Company plantations are perhaps correct,' said Wilfred, 'but who cares for the Company plantations! It's we p-p-private planters whose produce really matters.'

'Are all planters taking advantage of the present laxity of government, Wilfred? Aren't there some who try to show an example?'

Wilfred laughed. 'The s-s-saints are so few they can be numbered on half my hand. Your d-d-deeply religious Hubert himself is doing it. I'm doing it myself. I don't profess to be any s-s-saint. The only thing I deplore is the fact that the records are suffering.'

Very quietly Rosalind asked: 'How can you prove Hubertus is doing it?'

'Because he's admitted to me he does.' Wilfred laughed. 'Oh, don't look so shocked, Rosalind! I – I – well, by heaven! Why houldn't he do a bit of illicit trading while there's the chance! sn't he human?'

'Yes, he's human, but he also is a man of principles – or, at east, I have always looked upon him as such. However perhaps ou are right,' she murmured. Yes, perhaps Wilfred was right. he did not ask her husband, but she knew that her brother had ot lied. She remembered something Hubertus had said on an ccasion some years ago – it was before he had resigned as an fficer of the Burgher Militia. Something about God being able o see into our hearts and knowing when we acted in a spirit of orruption and when we acted because of urgent necessity. If he was not mistaken, the subject under discussion had been this ame matter of illicit trade. . . . An incomprehensible mixture, Iubertus, and every day he puzzles me more. Only Faustina eems to understand his inconsistencies. I wish I could know hat it is that makes her akin to him in understanding. What-ver it is I'm sure I must lack it.

n May of that year, 1772, there was great rejoicing in the ieker home when Jacqueline gave birth to a son. Hubertus was ery pleased with his grandson. 'It is such a relief,' he said to osalind, 'to know that he bears the name of Licker and not an Groenwegel. God has been good to me in not giving me any ns. I wish to have no hand in carrying on that foul name.' And ter a thoughtful pause: 'Yet it is a great name. We are no mean mily. We are traditional fighters, and for fighters there must e respect. "The Van Groenwegels never run." ' He wagged his ead slightly, and for an instant she saw on his face the old rtured look. He began to glance from side to side in baffled resolution. Then calm returned, and he shrugged and smiled, d, hands clasped on his stomach, tapped his thumbs lightly gether. He looked full of secret guile, and a trifle mad.

The christening took place at the end of August when the long y season was well in progress. Besides the families from ylands, Signal and Good Heart, respectively, the Liekers vited the Harkers of Sapphire, and their big house with its ther small compound ringed with orange trees became a bble of voices. The children were made to keep in the com-und, a table being laid for them at meal-time under the orange trees, and the older children being put in charge of the younger.

At gatherings such as these Hubertus, Rosalind noticed, was never ill at ease. He would attempt in the beginning to brew a solemn, high-toned conversation on morals and theology, but on receiving no encouragement – and he was never encouraged by anyone – he readily submitted to discussing the commonplaces of plantation living, and even grew good-humoured, especially if females joined the discussion. Feminine company never failed to stimulate him, though only Faustina caused him to cast away logic and take on an air of light-hearted banter really easy and sincere. At such times the sly smile and the trick of watching imaginary dust specks on his cheek-bones came into play.

About mid-afternoon he was in one of these moods, for sitting with him on the veranda besides Rosalind and James Harker was Faustina, and they were watching the children in the compound and discussing their physical development and general tendencies.

Clara Clackson, at twelve, was precociously developed in body but not in mind, and Hubertus said that this was no surprise as she was wholly her mother's child. Faustina disagreed that the child was wholly her mother's. 'If she were she would show more interest in the boys, but she doesn't.'

'That only proves,' said Hubertus, 'that she is, indeed, her mother's child. As a girl, Woglinde never took any interest in boys so that one could notice at a glance – therein lay her most dangerous mode of attack.'

'I know of one to whom Clara will never be a danger,' said Faustina, 'and that is Edward. He's so immune to feminine wiles he could be your child, Hubertus dear.'

James Harker uttered a loud bark of laughter. 'God, you're right, my girl! Strangest little fellow I've ever beheld – and the girls wait on him hand and foot, have you noticed? Without the slightest effort on his part, damme, they flock round him. Was his father like that?'

'Very much like that. I was only teasing Hubertus. Edward is really a replica of Jacques, though he has something else that Jacques hadn't. I can never make up my mind what it is.'

'Something good or evil?' asked Hubertus.

James Harker and Faustina uttered cries of reproach in chorus. 'If you dare start talking about good and evil again, Hubertus, I'll have some cold water thrown on you.' James agreed with this, adding: 'And we'll tie him to an orange tree until it's time to go home.' Then Faustina said: 'It's neither good nor evil. It's a way he has of talking and looking about him with a kind of contempt for everyone else, and yet it isn't that alone.' She added in English: 'I think you would want to say in English that he is bewitched. Is that not the word?'

'It is! It is!' laughed James. 'The hobgoblins must have brought him when you weren't looking, and planked him down beside Storm.'

'From a very small boy he was odd,' murmured Rosalind.

The afternoon was becoming clouded over with angry rows of blue-black thunder-cumulus that, they knew from experience, were too angry to bring rain or thunder, though Rosalind saw Hubertus every now and then glance upward in a troubled manner as though the oppressive quality of the air affected him, made him fidgety. Slaves had already moved indoors the table on which the children had eaten, but the children continued to frolic in the compound. Raphael sat in the uppermost branches of an orange tree where he had lured up Cornelis Lieker, Gert Lieker's grandson by his eldest son Jan. Raphael was known by everybody as the Tree Boy. He was quite obviously most happy when up in a tree. There were nights when he would steal out of the house and, unknown to the others, spend hours in the branches of a tree. He had confided this to Luise who had confided it to Susan, and Susan told everything to Rosalind.

Edward was patiently following the movements of ants along the ground, his red-brown hair falling frequently over his brow as he kept bending his head to watch. At nine, he was taller than his twin by an inch, and he had a wider face; otherwise, he resembled Storm very closely. Occasionally Rosalind would notice Graeme Clackson or Clara approach him and say something to him, but except for a casual glance, he seemed to ignore them. Then once Luise, who, at eighteen, was as tall as Rosalind and a very attractive girl, stopped to watch him, and Rosalind saw him tilt his head upward and return her stare. Saw him smile at Luise. Luise smiled, then abruptly turned off and left him, and Rosalind noticed that the girl's face held a tense, disturbed expression. In many ways, Luise, thought Rosalind, was as puzzling as Edward – especially in her attitude toward Edward. Once Rosalind had asked her: 'Don't you like Edward, Luise?' And Luise, immediately confused – indeed, unaccountably confused – had replied: 'I do, but he's so queer, Mother. I hate freaks,' she added in sudden impatience, with a heat that seemed uncalled for. 'And he *is* a freak! He just won't behave like the other boys. He ignores me when I say anything to him.'

A chilly wind began to blow from the south-east, bringing with it the strong smell of cane-juice from the mill on Good Heart, and driving the thunder-clouds in broken, ragged masses toward the north. One or two large drops of rain pattered down and died away, and the smell of the earth mingled with the smell of cane-juice. Rosalind heard a harsh wail of human agony that sailed on the wind and died weirdly as though abruptly drowned in an unseen spirit storm raging unknown about them. Later, Gert Lieker told them that it was Fries, the carpenter, having a bad tooth pulled out. 'He has been drinking rum the whole morning and most of the afternoon in preparation for the ordeal,' said Gert.

'Poor fellow,' said Rosalind. 'Oh, why must there be such suffering in the world?'

'See! A heart as soft as cotton,' smiled Hubertus, and stretching out, he took her hand, lifted it and kissed the tips of her fingers.

'What a foolish man!' she laughed, the blood in her face, her gaze moving diffidently out on the compound. The shudder of affection that went through her seemed to shrivel up, however, at the thought that it was Faustina who had put him into this flexible mood, but at once she scolded herself for being so narrow. What did it matter who had put him into this mood! Instead of being jealous, perhaps she should be grateful to Faustina.

Sunshine broke through the clouds in the west and came wine-red through the tree-foliage upon them, the wall of the veranda becoming shifty with the shadow-pattern of leaves. Through the rustle of the trees in the damp, strong wind came the Sunday sounds of the slaves: the thump of tom-toms and the wailing of their dirge-like songs. Clara Clackson's laughter occasionally created a separate category of sound; it flared through the air like magic-fire out of the earth, completely in disharmony with the soothing continuous rustling of the trees and the watery, red sunlight.

Rosalind, on her way upstairs, for it was nearly time to depart, glanced out of a small window half-way up, and had a glimpse of one of the two water-tanks, the sun shining on the top portion of it. In the deep shadow below she glimpsed something white, and paused. It was Luise. Luise stood watching Edward who, ignoring her, edged his way slowly round the rounded tank, evidently still observing the movements of ants. Without warning, he stopped, looked up at Luise, then straightened up. He was a full head shorter than Luise. Rosalind saw him smile, and then silently he put his hand up and patted Luise's cheek. He did it as he might have done it to some pet animal. Luise brushed his hand off, then almost in the same motion caught his wrist and pressed his hand against her breast. Rosalind was sure the girl trembled as she stood there half-leaning against the water-tank. Suddenly she released Edward's hand and turned and ran off.

They were on the *stelling* preparing to embark on their yacht when a planter, returning from a trip down-river, hailed out and asked them if they had heard the news. What news? . . . 'The Directeur-General's resignation has been accepted by the Directors in Holland! A ship has just come in! I heard it from an official at Borsselen!'

'Aha,' said Wilfred, who was also on the *stelling*. 'So it has come at last. G-G-Gravesande sent in his resignation eight years ago – since '64. He'll now be able to give all his attention to his p-p-plantation.'

'Yes,' said Mr Maybury, 'I've heard he's been planning to retire on Soesdyke. Good man, that. We won't get another like him.'

'It is the end of an era,' mumbled Hubertus. His grave mood had returned. Yet, unexpectedly, he looked at Rosalind and smiled and said: 'My dear, can you observe any grey hairs in my head?' He bent his head for her inspection, and she laughed and replied: 'There are two grains in the middle of your head. I saw them there a week ago.'

'I suspected it,' he murmured. 'A new era has begun.'

5

ABOUT the new era there could be no doubt.

Information soon reached the colony that an Essequibo planter, now on a visit in the Netherlands, had been appointed Directeur-General. His name was George Hendrik Trotz. According to this report, too, a new Commandeur had been appointed for Demerary, and the name of this gentleman was rumoured to be Paulus van Schuylenburg, a rumour that turned out to have been well founded, for on the twenty-seventh of November of that year, 1772, Paulus van Schuylenburg did arrive; he arrived in the same ship that brought the new Directeur-General.

Within the next few weeks it was announced that a separate Council of Policy and Justice had been formed for Demerary, so that though both Essequibo and Demerary would continue to be considered one colony, each river would have its own Council. Also, there would not be a separate College of Keisheers for Demerary.

'Hubert,' said Wilfred, 'was foolish to resign as a Burgher Officer. I'm p-p-pretty certain he would have been elected a representative for us private planters.'

The College of Kiersheers comprised the Burgher Officers of the colony, and it was this College that nominated the representative of the free planters for the Council. The choice was not restricted to the officers of the Burghery, it was true – any planter could be chosen as a representative – but in Essequibo the College had invariably selected one of their own number as a nominee, and the same practice would probably be followed in Demerary.

'I should not have wanted to be a member of the Council of Policy,' Hubertus said to Rosalind, but she could discern that his manner lacked conviction. He was secretly disappointed. 'I am not worthy of such a position. By a deed of weakness committed that day in December, 1766, I forfeited the right to be a representative of my fellow-men. I was disloyal to the principles I hold sacred, and I must suffer.'

130

'Why will you persist in wounding yourself, Hubertus!'

He said nothing; only stood frowning about him in a baffled, brooding manner. He seemed to forget her presence, and began to murmur to himself.

'Yet it was a moment of great beauty,' she heard him say. 'I have no cause to regret it in so far as that is concerned.' He shut his eyes and moved his head slightly from side to side. 'How can one be loyal to God and to the flesh at one and the same time? The flesh is not of necessity evil, yet to yield to its urges is to wound the spirit. The spirit cannot grow in stature while the flesh is being satiated.' He suddenly opened his eyes, shrugged and smiled as though aware of having made himself absurd. He patted her arm and said: 'Be not troubled over me, my dear Rosalind. God has decreed that I should pass through these conflicts. I must be like Job and endure it all with patience.'

It was a grey, rainy day in January, and they were on the front veranda watching the little rivers of water that patterned the compound. After a silence, he said very casually: 'I suppose you must know that Graeme Clackson is my son.'

She gave him a quick look. 'Your son? Why should you think so?'

He broke into a gradual smile, staring out at the wetness. 'I have known it for the last two or three years, but I said nothing, and I am sure Cranley knows it, too. The boy resembles me, haven't you noticed?'

She said nothing, too perturbed to decide what attitude to adopt.

'The living proof of my weakness, my disloyalty, my lack of restraint – my moment of loveliness. It was a day like this. The rain dripped on us. Oh, it was beautiful. Beautiful, my dear.'

She still said nothing.

'Have you noticed the children? They are developing. I understand Edward is very good at sketching. The tutor who visits them at Rylands has remarked on it. I believe it must be in our blood. Do you remember how you used to compliment me on my own sketching?'

She nodded. 'Yes, you had talent. A pity you did not follow it up. Hubertus, I have just thought of something. Speaking of the children, you reminded me. Luise is going through a very puzzling phase. Have you ever noticed her attitude toward Edward?'

'I can't say I have. What is her attitude towards him?'

'I'm not certain myself, but it strikes me she is attracted to him in a physical way – yet seems to dislike him in other respects.'

'But she's nineteen – she was nineteen in October. A young woman. How old is Edward? He is not even ten. How could he be physically attractive to her? Aren't you being fanciful?'

'I don't think so. I have been watching them carefully since last August.' She told him of what she had seen the day of the christening at the Liekers' home, and he began to pull slowly at his beard and frown. 'And there have been other instances since then,' she continued. 'At Christmas when they were here I saw her kissing him on the back veranda.'

'Does he respond?'

'In a strange way – a sort of teasing, mischievous way. You know what an odd boy he is. It is hard to make him out at all.'

He grunted. 'Perhaps it is the bad blood showing itself in them. We Van Groenwegels have had a long history of in-breeding and perversion behind us.' His hands began to clench and unclench. 'We are famous for producing monsters. Monsters. Am I not one myself? Am I not?'

'Don't upset yourself again, my dear. I'm sorry I mentioned it.'

'No, you were right to mention it. The situation must be watched. We must see that nothing evil comes of this unnatural attraction.'

After a silence, he said: 'You knew – yet you said nothing.'

'She's young, Hubertus. It may only be a passing phase. I thought it would have upset you, that's why I kept silent.'

'I am not speaking of Luise.'

'Oh.'

'Graeme. You knew.'

She said nothing.

'Have you ever discussed it with Faustina?'

'Yes.'

'At Christmas I was certain. I saw him smile, and I knew.'
She heard him sigh. He began to tap slowly with his hand on the

veranda rail. 'Damnation. Only damnation awaits me in the life hereafter.'

Then she became aware that he was watching her out of the corner of his eye, a slight smile of mockery curving down his mouth.

'You feel I can repent. Say it, Rosalind. God will pardon me if I pray to him and ask forgiveness. This is what you wish to tell me, isn't it so?'

She still would say nothing, and he began to laugh softly, affectionately. He touched her arm lightly with the tips of his fingers, and abruptly went inside, still uttering low laughter. And to Rosalind came a thought which, during the past few months, had more than once recurred — a thought that depressed and alarmed her so that she had wanted to put it aside as foolish. Foolish and unworthy.

I wonder, she thought, if he has ever truly believed in God.

PART FOUR

THE new era began with thunder – though as Wilfred remarked: 'We must not blame the new government. It is simply a m-m-manifestation of the times in which we live. The blame, strictly, rests on us, the Christian inhabitants of these colonies. Our own cruelty and inhumanity are responsible for these two terrible storms, and we can only be thankful that they were not far more d-d-disastrous.'

In Demerary, the rumbling of the first storm was heard only at a distance. On two plantations in Essequibo the slaves rebelled, and but for the prompt and strong measures taken by the Burghers, led by their captain, Van der Heyden, and the assistance given by the Indians, the rebellion might have spread and become really serious.

'There is a rumour afoot,' said Cranley Clackson during a discussion of the affair at breakfast after Sunday service at the Harkers' house, 'that this revolt was instigated by a Spanish agent from Guayana, and I wouldn't doubt that there is some truth in it. Governor Centurion, from all I can gather, is a man with no ordinary genius for creating trouble – within and without his own boundaries.'

Luise, who sat on his right, agreed. She was very fond of Cranley, even more than Jacqueline had been and still was. He was the kind of man, she felt, she could have married despite his being so much older than herself. Indeed, the older he got the more charming he seemed to become.

'Yes, he's a dreadful man,' she said. 'One or two of his own soldiers sometimes desert and cross over into Essequibo because of his harsh treatment. Kurt Lieker and Claas Hoorn met one of them at Borsselen, and he said that Don Centurion often raids our frontier posts and kills the Indians and our own people.'

Her uncle, who sat on Cranley's left, overheard and cried: 'True! Oh, yes, only t-t-too true! Centurion replaced Iturriaga in 1766, and he has been trying ever since to extend his frontier – at our expense. He raids our outposts very frequently, and does his best to create ill-feeling for us among the Indians. I have heard on reliable authority that he even sends agents among the slaves in Essequibo to stir up trouble, and I'm of the firm opinion that he had a hand in this d-d-disgraceful incident in Essequibo. Yet I still claim that b-b-basically we must blame our own inhuman methods for these instances of revolt. We ignore the circumstance that these poor black people are human like ourselves. They experience the same emotions as we do, and it is natural that at some time they will b-b-burn to wreak vengeance upon us. What better example do we need than what happened in Berbice not ten years ago!'

'Uncle Wilfred has always been a champion of the negroes,' Luise smiled. And Cranley nodded solemnly and said: 'One day, I am convinced, we shall see him leading them, standard aloft, pistol at the cock. Eh, Wilfred?'

Wilfred spluttered with good-natured laughter. That was what Luise liked about him. Her uncle never took offence easily, heated as he might become over an issue. Of all the grown-up-folk, she decided, she liked Cranley and her Uncle Wilfred best. Cousin Faustina was nice, too, but she sided always with her father in a discussion, and Luise more and more was coming to fear and dislike her father; anyone who was an open ally of her father she regarded with suspicion. For her mother she felt more pity than distrust. . . . Mother, she often thought, is Father's victim. She is devoted to him, and he takes advantage of this and forces her to do his will, even though she might not fully approve.

'Gravesande, when he was in office, could have handled Centurion's outrages,' old Mr Maybury was saying across the table. At eighty, he was still a man of great vitality, and his voice lacked none of the power it had possessed when he was seventy. 'Gravesande suggested to the Directors that he should be allowed to arm the Indians and let them loose against Centurion, but the Directors, as usual, were too mean to supply the necessary arms. Never seen such a state of affairs! They sit down in Holland and expect to batten off us here, yet they won't spend a guilder in the cause of our defence. Left to me, I'd hang and quarter the whole lot of them, not excluding Their High Mightinesses the Stadtholders!'

'Father, please be careful what you say,' cautioned Rosalind. Her father made a puffing sound. 'I don't care if it gets back to their ears. I'll say it again. I'd hang them all and quarter them.'

Luise joined in the laughter that wavered around the table. She said to herself: I forgot Grandfather. I like him, too. I like all people who are courageous and can say and do what they want to.

As the weeks and months went by the Essequibo storm – and the high-handed exploits of Commandant-General Don Manuel Centurion – disappeared into the oblivion of complacency where all such events inevitably faded in Demerary. Why should anyone trouble about what was going on far away on the north-western border? Why change their attitude toward the slaves? Slaves were slaves – black heathens from Africa intended to serve their Christian masters. Whip them, pour burning sealing wax into the wounds freshly inflicted on their backs, cut off their ears, saw off their arms and plunge the bleeding stumps into boiling tar. These things had been done for generations, so why make a fuss over them? One must be severe with slaves; it was the only way to preserve discipline.

'That is one thing,' said Luise to Edward, 'that makes me not hate Father as much as I could. He doesn't practise the terrible cruelties other planters do. He has them flogged when they deserve it, but that is all.'

Edward said nothing. Only smiled very slightly. The two of them stood watching the mill at work. The mules and horses went round and round, tirelessly, working the lever that set the machinery into motion.

Luise gave him a look and scowled. 'I believe you're going to be as cruel as any of the others yourself when you grow up.'

Edward pointed. 'That fellow nearly had his hand caught in the rollers – did you see?'

'No, I didn't. And I'm glad I didn't. I don't like horrible sights.'

'Have you ever seen it happen? I did – last year on the Harkers' place. The rollers pulled his whole hand in, and his wrist, too, was disappearing, but the other one standing nearby chopped his arm quickly with a cutlass – hacked it off clean. If not, his whole body might have been pulled through the rollers. The machinery would have been badly damaged.'

139

'The machinery! What of the poor man!'

'What's a slave more or less!'

'Oh, I hate you. I hate you terribly.'

He said nothing. Only shut his eyes and grinned like a demon. Opened his eyes and winked at her. His brown hair kept falling over his forehead, and every time it did she had the urge to brush it back for him. The urge was like a pain in her. . . . Nothing will convince me he is not a devil. Satan sent him on to the earth. I'm sure of it. Sure of it.

They stood in silence watching the canes being crushed in the rollers. The air around them was saturated with the fumes of the boiling juice in the brick shed adjoining the mill-house. Every now and then a wave of heat from the brick shed would reach them, adding to the heat of the July day.

'Do you know,' he said, 'that your mother watches us? When she isn't watching herself she sends a slave to watch us. That fellow standing near the mora tree over there pretending to mind the sheep is really spying on us. Do you know that?'

Without turning her head to look, she said: 'I knew that long before you did. Don't think yourself so clever. You're only ten. I'm nineteen.'

'Let's go in and watch the juice boiling.'

'No, let's stay here. It's too hot in there.'

Without a word more, he moved off and went into the shed, and she followed him, steeling herself against the dazing heat. The five large copper cauldrons hissed and bubbled, and to Luise it was an evil sound. It made her think of hell. Hell must be like this. Hot and hissing and bubbling.

'You would like this,' she muttered fiercely. 'You devil of hell.'

He ignored her, bending and craning his head to watch the flat-bottomed coolers into which the liquid sugar kept falling sluggishly. The whole darkish interior of the place was steamy, and the black faces and bodies of the slaves moving to and fro between the cauldrons and the wooden coolers looked unreal and sinister. . . . I hate being in here, thought Luise. If only I could run away and leave him and never see him again!

Perspiration was soon running down her cheeks and arms, and it was a relief when he said that they must go. 'It's far too hot,' he said. 'When I grow up I'm going to build a bigger shed and

140

have large windows so that it can be cooler. The man who built his was a fool.'

'It was my father who built this. Are you calling him a fool?'

'I am.'

She slapped his cheek, but he only grinned. 'One day,' he said softly, 'I'm going to pay you back for all these slaps you give me.'

'How?'

He looked up at her. She was nearly a head taller than he. 'In ced,' he said, and she turned aside her face, blushing and mur-uring: 'Little devil. Stupid, foolish little devil.'

They were walking along the path that led toward the house, nd he told her to stop. She said she would not, and continued o move on. He came to a halt, and a moment later she halted nd said: 'Don't be foolish. Come on and let's get back to the ouse.' He continued to stand where he was, and she retraced er steps and stopped beside him.

'If you dare touch me, Edward!'

'Why should I want to touch you! It's you who want to touch ie.'

'Why have you stopped here, then?'

They were on a dam that ran between the canefields, and save or the now distant clank and thump of the mill there was no und. Nor was there anyone in sight. After a moment, from far the south they heard the voice of an overseer – probably roud, the man who had succeeded Robert Guire. Many of the uthern fields were being reaped.

'I'm sure,' said Edward in a whisper, 'there's a man hiding that field over there, Luise, and it isn't a slave. I had a glimpse f him as we were coming along. He was ahead of us. It was a hite man.'

'Oh, don't be silly. You aren't fanciful. Is this something ew?'

'Let us go on, but I'm sure I'm right. A man dodged in among e canes just as we turned the bend, and it was a white man.'

'The only white men on the plantation today are Father, ncle Wilfred and the two overseers.' She glanced round ner-usly, however, even as she spoke, and caught his arm, pressing against her side. As they moved on they heard footsteps on e dam behind them, but looking round, they saw the man

141

who had been minding the sheep near the mill. The slave her mother had sent to watch them.

'Perhaps it was he you saw.'

'It wasn't,' he insisted. 'It was a white man, I tell you.

As they went round a bend and the man behind them disappeared from view, she stopped and said urgently: 'Kiss me Edward.'

He held up his face obediently, casually, and let her kiss him She shut her eyes and breathed as though in torture. 'You beast,' she murmured.

He uttered a soft chuckle as they went on, and she asked him what he was laughing at. 'At something I heard Cousin Hubertus saying to Mother.'

'What was that?'

'He said all we Van Groenwegels are doomed, because w have bad blood in us. We're all perverted monsters. That wa what he said.'

'Why should you have remembered that at this instant!'

He made no reply.

'How did you come to hear Father say that to Cousi Faustina?'

'I was spying on them one evening at the Beckles. It was th day when we all went to the Beckles for that anniversar banquet they gave.'

'It's Beckleses – not Beckles. I've told you that before. Kis me.'

'No.'

She did not insist, but she bit her lip hard. After a silenc she asked: 'Why did you have to spy on them? Were the alone?'

'They were – behind the water-tanks, under a star-apple tre And they were kissing. They kissed several times.'

'What! You're a liar, Edward!'

'I'm not. It wasn't the first time I'd seen them kiss. And I' heard them telling each other love-things. Just as you tell me

She released his arm, within her a sudden sense of numbnes 'Is this really true? Father and Cousin Faustina? You're n telling a lie?'

He put his hand on his heart, and she knew that he was tellir the truth. In any event, he was not given to telling lies – even white ones.

'But – but you've never seen them making love – I mean lying together or anything like that?'

'No. I can't say I have. It's in our blood,' he grinned. 'That's why you like me to kiss you. A big girl like you nineteen years old!'

She hardly heard him. She was thinking: Who would have dreamt such a thing! And Father who is so pious, so upright, so strict in everything!

'Your eyes always look greener when something astonishes you.'

Silently she took his arm again, and they moved on for a long distance saying nothing. Her eyes, indeed, had a more intensely green look as she stared ahead. They were deep-set like her mother's, and her cheekbones were low like her mother's. Her mouth was her own, the lower lip very full; it sometimes drooped as though too heavy to adhere to the upper, and at such moments she looked child-like with an open-mouthed innocence. It was like this she looked now in her shocked incredulity. . . . Cousin Faustina. It was very hard to believe. Both her father and Cousin Faustina had always seemed to her such noble beings. It was true that of late she had felt a great deal of resentment against him, had even tried to convince herself that she hated him. But, within herself, she knew this to be sheer melodrama; it was like telling Edward that she hated him when she knew that her whole inside was writhing with an ungovernable love for every inch of him. Her respect for her father could never be killed. He would never cease to seem to her invulnerable, invincible, deathless. She might rail against him because of his stern pronouncements and the subtle way in which he bullied her mother, but she had never for an instant thought of questioning his integrity. And now to be told casually by Edward that he had kissed Cousin Faustina near the watertanks at the Beckleses' – that he had done this more than once! When could this attachment have started, she wondered, and had it gone further than kissing?

She felt a contraction within her – and it was as though a new fiery ache were coming to life. She began to tremble, and when Edward asked her what was the matter she could only shake her head. If she had tried to speak she would have stammered so badly he would not have understood her.

Perhaps her father was right in what he had told Cousin Faustina. It must be the bad blood in the Van Groenwegels. She remembered Jacqueline and Robert Guire – though hadn't Dora Harker run away last year with a soldier? And hadn't the Council fined Mevrouw Hoorn, that widow down-river, for receiving men at her cottage – as many as ten had visited her one night! And only last week Goedlust Lieker had cruelly tortured a slave to death – an old man of sixty-seven! And a month ago Mynheer Grust had, in a rage, ravished a sick slave girl because she would not get well, and then tied her to a tree for a day and night until it was discovered that she was pregnant, and then he had set her free and had her beaten. Surely it was not only the Van Groenwegels who had bad blood!

No, it was simply that her father was what he happened to be. A strong man and good, but sometimes uncertain; sometimes a bully, sometimes kind, gentle. Pious, of high principle . . . yet now there was this that Edward had just told her. If it were true then he was an immoral man. He was a hypocrit who had deceived her mother. But again. . . .

'Edward, I've just thought of something.'

'Yes?'

'Father never scolds us. He never warns us about being immoral with men. I can't think of once when he has done so. Mother often advises us to be careful, but not Father.'

'He ought to begin, then. You need a lot of warning.'

'Kiss me.'

'No.'

'Please stop and kiss me. Edward, I beg you.'

'No. That man is behind us. Mother's spy.'

She looked back and saw that he was right. 'Edward, I can kill for you. If only you were older!'

'I'm growing every day.'

'Oooh! You beast!' She drew away from him, her face in a grimace of pain. For he had given her a hard, screwing pinch on her thigh.

144

2

SMALL things that might have left no impression on her sisters made a lasting impression on Luise. She had been born with a sensitive, easily impressionable nature. And she was mercurial; even the sudden rustling of the trees in a soft wind might affect her mood – cause her to fidget and glance about her with an abrupt longing for something she could not define. She became irritated over trifles. And trifles, too, might send her into ecstasies of pleasure. She lived intensely and richly; each moment was, for her, deeply shadowed or brilliantly lit; ripely coloured or blackly smeared.

One day about a fortnight after her encounter with Edward, she stared across the dining-table at her father and tears began to run down her cheeks. She stopped eating and dried them, but not before the others had seen them.

'What is the matter with you, Luise?' asked Rosalind.

'Nothing, Mother. Nothing.' And it was the truth. It was nothing that she could explain. She had just been touched by the stolid, lonely expression on her father's face, and the tears had flowed. Yet she had seen that expression a thousand times before. Ever since she had known herself.

Mary and Susan grunted, and Hubertus smiled vaguely. And her mother did not persist in questioning her. For they were accustomed to her moods.

Toward the end of the meal, Luise said: 'Father, has any strange man been seen by the overseers on our plantation?'

Her father did not look up from his plate, but he grew alert. She noted this. Mary exclaimed: 'A strange man! What do you mean, Luise?'

'A black man?' asked Susan.

'No, a white man.'

Her father suddenly looked at her. 'Have you seen a strange white man on the plantation?' he asked.

A tiny leaf began to shake in her. . . . He has taken notice of me. He so seldom does. If only he and Edward could take notice of me. . . .

'No, but Edward thought he did – it was a day a few weeks

ago when he was here. We went for a walk to the mill, and he said he saw a strange white man run into the canes as we were coming back along the dam.'

'I see. Very interesting.'

'I'm sure he imagined it. I told him so. Though he doesn't imagine things. Oh, I'm not hungry today. It's so hot. If only we could have some rain. A good terrible thunderstorm. I like lightning.'

'You like everything that's strange,' muttered Mary. And Luise laughed.

To her surprise, her father continued to question her. 'Can you remember exactly where you were when Edward thought he saw this man?'

'What is the matter, Father? Is there — I only mentioned it for the sake of saying something. No, I can't remember the exact spot. It was on the dam, and it was a hot day like this. And Edward kept teasing me. He's such a terrible boy. I could kill him sometimes.'

'Was this the only occasion you saw — or thought you saw — a stranger on the plantation?'

'Hubertus, what is this? Has something happened?'

They all looked at him now. He chewed slowly, stolidly; almost like a cow, thought Luise, and nearly sniggered. Then deliberately he turned his gaze on her mother and said quietly 'Overgaar has more than once reported the presence of a strange white man on our land. Lieker's overseers, too, have seen him. Some odd business is afoot, my dear, and we all want to discover what it can be.'

They looked at him in silence.

'Is it a soldier, Father?' Luise asked, breaking the silence after a slight scraping of her chair.

'We don't know,' said her father.

He can be so mysterious, thought Luise as they watched him. One never knows what he is thinking. I wonder if he hates me. No, I'm sure he doesn't. He hardly even thinks of me. I might not be his daughter. I might not be in the home here. He notices none of us. Only Mother. I believe Mother is the only creature he loves. . . . Unless Edward is right about Cousin Faustina. . .

'There is disaffection among our people. I have said nothing about it, because I didn't want to alarm you.'

146

'Our people are giving trouble, Hubertus?'

'Yes. Someone has been spreading mischief among them. Plotting evil. It is the same on several plantations in this area.'

'Has Father complained, too?'

'Yes.'

Through the doors and windows the heat came in persistent stifling tentacles that circled them as though bent on strangling them. Mary wagged her hand before her face, and Susan stroked her neck. Luise shifted about in her chair. Rosalind, adjusted her skirt, though it did not need adjusting. Only Hubertus sat still, eating. And heavily calm.

I feel safe with Father, thought Luise.

'Hubertus.'

'Yes?'

'On Saturday last I overheard you telling Overgaar to – to inspect the muskets in the store-room. I thought nothing of it, but now . . . did it mean that – would you use muskets against our people?'

Hubertus smiled slightly and rested a chicken bone. A tiny piece of food had stuck to his beard. He seemed to become aware of it, for they saw him fumble and remove it. 'You know me for what I am, Rosalind,' he said. 'I have always tried to be humane, and I shall continue to be humane.'

'I know that, my dear. I know you are not cruel. But – but the muskets – would you use them?'

'I would not hesitate to use them, Rosalind – if we were threatened.'

'I feel as if something is pressing down on me,' murmured Luise. 'Why doesn't it rain?'

'Hubertus, you would fire upon them? Our people? Hansa and Doork and all the others who work so hard in the fields?'

'I would weed them down like wild pigs, Rosalind, if they attacked my home and menaced the safety of my family.'

'Rain. Just a little rain. A mere drizzle.'

'At heart I'm a Van Groenwegel, remember that. The Van Groenwegels do not lie on their backs and let an enemy walk upon them. They fight. Fight to the death. Do you hear me? To the death.' His head trembled. The air around them seemed to grow doubly electrical. Taut. Luise felt that in a moment

147

she would whimper. Whimper and spring up and run. Run anywhere.

Her mother said in a soft voice to her father: 'You have always reproached Grandma Hendrickje, Hubertus, for her barbaric attitude.'

Her husband nodded. His gaze was out on the compound; he might have been communing with a ghost – with ghosts – out there. Luise saw the light in his eyes. It was a mad light. . . . We're all mad. It's the bad blood. Oh, I can laugh, but I wouldn't know what I'd be laughing at. . . .

'I have never met her in person, but I know, my dear, from what Faustina has told me, that there was greatness in her. She loved the truth. She believed in facing the truth – even the ugly, harsh truth. I believe in doing that, too. I try to be God-fearing, to be kindly, to be Christian, but in me there is a voice of instinct – of intuition, if you will – that tells me that kindliness, gentleness, humaneness do not win battles. And there are many battles in this life to be fought. The strong, the ruthless win. The weak, the timid, the kindly and faltering are annihilated. Grandma Hendrickje faced the truth when she impressed upon my half-brothers and sisters the precept of resistance. We must always resist, Rosalind. When we cease to resist and turn the other cheek to an enemy we are lost. In this I am against the teaching of Christ.'

A distant hissing in the bush. A breeze. Yes, it's a breeze. . . But it did not reach them. It must have died away a mile or two away. . . . I'm going to scream if we don't get some breeze. . . .

'This is a revelation, Hubertus. We must hate our enemies. And you have always preached against hate.'

'I have – and I shall continue to do so. I do not believe in hate. No, Rosalind, we must love our enemies – but when our enemies attack us we must butcher them without mercy. Or we shall get butchered.' He was rubbing his hands gently together Heavily calm . . . I love and respect him, thought Luise. I believe he is right. I don't know why, but I believe he is right. I love Edward but I don't respect him. I'd die for Edward but despise him. Edward is cruel and despicable. I know it, yet can't help loving him. Why? Why? Oh, I've never known such a hot day. I shall burn up. I feel like tearing off my clothes. But if I did I should want Edward . . . I should want him terribly

148

I'm depraved, dirty. It's only Father's calm that saves me. I feel nothing ill can befall me as long as he is near. . . .

'It seems strange to hear you speak this way, Hubertus.'

'Why strange, Mother? Father is right. I know he's right. We must love our enemies when they leave us alone, but when they move against us we have to fight them and kill them, or they'll kill us. What else can we do?'

During the silence that followed this outburst they again heard a hissing in the bush. And this time the breeze reached them. It moved around them in the room, gently and soothingly, but it was warm. Luise took deep breaths of it; it seemed to her a fulfilment. She shut her eyes.

'I have put muskets and ammunition in the pantry store-room,' said her father, rising. 'Should the need arise, you all know where to find the key for the store-room door.' He stood and looked from one to the other of them. 'I hope the need will not arise. I'm not blood-thirsty. But if it does and I am not here in this house with you – get the muskets. And fire upon them. Do you hear me? Fire upon them and kill.' He left the room.

With him went the wind, and the day once more was still and very hot.

On the day after the next the thunderstorm wished for by Luise broke; it broke suddenly at about two in the afternoon and lasted until after five. The heavy rain cooled the air, and Luise was on the back veranda with Mary at about six o'clock when Overgaar came to make his report. They did not usually pay attention to what their father and the man discussed, but this evening something Overgaar said caused them to listen. . . . 'I'm sure of it, Mynheer. Whoever he is, he has supplied them with arms and shot and powder. I've searched everywhere but cannot find the spot where they have hidden them, but I am convinced that the arms and shot are there. Groud agrees with me, Mynheer. He, too, feels from what he has seen and heard that this man has done evil work. . . . '

A silence after Overgaar had finished speaking. Then their father said: 'Tomorrow morning I want you to bring them all into the compound here, Overgaar. Every one of them. Tell them it's a muster. I'm going to speak to them. Words may help

– and they may not. We shall see. At six tomorrow morning have them all here in the compound.'

In their nightgowns, Luise and Mary and Susan leant out of their bedroom windows and listened. In the next room, their mother, too, listened.

'. . . I do not usually speak to slaves. The duty of a slave is to obey, and to work hard, and there should be no need to speak to him apart from to give him orders. But I'm speaking to you this morning because I feel that the conduct of many of you has been bad. You have been disobeying the orders of the overseers. You have been demanding more rations than are your due. You have been slacking in the fields. You have been talking amongst yourselves when you should have been at work. You have been speaking evil of the overseers and of myself. And you have been doing these things because you have been told to do them. A bad man – a devil – is wandering about on the plantations, and he has spoken to you and told you to take up arms against me your master.'

Hubertus looked round at them. Over a hundred of them. His serfs. The black men who toiled for him. Men with brown linen about their waists, their muscular bodies shimmering dully in the greyish light of early morning. The sun had not yet topped the trees. And there were women, too, and children, but these squatted on the edge of the compound, as though fearful of approaching too close to their master. They sat under the fruit-trees.

'There is nothing that goes on that does not come to my ears. I know all. I know of the arms this man has been sharing out to you, and I know that somewhere on this plantation you have hidden these arms – and the powder and shot that were also given to you.'

There was a stirring among them. And a mumbling.

'Yes, I know all. I know that you can be good people when you want to be. You can work hard and obey orders. I wish you well, as I have always done, but when you disobey my order and the orders of the overseers, then I shall not wish you well. I wish only to be kind and humane toward you, but if you show me that you prefer to heed the poisonous words of this strange man and persist in not obeying the orders of the overseers, then

shall be angry and I shall not be kind to you. I shall be harsh.
I shall punish you. For I have muskets, too, and shot and
powder. There are many in my house here, and my overseers
also are armed. And I tell you this morning that if you are
wise people you will behave yourselves as you did before and
all will go well with you. . . . Yes! You there! You said something. I hear you! Come out! Overgaar, bring him out!
Danrab!'

Overgaar dragged the man out of the mob and stood him
alone apart from the main body. He was a shortish fellow with
a slight stoop. Very strong-looking and with a sullen, stubborn
face. A black human being with character. Watching him from
upstairs, Luise felt almost as much awe for him as she did for
her father. . . . He's a slave and his skin is black but he is a man,
she thought. If he were free and had a house like this I could
respect him.

'What is it you said, Danrab?'

'I say you not give us the rations we should get, Massa. We
work hard and you give us little. Slave must eat, too. Not only
Christian massa.'

Overgaar clouted him. Shouted at him.

'Leave him to me, please, Overgaar. Danrab, since when
have you come to feel that you do not get enough rations? Is it
since this white man has been speaking to you in secret?'

'The white man tell us plenty what true. He's a good white
man from another country. He talk good things.'

'And he has given you arms and powder and shot, has he
not?'

Silence. Danrab stared past his master, his face blank.

'Speak. I'm waiting.'

Silence. . . . Yes, he has strength, that man. If Edward were
like him I would be less miserable. . . .

'Who is he, Danrab? Where is he now?'

No reply.

'Disobedience. You have earned twenty lashes, Danrab.'

'I shall string him up this minute, Mynheer!'

'Perhaps he will repent, Overgaar. Speak, Danrab. Tell me
where these arms are hidden.'

The man stood silent, stubborn, like the others. And rigid.

'I can make it thirty lashes, Danrab. I can be harsh when I

think harshness necessary. I can be as brutal as I can be kind.'

Danrab spoke. 'You can punish me, Massa, but I shall say nothing.'

Overgaar and Groud both grasped the man. Groud called to Heeban, one of the drivers. 'Bring the ropes, Heeban!'

Luise hid her face in her hands and turned away from the window. 'I won't see him beaten! Don't look, Mary! Susan, don't look!'

'Why don't you behave yourself, Luise! Father is looking up here!'

'Let him look! He's a brute! A coward!' She buried her face in Mary's lap, moaning softly. Mary told her not to be foolish. 'They're not going to beat him. Father has pardoned him. Why can't you behave yourself?'

Luise rose and looked out again. She saw that Overgaar and Groud had released the man. Heeban stood by with ropes, his face as dismayed as the faces of Overgaar and Groud. Their master was smiling. 'We must respect courage,' he was saying, 'and there is no doubt that Danrab has courage. For him we must reserve a greater punishment than mere lashes, but he has not yet earned this punishment, so we must send him away in peace. Go, Danrab. Overgaar! Groud! Take them all away to their tasks – and never fail to let them know that *our* muskets are oiled and ready, and *our* powder dry.'

About two hours before daylight, three mornings later, Luise was walking along the driveway toward the *stelling* where Edward and his mother were awaiting her. Faustina had asked her to meet them at the *stelling*, and Luise knew that the meeting would be a vital one. Cousin Faustina would tell her what Luise had been dreading for the past few years. . . . 'You cannot do this, Luise. He's a boy. . . . ' How chilly it was, and Danrab was following her. She could hear his breath, and his eyes must be steady on her back. He had grasped her arm now, but the voice was Mary's telling her to wake up. Her mother was also in the room.

'Dress quickly, girls. We are going to Borsselen.'

'What has happened, Mother?'

Rosalind told them. A messenger had just come with a circular from the Burgher Captain for their father to sign. A muster had been called at once on Plantation Dakker's Lust on the West Bank. The slaves were in revolt. Their father was leaving at once for Dakker's Lust.

A hammering came on the kitchen door, and they heard their father call out: 'Very well, Overgaar! I shall be down in a moment!'

'It's Groud, Mynheer! Mynheer Overgaar will be here shortly! Our people are giving trouble, and he is trying to reason with them!'

'What has been happening out there, Groud?'

'Danrab and twenty others are missing, Mynheer. It may be more than twenty, but as far as we can ascertain here is Mynheer Overgaar now!'

'This is so exciting,' giggled Luise. 'Oh, why have we to go to Borsselen? Mother, why can't we remain here and see what happens?'

Her mother had hastened out of the room, however, at a call from her father. They heard the kitchen door being opened by one of the household slaves. Heard the voices of Overgaar and Groud. In the lamplight the room looked peaceful and ordinary, and Luise felt excited but not alarmed. Susan had shed her nightgown and was looking for a petticoat. Mary, composed as always, was putting up her hair – long, light-brown hair that reached to her waist. Then Luise remembered what her mother had said. Their father was leaving at once for Dakker's Lust. Alarm and panic came upon her. The house was no longer safe. With a whimper, she left the room and went downstairs.

'Father, where are you? Where are you?'

Hubertus was in the living-room talking to Overgaar and Groud. He was fully dressed, and on the table Luise saw his musket. Overgaar and Groud also had muskets. Hubertus turned impatiently. 'Luise! What is the meaning of this! Why aren't you dressing? Didn't your mother tell you to dress?'

'She said you were leaving us to go to Dakker's Lust, Father. You mustn't leave us. Let us go with you. Or stay with us. I shall die if you leave us.' She spoke not in a shrill voice, but in a voice that was intense, low and almost calm. 'I'll never feel safe if you aren't with us.'

'Go upstairs and get dressed,' said her father coldly.

'I won't – until you promise to let us come with you.'

153

'Luise!' It was Rosalind on the stairs. 'Come upstairs and dress!'

'I'm talking to Father, Mother!'

Hubertus, unruffled, turned back to the two men. 'Overgaar, Groud, go and do as I've told you. Go at once. And be as harsh as you like – and as you think fit. I think we can trust Barkum to handle the household people, but have an occasional eye on the house whenever you can.'

'Very well, Mynheer.'

The two men left, and Hubertus waved his hand in a gesture of dismissal to Luise. 'I don't want any argument, Luise. Go upstairs and dress.'

Rosalind had come downstairs. She was trying to persuade Luise to go upstairs, but Luise would not move. There was no hysteria in her manner.

'I'm not dressing, Mother, until Father assures me he will let us come with him to Dakker's Lust.'

'You will not have that assurance, young lady. You are going to Borsselen with your sisters and your mother. Only members of the Burghery will gather at Dakker's Lust. Now, hurry. I want to see you on the yacht before I leave. Upstairs and get dressed.'

Luise stared at him, and then said: 'I'm ashamed of you, Father.'

Her father said nothing. He was occupied with his powder and shot.

'Luise, my child, please don't be so difficult. What is the matter with you? Come upstairs and get dressed and let us be going. It may be dangerous to remain here much longer. Do you know what has happened to the Hoofts? They were attacked in their house and killed. Both Mynheer Hooft and his wife. Heaven knows what has been done to the children!'

'Mynheer Hooft? They've killed him? And Mevrouw . . . Mother, I'm still not going to Borsselen. I don't care. I want to be with Father. I won't feel safe if I'm not with Father.' She wrenched herself free from her mother and said to Hubertus: 'I'm ashamed of you, Father. You're running. Have you forgotten our family motto? "The Van Groenwegels never run!" '

'Luise!'

'It's true, Mother! It's true! He's running. We're all running.'

Her father put down the powder keg and took two strides up to her. He grasped her by the shoulders and shook her, silently, savagely. She gave a shaky laugh and said: 'I don't care what you do to me! I don't care! You aren't a true Van Groenwegel! You want to run and leave our home undefended! Why don't you stay with us here and fight? Cousin Faustina wouldn't run! I'm sure she wouldn't! Cousin Jacques died fighting for the family. Grandma Hendrickje didn't run. But you're running.'

'Hubertus dear, take no notice of her. She's demented.'

Hubertus released her. His eyes had lost their wildly desperate look. Now they were the shifty, tortured eyes of old. Often, as a girl, Luise had wondered why they had looked like that. For the first time she thought she understood. It was his look of suffering. He never knew whether to be proud of their blood or ashamed of it. She felt sorry for him – and remorseful.

'I'm not demented, Father. I didn't mean to remind you. But I want you to be with us. Stay with us, or let us go with you. I'll help you to load the musket. You'll need a loader.'

Mary came downstairs, fully dressed, though her hair had partly fallen again about her shoulders. 'Susan is nearly finished,' she said. 'Luise, why are you still in your nightgown? Mother, isn't she . . . ?' She broke off, sensing that the air was taut. Luise looked at her, and thought: I wish I were like her. She never gets upset about anything. She's a Maybury, not a Van Groenwegel. Jacqueline and I and Father are Van Groenwegels. Susan is a bit of both. I'm not sure of her. I feel terrible. . . .

Her father was nodding. He said: 'You're a hysterical little fool, Luise, but you've spoken the truth. Cousin Faustina would not run. I hadn't thought of that. She has integrity – more than I have. I'm a hypocrite.'

'Hubertus my dear, why will you say such absurd things! To take notice of this silly child! Aren't you doing your duty by going to Dakker's Lust? You've been summoned there by the Burgher Captain. Captain Haley sent you the circular to sign, didn't he? How can you speak of not having integrity? Oh, this is too foolish! My dear, please be sensible.'

155

He patted her shoulder. 'Don't upset yourself, Rosalind. I know I'm being foolish, yet I know my failings. Luise is right. I'm a Van Groenwegel, and according to the traditions of our family I should stay here and defend our home against attack. When we were awakened this morning it was the first thought that came to me. I ought not to leave this house. Then I assured myself that I would be sensible – yes, sensible, not sentimental – and do as the other planters are doing. Send you to Borsselen and go myself to Dakker's Lust.' He passed his hand slowly down his cheek and wagged his head slightly. 'Yet before I could go my daughter reminded me of my real duty – my duty as a Van Groenwegel.' His hand shot forth. He grasped Luise by the front of her night-gown. 'Why did you remind me, you little she-devil! Why? Why? Out of sheer perverseness? Out of sheer maliciousness?' He released her and turned off. Strode back to the table and began to toy with the powder keg. And Luise stared at him, a half-smile on her face. She gripped her mother's wrist with one hand, and with the other fingered the torn front of her nightgown. . . . Once Edward tore my dress. I'd slapped him for not paying attention when I read something from Virgil for him. He hates Latin. I remember thinking then: This won't be the last time I'll get my dress torn. Many times before I die it will happen. But I have never imagined Father would do it. . . .

'Hubertus, what are we doing? Are we staying here?'

'No,' he said. 'We are doing what I said. You and the girls will go to Borsselen and I shall go to Dakker's Lust. Luise, go and dress.'

'Luise, go at once and get dressed.'

Luise went upstairs, but she did not hurry. In the room she shared with Susan and Mary, she stood before the mirror of the heavy oak dressing-table – it had come from Holland – and, taking off her torn nightgown, watched the marks of her father's fingers on her chest. There was a long, thin red scratch on her left breast. It fascinated her. She brought the lamp closer to see whether there were any traces of blood. . . . No, no blood. She deserved to have been more badly hurt. She shut her eyes and remembered the expression on his face: the tortured look. . . . I believe I'm like him. Things worry me. I never know what to do. Sometimes I feel I should stop being friendly with

156

Edward, and yet I can't. I despise myself for feeling as I do about Edward and yet I ask myself: Is it really wrong? What does it matter that he is so much younger than I? . . . I am not a pervert. I will not believe I am a pervert. She bit her lower lip hard, shut her eyes tighter, cupped a breast in each hand and squeezed it hard, moved her head from side to side, her breath making a lisp. She stood for a moment like this then suddenly relaxed.

From outside came shouts and the pop-pop-pop of muskets. Hastily she began to dress.

She heard her father's footsteps downstairs. Heard Susan utter a shrill cry of alarm. Half-dressed, Luise paused at a window as the crackle of flames came to her ears. She saw through the fruit-trees a reddish glow, and knew in that direction stood the chief carpenter's cottage. Her father was hurrying across the compound. Then the pop-pop-pop broke out amongst the trees, accompanied by red flashes. Her father paused, then turned and made for the water-tanks. He seemed unhurt. In the grey light of dawn she could barely make him out low in the shadows near the water-tanks. She saw two figures emerge from amongst the trees. There was a flash and bang from the water-tanks, and one of the figures yelled and ran, the other crumpled up groaning.

The flames at the chief carpenter's cottage began to die down. Luise decided upon action. Her father was alone near the water-tanks. He must have another musket. He must have someone to help him load.

Half-dressed as she was – in only a petticoat – she rushed downstairs.

'Luise! Why aren't you dressed yet? Child, are you off your head?'

Luise, ignoring her mother, moved into the living-room and saw a musket lying against the edge of a table. Another lay on the table. She snatched up both and ran out on the veranda. She heard her mother and sisters calling after her but did not heed. She ran down the steps and made for the water-tanks. A pop-pop-pop and flashes came from the fruit-trees, but she got to the tanks in safety. From the house she heard her name being shrieked by Mary and Susan. Breathing hard, she clutched her father, after letting go of the cumbersome weapons. 'I've brought them for you, Father. I'm going to help you load,' she gasped. He growled at her: 'You're mad! Mad!'

'I wanted to help you. I was afraid for you.'

Pop-pop-pop among the trees. The balls ping-pinged on the tanks.

'Keep in the shadows. Half-naked. Not even fully dressed. Mad! Mad!'

'I think both these are loaded. I'll fire one. I think they're over there near the sapodillas.'

'Leave it alone. Don't dare attempt to use it.'

'Father, look! They're coming out from among the trees. They've seen us.' She raised a musket and fired. Her father fired simultaneously.

Yells. One figure fell. The others ran.

From another section of the trees musket-fire broke out.

'They're firing at the house, Father.' Luise was loading, her movements calm. Even her voice was calm.

They saw a shortish figure crossing the compound toward the house. It was Overgaar. Musket-fire broke out again amongst the trees, but Overgaar reached the house in safety. Luise chortled: 'They can't aim at all.'

Her father gave a grunt of satisfaction. 'Good man, Overgaar. He'll take charge of them in the house.'

'Mary and Susan can fire muskets, but they must be frightened.' She suddenly gasped and hissed: 'Quick, Father! I saw someone dart across and hide behind the big tank here. I believe it's one of our people.'

They crouched alert, and almost at once the man Luise had seen showed himself. He was armed with a cutlass and had evidently intended to take them by surprise. Hubertus half-rose presented his musket and fired, and the man collapsed. Another appeared even as the first collapsed, and Luise backed away against the smaller tank. Hubertus dodged the slashing hanger and grappled with the man, and Luise with a step forward swung the musket in her grasp and brought it down with a crunch on the man's rump. She had aimed for his head but the weapon proved too heavy for her. The man groaned and crumpled, and Hubertus' fist smashed into his face. Luise backed away and gasped: 'Don't kill him, Father! Don't! I couldn't stand it!'

158

Hubertus, about to fire point-blank into the man's face, hesitated.

The man whimpered pitifully.

Then Groud and Bosch, the chief carpenter, came running up, blowing, Bosch bleeding down the side of his neck.

'Are you hurt, Mynheer?' panted Groud.

'No. What of the house? Are they attacking from the back?'

'No, Mynheer. There was some firing, but Mynheer Overgaar and Barkum scattered them. Everything is under control now.'

'A white man was leading them, Mynheer. The strange man there has been so much talk about. He came from up-river at midnight and left three muskets with Danrab, then moved on down-river.'

'Where is Danrab?'

'We've caught him, Mynheer. He's strung up awaiting your orders. The others were following him blindly. As soon as we caught him they threw down their arms and obeyed our orders to disperse. But it's that white man who put them up to do this. I'm sure he's a Spanish spy, Mynheer. There's a rumour he was sent from Spanish Guayana.'

'What of your cottage, Bosch? They tried to burn it down. I saw flames — '

'That was Hookan and some others. We've strung up Hookan too. Heeban and two others helped put out the fire they set. We should give them extra rations, Mynheer. They did good work.'

'Very well, Bosch. I'll bear it in mind.'

Luise, abruptly aware of her semi-nudity, though Bosch and Groud had hardly glanced at her, darted away toward the house. In the living-room Mary and Susan, in a tremble of excitement, caught her arm, babbling at her.

'Are you hurt, Luise?'

'What happened out there? Was Father hurt?'

Luise sniggered and replied: 'Father and I killed thirty men, one after the other. Oh, it was a terrible fight. We cut off their legs and arms and heads and Father flattened one of them — '

'Oh, be serious, Luise! Look! You're bleeding on your back!'

'Yes, I bruised myself against the water-tank. Oh, it was a

159

glorious fight! The Van Groenwegels never run!' She uttered a gasp as Overgaar came in, hugged her arms across her breasts and ran upstairs to get the rest of her clothes on. Mary and Susan followed her.

About an hour later, word came from Captain Haley that the muster at Dakker's Lust was off. The revolt had been put down wherever it had broken out. The leaders had failed to achieve any unified action, and the white stranger had escaped, but was being pursued. He had crossed over to the West Bank and was making for the Essequibo.

'And thus,' said Hubertus that evening, 'ends the first violent event in our branch of the family – the first test to which we have ever been put.' He smiled at Rosalind; they were all on the back veranda. 'You may think me sentimental, my dear, but I'm moved.'

Luise, her gaze out on the darkening compound, knew that he had turned his gaze upon her. A deep shuddering ecstasy moved within her. She thought: I don't think there will ever be a moment like this again in all my life.

'The blood I despise – or imagine I despise. It is uncivilised to feel a strong family pride. I'm convinced of that – yet it moves me when incidents like this occur. It awakens primitive feelings in me for which I cannot account.' He moved round to where Luise stood. Luise knew he would. Some intuition had warned her he would. She felt his hand on her shoulder. Heard him chuckle deep inside.

'You're mad, my girl. Luise. Do you hear me, my child? You're mad. Running outside there half-dressed – without a thought to modesty. With two muskets. Almost laughable. But how can you help it? It's the blood in you. There is madness in the Van Groenwegels, I'm convinced of it as I was never before. Yet it's a madness I admire and revel in.' He gripped both her arms and pressed her to him. 'I admired you this morning, Luise. There is something of Grandma Hendrickje in you. Despicable woman, from all reports. A monster. Yet, she was a Van Groenwegel. She died in battle. Mad. Mad like yourself. Mad like me.'

He went inside laughing softly. Wagging his head and laughing.

Luise giggled.

3

IT WAS nearly a fortnight before events on the Demerary sorted themselves into any coherent pattern. Meantime the wildest rumours flicked up and down the river. Gert Lieker came to Good Heart and said that he had heard from his Indians that Hubertus had been murdered near the water-tanks and Luise found naked beside him, raped and badly mauled about. And Hubertus returned the compliment by telling him that his own Indians, after rounding up one or two runaways, had stated definitely that Gert Lieker's house had been burnt down. Gert said that it was a barn that had been looted and burnt. It was nearly a week before news came from Rylands and Signal, then Wilfred arrived and told them that Bannister had been wounded in the head, but not seriously, and, on Cranley's place, a negro driver had been beaten to death because he refused to join in the revolt; a small boat of Cranley's had been holed and sunk. On Signal hardly any damage had been done at all, and Wilfred said he had had matters under control within half an hour; the old man had wanted to fire upon them, but Wilfred persuaded him to remain in the house and leave Wilfred to handle the situation. Wilfred admitted that he had had to use his whip freely. He, too, had heard a rumour that Luise had been raped.

When the situation had become settled again, it was known for certain that several white planters had lost their lives, including Mynheer Hooft and his wife. The white stranger, who had supplied arms to the slaves, and who had escaped toward the Essequibo, was captured. His name was Jan Pieter Caillaert, and it was definitely established that he had been acting on behalf of the Spanish governor in Guayana. He was formally charged with 'supplying weapons and ammunition to slaves and plotting advising and urging them to murder Mynheer P. C. Hooft and his wife, by which many whites, free people and negroes lost their lives.'

He was sentenced to be broken alive on the wheel, decapitated and then burnt.

For several weeks Luise found that she was the subject of discussion everywhere. On three successive Sunday services, she heard herself referred to as a heroine, though one Sunday, at Rylands, Edward told her as they sat alone behind the chief carpenter's cottage: 'Everybody doesn't think you behaved so bravely, I can tell you. I heard Mevrouw Baroon telling Mynheer Jahr that you had no modesty to be running out of your house naked. She said it was just the kind of thing a dissolute Van Groenwegel would have done. She knows all about our Canje relatives and their vileness.'

Luise sniffed. 'I don't care what anyone says. I was so afraid for Father I didn't even realise I was only half-dressed. I just knew I had to go and help him fight. They had fired upon him.'

Edward looked sly and murmured: 'I heard something even worse.'

'What do you mean? What did you hear?' She knew that he was not inventing these tales simply to be malicious; he was a beast but he never manufactured tales. She had never once caught him out in a lie.

'I heard,' he said, 'that something immoral is happening between you and Cousin Hubertus.'

'Something immoral? But that's foolish. Who could have said that?'

'Tantoon, our stable-man, was telling Sylla, our nurse. Clara and I were sitting in the loft, and they didn't know we were up there.'

Luise shifted and frowned. 'People are fools. They would say anything. Father is a fine man, and he would never dream of making immoral overtures to me. It's because that sort of thing happens between other fathers and their daughters that they think Father is after me, too.'

'Tantoon said he heard you and Cousin Hubertus were in bed together when the alarm broke; that was how you and he were fighting together near the tanks. You ran out of bed naked just as you were when the alarm went, Tantoon said. Clara nearly spoiled things by screaming out. I had to put my hand over her mouth quickly.'

'You're a fool to listen to slave gossip.' She stirred again

162

but she was not troubled because of what Tantoon had said. She gripped his arm and said: 'Why doesn't she leave you alone? She follows you all over the place, I suppose.'

'Who? Clara? Yes, I believe she likes me. But she doesn't follow me all over the place. It was I who asked her to go into the loft with me.'

'Have you – did you try to make love to her?'

He laughed, and somehow it was a relief to detect the scorn in his voice. 'Make love? You're love-mad – not me. I never want to make love to anybody. Clara and I are only good friends, and she's a much better friend than you. She doesn't keep pestering me to kiss her as you do.'

'Edward, don't be brutal. Please don't be brutal.'

'But you *are* a pest. We can't sit down for two minutes before you want me to kiss you or touch your chest. Clara is swelling out, too, in her chest. She has pointed ones, not quite as big as yours – the right one is a little smaller than the left. But she never once wants me to touch them, and I don't want to touch them, either. That's why we can be such good friends.'

She pressed her hands to her face. In the darkness behind her shut eyes there were green and blue whorls. The symbols of agony.

'And she's nearer my age, too. She's only two and three-quarters years older than I. You're nearly ten years older than I.'

Her breath came in a hiss through her fingers. In moments like this she felt so ashamed and degraded that she was afraid to open her eyes and watch the daylight. She listened to him whining with delight at her discomfiture, and a feeling of utter despair came upon her. It was in moments like this that she wanted to see him dead. Then abruptly a sense of weakness and dejection possessed her – a resigned inferiority. Let him torture her; it did not matter. As long as it was he who did it she could bear it. She was suddenly at peace, saturated with bliss.

She lowered her hands and murmured: 'You can do what you like with me. I don't mind. Hurt me. Kill me.'

He pinched her thigh, and she gasped but bore it. He asked her if she was trying to be brave, and when she made no reply he pinched her again – harder. She shut her eyes tight, shuddered and breathed deeply in pain, but made no protest.

163

He watched her for a moment as though she were an ant that interested him, then said: 'If I marry Clara when I grow up what would you do?'

She gulped and replied: 'I'd be your mistress.'

'A kind of whore? Like one of the slave women?'

'Yes.'

His hair fell over his forehead. He brushed it back, watching her, his brows lowered in a slightly puzzled manner. 'I don't understand you. You would have bastards by me, you mean?'

'Yes.'

'And if I kicked you and beat you with a balata whip?'

'I'd let you do it. It wouldn't matter. It wouldn't matter.' She put her hands to her face and sobbed quietly.

He uttered a soft grunt, smiling. Rose and kicked her in the small of her back. She sprang up. 'Are you mad, Edward! Are you mad!'

'No. I just wanted to see what you would do. You liked my kick?'

She was silent, her eyes on the ground. Then she nodded.

'Really? You liked it?'

'Yes.'

He shook his head, frowning. 'I don't understand you.'

Once again she had the impression that she was only an ant in whose habits he was detachedly interested.

There were many more occasions on which she saw that look on his face, but she did not always respond with feelings of pleasurable shrinking. Sometimes an intense resentment, a venomous hate, would bubble up within her and she would strike him; slap his face or pound her fists against his chest. And there was the unforgettable occasion of the Christmas breakfast. They were entertaining Cranley and Faustina and the children for the day.

It was Christmas of 1774, and her father and Cranley were discussing the canals which Commander van Schuylenburg was having cut at right-angles to the river with the object of opening new areas further inland for cultivation. Some people said Cranley, were laughing at the scheme. 'And some,' he added, 'seem to favour that plan of the Directeur-General's Trotz wanted to cut a canal linking the river here with Esse quibo remember? But, in my opinion, that was far more of a hare-brained scheme.'

Luise, who was sitting next to Cranley, burst out: 'Oh, I'm glad you think so! It was the very same thing I was telling Mary only last week.'

And Edward, sitting next to her, sniggered.

'Well, what are you amused at?' she said, turning toward him.

'Always pushing yourself into big people's conversation,' he murmured, his gaze on his plate. 'Haven't yet learnt that it's bad manners.'

'I don't need you to teach me good manners.'

He grunted, and then chewing solemnly, turned his face slightly in her direction and looked at her – a human regarding an insect.

Her hand trembled, and rising, she took up her plate, dashed its contents into his lap, dropped the plate and rushed out of the room on to the back veranda, the gurgle and trickle of water outside – it was raining – seeming to her like a dismal projection of the dazed anger that blurred her consciousness.

Out of the babble of amazed exclamations she had left behind her emerged the sound of leisurely footsteps, and she did not have to turn to know that it was her father who had come out after her on the veranda. She felt a gentle touch on her back and heard him say: 'You seemed to have lost control of yourself, my child.'

She continued to grip the rail and stare down at the rivulets of water in the compound. A desperate longing to be free of living showered through her spirit like a spray of rain from some other world – a world in which there was no resentment, no anger, no itching urge of passion.

'I understand. I have been observing you for a long time, and I know what has been happening within you. You're harrowed, my girl. Perpetually harrowed. It's from me you have inherited the capacity.'

'One day I'm going to kill him, Father. I mean it. Kill him.'

'You won't do it. At the last second the finger of reason will check you. I know, because I've wanted to kill many times. Sometimes I torture myself by thinking back to that morning near the tanks. I say to myself: "I believe I would have fired

165

point-blank into that man's face if Luise had not shouted at me to desist." I tell myself that the intention was there – the intention to murder – and that murder would have been done but for you. Then I reason that no – oh, no, in any event I would not have done it. The poor fellow was whimpering pitifully. I would have spared him even if I had been alone. Yet the doubt persists. I'm not so sure that reason checked me. I was in such a fury.' He chuckled and patted her back again. 'Come inside and take your place again, Luise. Compose yourself. Today is no day for ill-will.'

There were other footsteps, and Luise turned quickly and saw Faustina. Plump and almost as massive as her father, she came forward, smiling and shaking her head slightly in an indulgent manner. 'Comforting her like a good father, Hubertus? I hope you complimented her. He deserved it. I wish there were more people who would treat him like that.'

For one swift instant the incident in the dining-room vanished completely from Luise's consciousness: she was only aware of the expression on her father's face as he watched Faustina advance. Luise had no doubt about it now. Edward had spoken the truth that day. Her father and Cousin Faustina had known intimate moments; perhaps they were still lovers.

'No, I was telling her she had taken after her father,' said Hubertus. 'A wicked, unpredictable man. A self-torturer.'

'I might have conjectured you would.' Faustina gave Luise a hug. 'Take no notice of him, my dear child. His words mean nothing. It is always his actions you must judge him by. Remember that, and you will understand him; forget it and you will deem him a despicable soul.'

'Very pretty – and very consoling,' Luise heard her father murmur. The tone of his voice and the look on his face were new to her; she felt a sense of shock. Where was the old stolidity; the brittle mockery? Where was the pompousness; the heavy piety? . . . I see what it is now. Mother is too rigid for him; too righteous and principled. He is the kind of man who can only be appreciated by a woman like Cousin Faustina. Cousin Faustina is flexible. She can bring out things in him that would have remained buried for good if Mother had been the only woman intimately concerned in his life.

'Let us go inside,' said Faustina, her arm still about Luise

'I've put that young rogue to sit somewhere else. He has a mechanical mind, and he's cruel. That is where he differs greatly from his father. My soft, kind-hearted Jacques.'

Luise allowed herself to be led inside. Cousin Faustina could be very soothing.

4

THE following year, 1775, brought sharp contrasts in light and shade. In April, Mr George Radnor and his nephew, Timothy Herd, arrived on a visit to Demerary. They were from Antigua, and Mr Radnor was a planter and his nephew a surgeon in the British Army; he was attached to a regiment stationed permanently in Antigua, and was on a month's leave. Captain Herd fell in love with Susan and made an offer of marriage. Susan accepted, and they were married a week later, and left for Antigua early in May.

Luise was very happy for Susan, especially as she felt that Timothy Herd was a fine man and would be a good husband to her sister, yet the suddenness of the event upset her, and after Susan had left Luise experienced a great loneliness of spirit. She had been much closer to Susan than to Mary. Mary disapproved of her, especially of her unnatural attachment to Edward; she even suspected that her mother had elected Mary a spy to watch her when Edward was present. With Susan's going Luise found herself retreating further into the secrecy of her own ponderings.

Not two weeks after the lavish wedding feast, a slave arrived from Signal to tell them that old Mr Maybury had died in his sleep the night before. And once again Luise felt that the loss particularly affected her: from childhood she had been her grandfather's favourite; he had hardly ever made any attempt to disguise his partiality.

At the funeral, a young man called Anton de Riest paid a great deal of attention to Luise, but, as had happened with other young men who had paid her attention, she showed him plainly that she could not be responsive. On their way home, in the yacht, Rosalind said to her: 'Luise my child, don't you think it would be wise if you showed more interest in young men of your own age? I know I have said it often before, but I repeat it only because I noticed how coolly you treated that boy Anton de Riest. I think he is a gentleman – a gentleman in every way – and it is a pity you cannot allow yourself to be kinder to him.'

Luise could tell that her mother had rehearsed this speech. As she spoke she glanced at her husband who sat smoking his pipe and staring out at the bush, immured within his own reflections and apparently unaware of the presence of the rest of them.

Luise also glanced at him as she answered her mother. 'No man but Edward interests me, Mother. I think I have made that clear to everyone before – and often.'

Both Rosalind and Mary gave her startled looks.

'Luise! So it has actually come to open admission!'

'You have no shame!' Mary exclaimed.

'Hubertus, did you hear what Luise has just said?'

Her husband shifted slightly on his seat, breathed deeply and grunted assent, but continued to gaze imperturbably out of the cabin window.

'And have you no comment to make?'

He took his pipe from his mouth. His gaze was gentle, indulgent, almost teasing. 'How old is our Luise, my dear? Twenty-two in October, isn't she? She is an adult human being, Rosalind. Don't you think that we should give her the right to express her own feelings? Are you asking me to chide her because she has made an honest statement?' He suddenly leant forward, put out his hand and patted his wife's knee affectionately. Uttered a soft grunting sound, and resumed his smoking, his gaze out of the window again.

Rosalind grew very pale, and for a long interval was silent, her hands clasped tight in her lap, her narrow face lowered.

How tight-lipped, thought Luise. How self-righteous. Yet I'm sorry for her. How can one help being sorry for her! It isn't often she attacks me openly like this. Perhaps she honestly feels she is doing her duty as a good Christian. It was a little brutal of Father to take sides with me so directly. Now she must feel he is further than ever from her – and nearer to me and Cousin Faustina. I believe she must suffer more than we any of us suspect.

'Mother, I didn't mean to be disrespectful – or impudent, but – but – well, Father has told you. It was an honest state-

168

ment. I mean it. I can't help myself. Since I was much younger I knew it. I knew I'd never be interested in any other man.'

'Man!' exclaimed Mary. 'He's a boy! A boy of twelve!'

'Please, Mary dear! Say nothing. Let us all be silent. I should not have spoken in the first place. I'm sorry, Luise my child. Forgive me.'

She did not say it in a spirit of self-pity. Luise could see that she was genuinely upset, genuinely regretful. It confirmed her opinion that her mother was a person of sound character; she could no more help being rigid in her principles than Luise could being hopelessly enamoured of Edward.

'I've tried to explain it in a thousand different ways, but it has made no difference. I've tried to avoid him, to hate him. No one knows more than I how it – how unnatural it is. I've been ashamed until – until shame itself has become meaning-less.'

She fell silent, dabbing at her eyes.

And for the rest of the trip nothing more was said by any of them.

In June, the new master of Signal sent a message to say that his wife had given birth to a son – their first. It was a written message and read: 'Primrose has given to me a son, and when you see him you will not hesitate to agree that he is the picture of his grandfather. Come. Please will you all come as soon as you can. Come before Sunday if possible.'

They went up the next day, and Wilfred almost danced up the stairs in his excitement as he led them to the bedroom where Primrose and the new child lay. He had all his father's vitality, though it was far less restrained; Hubertus had once remarked to him that he wasted his vitality shamefully. His hair was completely grey now, though it was a grey more reminiscent of youth than of senility; Wilfred sometimes – especially in sun-shine – could well have been taken for a blond-haired small boy of six whom the fairies overnight had magically lengthened from three feet to six. With his green eyes flashing excitedly and his long, thin legs skipping jerkily up the steps he could, indeed, have been six years old.

'Look! Have a look! T-tell me if I'm not right! Isn't he an exact copy of Father? The mouth! The n-n-nose! The brow!

P-p-perfect picture of Father! Tell me if I'm not right!'

They all agreed with him, though Luise knew that they non of them saw a resemblance to anyone, not even Wilfred himsel or Primrose. To have disappointed Wilfred, however, was un thinkable.

Before they left, he mopped his brow – he was perspiring and told them: 'It's such a relief. Such a relief. We had p-p practically given up hope of having another child. Just on abortion after another. Excuse me, Rosalind my dear! Mary But I – well, it is the truth you know. And a boy. We had bot wanted a boy after Elizabeth. By the way, we want to arrang for the christening. The third Sunday in July might be p-p perfect, don't you think? Eh, Hubert? I thought I'd ask you –

'Perfect, Wilfred.' Hubertus gripped his arm. 'And if yo prefer, Rosalind and I will relieve you of all the arrangement As a happy father you must not be expected to be troubled b the prosaic details involved in arranging a christening. Am not right, Rosalind love?'

'Yes. Yes, it would be a great pleasure, Wilfred,' murmure Rosalind.

. . . and Edward will be present, thought Luise.

But Edward did not come. Luise, a cold hand seeming to clenc into a hard fist within her chest, heard Faustina say th Edward had asked to be left at home. 'He's building a bridg over the little creek aback of the coffee-lodges. He has such passion for designing and building, that boy. I'm certain he going to be an engineer when he grows up.'

Luise thought: That is true, but I believe this is a plot. Sh has left him home on purpose to keep him away from m Perhaps Mother asked her to do it. Yes, I'm sure it must be plot between them.

She went up to her room, and stared at herself in the mirro She hid her face in her hands and shook her body from side side. Abruptly she stiffened, removed her hands from her fac She went downstairs, walking calmly. And as calmly sl awaited her chance, and, unobserved, left the house by t kitchen way, crossed the compound and took the path that l to the Indian settlement.

Ten minutes later she was talking to Tananapa, Manaibc

elder son. The tide? It turned in a few minutes' time. Not long. To Rylands? Yes, it would be an honour to take the young lady in his *corial*. No, it was no trouble at all. Tananapa was very pleased to be of help. A message to the house? Yes, he would have a message sent to the house after they had left – just as she wished. The Mynheer and Mevrouw would be told that she had departed for Rylands.

Three hours later she was asking the house slaves at the Rylands house for Edward. Massa Edward? He was aback on the creek with some Indian boys. They were building a bridge.

Feeling very foolish under the surprised stare of the two women she turned off, mumbling that she would go and find them herself. She knew the way. Going down the steps, she heard them snigger.

She was hungry, but it would have been too humiliating to ask for food. On the path to the coffee-lodges she picked a ripe sapodilla and ate it. A small part of it was green and hard, and the stainy, astringent taste blended with her mood. . . . I'm a fool, but how can I help being a fool!

The day was hot and still, but the fruit-trees gave ample shelter from the sun. She was grateful to them. . . . I can kiss them. Once she paused in the track and looked at her hands, feeling a little light-headed.

Nearing the coffee-lodges – there were two of them, one in which the berries were stored and pulped, the other in which the berries were dried – she heard the voice of the slaves at work in some nearby fields. She took the opening to the right of the lodges and after a few minutes along this new path, found herself in the gloom of the bush. Lizards scuttled away in fright – shiny, black ones. The soil was sandy where it was not covered with leaf-mould.

Suddenly she came to a stop. She could hear the splashing of water – and voices. Edward and the Indian boys. A trembling came upon her. A trembling of ecstasy. In this moment she felt that the trouble had been worth it. The humiliation, the self-doubts, self-reproach. She hugged herself, uttered a thin whinnying sound, and went quickly on.

In two minutes she was at the creek, a narrow, black-watered stream, hardly twelve feet from bank to bank. And there were the boys – Edward and three Indians. They were all naked and

171

up to their chests in the water, and were struggling with thin logs which must once have been the trunks of mora saplings. The edge of the bank on which she stood was white with the flakes of newly cut green wood. The smell of water and green wood swirled strong about her.

The Indians stared at her in surprise, but Edward, tugging at two logs to get them securely fixed side by side on the opposite bank, merely glanced at her, spluttered as a wavelet engulfed his face, raised his head and shouted some orders at the boys. 'That's it! A little to the left, Hennaba! Mokka, you take that one over there, and bring it slowly! Slowly!' Abruptly his gaze shot back to Luise. 'Luise, throw that coil of rope behind you to Waini! *Behind* you!'

Luise, startled, looked about her confusedly. She saw the rope, bent and took it up. It was wet. 'What must I do with it?'

'Throw it to Waini! Go on! Throw it!'

Waini, clutching the end of a log, grinned at her, and she heaved the rope at him. It uncoiled, and one end fell half-way across the stream, the bulk collapsing at her feet. It was longer than she had thought.

'Oh, I'm sorry!' She stooped and gathered the coils up heaved again, and this time Waini was able to catch hold of i where he was posted against the other bank. The front of he dress got splashed, but she did not mind. She found hersel catching some of Edward's enthusiasm. The bridge was alread taking shape. The piles and cross sections on both banks ha already been erected and two logs joining them across th stream had been put neatly into place, tied together with bush rope made of strips of palm bark. She took off her shoe already wet, and stood waiting for further orders from Edwar He seemed to have forgotten her, however. She did not min Being close to him was enough. She sat on the ground, and l her bare feet dangle in the water, telling herself that this wa heaven compared with the hell she would have suffered had sh remained for the christening at Good Heart.

The boy called Mokka was struggling unsuccessfully to las his end of a log to the cross-section on the bank, and she ro and moved toward him. 'Can I help you, Mokka?' He grinne at her sheepishly for reply.

Edward, opposite them, had secured his end, and now l

172

plunged forward and began to swim, for in the middle of the stream the depth was greater than near the banks by about two feet. Edward swam across and came to Mokka's help while Waini and Hennaba were struggling with another log on the other bank. Edward had just caught hold of the cross-section and was about to lash the end Mokka was trying to hold in place when the other end across the way came loose. But Edward did not exclaim impatiently as Luise had expected. He simply grunted, and murmured: 'Miscalculated. I'll have to go over and do it again with a stronger piece of rope. Luise, help Mokka hold this. It's a bit heavy for him.'

Obediently she bent forward, and, her skirt trailing in the water, held the end of the log down on the cross slat stretched between the two piles. Mokka's brown hands got busy with a piece of bush-rope, and water kept spattering up into her face, half-blinding her. But she held the log down, refusing to be discouraged. The front part of her skirt was soaked several inches above the hem.

Edward shouted across with satisfaction as he secured his end again.

'Everything is all right here too!' Luise called back. She stepped back and began to wring the water out of her skirt.

Waini and Hennaba had just succeeded in securing theirs, too, and Edward clambered up on to the opposite bank, a lanky, but strong, rope-limbed boy, and surveyed the logs now in place. He seemed completely untroubled by her presence, completely unaware that she was warm-cheeked with discomfiture at the sight of his naked body.

'Five more and it will be good enough for us to wheel a barrow over,' he said with satisfaction. 'Are you tired, boys?'

'Yes, let's eat now!' called Waini. He seemed the youngest, and had a two-inch scar over his right eyebrow that made him appear to frown in a one-sided manner. He was the least shy of the three.

'Very well, we'll eat,' said Edward, and plunged in. In a few swift strokes he had clambered up and was shaking the water from his body only two or three feet from Luise. The other boys joined him, and Hennaba ran off toward the pathway, returning after a moment with a canvas bag.

Luise, uneasy, red-cheeked, clasped and unclasped her hands

173

and suddenly stammered: 'Edward, I – do you wish me to go
back to the house while you eat?'

He looked at her in surprise. 'Why? Don't you want to eat
with us? We've got cassava bread and meat and sapodillas.'

'Oh, very well.'

The boys were already seated. She sank down with them,
took a deep breath, and told herself that she must not be foolish.
If they were unashamed of their nakedness why should she be?
And the next instant the realisation that she was very hungry
caused her to forget everything but the food they handed to
her. As she ate a cool peace began to come alive within her, and
she wanted to laugh at her foolish modesty which had nearly
ruined the situation. She interrupted the chatter of the boys to
say: 'But, Edward, you never even expressed surprise at seeing
me appear!'

He hunched his shoulders, grinned like a demon and said:
'Why should I? If you appear you appear. Isn't there a christening at Good Heart today? Why didn't you stay for it?'

She averted her face. 'Don't ask me that. You – you know
very well – I preferred coming here, that's why.'

'How do you like the bridge?' he asked.

'Very good. What made you think of building a bridge here?'

'It saves having to cross over by the old log near the *koker*.
It will be useful to Father and Cousin Wilfred when they want
to go hunting. I designed it myself. I'll show you the plan I drew
when we go to the house.'

'Did you draw a plan first?'

'Of course I did. Anything you build must first have a plan
drawn on paper. I asked Storm to help me here but he preferred
to go to Good Heart.'

'Could I give you any help?'

'Well, you've already helped a bit, haven't you? If you want
to give us more help, take off your clothes and come in with us.'

'Take off my clothes! Are you out of your wits!'

'Well, you can't come in with your clothes, can you?'

'No, I suppose I can't,' she mumbled, her face averted.

He did not pursue the matter, his manner completely in-
different – as always. Out of the corner of her eye she watched
him, and wondered how it was possible anyone could be so
blankly unresponsive. Was it his age? Did he lack emotiona

174

fervour because of his youth? But he could be lecherous when he wanted to be. How often hadn't he said obscene things to her – though, she had to admit, he had said them in a spirit of cold wantonness; not because she had awakened any physical response in him.

When he and the Indians resumed work on the bridge, she sat glumly on the bank and watched them. Of a sudden she would stiffen and decide that she would shed her clothes and join them. It was so stupid to be ashamed of her nakedness. Then she remembered the morning near the tanks with her father. Look at the ugly gossip that incident had stirred up. Her action in running off from Good Heart would create enough talk, but should anyone say they had seen her in the water naked with the boys . . . She shut her eyes and gnashed her teeth. Why should she care what people said? So long as in her own mind she was clean. It would be so much fun paddling about in the water helping them with their logs. Yes, she would do it. . . . She was doing it. Shedding her clothes. The skirt, the petticoats, the bodice, the underpants . . . Now, walk forward . . . 'I'm coming in, Edward!' . . . She opened her eyes. No, she must not. She must restrain herself. Her father was always stressing the virtues of restraint. . . . He admires Mother for her restraint. I believe he admires me, too, but for other reasons. My courage in persisting with this friendship in the face of gossip. He is my champion, yet sometimes I feel I should be more at ease if he did not take my part so readily, if he didn't regard me as having inherited his capacity for self-torture. Somehow it humiliates me to think that I've inherited one of his chief weaknesses. . . . Yet his support is comforting. I like to know he is there for me to lean on – to take up my cause when Mother and Mary attack me.

She became so engaged in her reflections that it startled her to find Edward beside her. He waved his hand and said: 'It's finished.'

She rose unsteadily, flushing. 'Is it? Yes. Yes, it's good.'

The five remaining logs had been lashed into place, and the bridge looked solid and extremely serviceable. The Indians were running to and fro across it, shrieking and behaving their age.

Edward said: 'Come on. Let me take you across it. You can

tell them when you go back you were the first lady to walk on it.'

She gave him a stare of surprise. It was the first mature thing she had heard him say that did not contain an acid mockery. He really wanted her to walk ceremonially over the bridge so that she could boast of it.

Dripping wet as he was, he held her hand and walked with her over to the other bank. She was so moved with pleasure, with love for him, that she hardly felt the logs beneath her feet. It could have been her ghost walking over this bridge so aerial, so dissolved, did she feel. She continued to hold his hand as they reached the other bank, and her eyes were moist.

'What a pretty gesture, Edward! I shall never forget this moment.' She glanced about quickly. The Indians had plunged into the water and swum off up-creek. Their shrieks could be heard – and their splashings.

She gave a quavering laugh. 'I was just going to spoil things by asking you to kiss me.'

'I was waiting for you to do that,' he said. And held up his face.

She kissed him, and said: 'You're so much taller now. I haven't got to bend so much. I've loved you since you were half your height, Edward. Isn't that silly!'

'Of course it is. But you're a queer girl, so I'm not surprised.'

He spoke with the old detachment, the old indifference, his gaze on the bridge all the time, avid, calculating, so that she envied the bridge.

A resolve coalesced within her. She said: 'Edward, we can't go on like this. I mean, my always chasing after you. Do you know what I've just decided? I'm not going to attempt to see you again.'

'What! You mean no following me around? No trying to kiss me? No pestering me at all?'

She winced. 'No,' she murmured. 'None of it at all. I – no, I won't trouble you at all – unless you yourself ask me.'

He hunched his shoulders up, making himself into a hunchback, and looked up at her, grinning and squeaking grotesquely. 'Unless *I* ask you!' Abruptly he straightened himself and said: 'Well, that mightn't be so long because I'm going to need you.'

'Need me?'

He nodded, his face serious. 'Yes. Won't tell you what it is now. I'm doing a lot of practice. But I'm going to need you.'

'Well, that does sound mysterious.'

'Isn't it time for you to go?'

'Yes. Yes, I must go.'

'Wait a moment and let me dress, and I'll come to the *stelling* with you.'

She smiled. 'You're a gentleman. I can say that, at least, for you.'

5

DURING the next two years it came upon her that there was much more of her father in her than she had wanted to believe. For during those two years she held to her resolve made that day by the creek. She saw Edward many times when he came to Good Heart and when she went to Rylands and on the various occasions that arose, but she left him alone. It was an agony, but she succeeded.

The first test came only a few weeks after the creek incident. On the fourteenth of August of this same year, 1775, the retired Directeur-General Laurens Storm van's Gravesande died at the age of seventy-one on his plantation, Soesdyk, down-river, and Hubertus, among several other planters, journeyed with the corpse to Fort Island in Essequibo for the service of internment. In his absence Rosalind and Mary and Luise stayed at Rylands. At the end of their stay, on their way back to Good Heart, Mary looked at her sister and said: 'I'm glad you've learnt sense, at last.' Rosalind frowned: 'Mary!' in reproof. Luise made no reply, but stared out of the cabin window, her face as stolid as her father's.

During these two years Anton de Riest did not relax his efforts, and twice again proposed – and twice again was refused. She was kind but firm.

'I don't love you,' she told him. They were on the *stelling* of his father's plantation, Three Brothers, one afternoon in September, 1776. 'It isn't your fault, and it would be unfair to you to marry you without love on my side.' She touched his hand. 'You understand?'

He shook his head. 'I've told you I don't care if you're not in love with me. I'd marry you on any terms, Luise.'

'But I couldn't. I'm sorry, but I couldn't.'

A tall, blond young man of twenty-seven, he stood there and stared at her with his clear green eyes, his thin nose and thin lips very red with sunburn. He was his father's best overseer, and did not mind doing the duties of a servant. For an overseer was a servant. She admired him, and knew that he was the kind of man she could have married.

'Is it because – about a year ago I heard you were supposed to be very attached to a cousin of yours, then – then it began to be said you had come to your senses. I was so relieved. I . . . ' He broke off in confusion.

'The first rumour was true, Anton, but not the second. I'm still in love with my cousin Edward. And I shall always be in love with him.'

'But –'

She interrupted him. 'Don't say it. He's thirteen and I'm nearly twenty-three. Oh, how tired I am of hearing that! How tired!' It was only by shutting her eyes tight that she kept back the tears.

In November that same year Mother Lieker died, and Jacqueline, with her three children, all boys, became the mistress of the Lieker plantation. And early in January of the following year, 1777 – the year in which Commandeur van Schuylenburg celebrated the completion of three of his canals – Mary accepted a proposal of marriage from a middle-aged widower from Plantation Degries on the west coast of the Demerary estuary. During the interval when the proposal was being considered Hubertus said: 'I don't approve, my child, but if it is your wish – and the choice must be yours, for you are a person in your own right – then I will unhesitatingly take steps to have you ondertrowed.' At his use of this official term they looked at him, and after a moment he smiled and said: 'Yes, for me, Mary, it will be a marriage only in the sight of the law – not in the sight of God. God smiles only on marriages of love. That is my belief.'

Rosalind, tense, said: 'Does God smile on love-marriage outside of sanctified wedlock?'

Luise saw her father grow still, and his face, she noticed twitched – especially about the eyes. Only for an instant, how ever. He relaxed and smiled: 'I'm not accustomed to answering riddles, my dear, but perhaps I do understand this one, and my answer is: God does not possess the narrow, limited outlook of his puny creations who call themselves men. God, it is my conviction, smiles upon love, sacred or profane. The only measure He applies in judging such love is the measure of sincerity. So long as love is deep and sincere, whether the predicants or the law officials approve of it or not, such love is a joy in God's sight.' Chuckling, he stretched out and touched her cheek with the tips of his fingers. 'My love for you is like that, Rosalind. Deep and sincere.'

'And also your love for Faustina?'

'Mother!' Like her mother, Mary too, was white, a hand clutching at her bosom.

Luise saw her father grow still again. This time, however, his face did not twitch. He nodded slowly, the smile still on his lips. 'Yes, Rosalind – my love for Faustina – that, also, is deep and sincere.'

Mary was married to Mynheer Hubner in March, and with her departure a silence descended upon the house at Good Heart. Between Rosalind and Mary there had been a close bond; they had spoken the same language. Luise and her father were joined by another bond, though, in their case, neither would admit the affinity in demonstrative fashion; little had ever been said between Luise and her father. Mary, by her close and easy relationship with her mother, had provided the means of communication between them all, for though she was opposed to her father and sister, she had never been afraid to express her opinions to them. When she was present, the atmosphere, though troubled, had been positive. Now the atmosphere was negative.

On Sundays, after service, it was full of background tensions, or in the conversation of everyone there was reference to the war in North America. Cranley and Wilfred were both certain that the Netherlands would eventually become involved. 'I've heard it whispered,' said Wilfred, 'that the Dutch in St Eustatious are doing a big trade in smuggling. Yes. They smuggle supplies to the King's enemies in those c-c-colonies. Ugly business. The English won't t-t-tolerate it indefinitely, you take my word for it.'

179

'Should England declare war on the Netherlands,' said Cranley, 'our greatest difficulty will come from the privateers who never fail to take advantage of such a situation. Ruthless rogues those privateers.'

'Why must people fight among themselves!' Luise exclaimed. 'Why can't they leave such behaviour to the beasts in the bush!'

Her father, who sat on her right, smiled and grunted. 'It is because men, in their egotism, my child, are too disregardful of the beast in them. To be noble we must first recognise the ignoble in ourselves. To be aware of what is ugly and evil in ourselves is to be on guard against it. When, in our conceit, we think ourselves all pure and perfect, then the beast snarls and brings us down, reminding us of its presence.'

'Wisdom, wisdom,' tittered Wilfred. 'Old Hubert can always sum things up for us out of that old tome he has c-c-concealed in his brain.'

It was the first Sunday in September, and they were at Wilfred's house. The long dry season was at the peak of its heat and slaves were ranged at various points around the two dining tables wielding large palm-leaf fans. Not that these made much difference. Everyone perspired.

Luise, despite her very light attire, felt sticky and uncomfortable, and, at the end of the meal, was one of the first to rise and move out on to the side veranda. The glare of the day made her wince. Clara Clackson's laughter, gay and shrill, sounded at the western end of the veranda, and Luise saw the girl, shortish, but very shapely, standing at the rail with Raphael van Groenwegel and Alpheda Leuven from down-river. Luise was about to move in their direction when a quick footstep behind her caused her to pause. It was Edward. Edward, at fourteen, was as tall as herself. He had sat at the other table. She always tried to arrange to sit where there was little chance of seeing him or talking to him.

He touched her on her arm, and she started, feeling little tremors moving like wires throughout her stomach.

'Yes, Edward?'

The brown hair was threatening to fall over his forehead. 'Today is the day,' he said. His voice was changing. The male bass had come.

'Today? I don't understand.' Her own voice shook.

180

'Have you forgotten I said I would need you?'

'I – oh, yes. Yes, that day by the creek. I never really knew what you meant.' She gave a little gulping smile.

'Meet me under that big sandbox tree. You know it, don't you? It's not far from the sugar-mill. Take that path over there.' He pointed. 'It's the shortest way.'

'But what must we meet for?'

'I'll explain,' he said. He was perfectly collected, and might have been telling her to fetch him a mug of water. 'You go at once. I have to get something from upstairs. I'll follow in a moment.'

He left her, and, her whole body in a tremulous ache, she hurried toward the kitchen, trying to contain herself but certain that the house-slaves were staring at her in wonder. It was nothing unusual for womenfolk to go into the kitchen, but she felt it would seem so. Everyone must have seen Edward speaking to her on the veranda. Everyone knew where she was going. Blindly uncaring, she went down the kitchen steps and moved across the compound toward the path opening Edward had pointed out. She knew the sandbox tree he meant. She had gone there with him in the past.

The past. . . . What was the past? Somehow, her sense of time had grown blurred. Was it two years ago since that light-footed little journey over a log bridge had taken place? . . . She looked at her hand. It might still be wet with creek water from the hand that had clasped it. . . . I'm such a fool! Oh, why was I born such a fool! Why couldn't I have been simple and conventional like Mary and Susan? Even Jacqueline? I would have been married now to Anton de Riest. Jacqueline has four children. Susan has written to say she had a daughter. Perhaps Mary is pregnant already. I could have had two or three myself. Instead, I'm walking in the heat, trembling and upset, to obey the command of a boy nearly ten years my junior. Why must some people be born with a mad streak! I'm mad. I know I'm mad, yet I can do nothing to help myself. Nothing. Nothing at all. I'm like a dry leaf that must always be blown wherever the breeze wills. . . . She laughed. That is a bad analogy. I cannot see Edward as a breeze. A breeze is soft, kind. It would blow a leaf into cool, shady places. . . . Oh, this heat. . . .

It was very secluded under the sandbox tree. The huge,

181

thorny trunk itself was like a wall separating the spot from inquisitive gazes, from the babble of voices, and all the fuss of people. The sugar-mill and clumps of manicole palms with the sandbox trunk formed a kind of ring enclosing a small clearing overgrown with grass and ferns. Sunshine filtered through the spreading branches of the sandbox in small shifty patches that made the ferns glitter in desultory fashion, and gave them a vaguely watching, mysterious air. Every odd second an insect would send up a thin steaming tweet, as though it were in league with the ferns and the stunted grass. With the shiny black lizards that wriggled interminably on the loamy soil.

She had not long to wait. He was carrying a flat, square parcel.

'Come nearer to the wall of the mill,' he said. 'There's more sunshine here. A bigger patch, I mean. And not so much grass.'

She went to the spot he indicated, and seated herself on an old copper basin, half-buried, bottom up, in cane-trash and soil. They had sat here before. . . . In the past. . . .

He put down his parcel, squatted on the ground before her and smiled: 'You used to tell me you loved me. Remember?'

She nodded. Tense and curious.

'That means you'd keep a secret if I ask you to, doesn't it?'

'Yes.'

He began to rub his knee slowly, contemplatively. His gestures had always been so unboyish. Even at four he had had an adult manner.

'Yes, I think I can trust you. You're not bad. I like you. It's only that you used to bother me so much. I'm not the kissing kind. Seems foolish to me, always touching a girl and kissing her. What I like is making things. Building things and – ' He broke off, stared at her, then continued. 'This is the secret. I like sketching. For years and years I've been sketching. But I don't want people to know. Mother and Father know. I had to tell them, because I wouldn't have been able to get my pencils and paper if I hadn't. But they've promised they won't tell anyone.'

As he fell silent, his gaze on the ground, she said: 'But, Edward, why should you want it to be kept secret? I think you should be proud to be able to sketch. You must have a talent. Father used to sketch, too.'

182

'I know. It's in the family. But to me, it seems a girlish kind of thing to do. Building a bridge or a house would be all right. I'd like people to know I can do that – but sketching leaves, and faces, and trees – oh, no. And another thing.' He crouched forward until his face was almost touching her skirt. In a lowered voice, he said: 'Clara told me – years and years ago she told me. She said that Grandma Hendrickje's husband was a painter. An artist. And she used to beat him with a whip, because he was a weak, girlish kind of fellow. He was no man at all. You think I want to be like him? Perhaps it's his talent I've inherited. But I won't be like him. No woman is going to beat me with any whip. And I won't have people talking about me and saying I'm girlish. That's why I want it to be a strict secret. You understand?'

Her restraint went. She reached forward and caressed his cheek, biting her lower lip hard. 'Of course, I understand. It's silly – a silly reason – but I understand. But why did you have to tell me?'

'Because I think the time has come for me to try something else besides leaves and trees and faces. I want to do a whole body. I want to make a picture of you – the whole of you.'

'You mean – not with my clothes off?'

'With your clothes off? Whatever for? Oh.' He grinned as though suddenly remembering. 'Yes, I know. A lot of the masters used to paint naked women. Old Timmins, our tutor, has shown us one or two copies he has. No, I didn't mean that at all. I don't want to sketch you naked.'

After a silence, she said: 'I wonder how Clara heard that about Grandma Hendrickje's husband. It's a family tale. Father never liked to tell us about the doings of the old people.'

'Clara said she overheard Mother telling Father one evening. Mother knows all about the bad deeds the old people did. She won't tell us anything, but now and then we overhear little bits. I believe there is something in blood. Bad blood does come down in children.'

'Father believes that, too. It may be true, and it may not. You shouldn't let it trouble you, Edward. Pray to God and He'll help you to be good.'

He was unwrapping his parcel. He told her to sit back. 'Just sit still and look at me. We have the whole afternoon before us. I'll try to get your face finished first, and then another time I'll do the rest of your body, but you'll have to wear this same dress.'

At the end of what must have been an hour, he showed her what he had done, and she was astonished at the excellence of his drawing.

'Heavens! But you're talented, Edward! That's me. It's – that's my face – exactly how I look. Only you've . . . '

'Yes?'

She hesitated, then said: 'Only you've made me more beautiful – and very sad.'

'That's how I *want* you to look. I always think of you as beautiful and sad. You're the most beautiful girl on the whole river. Clara is handsome but she is not like you. I can't explain it, but I know what I mean.'

Her hand trembled. 'Do you really think me the most beautiful girl on the whole river?'

'Yes. But please don't want me to kiss you or touch your breasts because I've said that. I mean it. You are. Anyone with eyes can tell you that. Sit back again. I think we have time for me to do your throat and shoulders.'

She sat back again, and it was as though her body were melting from sheer happiness. What did it matter that his voice and manner were so passionless? He had said what he had, and she knew he meant it. He never told lies. It was the one trait about him she could vouch for. She kept watching his absorbed face bent over the sketching board. Such a small, determined mouth. A small, pointed chin. Deep green eyes with specks of grey. It was a sensitive face – yet cruel. . . . I feel like a ghost contained in a cloud of love. I could die now without regrets. . . . I don't mind being a fool if I can have moments such as this. . . .

The gossip began again, but she did not mind. She was happy. On every occasion when it was convenient Edward took her into a secluded spot to make sketches of her. Rosalind did not send spies to watch them; her attitude now was one of resignation. She made no comments; she lived within herself, as each of the three of them at Good Heart did. . . . We are like islands in a lake, though Luise, and how pleasant it is on mine!

How green the trees, and how peacefully the little creeks flow among the ferns!

What satisfied her more deeply than anything else was that as the weeks and months passed he began to be shaped by her will. She told him that it was foolish to try to prevent people from knowing about his art, and, at first, he growled and said that he wanted it so, then he began to yield to her point of view. One day – it was at Signal in February, the following year, 1778 – he had just shown her some of his sketches, the ones he had done during the two-year interval when she had seen virtually nothing of him, and she exclaimed: 'What beautiful work! Edward, I'm so proud of you! Why should you want to hide these things! I'm sure the family would be glad to boast of your talent.'

He grinned in his demoniac way and said: 'I tell you what it is. It's not that I'm really afraid because of what Clara told me – I mean about Grandma Hendrickje's husband, but I'm afraid people might want to make a fuss over me, and I'd feel like killing them. I want to be left alone.' He shifted about, frowning through the window of the loft; they were in the loft of Wilfred's small barn. . . . He looks a little like Father now, thought Luise. A little tortured. . . . The urge to stretch out and run her fingers through his hair made a burning in her when she tried to suppress it.

'Perhaps I shouldn't say that. What Clara said did make me think a lot – but since I've been sketching you it doesn't matter.' He looked at her abruptly, scowled as though annoyed because of the way she was looking at him, then said: 'Oh, I'll drop this secrecy before long – but not just at the moment. Let me do some sketches of you first. I did nine of Clara before I began to do you.' He sniggered. 'Mostly from memory. She doesn't know I've done them.' His hands clenched slowly – and unclenched – and he kept smiling at some secret thing in his mind.

'Edward.'

'Yes?'

'You're not – are you fond of Clara?'

'Fond of her?' He frowned at her in surprise. 'Why should you think so? I like her, but if you mean – oh, I see.' He began to shake his head in his adult fashion and laugh. 'You mean if I'm in love with her. Well, I'm not. I know two fellows who are. Kurt Haedeker and John Hartfield. They nearly had a fight over her three Sundays ago.'

'And does she like them?'

'I don't think so.' He hesitated, then said: 'I think she likes me. But she's a bit shy. She's not like you – bold like you, I mean.'

'But I do behave myself nowadays, don't I?'

'Yes, you're much better, I must say. You don't worry me so much.'

She laughed. 'How frank you are, Edward! A few years ago I would have felt like striking you for saying that, but now – well, I've grown accustomed to you. I know you don't mean to be cruel to me – though you do have a streak of cruelty in you.'

'That's from Grandma Hendrickje.'

Before the year was over she had succeeded in getting him to drop the secrecy, and now they did not have to be clandestine in meeting in their secret spots, for everyone knew why they were together. Not that the gossip grew any kinder. One day Edward said to her: 'We're being laughed at everywhere, and people are beginning to say it's *you* who are leading me on a string. At first, they said it was I who was leading you about. They're fools! No woman can ever lead me.'

'Do as I do and take no notice of what anyone says.'

'Oh, I don't care. People to me are like pebbles. I always feel like kicking them along the ground.'

6

AND all the time there was the talk of war. One Sunday Wilfred said: 'You'd be surprised to know what Schuylenburg said no t-t-too long ago. I heard it on good authority, and I have no d-d-doubt it's true. Schuylenburg was dining with that plante: fellow from Barbados, James Clarke, and he t-t-told Clark that if ever we did find ourselves at war with England he would prefer to have the colony captured by a King's ship rather tha: be attacked by privateers. Of course, you – well, you can se what prompted him to say that. He owns Plantation Land o: Canaan, and well, n-n-naturally, he wouldn't want to be raide by privateers.' Wilfred tittered. 'In a way, it's not such a bad thing that our Commandeur should own a private estate of his own, is it? G-g-gives him more sympathy with us private planters. He can see our p-p-point of view more clearly and reasonably.'

Cranley said: 'If it is true that he said so I think he spoke very wisely. But, then, of course, Wilfred, his words *could* be construed as treason – by the Netherlands. We are English, and we see the matter in a different light.'

Luise exclaimed: 'I'm sure Father would agree with you, Cranley! He may be Dutch but he's not bigoted!'

'Ah! What a loyal daughter!' Cranley glanced toward Hubertus who was at the other table, seated next to Faustina. Cranley gave her his charming, ironic smile. 'I believe you are right, my dear. Hubert is certainly not bigoted, and he's no fool, either – in a material sense, that is. Yet he can, you will admit, be extremely unpredictable at times.'

Both her Uncle and Luise gave him a swift glance, and Luise thought: I wonder if Uncle Wilfred noticed it, too. Cranley sounds bitter. Could it be . . . She glanced toward her father . . . No, Father and Cousin Faustina are too old and wise to be indiscreet. They have integrity. . . . And yet. . . .

For the rest of the meal she was a trifle disturbed.

At the other table, Edward ate with his usual absorbed air. He was seated between Maisie Haversham and Ludwig Gitt, but not once did Luise see him glance at either of them. Nor did he glance in her direction.

They were at Rylands, and it was a rather cloudy day in November, 1780. The long dry season was coming to an end, and during the past few days there had been light, brief showers.

When the meal was over, Edward came to her on the veranda where they always met after eating. He said: 'If you are ready we can start now. I don't think it will rain. I've found a new hiding-place. It's not far from that old bridge of mine.'

She smiled: 'Aren't you tired of sketching me, Edward?'

'I'll tell you when I am. I've done you in nineteen different poses. I counted them yesterday. And that doesn't include fourteen heads.'

On their way, he said: 'Today it will be different.'

'Different? What do you mean?'

'I'll explain when we get to the hiding-place.'

She knew that it would be futile asking him to explain at once, so kept silent. He was taller than she now by an inch, and often she thought he could be her own age. His masculinity was far more evident than Storm's or Raphael's but then he was quiet and thoughtful whereas Storm and Raphael still behaved like boys. Raphael, even at eighteen, had not lost his love for tree-climbing, and he and Storm and Cornelis Lieker went boating and hunting together. Edward never went with them, though sometimes he accompanied Wilfred or the Indians.

The hiding-place was at the top of a low hill just beyond the creek. The ground was sandy, and their feet made no sound as they ascended. Then after rounding a clump of wild pines, draped with the white webs of hairy bush-spiders, Edward led her into what seemed a clearing hacked out of the trees. The ground was still sandy, and the trunk of a fallen palm lay across the further side of the clearing – a prickly thing half-smothered with dried fronds and spider-webs. Aeta palms and swizzle-stick shrubs and an odd wild pine surrounded the spot, and the twilight was of a coppery hue, a trifle weird, though – when one was not alone, thought Luise – peaceful.

'How do you like it here?' he asked. 'I came upon it unexpectedly a few days ago. Strange I hadn't found it before, because I've been this way so many times.'

'It's an ideal hiding-place,' she admitted, looking round, but I can guess why you didn't discover it. It's those pines. If just two of them hadn't been missing where we entered, this place could have remained unknown for ever.'

'Yes, I thought so myself.' He frowned, and added: 'Now you mention it, I can almost imagine someone having deliberately cut down two pines to make an entrance. Probably my fancy.'

'Can you sketch in this light?'

'Of course I can,' he said, unwrapping his parcel. 'I've sketched in worse lights, haven't I!'

'Where must I sit or stand?'

'Just there – near that clump of swizzle-stick trees. But before you do I want you to take off your clothes.'

'What! Take off – '

'Don't be difficult, please. I won't touch your body – though you'll want me to, I suppose. Even with your clothes on you want me to –'

'Edward, that's not true. Not these past few years!'

'You don't ask me to in words – but your eyes do. You can't fool me. All the time you want me to kiss you and paw you over. It's nothing new. Are you going to undress and let me do you in the nude?'

She stood, biting her lower lip in indecision. A trembling had attacked her. . . . If only he had told me before so as to prepare me. . . .

'If you don't want to, say so and I'll do you with your clothes on. I've done enough of you clothed, though, and I think it's time I experimented with you in the nude.' His voice was as cold and detached as though he were talking about a bridge he was planning to build somewhere.

'I'm a bit shy of you, Edward – nowadays. You're seventeen and – and very manly. And, of course, I – well, I love you. I . . .' She broke off, gulping. Suddenly pressed her hands to her face.

She heard him grunt, and then there was another sound – the crackling of a dry leaf. She removed her hands and realised that he had taken a step toward her. He stood before her, almost touching her.

'Don't be foolish,' he said, and his voice held a note she had never known before today. She stared at him, feeling dizzy. 'If you weren't so blind you'd have known that I love you, too. Sketching you all these months and years and sinking myself in your beauty – you don't think it would make me love you? And you're good to me, too. You're a fool if you can't see I'm in love with you. But I don't make a big fuss over it, that's why you're blind to it, I suppose.'

She could say nothing.

'I'm only waiting until I'm a year or two older and then I'm going to marry you. I've been planning it for two or three years now. There isn't another girl about this river I could waste time on trying to court. They're all so giggly and stupid. Not one of them would make me a good wife. But you're different. I didn't mean to tell you this now, but I had to. You looked so sad standing there with your hands to your face.'

He turned away, clicking his tongue as though annoyed.

'Edward my dear, I – wish I knew what to say.'

'Don't say it. It's sure to be foolish. Look here, we'd better be going. I can't sketch you. Not today. You've upset me.'

'I'm sorry. I . . . Edward, I'll take off my clothes. I'll do it.'

He shook his head. 'Not today. I can't draw now.' She saw his head tremble. His hands were clenched. He kept staring at the fallen palm. Of a sudden he clicked his tongue again and stooping began to tie his parcel together. She saw his fingers tremble as they worked.

'You'll let us come back another day?'

He grunted. 'Yes. Father is going to Barbados to spend a month with his aristocratic relatives who are in Barbados on a visit there from England. Sir Graeme Clackson and his son.' His voice had grown normal again. 'Mother says she's inviting you three from Good Heart to spend the month here.'

'I see. But at a time like this – is it wise that Cranley should go to Barbados?'

'You mean the war in North America? It isn't certain that England will declare war on us. Why shouldn't Father go? And in any case, he's English. He'll be quite safe if war comes.'

'When does he sail?'

'Some day next week.' He had finished rewrapping the parcel. He stood up and said: 'Let's go.'

She did not move. 'Are you afraid to stay?'

'Yes.' He avoided her gaze. 'If you take off your clothes now I'd want to have you. Even with your clothes on I – let's go.'

'But I'd like you to, Edward. Please. I've lived for it.'

'When we're married. Not before. Let's go.'

There was so much finality in his voice that she did not argue.

They went.

At Good Heart, the following day, she said to her mother: 'Did you hear that Cranley is going to Barbados for a month?'

'Yes,' said Rosalind, quietly, her face emotionless.

After a silence: 'Cousin Faustina has asked us to spend the month at Rylands. Edward told me yesterday.'

'Yes.'

Another silence. They were on the veranda, all three of them.

Hubertus was smoking. In a short while Overgaar would come with his report.

'You didn't mention it,' said Luise.

No comment from her mother. Her father gazed at the fruit-trees, his face as blank as his wife's.

'Mother, are we going?'

Rosalind gave her a mild look of surprise. 'I don't know what *you* and your father are doing, Luise. How should I?'

Silence once again. The thump-thump of slave drums.

'Father, are you going?'

'Yes. Yes, I'm spending the month at Rylands, my girl.' He looked at her and smiled affectionately, then his face grew mask-like as before. Smoke curled upward from his pipe.

Luise rose and sighed. Rubbed her hands slowly down her cheeks.

'Mother, are you spending the month at Rylands, too?'

'No, Luise. I'm staying here.'

PART FIVE

1

LAUGHING and chattering like a pack of silly monkeys. I wish I were living by myself. I hate laughing and chattering.

Crouched up alone at one end of the *stelling*, Edward hugged his legs and scowled at the black water. It was a fine morning, with large grey-white clouds drifting in the sky, and the sun was not very hot – compared with what it could be in September and October. There might be rain this afternoon. A fine morning in November was not to be trusted.

At the other end of the *stelling*, Storm and Raphael and Clara were sitting side by side, their bare legs dangling over the water. And in the water, close in to the bank, Graeme and his sister Mathilde and two slave girls of about their own ages were swimming with loud splashes and shrieks. Storm and Raphael and Clara, with their laughing and chattering, made almost as much noise. Edward's lips moved silently now and then as he cursed them. . . . Fools – they would always be fools. Big girl like Clara. Twenty years old. Ought to have been married already and with children. And Raphael eighteen last February – nearly nineteen – and look at him! Like some ten-year-old! Tall fellow with hair like washed-out salt-fish. And Storm – sometimes I can't stand knowing he and I are twins. It makes me ashamed to look at him and know he resembles me so closely. Strangers are always taking him for me and me for him. I could kill him. Nothing in his head. He'll just be another gentleman planter when he grows up. Even his Latin isn't much good. Old Timmins has despaired of him. Raphael and Clara aren't so bad. Clara is good at Greek – much better than I. . . . Oh, she can be something, that girl – if she had somebody to sober her down. I could do it. I've often thought of doing it, but I look on her as a sister – just as the others do. We all grew up together, so how can we help looking on her as a sister. That's why Luise always makes me laugh when she asks me if I'm in love with Clara. . . . I could be, though. I've thought of it sometimes, and I believe Clara can feel that way about me, too. She has given me some queer looks – same kind of looks Luise gives me. . . . Goedlust Lieker has his eye on her, I've been told. A fellow I don't like, but I suppose Father and Mother would consider it a good match. The Liekers have bought a new plantation on the coast, and Goedlust is going to live on it. . . .

Why doesn't that yacht hurry up and come? . . .

The yacht with Luise and Hubertus was on its way. At th
moment it was only half an hour's journey away.

It was the first time for years that Luise could remembe
having been alone like this with her father. For the greater pa
of the trip they had been silent, but within the past few minute
conversation had suddenly blossomed forth between them. H
pipe had gone out, and he made no attempt to light it agair
He had begun by asking about her nieces and nephews – ha
she any favourites among them? Surprised, she had replied ne
She liked all of Jacqueline's children, and Mary's little boy wa
a lovely little fellow.

'I wonder if we shall ever see Susan's,' she said.

He gave her a sly look, and smiled. 'Your father, my gir
sometimes wonders when he will see yours.'

And now she understood what he had been leading up te
The blood began to gather slowly in her face, but she did ne
fidget. Nor comment.

'You are quite satisfied to be friendly with your cousi
Luise?'

'Yes, Father.'

'Have you been physically intimate with him?'

'Father!'

'You must pardon me asking such a question, my girl, bt
I ask it out of consideration for you. You have been in n
thoughts a great deal.'

'I see.'

Strange, she thought, that I should resent it whenever I
tries to be sympathetic or take my part. I know he means we
and yet . . .

'No, we haven't been intimate – but it's not through lack
ardour on my side, as you must know. Since you wish me
be frank, I'll say it.'

He nodded contemplatively, his gaze out of the cabin wir
dow. 'A very puzzling boy. He is so much older than his years
in mind. Do you know what he asked me one day a year or tv
ago? He asked me if I would let him rebuild my sugar-mill

196

a few years' time. He said that he had planned just how the structure should be, and that it would be a much cooler and more convenient building than the one that now stands. I was astonished, Luise. He did not speak like a boy. I believe he will get far.'

On impulse she rose and moved over beside him. She held his hand and said: 'Father, tell me. Suppose – he has already told me that he loves me and would like to marry me in a year or two. Would you oppose the match? And do you think Cousin Faustina would oppose it?'

His face remained expressionless for a moment, then he began to smile. She watched the crow's feet around his eyes. He was fifty-three. There were grey strands in his head and in his beard, but, if anything, he had developed more power and virility, more vitality, with the years. She could not look at his eyes for long, but had to avert her own. The great solid body beside hers seemed to exude a force she could sense in tingling waves that rushed through the whole soft slimness of her own person.

'Our family, Luise, has inter-married far too much. Inbreeding is not a good thing, and I must tell you that I don't approve of it, but as I once told your mother – and I think you were present – I am always in favour of a marriage that is based on deep and sincere love.' Of a sudden he began to tap his knee with the stem of his pipe, and she saw that his face had lost its composure. A haunted, hunted light had come into his eyes. His free hand closed over her wrist, and she found herself breathing hard to suppress a cry of pain. She shut her eyes. Then the agony was over, and his hand moved upward to his face, rubbing slowly up and down the high checkbone. He said: 'You have seen some desperate struggles, my child. I've watched you these past years when you might not have realised it. Our home is not the same now, and it is my fault. I've lost your mother's love – and it is a precious thing I have thrown away. No one knows it more than I, Luise, but no one knows it more than I, too, that what has happened could not have been avoided. Your faith in God is still strong, Luise, isn't it?'

'Yes. I pray often.'

He put his pipe down on the bench and took it up. He leaned forward, breathing deeply, nodding his head. 'Yes. My faith is still strong – yet I sometimes pause and wonder at God's purpose. If only I could understand the purpose behind events – behind our lives – I would be less harrowed. Sometimes I'm attacked by a terrible fear, my girl – it is the fear that I shall get old and still not have found peace. I am fifty-three, and I am baffled as at thirty-five. The twilight is still deep on every hand and though there are instants when a beam of true light breaks through, these instants are fleeting and – and perhaps more a source of perturbation than of balm – and enlightenment.' Abruptly he chuckled and patted her cheek lightly with the tips of his fingers. 'This is selfish of me, Luise. I have no right to impose my gloomy sentiments upon you. You are a lovely child. Your beauty increases with the passage of every week and month. Yes, I would approve, my girl. Let the colony gossip. What does gossip matter if you, within yourself, are happy with the things of your spirit!'

'Thanks. But – what of Cousin Faustina?'

'She will, too. I know she will.' He held her arm – very gently. 'And I think it would be good if you two lived at Good Heart. Our home would be a less lonely place. It might cheer your mother.'

She touched his hand. 'May I say something? I don't think you're right.' She hesitated, then went on: 'You haven't lost Mother's love, but – I think she feels alone in spirit. She knows that you and I – and Cousin Faustina – are closer in the way we see life. I don't think it's your fault, but there's one thing I've wanted to tell you. You shouldn't take my part as readily as you do in her presence. That hurts her.'

He grunted. 'I must remember that. Yes, it was thoughtless of me. But you don't know all, my child,' he sighed. 'You don't know all. I must relight my pipe. And excuse me. My thoughts are not consecutive this morning. You have noticed it haven't you? How – how I lack concentration?'

'Yes.'

'And you know why, don't you?'

'I think so.'

A silence came upon them after that. ...

Edward, too, was still silent at his end of the *stelling*.

I would be anywhere else but here, he told himself, but

198

can't be helped. I must endure these monkeys. I want to see her step off that boat on to the *stelling*. She has such grace, my beloved. Only I mustn't tell her so. I can't tell her many things now, or she'll want me to ravish her on the spot. She's so fervid. I am, too, but I know how to keep things hidden. I can keep my feelings as well as my thoughts hidden. These monkeys know nothing about restraint. They can just babble and chatter and scamper about. They think me odd because I can be silent and alone and not be bored. None of them will ever understand me. Only my beloved understands me and doesn't think me queer. She used to at first – when she was chattery and unrestrained as they. She has changed a great deal these past few years. In body and spirit she gets lovelier and lovelier every day. If only I were nineteen already! I'm older than that in mind, I know. Everyone says it, and in that they aren't wrong. I was born old. . . .

Luise my love, I could build towers for you. And strange pagodas in the jungle where no noise of fools would reach us. . . . Black water moving slowly. . . . I could drown myself in moonlight and all kinds of midnight magic – if you would drown with me. . . .

Black water moving slowly . . . I couldn't miss seeing her step out of that boat. What a pity that father of hers will be with her. Big hulking hypocrite! I don't know how Mother can be friendly with him. With his pious, pompous airs and his affected gestures. Smiling and patting people on the shoulder and simpering in his beard. Makes me itch to expose him for the grand hoax he is. I don't believe he's capable of uttering a sincere word. He speaks as though he were composing a book. . . . He fools even Luise. Luise believes in him. But Cousin Rosalind doesn't. I know she doesn't – not nowadays. She has found him out for what he is. She knows why he's coming to spend time here, and I believe Father knows, too. Father is a real mystery; I don't understand him. He never shows his hand – or perhaps he loves Mother so much he wants her to be happy at any cost. Yes, it may be that. He knows Mother and Cousin Hubertus make love in secret, but he lets them because he's generous. He's worth ten of Cousin Hubertus. Mother ought to be ashamed of herself, and yet . . . I know she's good and big-hearted; she's not a hypocrite like Cousin Hubertus. She's a mystery, too. One day I'm going to ask her outright what she finds in Cousin Hubertus. . . .

Oh, there! At last!

The Van Groenwegels' yacht came into view round the bend down-river, and the shrieks and laughter of the others, and the splashing in the water, rose to a new pitch of intensity. Storm looked at Edward and yelled: 'Edward, jump in and swim and meet them!' And Raphael: 'Go on, Edward! Swim out to your heart's delight!' A new explosion of shrieking laughter burst from them, Clara's voice high above the chorus like a long shuddering beam of sunlight. Though suddenly she cried 'Storm! Raphael! Don't tease him!'

'He calls us monkeys, doesn't he?'

'He's a baboon,' laughed Raphael. 'A love-sick baboon!'

'You shouldn't tease the poor boy.'

'Graeme! Not too far out! Remember the *perai!*'

'Yes, keep in-shore there! Mathilde! Come back!'

Ignore them all. Ignore and watch. . . . Black water slowly moving. . . . The curved bow coming closer. . . . He rose. . . . Oh my love. . . .

And now she was stepping on to the *stelling*. She looked toward him and smiled. Ignored the others and came toward him, and he scowled at her and growled: 'Let's hurry away. can't stand monkeys.'

'Good morning, Edward my boy!'

'Oh, I – I'm sorry! Good morning, Cousin Hubertus!'

' . . . he's a hypocrite, all the same, and I don't like hypocrites.

'He only appears to be, but he's sincere, Edward.'

'Then it's a kind of sincerity I don't understand.'

'He's good. Big and understanding.'

'You're always telling me that, but I still don't believe it.'

'Aren't you pleased that he's approved?'

'Yes.'

They were in the hiding-place, and it was mid-afternoon.

'You won't mind living at Good Heart?'

'No.'

She watched him, thinking: If only I could see into that dead head of his. I never know what he is thinking.

He had made no attempt to unwrap his parcel. He was very tense.

'Aren't you going to do your sketching?'

'Yes. Do you — are you going to take off your clothes?'

'Of course, Edward.' She laughed. 'I'm not shy — because I came prepared. Last time you took me by surprise.'

'Well, stop looking love-sick and undress.'

'Will you turn your back? I'll tell you when I'm ready.'

He clicked his tongue but obeyed, thinking: I feel as if I'm melting. If I don't take a grip of myself I'll be behaving like her. I hate being a fool over things like this. . . . I think this is the most terrible, the most exciting and the most beautiful moment I'll ever experience. Never again will it happen like this. . . .

'You can turn round now.'

He trembled, hesitated, and turned. The grim look on his face lasted a moment longer, then he smiled — and looked away, his hands clenched.

'Are you disappointed?'

He shook his head. Trembling. Everything, he thought, is singing around me.

In the silence they heard the lizards. And distantly the creek. The soft sucking of water at the bush. Tree-roots and ferns.

Two small patches of sunlight were mingled with the spider webs on the fallen palm. An insect went tick! And again tick!

'Your parcel. You haven't untied it.'

He shook his head, looking at the palm.

I can hear this silence. After I'm dead I'll still hear it. . . . I wish I could see into his thoughts. . . .

'You don't want to draw?'

He shook his head.

The silence. It seemed to whirr about them, alive with humid phantoms.

She rose quickly and moved over to him, and held him. And in silence he held her and kissed and fondled her. His hands were cold, and he trembled all the time. She whispered: 'You undress, too.' But he shook his head. Fondled her back and her cheeks and her throat and her breasts. Staring past her and shaking his head. Biting his lip.

'You want me, Edward. Have me.'

'No.'

She was fondling him. 'But you do.'

The sun had shifted on to a hairy spider. He saw one black leg curl inward, retreat. The webs glistened faintly. A magic world of menace.

'You want me terribly.'

He nodded. Trembled uncontrollably.

'Then have me.'

'When we're married.'

'Now.'

'No.' He sat very rigid, his face strained.

'Why?'

'It's – I didn't dream of it like this.'

'Have me now.' She fondled him unceasingly, but he was stubborn.

'Please, Edward.'

He began to tremble again. Kissed her in a frenzy. Whimpering.

'Oh, my dear! Oh, my dear!'

The trembling died down – with his breath. His eyes were shut, and she let him hold her, murmuring, fighting down her disappointment.

'I'm a fool,' he said.

'You're not. You couldn't help it. I over-excited you.'

'I'm a stupid fool.'

'It's my fault, Edward. Don't be upset, dear. Next time it will be different. You'll be calmer.'

He kept staring over her shoulder, still holding her but frowning, half-ashamed, all the trembling gone. 'Dress and let' go,' he growled.

'I will. Hold me like this a minute longer.'

'I feel – I feel terrible.'

'Never mind. Don't be ashamed. With me you must never be ashamed.'

He felt soothed. Less ashamed. He stroked her hair gently.

She touched his cheek. 'Why do you want us to wait until we're married? Are you so – so moral?'

'I planned it so years ago. I like things to go as I planned them. And besides . . .'

'Yes?'

He frowned and said: 'You're too lovely and precious to

202

me – to – to be ravished out of wedlock. I'd feel it was sacrilege.'

She kept looking at his face. Stroked his neck and murmured that she understood. 'Only, Edward, for me the waiting is terrible. I've waited so many years. I was twenty-eight last October.'

A silence. The insect began to go tick again.

'If you feel – I hate to know you have to suffer because of me. Well, then – we can come here again tomorrow if you like.'

The following day, however, the rain poured. And the day after was the same. He spent most of his time in the chief carpenter's cottage.

'What do you do there?' she asked him in the evening.

'Can you keep it a secret?'

'Of course. You're so fond of secrets!'

'Harrow is teaching me about building. We're good friends. For months now I've been going to his cottage.' He paused, then looked at her. 'This is a strict secret. I've made a plan for a new factory for Good Heart, and I showed it to Harrow, and he thinks it a good one. One day, when I'm a little older, I'm determined to build a new factory for your father.'

'I'm going to be very proud of you. Very, very proud.'

The following day there were only light, intermittent showers, and he said when she tackled him: 'I'll go and see if it's very wet and come back and tell you. Wait on the veranda here for me.'

He set out at once.

The trees dripped continuously, and everywhere was the sound of trickling water. The compound was a morass, and the paths were squelchy with mud. But the sun shone from a sky patchy with grey-white clouds that moved slowly toward the south-west. High up in the branches of a star-apple tree, Raphael, half-nude to his waist, was throwing down ripe fruit to Storm and Clara, both bare-footed and sloshing about in the mud.

It's sandy in our hiding-place, thought Edward. If this sun can keep on shining for another hour or so it might not be too wet there – though the sun never penetrates directly, it is true. . . . I don't feel it's right, though. I should be married to her first. To go and defile her beautiful body. God! And it's

203

even more beautiful than I'd imagined it. . . . When I turned and looked at her . . . Oh, I mustn't think of it. I'll go mad. . .

Approaching the coffee-lodges, he gave a groan. The sun was gone. A drizzle began to fall, and it got coarser and coarser

At the creek, he decided it would be useless to bother. The sand, already wet, would be wetter as this rain continued to fall. Perhaps it was just as well. Though he hated her to suffer. . .

After a moment's indecision, he took off his clothes and plunged into the water, swam around for about half an hour, came out, walked about until he was glowing, then hauled on his rain-soaked pants and with the rest of his clothes thrown over his arm, crossed by the bridge and took the path that led up the hill. The rain fell ceaselessly, and the sky had that grey, settled look of early December. There would be no more sun that day.

All the same, it will be good to have a look at our hiding place. I'll just take a peep in and imagine I see her lying there naked. There will be drops of water among the spider webs. I kept looking at those webs when I was holding her.

Ascending, he noticed that there were fresh footprints in the sand. The rain had not yet washed them out.

Odd, he thought, sudden alarm within him. Surely the others haven't been exploring here. . . . If they've discovered our hiding-place. . . .

He gnashed his teeth, his hands clenching.

His feet made no noise in the sand as he ascended. All about him the trees dripped. Plip, plep, went the rain-drops, some large, some tiny blebs.

Nearing the wild pines, he paused. Halted and crouched down.

Voices. Someone . . . two people. . . . In the hiding-place.

Moving like a snake on his stomach, he crawled along toward the pines, and, at length, he was near enough to be in no doubt.

He listened, his hands clenched.

Voices – and the soft rustle of clothes. And the voices were so clear and so recognisable.

2

WAITING for him on the veranda, watching the dismal rain, she began to be anxious, telling herself that he must have met with an accident. A snake might have bitten him, or he might have been attacked by wild pigs. Peccaries. She envisaged him, bleeding and calling weakly for help, up in the branches of a tree. Should she go and search for him?

Then she saw him coming. In pants, the rest of his clothes over his arm, his hair plastered to his head, he squelched his way across the compound toward the house. From upstairs she heard a chorus of laughter. The others were in the big room shared by Storm and Raphael. They were calling down, jeering at him. And, as usual he ignored them, not even glancing up at the windows.

'I was so anxious for you, Edward,' she said as he joined her on the veranda. He nodded, his face glum, and slung his wet clothes over the rail. 'When I saw the rain I knew it would be hopeless today, but – I still wondered why you took such a long time to come back.'

Still silent, he stood, his hands on the rail glaring out at the wet scene. She laughed and said: 'You seem so fierce. Shouldn't you go upstairs and change into dry things? Your pants are soaking.'

Then he turned abruptly and began to tell her what he had been doing, his voice low and savage, his whole frame taut. She was incredulous. She said: 'You must be mistaken. In the rain? They wouldn't – oh, not in the rain, Edward. It must have been two of Cranley's people. These slaves don't care about the weather –'

'I wasn't dreaming. It was Mother and your father. I heard them speaking. And they were making love. In our hiding-place. I felt like killing.'

'But why did they have to go there? He could have gone to her room at night. Don't let it upset you. I know how you feel about our hiding-place. We'll search for another deeper in the bush.'

'I'm going to be revenged on them for that.'

Something occurred to her. 'Edward, I've just thought . . . I

205

wonder if they haven't been going there before. It might have been Father himself who discovered the spot and cleared away those two pines. Remember we were a bit puzzled why a way should have been cleared so neatly into the spot?'

He grew rigid. 'I didn't think of that. You mean . . . then this isn't the first time. Even when Father was here they used to sneak off alone and go there! That makes it even worse.' His hands clenched. 'I feel like going to them now and telling them what I think of them. The traitors!'

'Please. Be calm, dear. Don't call them traitors. They're in love. For years they've been in love. From little things I've over-heard Mother saying to him I discovered that it's nothing new. Cranley married her knowing that she was in love with Father.'

'Then he was a weak, stupid fool! See me marrying a girl who was in love with another man! I'd kick her before I did! Stamp on her!'

'Control yourself, Edward. Why not go up and change?'

'Up there – with those chattering apes! I wish I had a room of my own. I . . . ' He broke off, and she saw a strange, half-mad glitter come into his eyes. He began to breathe quickly. 'Luise, let's go upstairs. Into *their* room. Mother's room where he goes into at night, the beast!'

'Edward, he's my father – and he's not a beast. You mustn't say that. You must be sympathetic. He still loves Mother, though you mightn't believe it. In a different way, but he loves her.'

'Let's go upstairs,' he said, ignoring her defence of her father. 'Into Mother's room.' He gulped and went on: 'We'll stay in there until they come. Let them come and find us in there.'

'Why?'

'Why? To be revenged on them, that's why.' He grinned – and she was reminded of him in his younger days. The cruel boy who used to pinch and hit her. 'I want to hear what Mother will say to me when she finds me with you in bed. I want to hear her tell me I ought to be ashamed of myself.' He chortled excitedly, and on his face she saw hate, warped malice. She felt a shrinking of fear. A shrinking and shrivelling, as though a cold rag had brushed her heart and it was her heart that was shrinking and shrivelling.

'I hate to see you in moods like this, Edward.'

206

'Why? Don't you know I'm vindictive? You've said so before. You've said I'm cruel. Well, I am. I can't stand people who are deceptive.'

She smiled. 'That's the one thing I've always noted about you. You've never indulged in deception. But you must be tolerant. We can't all be the same.'

'Are you going to come upstairs with me?'

'I couldn't. With the children up there. They'd hear us going into Cousin Faustina's room. And how could I let Faustina come home and find us in her room, Edward? I should expire with embarrassment.'

He nodded. 'I suppose you're right. I feel insane. I want to do something to hurt them. Hurt them badly.'

'I understand how you feel. It's the shock of finding them there.' She held his arm and said: 'For my sake, don't do anything rash, my darling. It would hurt me if you spoke harshly to Father. I love and respect him very deeply, Edward – and I understand him better than you do.'

He scowled. 'I suppose Mother does, too. I'm disappointed in her. I wish she weren't my mother – and this is the first time I've wished that.'

They stood listening to the rain. Dribbling down on the roof, dreary and menacing. Trickles of water kept running down from his hair on to his chest and stomach. . . . They could be tears, she thought, watching them.

'Build a factory for him. What a fool I was. I shall tear up the plan. Tomorrow I'm going to rip it to pieces.' He glared at her. 'Marry you and live with you at Good Heart! Live in the same house with that simpering snake! I'll kill myself before I do that! Kill myself.'

Dismal December rain. . . . The tears were on her own cheeks now.

'What are you crying for? You're a fool! You're all fools. I – oh, I didn't mean that. I . . . ' He held her and began to kiss her cheek. He stammered. Whimpered. 'Not you, not you! I'd do anything for you, Luise. I'd – Id . . . ' He turned away muttering to himself.

'Edward.'

'What's it?'

'Come upstairs – to my room.'

207

'No.'

'We'll lock the door.'

'I can't. I'd – I'd hurt you.'

'Hurt me?'

'Yes. I'd hurt anything now. I just want to hurt somebody. Anybody.'

She looked at him.

'Even you. And – and I'd want to kill myself if I hurt you.' He turned and gripped her arms, shook her. Shook his head, his hair in a wild, wet dance, 'Oh, my love! My love! Luise!'

The water from his hair mingled with the tears on her cheeks. She was attacked by a sense of unreality. A dizzy vacancy.

'I'll go up with you. Let's go. I'll kill anybody who tries to stop us. Strangle them. Come, let's go.'

Her room was in the north-western section of the house, above the pantry. They found Graeme and Mathilde trapping rain-flies at a window.

'What are you two doing in here? Get out!'

'Edward! Don't speak to them like that!'

'Get out!'

'We were only catching rain-flies, Edward.'

'Get out! Or I'll kick you!'

Graeme and Mathilde, frightened, ran out of the room. Edward slammed the door after them with a bang that thundered throughout the house. He turned the key in the lock, muttering. His head shook.

Luise stood beside the big mahogany wardrobe and stared at him, half-fearfully, half-indulgently. Beyond the locked door they could hear the animated voices of the others. There was no laughter.

'I feel mad, Luise. Mad. I feel . . . I don't know what I feel. I wish I weren't in this house. Everything seems dead now. Mother. My plans. Me, myself.' He sat down on a chair and held his head in his hands.

'Take off those wet pants of yours.'

'No. I . . . Don't let's . . . I can't make love to you. I'd hurt you.'

'That's silly.' She had already begun to undress. 'Calm yourself, darling. You're so wild and impetuous. You frighten me sometimes.'

208

'I can't stand monkeys – and hypocrites. All those fools in there! Jabbering and laughing. They have minds like mud.'

He sat shaking his head. Running his fingers through his hair. And, all her clothes off, she came and stood by him, and he gave a start and looked at her, then turned away his face, growling: 'You shouldn't have undressed. I don't know why you bother with me. I'm a lost soul. Like your father. We're both lost souls – only he doesn't know he is.'

She held his head and pressed it against her stomach and told him to be calm. 'Let me comfort you. There's nothing I want to do more, Edward.'

He grunted and gave her a hard, screwing pinch on her thigh. She gasped and withdrew, and he laughed: 'I told you I'd hurt you, didn't I?' Then abruptly his eyes grew watery. He stood up and held her, kissed her in an agitated, whimpering hysteria. 'Not you, Luise. I never want to hurt you. Let me go. Something bad will happen if I don't go now.'

'You only imagine that. Come and lie down with me. You'll calm down.'

'That's all you've ever wanted me to do. Lie down with you. Kiss you. Fondle you. Rape you. Ever since I knew myself. You're obsessed. Mad. You're mad like me. Like your father – and Mother. Out there making love in the rain. We're a mad family.'

She laughed. 'Very well. We're all mad. Come and make love to me – in the bed. Not in the rain.'

He laughed. 'Not in the rain. In the bed.' He looked around the room. 'I've slept in here. Storm and I used to sleep in here.' He winced. 'Up to a few months ago we slept in here together in the bed there. And I remember one night lying awake and thinking of the night when I'd sleep with you in a bed – when we were married. But it wasn't this bed.' He let his eyes rest on her, and she saw him bite his lower lip, saw his eyes get watery. 'Nothing ever happens how we dream it. Nothing. People disappoint us, and – and –'

'Have I disappointed you?'

He shook his head. He seemed unable to speak. He kept swallowing.

The rain. Not heavy, but steady, dismal. From a sky of settled grey.

'Not you,' he murmured. Went on murmuring it. He stared at her, and then put out his hands and held her head – very gently – and began to smile. Rubbed his hands along her temples. Let his fingers slip through her hair. 'I feel as if I'm turning to rain from the love in me for you. Melting away.'

'I feel like that, too. Take me to the bed. Lift me.'

'A big thing like you! You're twenty-seven. I'm eighteen next March. I can do it, though. Who says I can't! Ten of you I can lift!'

He lifted her and took her to the bed. 'I could throw you up you're so light. I feel better, Luise. I'm going to feel bad again, but now I feel good. I feel big. Not like a few days ago. I was a fool. I disappointed you. Remember? I was terribly ashamed of myself. I felt like a stupid boy. But not now. I'm going to pinch you and kiss you and hit you. I sound as if I'm mad, don't I? Tell me.'

'Yes. But I don't mind. Do anything you like with me.'

He took off his wet pants, rolled them up into a ball and hurled the dripping mass through the window. They were both sprinkled. He laughed, and she laughed, and then they lay still and listened to the rain. And the voices of the others two rooms away. And to the lisp of their eye-lashes against the pillows. Each knew that the moment was being etched irrevocably on their minds. The gurgle of water in the compound seemed to come from years ago. . . . All the years of waiting. . . . I feel calm now. Not so mad. . . . People gossiping. . . . 'Edward.' He grunted 'Calm now?' He grunted assent, then raised his head and said: 'Calm enough to kiss you and hurt you.'

'Do it.'

As though it were an agreed upon signal, they both became breathing, anguished masses, the day and its sounds shut off from their awareness.

After many years – more than twenty-seven, she was sure – she began to hear the rain again. It emerged out of the mist of blue whorls and the singing echoes that sagged criss-cross through the vast space being gradually emptied of feeling. Drip-dribble on the roof, went the rain, and she wondered why she had thought it dismal only an hour ago. Less than an hour ago. . . .

He was asking her something in a murmur.

She smiled and moved her head in a nod. 'Yes, Edward.'

'Very much?'

She shook her head, still smiling.

'What are you smiling for?' he whispered. Not aggressively.

'At your consideration of me. It's lovely.'

'You're lovely.'

'Everything is.' She touched his cheek, hearing the lovely rain.

And the gurgle of water in the compound.

'This time . . .'

'Yes?' she asked.

'No, I mustn't say it. It's silly.'

'I know. This time you didn't disappoint me.' She touched his chest.

'You liked it?'

She nodded. And he heard her breathing.

'I'm glad. I didn't dream it this way, but I'm glad. I'm going to live to see that you don't suffer – that – that you have a lot of things you like.'

She said nothing, listening to him.

'I feel sleepy. You?'

She nodded.

'Let's sleep.'

They were going into a doze when the knock came on the door.

'Luise!'

They lay rigid, silent.

Again the knock.

'Luise!'

'Yes, Cousin Faustina!'

3

'Is Edward in there with you?'

'Yes, Faustina.'

Silence.

'Could you come into my room and see me, Luise?'

'Very well, Faustina.'

Silence.

'Edward!'

'What's it, Mother?'

'I think – please go and see Cousin Hubertus in his room

Edward did not reply. He whispered to Luise: 'Let's sleep

'My darling.' She kissed his cheek. 'Yes, let's sleep.'

Huddled close, listening to the rain, they slept.

Twilight was deep when they awoke. She woke first, an
thought: Nothing could ever upset me again. . . . The rain ha
thinned off. It made just a whispering on the roof. She listenc
but heard no sound of voices in the house. Only the clatt
of pots in the kitchen. . . . The twilight was a deep sepia. Th
window-panes were blurred with moisture. Under the sing
blanket it was warm, but she could tell that the room arour
them was chilly with rain-damp. Demerary rain-damp. Humi
Damp yet warmish. Damp with earth and tree-smells. S:
could smell the dankness of the jungle. . . . All the gossip, :
the reproach, could not trouble me now. . . . She stroked h
cheek, and heard the lisp of his eyelashes against the pillo
He stirred and uttered a low growl. . . . She whispered if
was happy, and he growled yes. . . .

'They must be waiting to talk to us.'

He sniggered. 'Let them wait.'

She giggled. 'Yes, let them wait.'

Silence.

I can lie like this until tomorrow morning, he thought. Th
know well not to disturb us. I'd kill anybody who comes
here. It must be nearly dinner-time but I don't want to eat
only want . . . He trembled and began to fondle her, and wh
their murmuring and the whole new wild whimpering eart
quake had quietened to a cool breathing peace the brief tv
light had deepened into night. Through the rain-whispers th
heard the thump of slave drums. And the tinkle of trickli
water. And through the damp came the smell of food. .
'Are you hungry?' . . . 'A little,' he said.

Dinner was at an end when they went down. They sat alc
at the table, and the slaves gave them odd, knowing looks
they served them.

They heard the murmuring of Raphael and Storm and Cl:
on the back veranda. A murmuring and a muffled sniggeri

Of Hubertus and Faustina they had seen nothing, but on going into the room he shared with Graeme and Mathilde, Edward had seen light under the door of his mother's room, and in dressing he had heard her moving about; her room was the adjoining one.

'I'm not ashamed. Are you?'

She shook her head. 'Not in the slightest.' She touched his knee.

He touched her cheek. 'Tomorrow I'm going to sketch you.'

She nodded.

Toward the end of the meal, he said: 'Are you going into Mother's room to talk to her?'

'Yes. And you must go to Father.'

He growled.

'You will – for my sake.'

He nodded.

And so after dinner they separated, each knocking at a different door.

Hubertus told him to come in. He rose, a book in hand, from the chair near a small table on which stood the lamp. He was smiling very amiably.

'Sit down, Edward my boy. And be at ease. You look as though you would strike me down with a sabre if there were a sabre available.'

Faustina did not say come in. She opened the door to Luise and murmured: 'My dear child. I thought you would never come. You aren't angry with me, are you?' She embraced her briefly and, an arm about her waist, walked with her toward the bed where they sat.

'What's it you want to talk to me about, Cousin Hubertus?'

Hubertus settled himself again in the chair by the table. His face stolid, he said: 'About yourself chiefly, my boy – and about Luise. And even about myself. I can never escape talking about myself, Edward. I'm a very self-centred man. Selfish might be a better word.' He spoke in Dutch now, though he had greeted Edward in English. 'Yes, no one is more conscious than I what a selfish person I am.'

Edward said nothing. Sat uneasily on the edge of the bed, and kept scowling at the floor.

'I've noticed you for years, my boy – when you might have imagined I was unaware of your existence. You have always been a strange, precocious youngster . . .'

'The children told me,' said Faustina. 'Clara and Storm. I thought he might have been sketching you, then – well, it seemed when I passed your door that you were too quiet, and I felt that – that you were making love. I know you won't mind me being frank, Luise dear.'

'No. I want you to be frank.'

'It was a little indiscreet, my child – with the other children in the house. But I suppose you couldn't help it. You have always been so fond of him.' Her face was sad and reflective as she spoke. . . . She's still beautiful, thought Luise. Hardly a line on her face. Age has only made her plump. . . . A tiny greyish speck – a bit of dry leaf – was sticking to her throat.

'. . . very different from your brothers. And you have a splendid talent for sketching. Did you know that your Great-grandfather Ignatius was a painter? Grandma Hendrickje's husband. But we mustn't speak of him. It pains me to remember the tales of old, Edward. We have much behind us to be ashamed of. That is part of my perpetual agony. I want to be proud of our family, and yet I want to forget – to live down the infamies of the past.'

Edward found that he could not meet the eyes above the beard. . . . I'd never thought he could outstare me. He's got more strength in him than he makes people think. I feel like a leaf near him. . . .

'. . . I, too, am fond of him, Luise. Very fond of him, despite his strangeness; his alarming precocity. Cranley and I have discussed him often. We recognise that he has talent, and we have made plans for his future.'

Luise felt the breath in her quickening. 'Plans for his future.'

'Yes. We haven't told him, but we are arranging for him to go to Amsterdam to study land-surveying – and building. The colony is developing rapidly, Luise, and we shall need land-surveyors and builders. And we feel Edward would do well in

214

these pursuits. He won't make a good planter.'

'I – I – yes, perhaps you're right.'

'Cranley and I planned to send him abroad next June. . . . '

' . . . The old blood, Edward. Yes, I'm proud of it – and yet I gnash my teeth at the filthy deeds of my mother. She was a Spanish-Indian half-breed from the Orinoco. She was brought to the Essequibo plantation as a slave, and my father debauched her in the coffee fields and got her with child. Me, Edward. I was the child that resulted from that filthy union. She was a depraved woman. She drove my father to suicide on the Canje plantation. Between herself and Grandma Hendrickje.' His face was still stolid, but Edward saw his eyes . . . looked at them and glanced away, ill-at-ease. . . . I don't know whether to hate him or to admire him. . . .

'See.' He stirred and laughed softly, stretched out and tapped Edward lightly on the knee. 'See, my boy. It is an obsession with me. I cannot prevent myself harking back – though it rips me apart within. But never mind! It's about you I want to talk. You're in love with my Luise, I hear. I didn't suspect that. I knew she was very much attached to you. Since you were a mere lump of a child she has been attached to you. Incredible. I've never been able to fathom it, but there it is. It is the truth, and we must face it. And a few days ago, on our way here, she told me you love her and want to marry her in a year or two. . . .'

' . . . I know you're a sensible girl, Luise. You wouldn't want to spoil his career. You've been so good to him – encouraging him to sketch and even letting him sketch you. You will talk to him, I'm sure, and let him see how unwise it would be for him to marry you at so young an age. Your father says he has asked you to marry him –'

'Yes, he loves me. He's asked me to marry him, and I'm going to. I'm going to, Faustina. You mustn't try to stop us. If you sent him away from me I'd – I'd drown myself.'

'But, my dear, he's a boy. A boy, Luise. Eighteen in March. And you were twenty-seven in October. There are nearly ten years between you –'

'I don't care if there were twenty, Faustina. So long as he

215

loves me I'm going to marry him.' She pressed her hands to her face, shaking.

'You mustn't think I don't sympathise with you my dear. I do. I'm even thinking of your own happiness, Luise. Edward is so young. I don't think he's capable of judging his own feelings. He may imagine he is in love with you now, but in five or six years, less, he may have matured and come to a realisation that he was merely infatuated – then what? You would be both unhappy.'

'Perhaps – but we should still have had five or six years of happiness. It would have been worth the experiment. Nothing – nothing you say will change my mind, Faustina. I've waited – he is too much an essential part of my being for me to consider giving him up. . . . '

'I agreed – reluctantly. For I do not believe in in-breeding, my boy. We've had too much of it in the family. It produces bad types, I'm convinced of that. I told her you would be welcome to come and live at Good Heart. And you could build for me the factory you spoke of. You're frowning. Why? Have you changed your mind about the project?'

Edward kept squeezing his knuckles together, the scowl on his face having intensified. . . . If only I could tell him what I think of him. But I can't. Those eyes of his are too much for me. . . . And Luise asked me not to be harsh toward him. I'd do anything she asks. . . . No, I must restrain myself with this hypocrite. . . .

'You're a puzzling young man,' chuckled Hubertus. He was silent a moment, looking reflective. He took up the book – it was Spinoza's *Ethics*, and had been rescued from the Canje house in 1764 and sent to Good Heart with one or two other items. He grunted. 'This book has your grandfather's name written in it. Adrian van Groenwegel. I've often wondered how he came to acquire it.' He was silent again, grunting softly to himself. Then he said: 'We may soon be at war, Edward. I can feel it coming. The English are annoyed with us because we have been helping to smuggle supplies to the forces of General Washington. St Eustatius is a nest of smuggling intrigue; I've heard it on good authority. The English ships are waiting for an opportunity to pounce. Any day English privateers may swoop

216

upon us and plunder our plantations, as they did in times past. Everyone in the colony is concerned, anxious.' He heaved a soft sigh. 'I was speaking to your mother, and she told me she and your step-father had plans for you. When this trouble has died down they would like to send you to Amsterdam to study land-surveying and building – '

'They've never told me that!'

'Neither did they tell me, my boy. I learnt of it only a day or two ago. Your mother told me. Otherwise – I mean, had I known of it before I would not have spoken to Luise as I did on the yacht. Your career ought to come before – it would be wiser to fulfil your talent before thinking of marriage. You're so young. There is no need for you to rush into marriage. Wouldn't you like to go to Amsterdam, Edward my boy?'

'Yes. I would – but Luise will have to come with me – as my wife.'

Hubertus smiled. Stretched out and tapped Edward's knee. 'I would have spoken like that, too – at your age. I know the feeling, my boy. That wild, desperate urge to consummate the body's passions with the beloved, and the unreasoning despair that goes along with it at the thought of separation. At sixteen I fell in love with a Swiss girl on the Essequibo. Yes, at sixteen – even younger than you are now. And, oddly enough, she, too, had a talent for drawing and painting – as I had. When her parents took her lower down the river to their new plantation I fancied that the universe had collapsed around me. For days I could not eat. . . . Ah, there again! Reminiscing. Always reminiscing. You should scold me when you catch me doing it, young man. . . . '

' . . . when I decide to give him up it will mean I've decided to give up life.'

'And do you think I want to give him up, Luise? You must be a mother to understand. I love him as much as you do, and I want him near to me. I should hate you if you took him from me at this age – no. No, I shouldn't have said that. Forgive me. I – I could never hate you.' The tears were with her now. . . . I should comfort her, but I can't. She should not have challenged me. . . . 'It's just that I feel I have the first right on him, Luise. I brought him into the world – and under such desperate

217

circumstances. On that ship in the Berbice – '

'But you have so much, Cousin Faustina. I have nothing. Nothing but him. You have your children and Cranley – and and . . . ' She broke off, the blood coming to her face.

'Yes? And? . . . You mean your father,' she murmured. She grew very quiet, staring at the misted window panes. Then she sighed and said: 'Yes, your father and I have been in love for years. I admit it. We have both been living a double life.' She rose and paced slowly to the window. Stood there with her hands clasped tight, looking out. . . .

' . . . I live too much in the past, Edward. However, to come back to what we were discussing. You wouldn't like to go to Amsterdam without Luise, you say. She couldn't go with you, my boy, so that means you turn down the suggestion. Is that correct?'

'Yes, that's correct, Cousin Hubertus.'

Hubertus stared at him, and Edward's gaze fell, though the boy kept clasping and unclasping his hands defiantly, the scowl still on his face.

'Very well,' said Hubertus, at length. 'I shall not try to force you. Your mother asked me to talk to you, but I can see you have a will of your own. I admire will. Because I have a will of my own, my boy, and I can recall the day when I, too, turned down a proposal to go to Amsterdam. Odd how these events repeat themselves. I had a talent for sketching, and they wanted to send me to Amsterdam to study land-surveying, but I refused. Not for the love of a girl, though, but because I preferred planting, and wasn't sufficiently interested in land-surveying or sketching. I respect the feelings of other people, Edward. It is in this way I show my loyalty to humankind. Not in the petty, conventional ways. I believe this is the way God intended us to follow – the way of instinctive decency rather than the way of man-made morality and man-made convention. Ah! There again. I'm letting myself stray from the point under discussion.' He rose. 'Come with me, my boy. We'll go into your mother's room and have a word with her. . . . '

' . . . I didn't intend to hurt you, Cousin Faustina. I'm sorry if – '

'No, no, Luise! Don't be sorry. I know you didn't intend to hurt me. You've simply said what is true.' She turned and looked at Luise. 'By the way, does – do you know whether Edward suspects that your father and I have – have been friendly – in more than –'

'It was Edward who told me. He told me years ago. He once saw you and Father – at the Beckleses. You're not – you won't tell him I told you. I don't mean to betray his confidence, but – but you asked me –'

'Have no fear, my dear. I won't mention a word to him.' She was silent, thoughtful – then she said: 'Yes, I remember. Under a star-apple tree I think it was – near the water-tanks. Luise, has he – have you heard any of the children referring to anything else?'

'Anything else like what?'

Faustina hesitated, then murmured: 'Graeme.'

'Graeme?' Luise stared at her. . . . What can she be getting at?

Faustina came over and held her arm, 'As I've gone so far, I may as well tell you – and I know you'll keep it strictly to yourself. Graeme is your father's child, Luise. Not Cranley's.'

Luise could say nothing. A trembling awoke within her.

'I can trust you to say nothing to anyone, Luise?'

'Yes.' She gulped and asked: 'Does Mother know?'

'Yes – from the outset. But Cranley – it's still a mystery, Luise. I have never been able to get out of him whether he knows or not. I'm inclined to think he knows, though.'

There was a knock on the door, and they both started.

'Who is that?'

The door opened and Hubertus and Edward came in. Hubertus was holding the upper part of Edward's arm in an affectionate manner, and he was smiling. 'Your son, my dear – I've brought him. He refuses to be persuaded. He will not go to Amsterdam without Luise.'

Edward looked very uncomfortable, shifting his feet about and glaring into a corner. . . . I can kill them all, he thought. kill them. Why must I have to go through all this? . . . He was afraid to look at his mother.

'He has. Then I think he's foolish.'

Hubertus shook his head. 'I disagree with you, my dear. Let

him make his own destiny. He is an individual in his own right.'

'He's a boy, Hubertus. A boy.'

'Only in years. He has the will of a man.'

'I shall never see it that way. You ought not to encourage him to feel he is a man.' She spoke with a bitterness that Luise felt was directed at her. . . . It's I who made him feel a man; not Father.

'I cannot encourage him to feel what he is already, my dear,' said Hubertus, unruffled. Both Luise and Edward looked at him, and Edward thought: After tonight I shall respect him more. He's not such a hypocrite as I'd thought him. And he can stand up to Mother. Mother won't be able to influence him now that he has made up his mind about Luise and me.

'Hubertus, do you mean – will you sanction his marrying Luise?'

'I certainly shall, Faustina. They will live at Good Heart with me, and Edward will build me a new factory. Isn't that so, my boy?'

Edward nodded, his gaze lowered.

'We shall announce the betrothal in February, and they can be married in the following month when he is eighteen.' Hubertus moved over to Luise and gave her a hug. 'I think you will be happy, my dear girl, but can I ask you one thing? And you, Edward? Will you promise not to be as intimate as you were this afternoon until you are married?'

'Willingly,' said Luise. 'We can wait until March.'

Edward nodded.

'I ask this for your mother's sake, Luise. She does not approve of physical intimacy out of wedlock. We must think of her feelings.'

' . . . of Mother's feelings.'

'I'd meant to come to your room again tonight,' he said, and she whispered back: 'I'd have asked you to. I wanted you to come.'

It was raining steadily and rather heavily, and the other children were in the living-room. Pressed close together against the rail of the back veranda, they held each other and listened to the rain. The spray came in on them but they took no notice.

220

'I could have asked him why he doesn't think of Mother's feelings.'

'He's still in Mother's room. He'll probably stay with her all night.'

They listened to the rain.

'But it doesn't matter, Edward. We can wait until March.'

'I wanted to sketch you tomorrow – without your clothes.'

'You could, darling. Nothing need – we could be restrained.'

'No.'

'No, we couldn't. You're right. We'll talk – and go for walks. Long walks in the rain. Would you like that?'

He nodded.

The rain thinned off abruptly. They heard water trickling and gurgling. Dripping from the eaves. The damp air moved around them in swathes.

'It will soon be March. March will soon come, Edward.'

'Yes.'

They heard the rain coming again. Swishing in the trees, then spattering down spitefully in the compound and on the roof.

'I've changed my mind about him,' he said. 'He's not a bad fellow.'

'No, I think you were right. He *is* a hypocrite, Edward. And he's selfish. After tonight I shall think much less of him.'

'He's selfish, but he's not a hypocrite. He really believes in what he says. He wants to be honest – but things worry him. I can't explain it better than that. But things worry him. He's harrowed.'

After a silence: 'I'm a little sorry for him, Luise. Not for Mother. For him.'

4

IN many ways, it was a troubled Christmas. Cranley arrived two days before Christmas Day, and he told them that war was inevitable. His uncle and cousin had been sent to Barbados on a mission by the Admiralty, and were already on their way home aboard a frigate of the Fleet.

Added to the fears of war there were the smaller, personal tensions. Rosalind disapproved as much as Faustina of the projected marriage in March. And Luise's manner toward her father had grown colder; the new knowledge that he was Graeme's father had affected her deeply; no matter how she tried she could not prevent herself from seeing him as a hoax – a trickster who had been living a sham these past years. For Cranley a new sympathy and tenderness came alive in her. Toward Faustina her manner had grown cooler, but this was chiefly because Faustina herself had put up a barrier of vague resentment. And between Faustina and Hubertus, Luise noticed, relations seemed not as easy as of before; Faustina's gaiety was forced in his presence, and Hubertus, always jovial and relaxed when she was near, now seemed to hold himself in check, either broodingly silent or going off into a heavy philosophical dissertation.

Edward was openly hostile toward his mother, and whenever she spoke to him would scowl and growl at her, and fall into a sulk. He resented her not approving of Luise as a wife for him – and he could not forgive her for having made love to Hubertus in what he had looked upon as a sacred spot; in his way of seeing it, it was she who must have enticed Hubertus there in the rain; he sensed that his attitude was irrational but the resentment remained just the same. He sympathised with Hubertus; he saw Hubertus as a plagued man. Rosalind against him, Luise against him – and Faustina encouraging him to keep up an illicit relationship. . . . 'No one can fool me,' he had said once to Luise. 'It's she who must have encouraged him all these years. Women always entice and encourage men. Look at you. Haven't you been enticing and encouraging me since I was nine years old! . . . ' And when Luise had looked hurt: 'Stop biting your lip. With you it's different. You're a special creature. I like you to entice and encourage me. . . . '

The betrothal was announced early in February – and it came as a surprise to the whole river, for the secret had been well kept. Not even Clara and the other children at Rylands had been told. The banquet held at the Rylands home on the first Sunday in February was restricted to the family and it was a rather strained affair. Only Wilfred was at ease. Wilfred stopped Luise in the living-room and embraced her. 'My dear child, I'm so pleased. I b-b-believe you will be very happy with that boy. He's – he's an extraordinary young fellow. I've always thought so.' He glanced round swiftly, furtively. 'I know there has been a lot of gossip about you two, but never mind! P-p-people always gossip, Luise. Brush them off! Go your own way and make your own life. P-p-people mean no harm when they gossip. They like to talk – that's all there is to it.' He suddenly broke into low guffaws. 'They used to laugh at me because of my records. Oh, yes! Laughed me to scorn. But did I n-n-notice them! No! Snapped my fingers at them, and went my way. And today I am a happy man. My records are a joy, Luise. One day I'll show them to you. With the exception of one or two years, my figures are accurate, and the day will yet be when those who laughed will come to me. Yes, they will come to me and p-p-pester me to let them consult my records. Wait and you'll see! You take my word for it.' Another furtive glance around. 'You're going to live at Good Heart, I hear. Excellent! I'm glad Hubert has agreed to that, my girl. That boy has talent. He will get somewhere in the world, I'm convinced of it. Take good care of him, my girl. And give him sons. Four, five, six sons!' Red in the face, he broke into spluttering laughter, squeezed her arm briefly and hurried on into the dining-room to join the others already gathered in there.

Luise, whose spirits had been rather low because of the cool attitude of Faustina and her own mother, felt greatly cheered, and a warmth of gratitude for her uncle's self-conscious congratulation flooded her and lasted throughout the function. As usual, she sat between Cranley and Wilfred; it had become an almost understood thing at meal-times that the three of them should sit close together. Toward her Cranley was his old cordial suave, quietly affectionate self; he had congratulated her on her arrival, but not in the warm, gushing, spontaneous manner of Wilfred; she had gained the impression that he had been doing his duty. Whether he approved or disapproved of the match she probably would never learn.

Edward, on the opposite side of the table, looked uncomfortable, and wore his most thundery scowl. He looked neither to right nor to left, and when anyone congratulated him merely growled acknowledgement. Not once throughout the whole meal did Luise notice him glance at her, and to herself she thought: He must be in agony, poor boy.

And Edward, behind his scowl, thought: More and more

223

people seem to me like pebbles. To be kicked along the ground. So few of them are worth picking up and treasuring. I detest ceremonies. I wish I never had to be present at another gathering in all my life to come. . . . And behind this mood there was the memory of what had occurred that morning before the others from Signal and Good Heart had arrived. . . . Meeting Clara on the front veranda, he had stopped and said: 'You've heard, I suppose?'

Quietly she had replied: 'Yes. Mother told us last night. My congratulations, Edward.'

'I've practically had to beg you for them.'

She blushed, and her eyes grew shifty. 'I didn't mean – I hadn't a chance before. The others laugh so much at everything about you . . . oh, you know what I mean, Edward.'

He sniffed. 'You laugh at me, too, so what are you pretending?'

'I don't. You know I don't. I – ' She turned away her face, and he saw to his amazement that she was going to cry. . . . The tear ran down.

'What is the matter with you now?'

She made a choking sound, stammered: 'Nothing. Nothing at all. I – you shouldn't say that. I never laugh at you.' She gulped and smiled, gave him a quick glance and said: 'I wish you a lot of happiness, Edward. I mean it. Don't mind if I seem silly. I mean it.' On the last three words her voice grew husky, and she hurried off inside.

His suspicion of years had now been confirmed. She loved him in more than a sisterly way. . . . But why, he kept asking himself throughout the meal, why should she? What's there in me for her to like? Raphael is more handsome than I. And Storm resembles me. . . . Could it be because I have never been close to the rest of them? It might be that. I have always held aloof from them. They must see me as a kind of stranger. . . . It disturbed him, because he was fond of Clara, and hated to think of her being unhappy on his account. She had more in her than Storm and Raphael put together. At one time he could even remember being anxious over her. In the secrecy of his fancies he had fought battles with various men who had married her – fought them and killed them because they had been unkind to her. . . . I'd be like a tiger to any man who ill-treated

her, he assured himself, the scowl on his face intensifying. . . .
He was aware of her frequent glances from across the table, but
he would not look at her. . . . If I did I'd show how I felt about
her. I hate showing people my deep feelings. What I feel deep
in me I hold to be sacred and therefore secret. . . .

The marriage had been fixed for the last Sunday in March, but
it did not come off on that day. For in the meantime the war
came.

On the third of the same month, February, unknown to the
colonists of Essequibo and Demerary, Admiral Rodney had
appeared off St Eustatius and forced that island to surrender.
As with all the Dutch colonies in this region, the defences of St
Eustatius were hopelessly weak, and the governor capitulated
without a struggle. Rodney immediately proceeded to confis-
cate the property of all the inhabitants, and ordered the banish-
ment of every male colonist. The two hundred and fifty ships
in harbour were seized, and the goods confiscated, made up into
bales and sold at auction to British traders from Barbados and
Antigua. The Jews on the island sent in a petition to the
Admiral, but Rodney, determined to wipe out all smuggling
activities – for St Eustatius had been doing an undercover
trade with the rebel forces under General Washington – was
firm, and the plan went through.

Toward the end of the month – on the twenty-first – the
privateers swooped upon Demerary, seized fifteen vessels that
happened to be in the lower part of the river, and sent an
ultimatum to Commandeur Schuylenburg.

'We have the pleasure to acquaint you,' said their ultimatum
'that St Eustatius is now under the English flag and that there
are five ships gone against Surinam.'

They had been commissioned, said the privateers, by Admiral
Rodney, and if the river did not surrender within two hours it
would be taken by force. Schuylenburg and the Council decided
that nothing could be done to defend the colony, and orders
were given to strike the flag and surrender. News was sent to
Essequibo on the twenty-fourth, and it was decided that Fort
Zeelandia also could not put up a defence, therefore Essequibo
must surrender. Fort St Andries in Berbice was captured about
a week later – on the sixth of March.

The privateers had no sooner departed from Demerary with their spoils when – on the twenty-seventh of February – two naval vessels – H.M.S. *Surprize* and H.M.S. *Barbuda* – arrived. Their Captains presented letters to the Commandeur stating that Rodney had directed them to come to this coast and 'attack, seize and destroy all ships and vessels belonging to the States General or their subjects, and finding at our arrival off here that the privateers from your defenceless situation have taken most of the ships out of the two rivers Demerary and Essequibo, we are to request that no more are given up to them but that the remainder be put in our possession. . . . We shall give you the same terms as those granted to St Eustatius.'

There was also a letter from the Governor of Barbados to Schuylenburg; it was of a more personal nature, and stated that 'having received information from Mr Clarke, who lately arrived from Demerary, that, upon the supposition that hostilities were likely to commence between Great Britain and the States General of the United Provinces, Your Excellency was apprehensive of privateers. . . . To avoid such consequences we understand you are willing to surrender to one of His Majesty's ships of war. . . . Lieutenant Forrest of 90th Regiment therefore sent with flag of truce to afford you an opportunity of surrendering to the King of Great Britain. Captain Pender of H.M.S. *Barbuda* will be able to accomplish this object when a proper force shall be sent to keep possession for the King my Master.

> 'I have the honour to be
> 'James Cunningham'

'That is the fate we must endure,' said Gert Lieker to Hubertus, 'because of our weakness. A contemptible little island like Barbados can send us terms of surrender, and we accept without a protest.'

Hubertus smoked imperturbably, watching the fruit-trees. It was a fine, not too hot day, and the sun glittered on the leaves.

'What is troubling me,' said Luise, who was very upset, 'is this reference to St Eustatius. They've said something about giving us the same terms as were granted to St Eustatius. But what were the terms they granted to St Eustatius, Mynheer?'

'That is what no one knows, my girl. That is what makes it

even more shameful. We have surrendered on terms of which we are unaware. When the English ships arrived none of us here had heard that war had been declared. It was the English who brought us the news that St Eustatius had been captured. Those privateers – they brought the first word, but they gave no details.'

Later that day, Wilfred arrived at Good Heart, after a trip down-river to garner information on the situation. He said: 'Essequibo has capitulated. That's the latest. And the C-C-Council has been told that two delegates must be sent to St Eustatius on the *Barbuda* to arrange the terms of surrender with Admiral Rodney. I understand they've p-p-picked on Joseph Bourda and John Haslin. Don't know much about Haslin, but Bourda is a sound fellow. He ought to be able to put our case fittingly and obtain the best terms.'

Gert Lieker, who was still there, shook his head gloomily. 'Bourda won't do much against Rodney. These English naval officers are a ruthless pack of curs. They'll strip us bare of everything we've worked so hard to build up, you wait and see.' He added bitterly: 'You English will probably be let off lightly, but it's we Dutch who are going to suffer heavily.'

There was an awkward silence. Awkward for Luise and Rosalind and Wilfred. Hubertus seemed, as before, unruffled. Eventually, Wilfred shifted his feet about and said: 'I suppose you have a right to feel as you do, Gert, and I – I – well, what I feel is that we must form no hasty c-c-conclusions about anything until Bourda and Haslin return from St Eustatius. What I do d-d-deplore most heartily is the way some of the English fellows are c-c-crowing over the surrender! Disgusting! Extremely bad taste – and most embarrassing. After all, we've always got on very amicably with you Dutch fellows, and it's just sheer misfortune that this c-c-catastrophe should have come upon the colony. I – I – yes, it's really most disgusting.'

'Jim Harker is one who has been crowing,' growled Gert.

Hubertus removed his pipe from his mouth, and said: 'I think you summed up the situation very precisely this morning, Gert. You said that weakness is the cause of the plight we are in. I agree. And I feel that we have no right to reprove the victorious when they crow.' He smiled at Wilfred, holding up a solemn forefinger. 'They have every right to crow, Wilfred. It

227

is good that they should crow, for it will bring home to us the lesson that the weak must suffer. Our instincts should tell us that is the law of Nature. When we are slack, neglectful of our defences, passive in our policy toward our neighbours – take the raids we suffered from Spanish Guyana some years ago as example – then we must suffer defeat. It is inevitable.'

Wilfred tittered. 'Thus spake Confucius. Eh? Hee, hee! I say, don't look so utterly d-d-despairing, Gert old fellow! Hope for the best. Hope for the best and b-b-bury your valuables where they can't be found. There's a good m-m-motto for you. Eh? A lot of your ancestors followed it, and it profited them, too. Yes, by George! I hear it's amazing the number of jars with jewellery people keep digging up in Essequibo and Berbice. Jewellery and coins. In the old days, at the first alarm, the planters took their valuables aback and buried them. Good policy! Sound!' He turned to Luise. 'And you, Luise! That wedding will have to be p-p-postponed, I take it. But never mind! Things will soon settle down again. Oh, they'll settle down, you take my word for it! And you're still as young and fresh as ever. Seem to get younger and more beautiful every day. A fact!' He was red in the face. 'Oh, yes, I can well understand that boy losing his head over you. Eh? Hee, hee!'

Luise, too, was blushing.

Rosalind smiled brittlely.

Gert Leiker grunted uncertainly, growling: 'I wish I could be as cheerful as that, Wilfred. Ruin. Ruin is all I can see ahead, and I can't be cheerful with such a prospect in view.'

At Rylands, Edward was as gloomy as Gert Lieker. In his imagination the situation was dismal and entirely without hope. The marriage would never take place, and his dream of building a factory for Hubertus would go unrealised. The English would seize all the plantations, and everyone with a Dutch name would be treated with scorn. It was over three weeks he had not seen Luise, for in the state of emergency that existed it was considered wise that families should remain at home. Banquets and Sunday gatherings had been mutually called off. At any hour of the day or night some alarm might come and it might be necessary to flee into the bush.

Edward went for lonely walks, and sometimes sat on the

back veranda and sketched or made plans for bridges, fac-tories and residences which he tore up the moment he had com-pleted. On one or two occasions, despite his policy of aloofness, he became involved in arguments with his brothers who persistently threw out taunting remarks at him. He would ignore them until some direct mention of Luise was made when, in a fury, he would snarl at them and express his opinions of their mentalities.

Clara, he noticed, was generally silent and unsmiling. For the past few weeks he had hardly heard her laugh, and more and more she seemed to be withdrawing from the company of Storm and Raphael. If she was not in her room – which was the small north-eastern one adjoining the store-room where Cranley kept his muskets and ammunition – she had gone off somewhere on the plantation with Graeme and Mathilde. She avoided Edward as much as she did Storm and Raphael, and Edward heard Storm mutter one morning: 'She's a queer girl – and ungrateful, too.' And Raphael, with a shrug, said: 'All girls are queer and ungrateful. I believe she's in love.' Edward did not hear more for they passed out of earshot. He was on the veranda sketching, and they were strolling by in the compound.

The days were fine and dry, and it was a pleasure to be in the open.

One afternoon, on his way to the creek, his parcel of drawing materials under his arm, he met Clara and the two younger children on the path, and on impulse stopped and said: 'Where are you three going? I'd like to do a quick sketch of you.'

They straggled to a halt and gave him surprised stares, and he flushed and said in a harsh, self-conscious voice: 'You needn't if you don't want to. I only thought it would be – it would make a good picture.'

'Certainly, if you wish to, Edward,' said Clara in a shyish voice, her manner rather tense. 'Where must we sit?'

'Come with me to the old bridge.'

They accompanied him to his old bridge which was still in use, though he had had it repaired twice within the past few years. He made them sit on the ground – and with the bridge as background began to sketch them rapidly in outline. Clara, in the middle, held her pose, but the two younger children kept shifting about, Mathilde giggling often.

229

After about half an hour, he waved his hand and said: 'That will do. Thanks. I've got enough down. I'll have to fill in the rest from memory.'

'Can we go now, Edward?' asked Graeme.

'Yes, run off.' He glanced up briefly and added: 'Thanks, Clara.'

Clara smiled slightly and murmured: 'It was a pleasure,' and hurried away, and presently, in the distance, he heard her gay laugh flare up and fade off. He was satisfied with what he had done, and worked for another hour or so, filling in details from memory and sketching in the bridge. In moments like this he was not lonely, nor in any way worried about the future.

5

GERT LIEKER'S pessimism was refuted. Joseph Bourda and John Haslin arrived at St Eustatius on the evening of the twelfth of March, and Admiral Rodney received them not in the manner of a ruthless cur but very graciously. Rodney invited them to dine aboard his ship, the *Sandwich,* and throughout the meal there was friendly, pleasant conversation. And the terms of surrender finally agreed upon were in no way as harsh as those imposed upon St Eustatius early in February. The inhabitants of Essequibo and Demerary were to 'remain in full possession of their property and to be governed by their present laws until His Majesty's pleasure be known.' The Company plantations, however, and all property belonging to the Dutch West India Company, were to be delivered up to His Majesty's officers. And the inhabitants were to take the oath of allegiance to Great Britain, and would be 'allowed to export their produce to Great Britain and the British islands of Tobago and Barbados in British bottoms and be treated in all respects as British subjects till His Majesty's pleasure be known.' Lastly, the 'Commandant and other officers have leave to go to Holland in a Cartel, taking with them all their effects, the troops to have the same indulgence.

> '14th March, 1781 at St Eustatius,
> '(Admiral) Geo. Brydges Rodney
> '(General) John Vaughan'

Bourda and Haslin arrived back in Demerary on the fifth of April, aboard H.M.S. *Hyaena*, accompanied by Lieutenant-Colonel Robert Kingston who had been sent by Rodney to make an inspection of Essequibo and Demerary, though it was Captain Thompson of the *Hyaena* who took control of the two colonies.

As usual, Wilfred was one of the first to investigate and return with a report on the state of things. On the morning of the ninth, he arrived at Good Heart, having collected James Harker and Gert Lieker on the way up. He was in one of his dancingly excitable moods. His arms moved about his head like cane leaves in a strong wind. 'A gentleman! A true gentleman, that's what he is, Hubert! That's Rodney! It – it would have done your heart good to hear Bourda and Haslin speak of him.'

Gert Lieker grunted, still trying not to look as pleased and relieved as he felt within. 'Why don't you tell Hubertus what the true gentleman did to the poor people of St Eustatius? I don't think the St Eustatians look on him as a gentleman.'

'Their fault!' Wilfred's arms whirled. 'Their fault entirely! Smuggling arms and supplies to General Washington's forces! What else could Rodney do but be severe! They asked for it, damme! Yes, they asked for it. Rodney is a gentleman, I tell you, Hubert. Only a gentleman could have granted us the terms these two colonies have been granted. And Kingston – another gentleman! Most agreeable fellow. I managed to get in a word to him. Told him he must come up to Signal at the first opportunity and spend a few days. We must arrange a hunt for him, Hubert. Or a better idea! My little sweetheart! Yes, that's it! The wedding, Hubert! Luise, your wedding! We'll ask Kingston to attend. He – he'd be p-p-perfectly delighted, I'm sure!'

'But we haven't fixed a date yet, Uncle Wilfred.'

'Eh? Well, let's fix a date – now. The clouds have all melted away. No more anxiety. This is a time for rejoicing. Fitting time for a wedding. Just as well it was postponed. Come, we must fix a date, and I'll send word to Kingston to come and see what we planters can do in the way of entertaining. Most charming fellow. You're bound to like him, Rosalind. Tch, tch! Don't look so d-d-downcast, my dear.' He gave his sister a brief hug. 'Come, come! Cheer up and let's p-p-plan our festivities.'

Luise, seeing her chance, said: 'Take me to Rylands, Uncle Wilfred, and let us discuss it with Cranley and Faustina – and Edward.'

'The p-p-pleasure is entirely your uncle's, my dear child!'

The wedding was fixed for the Sunday after the next, and Lieutenant-Colonel Kingston not only accepted the invitation but actually presented himself at Good Heart on the day. The general opinion was that at the last moment he would have pleaded an excuse on the grounds that his strenuous activities made it impossible to attend. Wilfred claimed it as a personal triumph, and was so stutteringly happy that, as Jim Harker put it, anyone would easily have thought he were the bridegroom and not Edward.

Kingston was, indeed, a charming man; in this Wilfred had not exaggerated. Everyone, Dutch and English, agreed upon this point. Gert Lieker said to Hubertus: 'A man like this makes us not too ashamed of having to take our oath of allegiance. I wish they had made him Governor instead of that stiff-backed Captain Thompson.'

Luise overheard her father reply: 'There is already a movement afoot, Gert, to have a petition drawn up asking Rodney to appoint Kingston.'

Despite Kingston's charm, the day, for Luise and Edward, proved a burden. Edward, forthright as always, did not fail to scowl and sulk, and when the last guest had departed in the evening and they were in their room – the large room Hubertus had had originally added for Faustina – Luise said to him: 'You're going to be known as the fiercest bridegroom that ever got married in this colony, Edward.'

'I don't care,' he grinned. 'Let them say what they want. When we have our own plantation I shall take care never to entertain anyone. I shall be known as the most selfish planter in the colony.'

'I'm not fond of crowds myself.' She suddenly pressed herself against him. 'Edward, you are happy, aren't you? You don't – you don't regret having married me, do you?'

'Of course I regret it. Take off your clothes and I'll show you how much.'

'What a crude thing to say!' She giggled and rubbed her

cheek against his chest. 'I hope I'll make you a good wife – and model.'

'That reminds me. I ought to have told you, but . . . '

She looked at him. In the lamplight his face had gone troubled.

'What is it, darling? What is it you ought to have told me?'

'It's nothing that matters, Luise, but I thought – it has been bothering me, and you know how I hate being deceitful.'

She stood very still, touching his arm, waiting.

'One day, a few weeks ago, I stopped Clara and Graeme and Mathilde and asked them to pose for a sketch. . . . '

She waited for him to go on.

'And a few days after I was doing a study of the ferns near the coffee lodges. You know the ones I mean? You said you like the dark-green ones better than the yellowish – '

'Yes, I remember.'

'Well, I was sitting there sketching, and Clara came upon me. She sometimes goes for walks alone. I think she's not so close to the others now. She asked me if I'd like to sketch her, and I said yes, and she sat down and I worked for nearly an hour. She sat still and didn't give me any trouble at all. Then she got up to go, and I thanked her. She waited for me to get my parcel tied up, and when I got up I – she just looked at me and then held me and kissed me.'

She said nothing, looking at him.

'She was going to turn off and rush away, but before I knew it I – I caught her quickly and held her and kissed her, too. I don't know why I did it. Luise. I don't know why, but I did. It upset me afterwards.'

'Afterwards?'

'After I'd kissed her – yes. Oh, I see. . . . No. Nothing happened but that. I just kissed, and she pulled away and ran off toward the house. For days after I hardly saw her face, except at meals – and even some meals she missed, saying she wasn't feeling well. I – I knew from her face that she'd been crying a lot in her room. I felt very upset, Luise. I wanted to kill myself because it seemed so – well, I felt I'd been unfaithful to you kissing her like that. But I couldn't help it. I don't know why did it. It simply happened before I knew what I was doing.'

He gave her a furtive, frowning glance, and she thought: I could be his tutor and he's waiting for me to reproach him for a neglected lesson.

She gave a nervous giggle and stroked his hair. 'Don't let it trouble you, dear. I'm sure you couldn't help it. She's very attractive – and she kissed you first. She's in love with you, Edward.'

'I know. It's terrible. I'm sorry, Luise. I hate to know she's unhappy. I like her – and I don't like to see people I'm fond of unhappy.'

'Yes. You're cruel – but only to your enemies. I'm glad I'm not your enemy.'

'Don't be so foolish.' He shifted about his feet uncomfortably. 'I can be cruel to anyone – even you.' He clutched her to him. 'Please, Luise, don't let me hurt you. I'd feel like dying after if I did. I'd shoot myself.'

'I know you would, but you won't. You won't, Edward. Only . . . ' She was silent a moment, and then said: 'Only I shall have to be careful after what you've just told me. I mean about Clara. If she tries to take you away from me I shall be a tigress. A tigress, Edward. And that applies to any other woman.'

PART SIX

'YOU needn't,' said Wilfred, 'enquire t-t-too closely into how I succeeded in getting an exact copy of this letter.' He tittered. 'But I did. I did. And here's the part that really concerns us. I'll read it slowly so – so as not to stammer. "When I parted with Captain Day I issued a proclamation to the inhabitants recommending them to take the oath of allegiance if they shipped any produce, or it was liable to confiscation, according to the terms of the capitulation. But the colonists, deeming themselves in a state of neutrality from ninth April to ninth October chose to frame a neutral oath, under the direction and advice of Mr Schuylenburg. To this the English inhabitants objected and framed another. On my return I made a third neutral oath for the tender consciences of the Dutch gentlemen who would not take that framed by the English, who had all objected to the first. This was a matter settled for the security of the capitulation in the intermediate state of neutrality, for those who shipped cargoes for Europe and the Isles, but is distinct and separate from the capitulation and its terms.

' "But though I recommended, at this period, the oath of allegiance, it is obvious I had no authority to enforce it when I admitted a neutral one, which became of no effect, or force, or consequence, after the ninth day of October, when you pledged yourselves to become British subjects and take the oath of allegiance to the British King, and which I now demand of your hands, in consequence of the solemn ratification you made with me for that purpose on the ninth day of April last, therein pledging yourselves, after the expiration of six months, to perform the same. If you do not I shall be under the disagreeable necessity of declaring the capitulation violated and void and command a confiscation of the properties of those so refusing. Edward Thompson – H.M.S. *Hyaena.* Fourteenth October, 1781." ' Wilfred waved the paper. 'There it is! Addressed to Schuylenburg and the Council. Just as I predicted! What else could Thompson do, Hubert! What else! The fools! Instead of being grateful that the terms of c-c-capitulation were so moderate they go making a fuss about the silly oath of allegiance! Fools! Just fools, that's what they are.'

There was silence.

Luise watched her father's face, and knew that behind his outward composure, he was unhappy. He was in the grip of another harrowing crisis.

Edward, too, watched him, and Edward thought: I'm sorry for the old fellow. People are narrow and stupid. I admire him for what he's done.

Rosalind, her gaze on her lap, was seated in the most shadowed corner of the living-room. She thought: This time he has cause to be harrowed – sound cause. For the first time he is struggling with a problem not created out of his fancy.

Wilfred broke the silence. 'Ignore them, Hubert. Let them ostracise you. You have us on your side, so what does it matter?'

Hubertus stirred slightly in his chair. He looked at Wilfred and said: 'I have reasoned that way, too, but it is hard to forget, Wilfred. We Dutch have flourished on this Wild Coast since early last century. One cannot forget the past hundred and seventy years in a few weeks. And remember the name I bear. Aert Adriansen van Groenwegel came to Essequibo in 1616.' He rose. 'My Dutch fellow-colonists have every right to ostracise me, Wilfred. I of them all should have refused to take the oath you English framed – yet I took it. And I took it because my personal principles dictated that I should. From youth I have believed that one should be loyal to no one group – to no one nationality. My loyalty has always been to humankind – not to a nation. That is why I found it no problem to marry your sister. That is why I took such pains to learn your language, and saw to it that my children learnt it, too. I wish it were in my power to learn all languages on the earth. I believe in the brotherhood of men on earth – not in the brotherhood of separate nations. An eccentric philosophy, no doubt, but it is mine. Mine.' He began to pace about, hands clasped on his bulging stomach. Suddenly he came to a halt and said: 'But whatever my own philosophy may be, the past cannot be pushed aside, Wilfred. That is the great trouble for me. However much I may want to I cannot forget the blood in my veins. Van Groenwegel blood. Blood that part of me venerates though the other part may despise it. Faustina and I are the only two Van Groenwegels who know the Tales of Old. The tales of our family's heroic deeds. We have never repeated those tales to our children, because we do not wish to keep alive an overweening pride in family. That is wrong. Grandma Hendrickje went too far. But those tales are a vital part of me. Their impression will never be wiped out until I die. Oh yes, Wilfred, by swearing full allegiance to the English I have been a traitor to our family traditions. The Van Groenwegels never surrender. They die rather than surrender. But there it is – the other half of me rejects this principle.' He patted Wilfred on the shoulder. 'Never mind, my boy.' His eyes were moist but he was smiling. Don't upset yourself about my feelings. I shall be plagued to the day of my death. It is my lot. I know it. There is no escape for me. Now tell us some more about what you learnt on your visit to the seat of government.'

'Oh – ah – yes, yes. Well, there was a meeting at Joseph Bourda's house, and I understand that the whole Council is to go to – to this new fort – Fort St George – to take the oath. Kingston has been appointed Governor, and that includes B-B-Berbice as well.'

'Excellent. Excellent. I'm glad Kingston has been appointed Governor.'

'I am, too. B-b-best thing that could have happened. But I'm sorry for Schuylenburg. Like yourself, Hubert, he's under a cloud with his f-f-fellow Dutchmen. They're saying he's too sympathetic with the English. And I hear he may have to answer a charge of treason b-b-because of what transpired between him and James Clarke of Barbados. When hostilities are over he'll probably have to go back to the Netherlands to explain a few things to the Directors of the Company.'

'I think that's too narrow and silly!' Luise exclaimed. 'He was quite right to tell Mr Clarke he preferred to have the colony captured by a King's ship. Those privateers would have stripped us of everything.'

'P-p-precisely, my child!' agreed Wilfred. 'As it is, we did have a taste of the privateers before the naval vessels arrived. Did you know that they took away fifteen ships? Yes. And they p-p-plundered one or two plantations down-river before they went off. D-d-dastardly rogues!'

'Did you say a new fort has been built, Uncle Wilfred?'

'Yes.' Wilfred glanced at Edward – as did Luise and Rosa-

239

lind. 'Yes, my boy. Very near to Plantation Labourgade – at the very mouth of the river. East bank. Fort St George they've called it. Most of the official business is being done there now. It was there my friend got me the copy of this let – ssh! Didn't mean to let that out. Hee, hee! Look here, I'll tell you something else in strict c-c-confidence. Kingston has whispered it that he wants to choose a new site for the capital of the colony. Borsselen has always been hopeless. Kingston says he may choose a spot somewhere near the mouth of the river. P-p-probably near the Brandwagt. But not a word of this must be m-m-mentioned, mind! Not a word!'

A few minutes later as Wilfred was going down the steps with Edward and Luise, who had offered to see him to the *stelling,* Rosalind thought: I wonder why Edward showed so much interest in the new fort. I think even Luise noticed it. . . . Vaguely she felt troubled. . . . I do hope he isn't contemplating any mad scheme that will make Luise unhappy. . . .

At the *stelling,* before he got aboard the yacht. Wilfred said: 'Take care of yourselves, my children. You in particular, my sweetheart,' he smiled at Luise. 'Have a lot of rest. Moderate amount of exercise. I'm taking a wager it will be a b-b-boy! Yes. Oh, yes! It *must* be a boy!' Red in the face, he gave her bulging stomach a quick, nervous pat, tapped Edward lightly on the arm and hopped agilely aboard the craft. Even Edward had to laugh aloud. Luise giggled uncontrollably.

As she and Edward walked back toward the house, however, she grew serious and said: 'Edward, why were you so interested in the new fort?'

He scowled, but she noted the slight start that went with the scowl. 'Why shouldn't I be interested in it?'

She sighed. 'I suppose it's some new secret between Father and yourself. You and Father do nothing but wander all over the plantation discussing projects you feel nobody else should hear of.'

'That's because they're important. Cousin Hubertus is a sensible man. Before very long you'll agree with me.'

'There was a time not long ago when you didn't think very well of him, Edward. Have you forgotten?'

'That was because I didn't know him well. He's a grand old

240

fellow. All his schemes are good, and I mean to help him with them all.'

She smiled and squeezed his arm. 'I'm glad you get on so well, dear. But sometimes I get a little jealous. Sometimes you make me feel you're more interested in him and his schemes than in me.'

'That's foolish,' he frowned.

'Nowadays you even see nothing wrong in his friendship with Faustina.'

'There isn't. Cousin Rosalind sulks like a bear all the time and hardly even speaks to him, so how can he be blamed for – for seeking Mother as a companion. It's only since I came to live here that I've discovered how Cousin Rosalind really treats him.'

'Yes, there is some justification in that. Mother certainly doesn't make an effort to be – to be wifely to him. She feels that he is the guilty one and it is in his place to make the first move to heal the trouble. I suppose it's a matter of pride – and she has always been very self-righteous.'

'Then she must suffer for it.'

'Edward! That sounds so brutal.'

He growled something inaudible.

'Stop here and kiss me.'

He kissed her, but did not hold her tight against him. During the past two or three weeks he had grown afraid of injuring the child. 'If I squeeze you tight I might kill the little thing in you,' he had said. No matter how she laughed at him she could not convince him to the contrary.

'Look how you're holding me,' she smiled. 'You're such a queer boy. Brutal in some things, and so tender and considerate in others.'

'Cousin Hubertus is hoping it will be a boy. Has he told you?'

'No, he hasn't. He says very little to me, as you know. But I should have thought he would have preferred a girl. Didn't he once say that he was thankful all his children were daughters and not sons?'

'That's because of the horrible things the family did in the past. He said he's not sorry he didn't have a son to carry on the name, but now that you and I are married he'd be proud to have a grandson bearing the name Van Groenwegel. He's very fond of you, Luise. He's told me so, and I know he meant it. He's a grand old fellow.'

'I'm going to begin to take count of the number of times you say that, Edward,' she laughed.

'Say what?'

'That he's a grand old fellow.'

'He is. I have a lot of talks with him and I know he is. We've got a whole pile of schemes we're going to carry out. Big things are going to happen before long.' He uttered a boyish, excitable chortle.

2

AT shortly after nine o'clock on the morning of the thirty-first of January, 1782, Luise gave birth to a son.

When Rosalind came downstairs into the living-room and announced it to Hubertus and Edward there was moisture in her eyes. Hubertus rose and embraced her, and Rosalind responded, trembling and murmuring incoherently. Edward, embarrassed, asked quietly: 'Can I go up and see them?'

'Yes. Yes, my boy, you may.'

'We shall all go up,' said Hubertus. 'This is a historic moment – a historic day.' His voice was a whisper. A tear glistened on his beard, and his great bulk shook.

A little later, when they were gazing at the tiny creature lying beside Luise, Hubertus shook his head and murmured: 'A historic day.' He kept murmuring it at intervals, as though in a hypnotic trance.

Edward said nothing. He smiled reluctantly, frowned, and bent and kissed the exhausted face of his wife who smiled up weakly at him.

'A historic day.'

And it was indeed, an historic day. At eight that morning, a French fleet of three frigates, four brigs and a large cutter, had drawn up in line of battle across the mouth of the river. By afternoon Governor Kingston and the Council of Policy had agreed to surrender to the Admiral of the French fleet, the Comte de Kersaint.

James Harker, who brought the news to Good Heart, told them: 'There's nothing we can do. We're hopelessly out-numbered. They have a hundred and thirty-six guns and eighteen hundred men against our ninety guns and three hundred and seventy men. Kingston has spiked the few guns at Fort St George.'

'The fort has been abandoned, then?' asked Edward.

'Yes. So far as I can gather, my boy, it has. Terrible. Terrible. To pounce on us like this. The damned rascals! No fear though, they'll wait until Doomsday before I take an oath of allegiance to them!'

Hubertus chuckled. 'Now, James! Now! This is where you must show your English sense of humour. The French are the allies of the Netherlands. By swearing allegiance to them you're merely swearing allegiance to your old comrades the Dutch. That is how you must regard it.'

'Bah! You're an old twister, Hubert. Can argue the hind-leg off a mule. Anyway, I'm damned pleased about your grand-son. Lucky dog. Four daughters, and yet you land up with a grandson bearing the family name!' James broke into his ear-splitting guffaw. 'What are you going to call the young devil? Have you decided yet?'

'On my suggestion, his parents have agreed upon the names Willem Hendrink. Willem was the name of a very worthy mem-ber of our family, James. He was the son of the first highly respected Commandeur of Essequibo.'

'And who was Hendrik?'

Hubertus was silent a moment, his gaze on the compound, then he murmured: 'After Grandma Hendrickje.'

'Ho, ho! The old she-devil you're always cursing in one breath and venerating in the other!' James slapped Hubertus on the shoulder. 'Just the ruddy inconsistent thing you would do. Ho, ho!'

On their way back to the house, after they had seen him board his yacht, Hubertus and Edward were in a thoughtful mood. Edward broke the silence between them with a question. 'How do you think this will affect our plans, Cousin Hubertus?'

'We shall simply have to wait and see what happens, my boy,' his father-in-law replied. 'No one can predict what turn events will take.'

'If the fort is abandoned it wouldn't matter.'

'No, I suppose it wouldn't, but, in any event, I have my doubts about purchasing a place like Labourgade. The sea frequently inundates the land about there, I've been told. But don't be troubled, my boy. I'm investigating the possibilities of another site not far off and safe from the sea – and from that annoying fort.' Hubertus gripped his arm. 'Impatient to get started on your building schemes, I know. Never mind. It won't be long now before you have a great deal to occupy your attention.'

'I can wait, sir. I have confidence in you.'

As on previous occasions, Wilfred kept travelling up and down river, ferreting out information, and passing on bits of news to all his friends and relatives. Through him they learnt that a meeting took place at the house of John Haslin, down-river, and that the new articles of capitulation had been signed by the Comte de Kersaint on the one side and on the other by Governor Kingston, Captain Tahourdin of H.M.S. *Oroonoko* and Schuylenburg and the Councillors of Policy. This was on the third of February. Shortly after, a proclamation was issued informing the population of the capitulation. It was made known that, according to the terms signed to, all private persons were to retain their property but that the Company plantations must be regarded as confiscated to the King of France. As soon as the oath of allegiance was taken, the population would have all the privileges of French colonists and would be free to trade with any nation except the English. The Dutch flag would enjoy the same privileges as the French and the Spanish and that of the United States of America until peace was proclaimed. The oath of allegiance must be taken within twenty-four hours. The Comte de Kersaint himself would be present at the home of Joseph Bourda to administer the oath. Wilfred told them that, on second thoughts, it had been decided to allow fourteen days instead of twenty-four hours, as it was realised by the Frenchmen that it would be impossible for all the planters to travel down at such short notice, especially those very high up the river.

'If they were all like me it would be no d-d-difficulty,' laughed Wilfred, who was in no way upset over having to swear

244

allegiance to the French. 'I'm a swift traveller. Here one hour, there another. B-b-best oarsmen on this whole river, b'God! But I say, let me read you some of the choice bits from the proclamation. Hee, hee! Listen to this slice of p-p-pomposity! "We, Comte de Kersaint, Commander-in-Chief of the land and sea forces of His Most Christian Majesty in this river, et cetera ... et cetera ... and the Governor and Councillors of the Colony of Demerary and its dependencies!" How do you like that, Hubert! But wait! There's another p-p-pretty little morsel. This is the c-c-cream of the whole thing, you hear my word! Listen!

' "To all whom it may concern, be it known that it is considered necessary, from the great extent of this river and its banks, to have a capital which will become the business centre, where religion will have a temple, justice a palace, war its arsenals, commerce its counting houses, industry its factories and where the inhabitants may enjoy the advantages of social intercourse.

' "This is perhaps the only instance of a European colony, among thousands throughout the world, which has arrived at some magnificence without the establishment of either town or village – " '

'It's the truth,' Edward interrupted. 'It's absurd that we have no town or village in a colony as big as this. I've always thought so myself.'

'I agree, my boy. I agree heartily. But wait. I have more of interest to read to you. Listen! "We propose now to establish, on the land formerly known as the Brandwagt – " Hang! I've lost the place. Anyway, it doesn't matter very much. They want to establish a town near the Brandwagt, Hubert. Oh, here we are! Listen! "Herewith we m-m-make known to the colonists that those who wish to have lots must make their application as soon as possible to Monsieur le Comte de Kersaint and the Ordonnateur Monsieur Gourg who will take n-n-note of their petitions and refer them to Monsieur Desprets, the Royal Engineer, by whom the plan will be submitted, the size of each grant fixed, and possession given, on condition of an annual contribution of five Dutch stivers per square toise. This tax, the aggregate of which is to be specially applied to the m-m-maintenance and improving of the town, is to be paid on delivery of the grant, and yearly in advance. All g-g-grants will be forfeited if after six months the holder does not fulfil his engagement of b-b-building a house thereon.

' "Done in our Assembly at Demerary, twenty-second February, 1782." Edward my boy! There's a chance for you! Take a grant and build yourself a house. Build two, three houses! Hee, hee!'

Edward, however, had not taken it as a jest. His eyes glittered. 'I will. I will. Cousin Hubertus, this is our chance. Get me a lot of land. We can have a town house as well as – as well as – ' He broke off, flushing.

Rosalind, who had just joined them on the veranda, gave him a look of surprise. 'What is the matter, Edward?'

Hubertus smiled. 'You shall have the land, Edward. This very day I shall take steps to procure a grant.'

'G-g-good God!' Wilfred gaped from one to the other of them. 'What's all this about! I mean, surely I haven't – Hubert, are you serious about this? You – you really mean to apply for a grant near the Brandwagt?'

Hubertus nodded. 'Yes, Wilfred. Edward, I think the time has come for us to drop our secrecy. Rosalind, I had intended to tell you in a day or two, my dear. I have purchased a new plantation on the coast. The sale was effected three days ago. We are abandoning Good Heart.'

. . . abandoning Good Heart.

' . . . Edward, it's your influence on him. It's you who persuaded him.'

'Yes, I advised him to abandon here. He's sensible. A grand old fellow.'

'Sometimes you frighten me, darling. Frighten me.'

3

'THIS step,' Hubertus told them at the dinner table, 'is no suddenly planned one. Long before you and Edward were married, Luise, I had been considering it. Please get it out of your head, my girl, that your husband has influenced me into doing something I should not otherwise have done. Edward is far too clever a young man to imagine that he could sway me in

246

any decision I regarded as unwise.' He exchanged a look with Edward, and Edward smiled a smile of perfect understanding. . . . They might be two conspirators, thought Luise, the alarm within her abating.

'I am not as methodical as your brother, Rosalind,' Hubertus continued, 'but I have kept my records from year to year, too, as every planter does, and I can give you this information so that you may see why it is compulsory for us to abandon Good Heart. The land, during the past five or six years, has shown a rapid diminution. Despite rotation of crops, which I had hoped might have been the solution, the soil has become exhausted to such a point that in less than three years we may be beggars if we remained here. Here are the exact figures: in 1778 our crop of sugar canes yielded three thousand, two hundred pounds per acre; in 1779 two thousand, one hundred; in 1780 one thousand, four hundred; last year, 1781, the yield was seven hundred and sixty pounds.

'The place I have just bought is well situated on the rich coastal lands, on this same bank of the river. It is a tract of land only partially developed; the owner, a Mr Harrison of Antigua, is on the verge of bankruptcy and has sold me for about a quarter of what the place, as it stands, is worth. This purchase has meant no strain on my finances, for in spite of the poor yields of the past few years I am glad to say we are still a very wealthy family.

'The flourishing years before the decline set in were *very* flourishing. Our cash in hand amounts to a considerable sum. On this new plantation we shall start out not modestly but on a generous scale. On a scale worthy of the Van Groenwegels.'

Erect in his chair, he took up his glass of wine, and Rosalind thought: He might just have finished addressing the Council of Policy. Poor Hubertus. I do believe he is still unconscious of what an absurd figure he cuts. . . .

People might think him pompous, thought Edward, but to me he has dignity. It will take a lot to shake my confidence in him. . . .

A hypocrite, Luise was thinking. But only by accident. I believe that at heart he intends to be sincere.

The prospect of the change did not perturb Rosalind. If anything, she was looking forward to it. Vaguely a hope was coming to life in her. Could it be, she thought, that he has decided to abandon his relationship with Faustina as well? I wonder. Surely there will be very few opportunities for them to meet when we are on the coast. I would give a limb to know how he has settled matters with her.

It was not long before she was given a hint as to the state of his mind. Coming out on the back veranda one afternoon, she found him standing by the rail smoking and watching with doting eyes the young Willem who was being fed by his mother. In such moments he lacked all absurdity and pomposity; tenderness and satisfaction replaced the mask of stolidity. Rosalind always felt nearer to him when he was like this.

'I was just saying, my dear,' he smiled, 'that Willem reminds me a little of Grandfather Aert. That brow – and the chin. What do you think?'

'Yes, there is some resemblance,' Rosalind nodded, though she saw none. At all costs, he must be humoured, she decided. This mood is so rare; it would be a pity to ruin it. . . . The old warmth moved in her.

'What did I tell you, my child,' he said to Luise. 'Your mother sees it, too. Old Aert comes to life again.'

Luise smiled abstractedly and agreed, her voice a murmur. Her thoughts were down-river, for Edward was spending a fortnight on the new plantation; he and the carpenters had left two days ago to begin building operations.

'He will compensate for much,' said Hubertus. He turned and looked at the fruit-trees and the outbuildings. 'He will comfort me when Good Heart has been left behind, when everything here has become a mere memory.'

They heard a wind far away in the bush. Like a shower of rain approaching. The sky was cloudless. In the west the sun had already disappeared behind the fruit-trees, and streaks of orange and pink were beginning to appear, splayed out like a pastel fan against the paling blue. The smell of dry-weather leaves and dry-weather grass moved in the cooling air.

'Yes, he will compensate for much.' His eyes had gone dreamy, and he might have grown unaware of other presence on the veranda. 'For the loss of old friends. Dear faces. . . . Change. New life. New interests. Inevitable in the affairs of men. We must stand up to them with courage, and adjust ourselves to the losses incurred. . . . '

It was announced from Rylands in April that Clara was engaged to John Hartfield, and that the wedding would take place in June or July.

Gert Lieker and his family were the only Dutch people present at the banquet held on the last Sunday in April. The events of the past year had estranged the other families. Though Gert told Cranley: 'We're as much disgusted with these Frenchmen as you English. Supposed to be our allies, and look what they're doing! Putting their own officials in all the important government posts. Schuylenburg and the Councillors are mere marionettes on a string. Do you think the Council would have approved of all these new prices! Sugar two and a half stivers a pound, coffee five stivers, cotton fourteen stivers. And this elaborate census of theirs. Demanding a list of one's whole family, servants, slaves, firearms, houses, mules, cattle.'

'That's so they can tax us more heavily,' Cranley chuckled.

'Edward likes them,' said Luise. 'He thinks they are progressive.'

'That's because he's building mad,' growled Gert. 'By the way, how are the new houses coming on?'

'Very well. Edward had them break down all the old buildings on the new plantation Father bought, and he's putting up places he himself designed. I saw the sketches he made. They seem very sensible houses. The factory is going to be of brick entirely. In fact, he wanted originally to build all the houses of brick – save the slaves' logies – but the chief carpenter says the expense would be too great, and Father agreed.'

'Why does Edward prefer brick?' Cranley asked.

'The risk of fire, he says.'

Gert snorted. 'Influence of the French! Remember that law they passed about kitchens! All kitchens for the new houses in the town must be of brick. Wood has always been good enough for us, but they insist on brick.'

'Edward was always in favour of brick – even before the French came.'

'That's right. Defend him. Nineteen years old, and he's mesmerised the whole lot of you.' Gert began to shake with laughter. 'I never thought I'd live to see the day when Hubertus would be dictated to by his son-in-law. That boy must have a lot of old Hendrickje in him.'

'Heaven forbid,' Cranley murmured.

Luise made no comment, her manner suddenly frosty. There were times when she found Gert Leiker detestable.

On the opposite side of the table, Edward gave her a look and began to smile. She was sure he had overheard Gert's remarks.

When they were on the yacht, later that afternoon, she said to him: 'I shall never sit near to him again at table.'

'He may not exist so far as I am concerned,' said Edward shrugging.

'The trouble with Gert,' smiled Hubertus, 'is that he is in difficulties. He knows that within a year or two he must abandon his place or be satisfied to grow coffee or cotton, and it is my belief that he cannot afford to start afresh on the coast. For Jacqueline's sake I may soon have to give him a helping hand.'

'Jacqueline says he's miserly. I believe he has more money than you think, Father. It's probably stored away in jars and buried somewhere.'

'Perhaps. In any event, I shall not be precipitate, my girl.' He glanced at Rosalind. 'Your mother and I have already discussed the matter of Gert's finances and the prospects for Jacqueline and her children. We are agreed on what steps should be taken if Jacqueline is ever in need.'

Rosalind nodded, and Luise thought: There can be no doubt now. They are getting closer. Cousin Faustina is already in the background.

Edward, too, noted the relaxed relations between his father-and mother-in-law, but he thought: I cannot see Mother giving him up without a struggle. Today she hardly exchanged a word with him, but that may have been a deliberate strategy meant to fool the rest of us.

To herself Rosalind was saying: I should like to think it is their integrity triumphing over the weakness of the flesh, but I'm not sure yet. She went out of her way to be friendly to me today, which was most unusual. I shall continue to hold an open mind. . . .

In the silence that came upon them Edward relived an incident not an hour old. He had gone upstairs to the small attic-room to hunt for some old sketches and plans of his, and emerging, had encountered Clara in the corridor. She said: 'I saw you come upstairs, Edward.'

'Yes?' He gave her a look of surprise, frowning uneasily.

'What have you been searching for? Your old sketches?' She glanced at the batch of paper hugged against him.

He nodded.

'I hear you're building a house in the new town.'

'Yes. Cousin Hubertus secured an allotment.'

'John's father, too. Building is going to start next month.'

'I see. I didn't know that.'

'It will be a shop and dwelling combined.'

'A shop?'

They kept avoiding each other's gazes.

'Yes. John is going to start a shop. General merchandise. We'll live upstairs.'

'I see. You'll – I hope you'll be happy, Clara.'

'Edward, I . . .'

'Yes?'

'I wanted to ask you something. Could you – would you please not come to the wedding?'

'You don't want me to?'

'No.' Her voice had become a whisper. 'Please don't. You could make an excuse that you have to be on the coast.'

He kept staring at her.

Head bent, she mumbled: 'I couldn't stand your being present.'

He nodded.

'You know why, don't you?'

'Yes. Very well. I won't come.' He began to turn off. 'I must be going down.' He paused and glanced at her. 'I do hope you'll be happy, Clara.'

'Thank you.'

He hesitated a moment, then hurried away. . . .

Should he tell Luise?

He felt her hand on his knee. 'Stop thinking about your ugly buildings for a minute, Edward.'

He started and grinned. 'I wasn't thinking about them.'

251

'Then what were you thinking about?'

'Nothing. Nothing in particular.'

Later, alone in their room at Good Heart, she said: 'Did you have an opportunity to wish John and Clara prosperity for the future?'

'Clara but not John.' Then he told her.

'She went upstairs deliberately to meet you'. She was breathing in a laboured manner. After a silence she said: 'It was a chance. Someone might have surprised you in the corridor.'

He nodded, frowning.

She watched his face closely, then abruptly turned away and began to cry softly.

It was only by an effort of will that he resisted an impulse to strike her. 'What are you crying for? Don't be a fool!'

'I'm sorry we're leaving here. I'm afraid, Edward. Afraid.

He scowled at her in disgust, then gripped her and began to fondle her and reassure her. 'You have nothing to be afraid of. Nothing. Aren't you married to me? It's I who must be afraid. If I were disloyal to you I'd want to kill myself. I'd blow out my brains.'

Gradually they both grew calm. Clasping each other still they stood by the window and looked out at the dusk. The sky was overcast, and though no rain was falling, there seemed a chilliness in the air that might mean rain later. Fire-flies were flashing under the fruit-trees, and far off they heard the goat suckers . . . Hoo-yoo! . . . Hoo-yoo!

She muttered something, and he asked her what she had said.

'It may rain tonight.' And after another silence: 'I still can' understand why.'

'Why what?'

'Why they made love in the rain that day,' she said. In murmur, as though addressing herself. 'Father and you mother.'

4

THE move to the new plantation was effected in July, shortl after Clara's wedding. Situated not far from Pierre de Saffron two plantations, Le Repentir and La Pénitence, it was renamed by Hubertus. Rosalind knew that he had had a struggle with himself before deciding on the name, and somehow she found that, though she did not approve of the new name, her sympathies were with him: even more so when Wilfred told them of the jeers he had overheard among their friends.

'Damned fools,' snorted Wilfred – and immediately apologised for his language. 'P-p-personally I think it's a beautiful name, and no more absurd than m-m-many another. Plantation Kaywana. What's the matter with that? Is it any worse than de Saffron's La Pénitence and Le Repentir?' Wilfred suddenly broke into sniggers. 'Which reminds me! I heard a good story about how de Saffron came to name his places as he did. It's like this: he and his brother came from France together about the m-m-middle of the century and they p-p-prospered considerably, as you must have heard. Then it appears they had a row and de Saffron m-m-murdered his brother – though he made it appear as an accident. He was so depressed and remorseful that he t t-turned to religion and became a recluse – and he renamed his two plantations La Pénitence and Le Repentir as a way of expressing his feelings.'

'Where do you pick up all these tales from, Uncle Wilfred!' laughed Luise. And her uncle wagged a playful forefinger at her, and returned: 'No fear, my little sweetheart, I have my sources! Oh, I have my sources!'

The house-warming was a very pleasant one. Every member of the family came, including Clara and her husband, who were less than half an hour's journey distant by boat. Gert Lieker and Jacqueline and her children spent two days, as did Faustina and Cranley and Storm and Raphael and the two younger children. The house held them all with ease.

Instead of the conventional box-like structure with a slated or shingled roof, Edward had designed a house cruciform in shape. The façade section consisted of a latticed portico-veranda above which was one large bedroom. Further in came the north and south wings, the lower storey of the south wing comprising a large dining-room, and the lower storey of the north wing a room of corresponding dimensions – the drawing-room; the upper stories of bedrooms. The elongated wing, which was a rearward extension of the façade section, contained six bedrooms and two bathrooms on the upper storey, and on the lower a small living-room opening directly from the hall-way and, beyond, pantry and kitchen and a servant's room. Access to the upper storey was by two curved stairways that led up from the hall-way to a balustered landing.

Everywhere such nicknames as Hubert's Mansion and Van Groenwegel Palace were being whispered about to the accompaniment of muffled sniggers. Hubertus heard of and over-heard them but smiled aloofly. At the portico doorway, in carved letters above the lattice-work. *Huis Kaywana* had already been inscribed.

Whenever asked, Hubertus explained in a quiet voice, his face impassive: 'Kaywana was the name of a remote ancestress. A very brave woman, tradition has it.' To Edward he had confided: 'The truth is, my boy, I had completely forgotten her name – and her exploits. It was your mother who refreshed my memory. The K on our tent-boat pennant stands for Kaywana.'

'Yes, I did hear Mother say something about her. Isn't she supposed to have been part Indian like yourself?'

'Yes. She was half Indian,' Hubertus nodded. 'Her name means Old Water.'

The room Edward and Luise chose was the southernmost of the three in the south wing. From their windows the red brick of the factory was visible in the distance through the trees, and more than once during those first few days Edward would stand gazing contemplatively out of the window until Luise came up behind him, touched his arm and said: 'What new improvements for the factory is my master brain thinking out?' He would start, frown and mumble something indistinguishable and begin to pace the room, seemingly oblivious of her presence.

She tried not to show that she was hurt because of his neglect, for intuitively she knew that in these moments he must not be reminded of their love. He was a man of two loves – his love for her and his love for his art and his buildings. To grumble when he neglected her for his other love would be one of the sure ways of losing him. She must resign herself to the situation and be content with the half of him that he gave to her. So long, she reassured herself, he gives the other half to buildings and not to another woman I won't mind.

One evening he stopped pacing and said to her abruptly: 'I've come to a decision, Luise. I want to work in oil paints.'

'Oil paints?' She never failed to show interest in his work – and, fortunately, it was not a feigned interest. His work did interest her. 'Do you think you'll be able to handle colours, Edward dear?'

'I'll try. I don't see why I shouldn't make a success of it. But don't say anything to anyone yet. I'll set up an easel in the next room. I'll use the next room as a studio. I'm determined to do a portrait of you for the living-room – and one of Cousin Hubertus for the dining-room.'

'And what of Mother?'

'Yes, Cousin Rosalind, too. She could go in the dining-room opposite Cousin Hubertus. I'll get some paints and canvas and brushes, and perhaps next month I'll make a start.'

It was nearly two months before he was able to secure all the materials required. In the meantime he had completed the house in Longchamps, which was the name the French had given to the new town coming to life in the vicinity of the Brandwagt. It was much smaller than *Huis Kaywana*, and because of the expense he had had to stick to the conventional box-like design. Even so, it differed from the others in the vicinity in that the lower half was of brick, the walls of the upper storey being of wood. There was a latticed gallery-veranda and a small portico. Because of the swampy nature of the soil the whole structure had to be built on four-foot brick pillars. Though Edward demurred, Hubertus insisted that it should be named Edward House.

There was no house-warming, and the tenant they found for it, Richard Granger, a tavern-owner, moved in immediately. The agreement, however, was that a guest-room should always be kept available should any member of the family need it when on a visit to Longchamps. Though an unusual arrangement, Mr Granger put up no objections. There were six bedrooms, and besides Mr Granger the only other occupants were his wife and widowed sister. Mr Granger's tavern stood not fifty yards from Edward House, and the gentleman had considered himself fortunate when he had heard that there was to be an unoccupied

255

house so near. Formerly he and his wife and sister had lived in two small rooms above the tavern.

About a hundred yards west of the tavern stood the Hartfield shop-residence, the kitchen and store-house almost on the brink of the new canal that was in the process of being dug. Slave labour had been requisitioned from the planters by the French, and two canals, running west to east, were already under way – South Canal and North Canal. These were the boundaries of the new town, and between them were two lines of lots – without cross-streets – and between these two lots a middle avenue, or what passed for an avenue; in actuality, it was nothing but an earth dam which, when it rained, became a squelchy morass of grey mud.

All the lots had been taken up, and buildings were springing up rapidly – shops as well as residences. Only the builders and the owners of the buildings, however, showed any enthusiasm for the scheme. The majority grumbled. Charles Bentley, a neighbouring planter, said to Hubertus: 'We're just being exploited by a pack of upstarts, that's what it is, Van Groenwegel. Taking our slave labour to dig canals. Putting up all these houses on what is virtually a swamp. I hear the foundations of some of them have begun to sink already – '

'That's because of bad construction,' Edward interrupted. 'Some of these builders don't know anything about underground drainage. If proper underground drains aren't dug a building must sink. It can be done – even in this soil – but some of them don't want to go to the expense, and some of them are simply incompetent. Fools,' he added, scowling.

Mr Bentley pulled at his whiskers and stared in some surprise at Edward. Then he smiled and said: 'Didn't know you were so versed in building, young man. Well, perhaps you're right. Yes, perhaps you're right. All the same, I insist that it's a badly planned town. It's aptly named Longchamps. A mile-long strip of territory stretching from the sea to the bush, and canals the only means of access to the sea. No cross-streets. It's absurd.'

'Those dams that pass for avenues are certainly most depressing,' Hubertus nodded, 'yet I feel that, as a colony, we have made a significant step forward. I am Dutch myself, Bentley, but I don't hesitate to admit that we Dutch have been too slow, too smug, too content to amble along. These new regulations and schemes may be irksome but they are necessary for our advancement. Indeed, I am ashamed that we Dutch allowed the French to come here and do what we ourselves should long ago have done. That is why, my friend, I am so disinclined to give my loyalty to any one nation or race. Each nation, each race, has its faults and its virtues, hence why extol one's own and despise others! Why not be loyal to all men of Christian faith?'

Mr Bentley, who was a very even-tempered man, chuckled and said: 'A most charitable way of looking at the matter, I warrant, but you must be careful when you say "race". All races aren't Christian. The Orientals and the Africans are heathens.'

'Perhaps I used the wrong word when I said "Christian",' smiled Hubertus. They were in the spacious portico, and the mid-morning sunshine striking through the lattice-work made a chequered pattern on the floor. A north-easterly breeze, laden with the smell of mud and water from the dams and canals of Longchamps, relieved the heat of the day. It was very pleasant in the portico. 'I should have said instead, civilised.'

'That is so,' said Bentley, 'but in that case you would have to include these free negroes and mulattoes who are steadily growing in numbers. They are becoming quite civilised, I can assure you. At least three mulattoes I know have opened shops in the town, and they've all adopted the Christian faith, to boot.'

'They are free men, Bentley. They are being given equal opportunities to become respected citizens. I should certainly include them among those to whom I feel loyalty is due.'

'Oh, I agree. I know some very decent fellows – and I rather like them, too – and I do feel they should be given equal opportunities to rise in the community. In fact, I have a mulatto lad on my place for whom I've just made an application for manumission. Yet I still feel that such people cannot be considered on a social level with people like us, Van Groenwegel. They must be respected and given fair opportunities, but – well, I don't think I could be persuaded to feel that I owe them any loyalty, socially speaking, I mean.'

'At the moment their manners and education do not make them fit persons for our company, but I see no reason why they may not eventually become ladies and gentlemen in their own rights. In that case I should have no objection to meeting them as equals socially.'

'Yes. Yes, I might even stretch a point there myself. After all, the white blood in them does give them some pre-eminence over the coal-black fellows who toil for us. Yet I still do feel they have their place. I'm sure you wouldn't sanction marriage between a member of your family and one of them, would you?'

'Most decidedly not,' said Hubertus. 'No, I would draw the line there, Bentley. I admit that my liberal spirit has its limitations.'

Bentley looked at Edward and laughed. 'I'm sure our conversation must be proving tiresome for Edward. He sits there frowning at the floor.'

Edward grinned. 'I'm interested, sir. Very interested. But to be honest, my mind had strayed a bit. A Monsieur Deganne from up-river has asked me to design a house for his new plantation.'

'Aha. You'll soon be famous throughout the colony. I knew it wouldn't be long before people began to commission you to do their houses.'

'Yes, Edward is becoming very well known. The new owner of Good Heart wants him to suggest some renovations for the buildings up there.'

'You've succeeded in disposing of Good Heart, then?'

'Yes, a Jewish merchant from St Eustatius has bought it. He was one of the very few who managed to evade Rodney and leave with a solid sum of money hidden amongst his belongings. Seems a decent sort of fellow.'

'What is he going to do? Grow cotton?'

'Yes, cotton – and some coffee. I think he told me. He will do well, I'm convinced. He has the will to succeed.' Bentley nodded, and Edward fidgeted. 'It was something of a wrench parting with it, Bentley,' said Hubertus. 'It was my first venture, I plucked it straight from the jungle, so to speak. It was one of the first plantations in this colony. But there was no help for it. A time always comes when we must put sentiment behind us.'

'Too true, too true,' nodded Bentley. 'In a country as new as this it pays to be practical rather than sentimental.'

Hubertus stirred in his chair, his face twitching slightly.

Bentley, Edward noted, gave him a curious look. Edward had been paying close attention to the conversation, though he had appeared abstracted, though he had made an excuse for appearing bored. There was not a moment, when in the presence of his father-in-law, that he did not pay attention to what he said – and study his mannerisms and responses. To Edward Hubertus was not only a figure of respect and admiration but also an object of interest. He observed him as he would observe, when a boy, the movements and habits of ants – only in this case his attitude was governed by a deep affection as well as by scientific interest.

What he was wondering now was: I can't yet decide how I shall depict him on canvas. Sitting won't be right. Standing would be better, but that might be tiring for him. And yet I'm not even sure that a standing portrait would express him in this way I envisage him within myself. . . . Look at his face twitching. What he wants to tell old Bentley is that practical things should come before sentiment but that the family means a lot to him. Family sentiment isn't easy to put aside. He's having a struggle with himself to decide whether to seem loyal to material things – or to the family pride.

'Yes. Yes,' he said. 'The practical, Bentley, should always come first. Yet, of course, when one thinks back into the past . . . Foolish of me, but certain sentiments cannot easily be thrust aside.'

'That family of yours. Yes, I know, my dear fellow,' chuckled Bentley. 'I've heard a lot about your ancestors. Very right to be proud of them. Such things do count, I agree.' Mr Bentley rose and said he must be going. A medium-sized man with blue eyes in a narrow, distinguished type of face, he wore a wig despite the climate.

5

THE next six or seven years were, for the family, as uneventful as they were eventful for the colony.

Plantation Kaywana flourished to the same extent that Good Heart did in the early days. Rylands, comparatively still young, continued to flourish; Cranley had gradually switched to sugar. Gert Lieker, less gradually, switched to cotton and coffee, much as it hurt his pride to do so; he refused help from Hubertus, though expressed his gratitude and seemed genuinely touched by the offer. Goedlust Lieker, who was managing the small West Coast plantation bought in 1780, struggled against incursions of the sea and disturbances among his people; he was a cruel master, and often gave short rations. Further along on the West Coast, Mary and her son lived contentedly on a fairly flourishing place, though her husband was suffering from cancer and not expected to live much longer; he died in 1786, and Raphael, at Mary's request, went to live at Degries as manager; Raphael, to the surprise of everyone proved a success as a manager and Mary sold him a share in the estate. One or two embarrassing tales about Raphael began to circulate; it was said that he was fond of the company of boys, and had no use for women. He became noted for his dandified dress and his over-refined airs and mannerisms. Like Mr Bentley and one or two other gentlemen, he affected a wig even on the hottest days.

It took Edward over eight months to be satisfied with himself as a painter; he scrapped canvas after canvas, despite what Luise considered good work. Eventually, however, he produced a portrait of her which he considered the ideal he was striving to achieve, and it was hung on the northern wall of the drawing-room. One day when Faustina saw it she said in a barely audible murmur: 'He must indeed be in love with her,' and turned away with moisture in her eyes. Within another year he had done Hubertus and Rosalind, the portraits being hung, as he desired, in the dining-room, one on the east wall and the other on the west, directly opposite. Meantime his building activities grew. He designed two sugar-mills and several private residences, three on the West Coast. His buildings never sank, and when he encountered clients who proved miserly he would refuse to take on the commission rather than produce a structure on poor foundations. At first he would take no fees for work done, but eventually Luise and Hubertus convinced him that it was foolish to give his labour for nothing.

Luise gave him two daughters, who, with their firstborn, Willem, were the central point of interest in *Huis Kaywana*. Hubertus and Rosalind often behaved as though they were the parents and Luise and Edward merely visiting relatives. Hubertus took Willem for walks about the compound, and Rosalind took charge of the two girls, Beatrice and Alpheda, to such an extent that Luise complained that Karena, the children's nurse, was being left with nothing to do.

John Hartfield's shop had grown into a much larger concern within two years; Edward had enlarged the lower storey of the building, and John was planning a new and separate building further west along South Canal. Year after year went by without Clara bearing a child, and soon it came to be taken for granted that she would be childless.

On the fifteenth of July, 1782, the Marquis de Lusignan had arrived as Governor of the three colonies, but he died in September and was succeeded by the Comte de Kersaint. Peace came in September of the following year, 1783, and in February of the following year the French announced their intention of handing back the colonies to the Dutch. On the sixth of March, 1784, the official transfer took place, and once again the populace was called upon to take oaths of allegiance. Again Demerary and Essequibo were the property of the Dutch West India Company.

Longchamps was renamed Stabroek, after the President of the Company, Nicolas Geelvink, Lord of Castricum, Backum and Stabroek, and the fort at the mouth of the river ceased to be known as Fort St George, its new name being Willem Frederik, after the eldest son of the Stadtholder of the Netherlands.

In February, 1785, Wilfred's voice was one of the loudest and shrillest raised in protest when Joseph Bourda decided to oppose the new government. Wilfred's protest – not against Bourda but, like Bourda's against the government – was by no means isolated. A number of planters, indeed, headed by Bourda, led the opposition to the new regulations announced from Holland. Wilfred held public meetings in Stabroek, and on Rylands and at Sapphire – Sapphire which had not been abandoned by the Harkers who had gone to Tortola in the Virgin Islands. Wilfred described it as 'd-d-disgusting tyranny' that the Company in Holland should decided to appoint the unofficial members of the Council of Policy. 'Haven't we always elected these members ourselves? Why should these new regulations be foisted upon us? We must resist them! Resist them with all our energy!'

No one disagreed with him, and on the arrival of the new Directeur-General, Jan L'Espinasse, the atmosphere grew tenser. When L'Espinasse announced that Joseph Bourda and a Mynheer Helsdingen were the new members appointed, both these gentlemen refused to serve. L'Espinasse, furious, announced new appointments, but again the gentlemen appointed refused. More furious, L'Espinasse imposed a fine of three thousand guilders on anyone else refusing to serve when appointed. The situation degenerated into a farce, and eventually L'Espinasse could get only one poor obscure planter, a Mynheer Hecke, to serve as Colonial Representative.

When the Council sat and imposed a head-tax of six guilders on slaves – the old tax had been two guilders, ten stivers – the planters laughed and refused to pay, claiming that the Council had been irregularly constituted. 'The fool!' cried Wilfred, dancing. 'Does he think we're going to p-p-passively hand over our money simply because his ludicrous Council has passed this new bill! He'll wait until the Trumpet sounds up there! Hee, hee!'

No taxes were paid during the years 1785 and 1786, and the Directors were obliged to send out delegates to review the situation. These delegates drew up what came to be known as the Plan of Redress. It was signed on the nineteenth of March, 1787, and presented to the States General. It recommended that the Council of Policy of Essequibo should be abolished and one Council created to represent both rivers, the Commandeur of Essequibo being made subordinate to the Directeur-General, who now resided in Demerary. Representatives of the planters, said the Plan, should be elected, as before, by the College of Kiesheers in each colony, each College to consist of seven members instead of five as formerly.

The planters looked upon the Plan of Redress as a triumph, but the Directeur-General refused to recognise it, and Wilfred and his friends again became vociferous. They sent in a protest – a sort of colonial bill of rights – and after some delay the matter was again taken up by the authorities in the Netherlands, and two commissioners, a Baron van Grovestins and a Mynheer Boey, were sent to Demerary to make peace. The planters had their way, and the Plan of Redress was put into effect, the two colonies now being officially termed the United Colony of Demerary and Essequibo. Directeur-General L'Espinasse resigned in a huff.

'Let him go!' shrilled Wilfred. 'The stubborn old monkey! Should have been b-b-bundled out of the colony a long time ago. Arrived here on the second of February, 1785. And what's today's date? The eighteenth of August, 1789. Took him four and a half years to do what he should have done since February the third, 1785. Eh? Don't you agree with me, John? Eh?'

'Yes, I agree,' said John in his mild voice, smiling.

Clara laughed. The years had not robbed her of her gay, shrill laugh. To himself, Edward saw it always as a long red or orange streamer curving swiftly, then languishingly, through space. It never failed to disturb him. He and Sidney Bentley — old Mr Bentley's son — and Wilfred were having breakfast with John and Clara and Graeme. Graeme, now a young man of twenty-two, had for the past year or two been assisting his brother-in-law in the still growing shop; Graeme managed the new branch further west along the canal.

'I don't know where Cousin Wilfred finds all this energy for politics,' said Clara. 'Some more fried plantain, Edward?'

'Thanks,' Edward murmured.

'I made it specially for you, because I know you like it.'

'Do you cook yourself?' Sidney smiled. It was no secret that Sidney was in love with her.

'Yes, sometimes. Don't speak so accusingly, Sidney.'

'She gives the cook no peace,' sighed John.

Edward suddenly looked at him and said: 'I'm still waiting to do that portrait. When are you going to find the time to pose for me?'

'Time, Edward my dear fellow. Time,' sighed John, shaking his large head on which his hair forever stood up in a bristly red-brown mass. Edward had always thought him a good subject for a portrait. 'If I'm not messing about in one of the shops I'm in the store-house, or in the little office where I have to see after the books with Graeme and Mr Thomson.'

'You work too hard, John my boy,' Wilfred scolded. 'Not enough play. The n-n-number of times I've invited you to a *labba* hunt up there with me! And every time you refuse. Too busy. Too busy. Won't do, my boy!'

'Yes, I know. I ought to take more recreation, but it's to tear myself away – I can never bring myself to do it.'

'It's a pity you don't paint, Sidney,' Clara said. 'I'm sure you wouldn't have neglected, as someone I know has neglected, to offer to do a portrait of me.'

Edward scowled and stirred in his chair. Even at twenty-six he was self-conscious and had not rid himself of many of his boyish traits. 'Stop making nasty insinuations Clara,' he said, trying to grin and frown at the same time. 'You know very well I intend to paint you. But I thought I'd do John first, because he has an interesting head.'

'That big bullet head of his! What's interesting in it!'

'Don't take any notice of her, Edward,' said John. 'I'm well accustomed to such slanderous remarks.'

'Talking about painting,' Wilfred put in, 'have you seen the portrait he's done of me? It's the m-m-most slanderous thing I've ever seen! Makes me look like a d-d-dissipated chicken-hawk. But look here, Edward, I want you to come up and do the whole family one day very soon. Something on a big scale, like the sort of things I've heard that fellow G-G-Gainsborough in England has done. He d-d-died last year, Cranley told me.'

'By all means,' said Edward. 'I'd be glad to try a family group.'

'But it's got to be very soon, my boy,' said Wilfred, and a serious note came into his voice. He seemed to hesitate, then looked round at them and said: 'I'm afraid in a few m-m-months' time you people won't be seeing much of me.'

'What do you mean?' asked John.

They all turned their gazes on him.

Wilfred fidgeted and passed a hand over his tangled mass of white hair. His nervous, alert green eyes blinked rapidly. 'I've bought a new place in Berbice. Last year Signal yielded only five hundred pounds to the acre. No good. The time has come to abandon it. D-d-depressing, but there it is.'

There was silence.

'Time,' said Wilfred, with a smile that was a little forced. 'Time and change. Nothing ever remains the same. Eh? Oh, well! Storm is coming with us. Perhaps he'll find a p-p-pretty young lady of Berbice to suit his fancy, and will get married there. Eh? Hee, hee! Oh, we mustn't complain. Come and pay us a visit once in a while. The sea voyage will do you good, I'm sure. Welcome at any time,' he said, brushing hastily at his eyes.

'I'll come up next Tuesday and spend a week with you,' said Edward, 'and get that portrait done. I think I have a large enough canvas.'

'I shall treasure it, my boy. Treasure it. You have a big t-t-talent, Edward. You must do Clara, too,' he hurried on, with a titter, just in time to cover up the break in his voice. 'The leading b-b-beauty of Stabroek! Eh? It'll be a famous picture!'

All Wilfred's efforts to be cheerful, however, did not succeed in lightening the gloom his news had brought upon them.

6

THE farewell banquet Wilfred held early in November at Signal might have been a sadder function but for the surprise announcement that Storm and Elizabeth, Wilfred's daughter, now twenty-one, were engaged to be married. The wedding would take place at Christmas, a few weeks after their arrival in Berbice.

Elizabeth was tall like her father, and of the same slim build, but had her mother's round pretty face and auburn hair. She was a shyish, charming girl, and Edward, in his large portrait of the family displayed over the sideboard in the dining-room, had brought out her personality with great effect. Elizabeth and Wilfred dominated the picture which was the centre of everyone's gaze during the function. 'It will be hung in our living-room in Berbice,' said Wilfred. 'And when Edward comes to visit us I shall m-m-make him do one of Mr and Mrs Van Groenwegel and sons and daughters. Yes, oh, yes!' tittered Wilfred, red in the face. 'I'm going to see to it that my house warms with g-g-grandchildren. I won't be satisfied with less than ten of them. Did you hear that, Storm my boy? Eliza! Hope you're listening to me!'

'Oh, Wilfred! Shame upon you!' cried Primrose his wife. 'You're making them blush!' But, like Wilfred, every inch of her two hundred pounds was shaking with laughter.

As in the old days, Wilfred sat on Cranley's left, with Luise to the right of Cranley. On the opposite side of the table, Edward sat between Clara and Hubertus. Often Luise would glance from Edward to Storm, who sat between Rosalind and Elizabeth, and think: The only difference between them, at a glance, is that Storm is always smiling and Edward always frowning. And Rosalind, exchanging a word now and then with Storm, thought: He lacks Edward's intensity and remoteness. Sitting next to him, no one could mistake him for Edward. He's just a very ordinary cultivated young man.

'How long,' asked Clara of Edward, 'did you actually take over it?'

'What? The picture up there? An aggregate of exactly thirty-seven days between August and last week.'

'It's lovely, Edward. Lovely. The likenesses are so good. When are you going to do me? Must I go down on my knees and beg you?'

'Don't be foolish. I'll come next Wednesday and make a start. Will that be convenient?'

'Of course. I'm at home every day and all day – all by myself.'

He stirred in his chair.

She gave him a quick glance and he thought her breath hissed in a way that was not usual.

'Perhaps . . . '

'Yes?' she prompted.

'No, I was just wondering – I mean, if John could have posed with you – mightn't it be better to do the two of you instead of you alone?'

'Can you see John leaving his wonderful shops to pose with me during the day. Why, even Saturdays and Sundays he's downstairs checking something or writing up his books. He – – oh, Edward, don't you want to paint me?'

He said nothing, his face troubled.

She murmured: 'Don't come if you feel – if you feel you shouldn't.'

'I'll come – on Wednesday. At about one o'clock.'

On Tuesday, after morning coffee, Hubertus said to Edward

'I'm taking Willem for a walk. Why don't you come with us, my boy?'

'I have work to do, sir,' said Edward, surprised; it was not often Hubertus invited him to go walking. Luise had just gone upstairs; she was four months pregnant. Rosalind, still seated at the dining-table, had an odd smile on her face. White-haired like Wilfred, she was acquiring a tranquillity and dignity as she aged. The lost, vaguely anguished expression had entirely gone. Now and then a sly irony was evident in her eyes, as though memory of the past gave her reason to be amused rather than bitter. There was this sly irony in her eyes now, and Edward saw it and was puzzled.

I wonder if she and Cousin Hubertus have been discussing me. But what could they have to discuss about me?

'You work too hard, Edward my boy. Come. Look at the sunshine. The dry season is lasting longer than I had expected it would. Come with Willem and me. We'll walk in the shade of the mango trees.'

Edward went with them.

Willem, at seven, had his mother's face but his father's shifty brown hair. A slim, blue eyed boy, he lacked his father's taciturnity, and asked innumerable questions, every one of which Hubertus dutifully answered.

'Are these the special mango trees you planted when you first came to live here, Grandfather?'

'Yes, my boy. They were imported from the East. What are you doing tomorrow, Edward? Painting anyone's portrait?'

'Yes. As it happens, I am. I promised Clara Hartfield to start on a portrait of her.'

'A charming young woman. A regular beauty. I understand there are a number of men in Stabroek who would sacrifice a fortune to receive a smile from her.'

Edward said nothing. He began to squeeze his thumb.

'I just saw something move in the grass there, Grandfather. Do you think it could be a snake?'

'No. Probably a salampenter, my boy. Or a lizard,' smiled Hubertus. 'What a lovely morning! A pity she has not been able to have any children. I'm sure it must be a great disappointment to them both.'

Edward was silent.

'Does Luise know you are going tomorrow to begin on this portrait?'

'Yes. I've told her. We have no secrets.'

'I've observed that. An excellent plan. I must say, Edward, it has done my heart good these past few years to note the harmonious relations that exist between yourself and Luise. You understand each other so perfectly, and the bond between you is so firm, so sincere, so warm. It moves me deeply to witness such a relationship, because – well, it was like that between Rosalind and myself. For the first fourteen or fifteen years of our marriage we were immeasurably happy; the harmony between us was so perfect that I believe now and then it even made us a little afraid. Afraid that something would intervene to disturb it.'

Edward said nothing.

Willem, running ahead of them, was throwing pebbles up into the foliage of the mango trees. The air was fresh with the smell of mango leaves and dew-damp grass. Off and on came the swift sweet smell of cane-juice.

'Your mother and I had a very beautiful friendship, my boy. We neither of us regret it – and yet – well, we have both had to pay for it in other ways. It shattered my home life. It destroyed forever the beautiful intimacy that had existed between Rosalind and myself. We have never recaptured the harmony of those first fourteen years, even though there is peace between us now.'

'When did your friendship with Mother cease? Is it since you came to Kaywana?'

'Approximately then – yes, my boy. We agreed that the time had come to end the beautiful dream. The longest shower of rain must end.'

'Why rain?'

Hubertus chuckled. 'Rain, for your mother and me, holds a special significance, Edward. I fear I cannot explain. It's something that must remain sacred with her and me. But we've strayed. I was speaking of Clara. I overheard your conversation at table a few days ago. Couldn't avoid overhearing it. I was sitting next to you, if you recall.' He was silent a moment, then continued reflectively: 'I knew her mother very well. Woglind Prutt. I was friendly with her on the Essequibo. A beautiful

268

woman, too. Beautiful but extremely unstable.'

'Clara isn't. She's very steady – and very upright.'

'And so are you, my boy.' Hubertus squeezed his arm. He turned, and Edward saw him smiling slyly within his thick grey beard. 'And so were your mother and I. Very steady, very upright, Edward.'

'I – oh, you don't have to explain, Cousin Hubertus. I understand perfectly. In fact, I didn't want to do her alone. I've been trying for months to avoid such a – such a situation. But she persisted, and I couldn't refuse without seeming boorish.'

Hubertus nodded and sighed softly. 'Events have such a way of repeating themselves,' he murmured. After a brief silence, he said: 'I can recall a day – it was at Rylands. We had just decided to keep her until things were more settled with Cranley. Her mother had just died. I remember experiencing a feeling of deep foreboding. She was such an attractive child. I could picture her growing up into as beautiful a woman as Woglinde. But I felt afraid – afraid that one day in the far future she might be a threat. Foolish of me, no doubt, but there it is. Just a feeling, Edward.'

Edward made no comment. He kept squeezing his thumb.

'Luise is not like her mother in temperament. There would be desperate trouble if – if anything should develop between you and Clara.'

'I know, sir.'

'It would be as much a disaster to me as you two. I live vicariously in you, Edward. Your happiness is mine. If I relaxed in thought for a mere moment I could feel Luise my wife and your children my own. I'm as close to you as that, my boy. It is probably senility creeping upon me. I'm sixty-two. Very hearty in body, but my mind is growing befogged.'

'Not in the slightest, sir. I think you're very wise – and you have every right to warn me. I feel – I've always been uncertain of myself in Clara's company. She disturbs me. I've told Luise, but she says she wants me to go tomorrow – just to prove that I can keep myself in check. She says it would be worse for me to go on avoiding Clara in the belief that I could not resist her charms if alone with her. Luise is right. Like you, she's wise. I must face it out, and – stop being a fool.'

His father-in-law nodded slowly and lengthily. Edward

thought he would not stop. 'Yes, Luise is wise in her way, yet
. . . ' He began to nod again. Suddenly stopped and jerked his
head in negation. 'Yet, Edward, the physical is so imperative.
I discovered that for myself – with your mother. Had we not
taken a walk in the rain on a certain evening in December, 1766,
we might never have set into motion all that happened during
the years that followed. According to the rules that men have
created, your mother and I have committed adultery many
times since that first evening in the rain. Now I have told you
why rain means so much to us.' Edward saw him smiling – an
abstracted smile. . . . He's going off into another of his sentimental trances, thought Edward. 'Yes, adultery. It's called
adultery – but to us each occasion was an instance of supreme
beauty. A jewel moment to be looked at in retrospect with
warmth and delight. No regret.' He started and chuckled.
'There, there! Straying again. You must pull me up, Edward.
It's a bad habit. We're speaking of Clara, aren't we? Yes, if I
were you I should be careful of being close to her – feeling as
you do about her.'

'But I'm not in love with her, sir!' Edward said quickly. 'It's
only – well, you know what I mean. She has a lovely body, and
I've always been attracted by her. Somehow, I've never seen
her as a sister as I ought to have. I've grown up with the others
at Rylands, but I was like a stranger. I was never interested in
what they did or said. I kept to myself. In fact, you and Luise
are the only people I've ever succeeded in getting close to.
Everybody else – even Mother – might be a stranger.'

'I know what you mean, my boy. I feel an affinity with you.
In your spirit you're probably as harrowed as I am. For people
like us, Edward, life is never simple. Our consciences are too
sensitive. We live richly, intensively, but we examine ourselves
too closely. We are perpetually accusing ourselves of faults
other people would consider trifling but which, to us, seem
mountain high. We strive after perfection too zealously. It is
because I know how deeply you love your wife and how disas-
trous it would be on your conscience should you – should you
lose control of yourself when with Clara – it is because of this
as well as my desire that nothing should happen to destroy your
marital happiness that I thought I would speak to you and ask
you to be careful. I've discussed it with Rosalind, and she

270

agrees with me – but there is irony in her agreement. It is natural that there should be. There is something I've never told you, Edward my boy. It is because I know you have a high opinion of me, and like a coward I did not want to destroy it, even though I knew that telling you would not destroy what you feel for me.'

'I know already – and it hasn't destroyed my respect for you.'

Hubertus gave him a quick glance, a tenseness in his manner.

'It's the one secret Luise kept from me, until about a year ago. Mother told her that night at Rylands when – you know the night I mean.'

'I see. Yes, your mother told me she had told Luise.'

They walked in silence for a while.

'Do you know if Graeme himself knows, Edward?'

'I don't think so. No, I'm sure he doesn't.'

7

DURING the night it rained steadily and heavily, and though Wednesday morning broke with sunshine, the ground was muddy.

Stepping ashore at Stabrock shortly after mid-day, Edward and his slave walked in mud ankle-deep until they came to the built-up causeway that began not far from the *stelling* in the vicinity of the Brandwagt. It was known as the Brickdam, for it had been constructed entirely of bricks on edge. In the rain season the Brickdam was the only solid thoroughfare in the whole town. All others consisted of mere banks of mud – mud that had been dug up from the canals and piled up to form rudimentary paths or streets – dams, as they were popularly called. Muddy plots of land, known as greens, separated one building from another, though not all of them were grass-covered.

The town had not developed as rapidly as had been hoped. From what Edward had heard, there were now exactly eighty-eight houses standing to accommodate a population of two hundred and thirty-eight whites, seventy-six free coloured people and four hundred and sixty-six slaves. Groud had given him these figures a few days ago, and he had no doubt they were correct. Groud was a reliable overseer and took an interest in statistics.

The houses stretched in two long rows for about a mile, from the bank of the river to the bush, each with its spacious green on either side and each within a few feet of the bank of either North or South Canal. Every one looked like a big box with a slated or shingled top. Some of them were painted pink, some a dull sienna, some a dull green, some terra-cotta. Sight of them never failed to make Edward groan and shake his head.

The free mulatto hucksters greeted him with smiles and affectionate glances. One or two of them called out to him, for they knew him well. He bought fruit from them sometimes. Each had his square of tarpaulin spread out in his favourite spot at the side of the road, and sat among his baskets of fruit and vegetables waiting for customers. The housewives of Stabroek depended upon these hucksters for their yams and eddoes and cassavas.

Among them were one or two free negroes, but these were aged and seemed half-asleep over their baskets. Planters had soft consciences when it came to the mulatto bastards produced by their slave women and released them from their bondage at a young age. But no negro slave was ever manumitted until he was so old as to be useless and, indeed, a burden whose riddance was worth the hundred guilders the government demanded as manumission fee. There were two mulatto planters on the Mahaicony Creek, Edward had heard; they had been granted concessions some six years ago. Which reminded him. Cousin Hubertus, he was sure, had of late begun to have sexual relations with his slave women. Overgaar, loyal as always, denied it, but Groud had smiled significantly at Edward that morning two months ago when he and Edward had passed Hubertus returning from a supposed inspection of the new logies on the south side of the factory compound. Not that Edward blamed him. Cousin Rosalind seemed so frigid in respect to such matters, and Cousin Hubertus was still very virile.

A pink-painted building, the Hartfield shop-residence stood on the bank of South Canal, as did Edward House further east. All the best houses were to be found on the bank of South Canal.

272

Edward went into the shop to have a word with John before going upstairs. In one half of the shop the air smelt of tar and oakum and iron, for in this half were stacked all the plantation hardware requirements that John stocked. In the other half the smell of salt beef and salt fish carried the day, for this was the Provision Store, as it was called. The shop had started out as a provision store, the hardware section having come into being a few years later.

'Never fail to keep your word,' smiled John from behind a barrel of salt pork. In shop-apron, he was no different in manner from when at the dining-table or in the living-room. On the point of sighing, it seemed, his eyes about to shut wearily, he went on: 'Go upstairs and get started on the work of art. You'll find her itching to pose for you. She's so vain.'

'I wish you were a little vain yourself. Can't you leave someone in charge down here for an hour or so, John! I would have preferred very much doing you both together.'

This time John sighed. 'Nothing would have pleased me more, Edward, but it isn't possible.' He glanced toward his three mulatto assistants. 'Reliable fellows, all three of them, but they don't know the stock as I do. If I ventured to step out of here for a minute you may be sure an order would come in for some item no one but me could attend to.' The threat of another sigh was arrested. His eyes grew wide-awake, pale-blue and a trifle fishy, thought Edward, following the direction of his gaze.

It was Mynheer van Huyn and two slaves who had just entered. The short, paunched, red-faced old gentleman was making an enquiry of one of the assistants, and the assistant smiled and began to move toward John.

'Illustrated for you as though I had arranged it beforehand,' smiled John triumphantly. 'Yes, Malcolm! What does Mynheer van Huyn want?'

Edward mumbled an excuse and hurried out. With his slave he moved round the side of the building to the stairway that led up to the enclosed veranda, called a gallery. He did not have to knock.

'I saw you coming along the dam,' said Clara, opening the door.

'Yes, I was talking to John downstairs. God! But you're decked off as if for a banquet,' he added with a scowl.

273

She laughed. A streamer going out into the heat, gamboge rising and falling and merging with the sunshine, became scattered amidst the voices of the hucksters and their customers. He glanced round, almost certain he would have seen the phenomenon. A mist moved through his stomach, troublous but exciting and charged with delightful dangers.

'You don't want to paint me in my worst house-frock, do you?' She waved toward a doorway. 'Let's go into the small living-room, Edward. It's coolest in there at this time of the day.' Leading the way with a multitude of little swishes from her silk dress – it was full of billowing folds and pleats all shimmering emerald green – she was perfectly self-possessed, and he began to feel foolish. The slave came after them with the easel and canvas and paint-box.

The small living-room was situated on the northern side of the house, well away from the rays of the early afternoon sun. At a glance Edward could see that the furniture was not the same as when last he had visited here. A couch had been brought in and placed near the northern wall, between two windows. He asked her about it, and she said: 'I had it brought from my bedroom. I thought you might want me to recline on it to paint me. Isn't that supposed to be the fashion with the great portrait painters in England?'

'I hadn't heard of it,' he frowned. 'Anyway, we shall see. The pose is something I have to decide after considerable thought – and boring hesitation. I may want you to stand on your head for a start.'

The laugh. 'I'll bow to all your decisions, Edward dear.'

After Jacob had set up his easel and laid out his palette and brushes and paints, Edward told him he could wait in the kitchen. 'I'll call you at about four, Jacob.'

Clara, meanwhile, had seated herself on the couch. Not coquettishly, however, Edward noted. Not for an instant could he accuse her of ulterior intentions. She had certainly gone to a lot of trouble to dress herself attractively, but she did that on all occasions when there was company. It would be unfair of him to say that she had worn this green dress with its low neck that revealed more than half her bosom because she wanted to seduce him. Her posture on the couch was in every way decorous. Not by glance or motion of a hand or shoulder had she tried to attract attention to her bodily allurements. It was he himself who was absorbing these.

Seated on a small upright chair, he regarded the gold-brown hair piled on the well-shaped head with its pleasing face. She lacked Luise's richly spiritual, mysteriously tantalising beauty, but she was lovely in her own way, nevertheless. A gay, open, earthy way. He liked the short, slightly upturned nose and the full-lipped mouth that pouted a trifle above a vaguely dimpled chin. And the long but too thick throat he approved of, also, for it merged downward with symmetry into the solid but not massive torso, and especially with the full, half-pendulous breasts. She could have been an inch or so taller, but her legs were long and shapely, as he remembered from the Rylands days. Pity this green dress had to conceal them.

'You'll have to get used to me staring at you,' he grinned. 'Get up from there and walk across the room.'

With a soft laugh, she obeyed. 'I don't mind you staring at me. I've heard all about your methods of drilling your subjects before deciding on the pose that suits you.'

'Sit in that chair over there.'

She obeyed, but he shook his head and told her to get up. 'Let's go into the big living-room.'

They were greeted by the smell of the canal – a bilgy aroma that was a mixture of rotting vegetable skins, carcases of animals and soft mud. 'That's why I'm not fond of being in here,' she said, with wrinkled nose. 'That canal is unhealthy. It's going to breed disease before long.'

Silent, he glanced around, considering, frowned and shook his head. 'No, in here won't do. Let's go back into the small room.'

Eventually, he decided on a large, very comfortable easy chair. He stood over her to arrange her arms in her lap, shuddered deep inside at the coolness of her forearms. Was afraid that the shudder would project itself into his hands so that she would notice, but he kept it in check. He wondered whether she, too, were feeling as he was feeling. She did not show it – not by the flicker of an eyelid or the quiver of a lip. He began to gain confidence in himself – and in her. There would be no trouble. He had been an idiot to think there would be any awkwardness.

'You can say anything you like while I sketch,' he told her.

'It won't put you off?'

'No. But don't expect me necessarily to reply.'

'It isn't yesterday I've known you, Edward.'

He worked until four o'clock – they heard the clock striking in the big living-room – and at the door as he was leaving, she smiled: 'Are you enjoying doing this, Edward? You're not finding it a bore.'

'Don't be foolish. Why should I? I'm never bored painting a portrait – or doing any kind of painting, for that matter.'

The silence that followed was uncomfortable. He knew she was looking at him as she had not looked at him once for the whole afternoon. A breeze came from the north-east, and out of the corner of his eye he was certain he saw a strand of her hair wave. He could smell the silk dress – delicately perfumed. Old flowers and feminine musk exciting and defying definition.

He gave her a swift scowling look and mumbled: 'Clara, I'm a fool. I . . . Cousin Hubertus is right. I shouldn't have . . .'

'You shouldn't have come to paint me?'

He nodded.

'Cousin Hubertus warned you against me, I suppose. He would.'

'But he was right! He was right! Oh, I'm a fool.'

'I am one, too. You haven't got to curse yourself alone. Go quickly. Quickly. Shall I expect you tomorrow at the same time?'

'Yes.'

'You will come? You won't fail?'

'No.' He gripped her hand, released it quickly, and hurried down.

On his arrival home, Luise gave him a questioning, amused look and asked: 'Did she take you into her bedroom, strip and demand that you paint her in the nude?'

He grinned and returned: 'She did – and I painted her passionately. Now rush off and assault her with your sharpest axe.'

And later that day when Hubertus, too, looked at him with enquiry, asking in an innocent, polite voice: 'How did you get on with the portrait, Edward my boy?' Rosalind, who was present, thought: Poor Hubertus. He seems almost disappointed to hear that everything went well and that Edward doesn't appear weighted with guilt at some gross misdemeanour. Perhaps if Edward had confessed to having misbehaved himself with Clara Hubertus would have felt relieved. Yes, relieved. It would have given him more than ever a fellow feeling for his dear son-in-law. Father-in-law and son-in-law adulterers alike. What more could be required to create a greater bond of sympathy between them! But that is wicked of me. I'm growing nasty and acid in my frigid old-lady way. No wonder poor Hubertus takes so long over his logic inspections. The godly and spiritual in him needs a woman's body for expression – even the body of a slatternly slave.

Edward himself thought: It is in moments like this that Cousin Hubertus seems most pathetic and lovable – at least, to me he seems so. I think I can put myself in his place. I know just how he feels now. He is as much an idiot as I am. Hell! I wonder what I shall do when I come home one afternoon and tell him I have been weak. I feel it in me such an afternoon is going to come. Soon. I may ask him to shoot me.

The rest of the sittings, however, proceeded without event. Clara, in her green dress, sat in the easy chair exactly as he had instructed her to the first day, and her behaviour was as restrained as always. She was silent most of the time, though became more inclined to conversation as the portrait entered its last stages. She talked of everyday matters. John and the shop. Sidney Bentley and his dislike of planting. 'His father is somewhat disappointed in him.' Raphael and Mary at Degries. 'I hear Mary spoils him. Treats him as if she were his mother. He nearly created a scandal with Mr Larkine's nephew. Mr Larkine was very annoyed, Margaret told me. It's a terrible pity Raphael had to turn out like that.' Of Rylands. 'I was hearing that Graeme might one day inherit the title. Can baronetcy be passed down to a nephew, Edward?' No reply from Edward. . . . 'Anyway, Father would have to die first. It would come to Father first. Can you imagine Graeme as Sir Graeme?' Of Storm and Elizabeth. 'I think they'll be happy. Cousin Wilfred hopes they'll give him a dozen grandchildren . . . ' She broke off suddenly, and Edward shouted: 'You've shifted your arm!'

:.. 'Oh, I'm sorry! Is that all right?' ... He grunted and painted on.

One day – it was the day of the sixteenth sitting – he said in the middle of a silence: 'I'm sorry you haven't any children, Clara.'

She started. Shifted her left arm. Apologised and adjusted the arm back into place. He saw that the blood had come to her face.

'I didn't mean,' he began to mumble, then grew silent without finishing his sentence, feeling his own cheeks getting warm.

After another silence, she said: 'Beauteous but barren.'

'What!' He gave her a shocked look. It was the first time he had ever heard her use such a tone of voice. He had not suspected bitterness in her. 'Clara, I'm sorry. I didn't realise ... I'm a fool. I can never say what I ought. It may happen when you least expect it.'

She laughed. No gamboge streak rose and fell. What came from her was a sound like the dried fruit of the sandbox tree exploding in the heat of the day. In his fancy he saw the flattish kernels flying in all directions.

'Have you seen a doctor?'

'Several surgeons have seen me. They can find nothing wrong with me. "It must be God's will, Mistress Hartfield." That's what they all say in the end. Don't look so glum, Edward. I'm accustomed to being barren. Do I impress you as though I'm pining to death because of the circumstance?'

He said nothing, but she did not fool him. A deep compassion moved within him. It depressed him immeasurably to know of the sufferings of anyone – especially when it was someone with whom he was well acquainted and for whom he had great fondness.

On the day of the nineteenth sitting – he had assured her that that day would see the final touches done – he lowered his palette and brush at about three o'clock and smiled slightly, taking a step back from the easel.

She sat forward, an eager look on her face. 'Is it – you've finished it, Edward?'

He nodded, and, silent, moved over to the window nearest. Half-leant, half-sat on the sill, staring dully before him.

She rose, approached and looked at the canvas. Took a swift breath.

Across the face he had smeared a large cross of green paint.

She looked at him. 'But . . . Edward, I don't . . . '

'No, you won't see it as I do. I understand. It's no good, Clara.'

'No good! But it was superb! A masterpiece! John, Sidney, Margaret – everyone I've brought in here to see it has said so. And now – now – ' She turned off with a sob.

'Nevertheless it was lifeless.' He grunted. 'That! *That!*' He took a step up to the easel, and casually slashed the canvas down with his palette knife. 'That's only a foolishly realistic representation of your face and body. It contains nothing else. Allow me to know. I've been working on it.'

'I believe you never wanted to do it. You – you've been forcing yourself to be polite. Isn't that it?'

'Stop being absurd. I never force myself to be polite to anyone. You know me well enough to know I wouldn't.' His manner softened. 'Clara, you must believe me. This isn't a mere show of temperament. I really feel this thing is a failure. Two or three sittings ago I began to feel so.' He added this in a mumble, and she gave him a quick glance.

An awkward silence came upon them.

The afternoon was overcast. They could hear the squelch of foot-treads in the mud outside. The murmur of voices – the voices of the hucksters and of people in the shop beneath them – blended with the smell of vegetables and salt meats that drifted up indefinitely to their nostrils. He became aware of another smell. Hers. The silk dress. Her hair. Without looking at her – he was staring at a knot in the floor-board on which he stood – he knew the expression on her face. A mist wreathed in his senses. He put down his palette and brush on a small table nearby, splayed out his fingers and wiped them slowly down the front of his apron. Murmured that he must be going. 'Some other time I'll try again.'

Quickly she held him and kissed him, and he kissed her back, and in the dizziness it was the swish of the silk dress that impressed itself on his awareness. The lisping swirl of its green folds made an image in his fancy so tangible, so palpable, that he wanted to grasp it. But it was her arms he grasped, smooth and firm and cool, murmuring that he must go.

'You've always been going – from me. Always – since we

279

were children. Won't you stay with me, Edward – this once?'

The smell of his paints tried to obtrude, but it failed to achieve the reality of the bare shoulder pressed against him. Of the thickish throat merging down to the half-exposed bosom. Of the smell of hair, dryish, brushing his cheek. . . . Of Cousin Hubertus asking politely how he had got on today.

He put her away gently, trembling.

She was trembling, too, but she made no attempt to touch him again.

'We've been afraid of each other since – I think since that day you stopped me with Graeme and Mathilde and asked us to pose for you. I've always been jealous of Luise, but I was afraid to let you know how I felt about you. I can never get at you, Edward. And yet I want you so much. It's something beyond me. I try to fight it down but its useless. Whenever I see you I – a kind of agony is set up in me. I know it's wrong to feel as I do. I ought to remember – '

'It's not wrong!' he snapped at her. 'Not wrong. Cousin Hubertus and I discuss such things. Passion between a man and a woman could not be evil. Human beings can and do make it evil. Human beings – Clara, I – human beings make me want to spit. Pebbles. As a boy I used to see people as pebbles I wanted to kick along the ground. People take lovely things and turn them into filth.' He softened. 'Yet there are a lot of people I like. I can't hate anyone. I want to kick people, but the next minute I'd want to kick myself for doing it, and – and I'd cry. People make me sorry for them – and then I want to snarl at them. Curse them. I must go, Clara.' He gripped her wrist. 'You're beautiful. The belle of Stabroek. They're right to call you that. I could – I could hold you . . . oh, I'm a fool. I must be going.'

'You will paint me, won't you? You'll try again?'

'Yes.' He laughed. 'Shall I tell you something? It's only when you look at me as if – as if you want me to make love to you that I can paint you in the way that would put life into the result. Yet I shudder every time you look at me like that. You're the one person I'm – you're the one danger I really fear.' He put his hands to his face. 'You're looking at me like that now. Stop it. I can't stand it. John. Luise. Cousin Hubertus.

280

I'd have to end my life if I hurt them. I don't understand myself. I'm an imbecile.'

'Why would Cousin Hubertus be hurt? He of all people!'

He snapped angrily: 'Don't speak contemptuously of him. He's the one human being I'd be miserable over if I hurt – desperately miserable. Because I know he would feel it deeply – more deeply than Luise or John. Luise might forgive me – and John. But Cousin Hubertus would be too wounded to forgive or to forget or to – to recover from the shock. You know about him and Mother, and he's afraid. . . .'

'I understand. You have no need to explain. I'm glad you've told me. I think I know you a little better now.'

The voices outside and downstairs in the shop.

'I'd never taken him into reckoning,' she murmured.

'What?'

'Nothing.' She laughed. No gamboge. 'Next time I'll try to be a better model – I promise.'

'I must be going.'

'Yes, you *must* be going.'

They both laughed.

'When will you start again?' she asked. The look on her face. The lower lip sagging. He could have held her again. The shudder moved in him.

'I don't know,' he said, avoiding her gaze.

'As soon as you can, Edward. Please.'

'Next week. Next month. Next year.' He grinned and shrugged.

'Luise is pregnant again.'

'Yes,' he said.

8

HUBERTUS complimented him on his strength. They sat alone on the portico watching the December drizzle. The mango and avocado pear trees drooped with the burden of moisture, and the smell of wet vegetation was mixed with occasional whiffs of cane-juice – there was no smell that moved Edward more than the smell of cane-juice; it brought back memories of Good Heart . . . He and Luise wandering over the plantation.

And that day in July watching the mill at work. . . . An afternoon like this soothes rather than depresses me. Cousin Hubertus, of course, likes nothing better than a rainy day. . . . Because of that evening in December, 1766, when he and Mother. . . .

'I don't know that it was strength, sir. No, it wasn't strength. It was the thought of letting you down.'

Hubertus tapped the tips of his fingers on the stem of his pipe, like a flute-player. It was a mannerism he had cultivated of late. He shook his head. 'It is strength of character, Edward my boy. I insist. I am proud of you. I feel as though it is I who fought the flesh and won. No doubt, it is because I have lost all my battles – and am still losing them – that I can feel such deep respect for you. I rate the conquests of the spirit very high, my boy, and that is because I myself am weak in spirit. Yes, I confess it. I used to confess it to your mother. She denied it, as you deny it, too. Nevertheless, I know it.' He uttered a reminiscent chuckle. 'I prefer to face the truth, as our ancestor did.'

'Which one was that?'

'Old Hendrickje. Your mother said that Hendrickje never failed to impress it upon her grandchildren. Face the truth, no matter how ugly, how terrible it might appear. This world would be a better place by far, my boy, if we would only stand up to the truth instead of evading it. You have confided in me that you once thought me a hypocrite. You were right, Edward. A hypocrite. I have always been a hypocrite.'

A gust of rainy breeze blew in upon them. Hubertus smiled. 'What a splendid afternoon! My weather. Yes, my weather. One of the things I will not do is deceive myself about myself. I know where my falsity lies, and I recognise it and when challenged am prepared to admit it.'

Edward leant forward suddenly. 'Sir, do you still believe in God?'

Hubertus took his pipe from his mouth and tilted his head back. 'That is the question I fear most, Edward, because it is a question I have often asked myself in recent days – without being able to find an answer that would seem to be in harmony with the truth of things.' He smiled and nodded lengthily. Stopped abruptly and said: 'I still hold prayers in the dining-room every morning, do I not? Yes, and my prayers are fervent, are they not? I'm sincere when I pray, Edward, but I must tell you that my conception of God has altered considerably during the past two or three years. I used to think of God as an austere Spirit whose one purpose was to punish mankind when the flesh triumphed, and scatter rewards when the spirit showed its superiority. Now . . . Well, now I am doubtful what my conception is, because I have changed in my attitude toward the flesh. Now I ask myself at what point does the flesh end and the spirit begin. Today you won a victory over the flesh – that is clear. But remember what we have said about human passion? We agreed that human passion is not necessarily evil. Then surely if we can find food in human passion – the flesh – there must be some element of the spirit contained in fleshly indulgence?'

Edward saw the sly smile amid the beard. Hubertus held up a solemn forefinger. 'You look at me with suspicion, my boy. I know what is moving in your head. You think I'm trying to explain and excuse my recent excursions to the logies. No, don't start. I thought you might have heard of them. There can be no secrets on a plantation. Rosalind knows – and Luise either knows or suspects strongly. I am not concerned with gossip, my boy. What occupies my thoughts far more is the rightness or wrongness of my deeds – the struggle within myself. It is always like that with me, Edward. So long as I myself can convince myself that I have acted in a spirit of purity, the chatter of other people affects me not in the slightest.' He uttered his chuckle again. 'You ask about God. Sometimes, my boy, I want to believe that I myself am God. Sometimes I feel that when I pray it is to myself I am praying. I control my life. I.' He rose, and Edward saw that he was agitated. His beard kept twitching slightly. His pipe had gone out. Edward heard him murmur to himself: 'Presumptuous. A presumptuous thing to say, but who knows but that it may be the truth.' He sat down, looked at Edward and said: 'Another thing I sometimes wonder, Edward. Should there really be a Supreme Being, a mighty central Intelligence somewhere in the universe, do you think He cares a jot whether we praise Him or think about Him? Does it not often strike you that we give ourselves an absurd importance? If God does exist, Edward, to Him we would be mere grains of dust. We would exist for Him as that mud out there exists for you and me. Do you and I expect homage from mud?'

Edward smiled, fascinated. 'You certainly think deeply, sir. I'd never looked at it in that way. Yes, you're right. I can see what you mean.'

Hubertus grunted. 'Yes, you can see. You have a big mind. Very few big minds exist, unfortunately, my boy. Rosalind can never see. To her God is the God she reads about in the New Testament, and there ends the matter. Now, there! Look what you have made me touch on! And we started out by discussing your strength of character. Oh, I'm pleased, Edward. I would have been disturbed if you had ventured into an intimate relationship with that young woman. Very disturbed. That mother of hers . . . So unstable.'

Edward made no comment.

'Very unstable. . . . '

Another gust of rainy breeze. . . .

Feeling the breeze, he remembered. But there was no rain in it, for March, as usual, was dry. The dams were hard, cracked in places.

'He said your mother was unstable.'

'Not me, too?'

'No, he admitted that you seemed steady. I told him you were.'

The breeze again. It smelt of fish and the bush. The sea was not far.

'Are you satisfied with this one? You won't smear it?'

'No. This is how I wanted it last year but couldn't do it.'

The flesh. . . . At what point did the flesh end . . . ?

'You look so worried, Edward.'

He nodded.

'You needn't tell Luise – or Cousin Hubertus. Why can't it be between you and me? No one need ever know.'

He said nothing, telling himself that he liked the smell of her hair – and of her flesh. Lovely flesh. So real to touch. The real and the beautiful. Surely there must be spirit here.

'I won't tell John. He'll never know from me.'

'He spoke about events – how events have a way of repeating themselves. He was so right.'

284

She laughed and rumpled his hair into greater confusion. 'You seem to be thinking more of him than of me. It's not flattering, dear.'

He said nothing, his gaze on the windowsill, but his thoughts on the move. . . . The death-urge will come later. Now I have the flesh.

'Only one thing I regret. That it wasn't when I was younger. Twenty. I looked much better than this, Edward.'

'I wasn't blind then.'

The breeze . . .

A soft bitter sound. She stirred, and the couch creaked.

'What's the matter?'

'He wasn't quite right about events,' she said, no laughter in her eyes now.

'What do you mean?'

'I mean they won't repeat themselves as – as with him and my stepmother. He forgot a very important factor.'

'What factor?'

'Don't be so dull, darling. I'm barren – that's what I mean. I won't bear you a Graeme.'

That shocked feeling moved through him. He gripped her shoulders hard. 'You mustn't speak like that, Clara. It tears at me.'

She pulled his head down so that their lips could meet.

A little later she said: 'You don't love me, but you do appreciate my body, Edward dear.'

' Every inch of it.'

'That's so easy to see. You're delicious, too.'

Again the breeze . . .

'I like to watch your hair wave in the breeze.'

'I like to rumple yours.' She rumpled it again.

Silence.

'You've left me again, Edward. You're with Cousin Hubertus.'

He winced.

'Tell him everything happened as it did yesterday. You painted me, and Friday next you'll come back to continue. Don't let him obsess you so much, Edward. Why can't it be *our* lovely secret! Why have you got to tell him – or Luise – or anyone?'

'Because I am myself, Clara. I wish I knew how to be a hypocrite.'

'Let me teach you to be one.'

He smiled.

'Aren't you going to finish the portrait?'

'I feel like finishing myself, Clara.'

'You were always so tragic. Don't be silly. You're – I believe you must be the only man in the colony who has never had any relations outside of marriage. Even strait-laced John now and then has his mulatto girl.'

'I am myself, Clara.' He shut his eyes. 'I can't escape from myself.'

'What you're trying to be is Cousin Hubertus. And look at him! Is he any saint! I don't care how you scowl. I will say it. You let him influence you too much, Edward. Sometimes I hate him.'

He was silent.

'It's absurd the way you worship him.'

'He has a big mind.'

'You have a simple mind. You're a dear, good boy. You're far more honest than he is. Too honest. You even let your honesty hurt you.'

'That's true.'

'Edward, please don't tell him. As a special favour for me. You'll hurt me if you do. Lie for my sake. Is it too much to ask?'

He shook his head. Rippled his hands across her breasts.

'You don't lie, I know. But this is the first time when you must. Luise is pregnant. It might endanger her life is she were very upset.'

He winced.

'It might bring on premature labour. I've heard of such cases.'

Silence.

'Say yes. Say you'll keep this to yourself.'

He nodded. 'You're right. I shall have to say nothing. I shall have to be a hypocrite. Take on another personality.'

'You'll come again on Friday to continue the portrait?'

He nodded.

'And to make love to me again like this?'

The breeze. . . . More chilly now than pleasantly cool.

'Edward?'

He kissed her throat and grunted in assent.

It was a longer silence than any of the others.

'Edward?'

'Yes?'

'It must be nearly four. We must get dressed, dear.'

He gripped her shoulders. 'Tell me. Did you say – you said John – is it true? About his having mulatto girls?'

'One.' She laughed. 'I don't mind. Poor fellow. He's so good to me in his plodding way. Her name is Lizzie. She sells plantains and yams on the Brickdam. You can see her any time you pass there. Rather pretty. Her little daughter is generally with her. Old Mr Darke's child. He supports it, I've heard.'

'And John goes to her?'

'Off and on during the past year or two. I believe he keeps her. Sidney says he once approached her, but she rebuffed him.' She laughed again. 'She's very faithful to John.'

'You really don't mind his going to her?'

'No.'

'And he's never guilty because of his – of his infidelity?'

'Not so that one could notice – no, Edward.'

'Does he sleep with you still?'

'Twice a week regularly.' She fondled his neck. 'Does that make you feel better?'

He said nothing. Rose and began to dress. And she, too, got up.

9

FOUR sittings later – a fortnight had elapsed – she told him: 'It's because you've never been a hypocrite that you can succeed so well at being one.' And he returned. 'Yet the role is bringing me no happiness, Clara – and sometimes I wonder if Luise is really fooled.'

Luise, however, suspected nothing. At any other time she might have, but her day of confinement was near. Indeed, on one occasion she had said to herself: Edward seems more agitated and abstracted than usual. He's probably catching some of my mood.

And another day: 'Your mind isn't with me, Edward.'

He started and frowned: 'Why should it perpetually be with you? It may be with Clara, for all we know.'

'How is the portrait getting on?'

'As it should. I'm tired of talking about that portrait. Tell me. Are you feeling well? You feel you'll get through the confinement safely?'

'Yes, I'm perfectly fit – but I keep thinking of it every minute of the day. It was the same with the others. It's very tiresome waiting.'

And to herself she thought: I see what it is. He's concerned over my condition. In his morbid fashion he always anticipates the worst instead of the best.

As though to confirm it, he rose – they were in their bedroom – and said: 'I wish it were over and done with myself. I can hardly sleep well at night now wondering what moment your pains will set in.'

She laughed softly, and he thought: What a difference, her way of laughing. No gamboge streak rising and falling. Hers is like a soft bluish cloud of morning mist melting amidst the cane-tops. Or wood-smoke rising slowly in the distance.

'Would you be relieved if I died? You could marry Mrs Houde.'

'If you died I'd be dead an hour later.'

'Would you really commit suicide, Edward?'

He said nothing, standing at a window, staring out.

She grunted. 'I believe you would be as foolish. Poor dear heart. You still do love me a little bit, then?'

He turned and gave a self-conscious grin, and she saw that his eyes were moist. 'What nonsense is this about Mrs Houde?' he asked – to cover up his emotion.

'The French widow on La Belle across the river. Now, don't pretend, Edward. She's madly in love with you. Everyone knows that. She makes it obvious enough, too, I'm sure.'

'Giggling idiot. Her brother has commissioned me to build him a cottage for his Head Carpenter. A new man expected from Martinique.'

'Yes, I heard Father talking about it. A new man with a wife and two children. I hear he's some poor relative of the Poussin and knows as much about carpentry as I do – but, of course, they have to help him out. He's not in good circumstances in Martinique.'

He approached and began to stroke her cheek. 'You do pick up a lot of gossip, don't you? We're having too many visitors nowadays – at least, for my liking.'

'I know. You'd prefer to be in this room with me from day to day and never see another mortal – except dear big-brained Cousin Hubertus, my estimable father.' She frowned suddenly. 'That reminds me. I heard him remarking to Mother yesterday that you've been avoiding him of late. He almost sounded hurt. Have you had a quarrel with him?'

'No I haven't been in the mood for philosophical discussion – that's why I've been avoiding him.' He grinned, kissing the top of her head. 'If you think I'm such a devoted follower of his that ought to prove to you I can be quite unfaithful when I want.'

It caused him anguish to say this, and he was glad that she could not see his face. He went on quickly: 'The truth is I'm planning that cottage for Emile Poussin, and you know I like to be alone when I'm doing that.'

'Yes. I know. I'm only teasing you.' She looked up, and he saw the old mischievous twinkle. 'And there's the portrait, too. When do you hope to complete that, Edward?'

'In another two sittings, I hope.' He glanced away, and mumbled: 'It will be a relief, too. I want to give all my time to the cottage.'

'Are you satisfied with this one? You won't smear it and rip it across as you did the last?'

He shook his head. 'No, it's turned out well. I've caught what I wanted to catch this time.'

'And what is that?'

He hesitated, then said: 'Her fleshly self – and the colour of her laughter.'

'The gamboge laugh. What a silly fanciful darling you are!'

Four days later, Clara agreed with him. 'It is different from the other one, and you have put something – something living into it. It's going to be my most precious possession, Edward.'

'I'm glad,' he murmured.

She pressed herself against him. 'You haven't grown up.

You're still the same, Edward – remote, sensitive, naïve, half-shy. Oh, my darling, I'm glad you've finished and yet desperately sorry. Edward, can't you come and see me sometimes – alone like this, I mean?'

'No.'

'I can't believe that today is going to be the last. I knew you wouldn't want to come after you'd finished the picture, but I've kept hoping you . . . ' She put her hands to her face.

He caressed her arm, but was silent.

Outside there was weak sunshine, and the dams were muddy. Rain had fallen during the morning. They could hear the hucksters' voices – some in English, some in Dutch. The smell of salt beef and vegetables came up to them as they sat side by side on the couch, half-dressed. He thought: A smell I shall never forget. To me it will be like rain to Cousin Hubertus. Out of the corner of his eye he watched her, trying to impress the picture on his mind. The fingers of her hands splayed out on her cheeks, the eyes sad, moist, the gold-brown hair slightly in disarray. Pity there was no breeze to make the loose strands wave. The thickish throat merging down . . . pale brown areolae on full, half-drooping breasts. The mauve silk dress. . . . He glanced at the canvas. . . . Yes, mauve had been just right. . . . I'm pleased with that portrait. Satisfied. It is one of the best I have done. . . .

'It's getting late, Clara.'

'Yes.'

Neither of them moved. . . . Beneath them they heard heavy, thumping sounds as of some piece of machinery being moved. John busy with his customers. . . .

'I'll remember this,' he murmured.

'You will?'

He nodded. 'Cousin Hubertus is right. It's not easy to tell where the flesh ends and the spirit begins. These afternoons with you have been beautiful. It wasn't simply lust. There was the beauty of the spirit in them.'

'You say things so prettily, Edward. You should have written poetry.'

'I do – in my mind.'

After a silence: 'Isn't Edward House vacant now?'

He gave her a glance of surprise. 'Yes,' he said. 'Mr Granger

290

has built himself a house. Why do you ask?'

'I was wondering – I thought it would have been so nice if you were living there. I could have seen more of you – not to be as we are now necessarily, though that would have been lovely. Seeing you, even with Luise, would have made me happy.'

He grunted. 'Luise has often suggested that we should live at Edward House. She thinks it would be more convenient for my building commissions. People could reach me more easily here at Stabroek.'

'Then why don't you come?' She laughed. 'Don't trouble to answer. I should have to be incredibly dense not to know why.'

He grinned and shifted about. 'Yes, I am very attached to the old fellow. I'd miss him a great deal if we left *Huis Kaywana*. He would miss me, too – possibly even more than I'd miss him. I am the only one who understands him, Clara.'

'I know. And he's such a big brain. Say it all.'

He nodded, and rising, finished dressing. Before he left he said: 'I'll come in one day next week to see about a good frame.'

That same night Luise gave birth to a son, and in the afternoon the note that John wrote to Edward congratulating him mentioned the portrait. 'Clara says you told her you consider it the best portrait you have ever done, and I am in complete agreement. It is beautiful, and we shall both treasure it, and are very grateful to you. You are foolish not to want to accept a fee. I would pay five hundred guilders cheerfully. Instead, however, I am sending this sum as a gift for your new son.'

The gift depressed Edward, for it increased his guilt. Nevertheless, a few days later when he went to Stabroek to arrange for the framing of the picture he called at the shop to thank John. It was the last visit he made to Stabroek for several weeks, for the Poussin cottage compelled his being on the West Bank for long periods. Luise teased him about Mrs Houde, the widowed sister of Emile Poussin who certainly did not make it a secret that she was greatly attracted to him. She embarrassed him on several occasions during his stay on the Poussin plantation, and Emile and his wife laughed at him and asked if he was a woman-hater. They were a very free-and-easy couple, and Emile, to Edward's consternation, fondled the female slave girls even in the presence of Denise, his wife – and Roxane, his sister. 'See what a very wicked man he is!' Denise would cry, laughing. And Roxane would giggle and look at Edward almost as much as to say: 'Pity you won't try doing it to me, too, you silent, handsome man!' He enjoyed staying with the Poussins, and when the cottage had been built he readily accepted their invitation to the house-warming. Hubertus and Rosalind and Luise were present, as were several people from the East Bank.

Edward, at table, found himself between Sidney Bentley and Margaret McGarret, a good friend of Clara's, and, to Edward's embarrassment, both Sidney and Margaret insisted on talking about the portrait. They were both agreed that it was a masterpiece. 'It's the sort of thing that should be handed down in the family as a valued heirloom,' said Sidney. 'What a pity poor old John hasn't had any children yet!'

Margaret, a very thin, but pretty girl, of about twenty-five, suddenly looked wise, and said: 'Clara may yet give us a surprise, Sidney.'

Sidney shook his head. 'I think she's given up hope, poor dear.'

Margaret grunted. 'Shall I whisper something to you two – and it's a strict secret! The miracle has happened.'

Edward felt a cold rag beginning to encircle his heart, but his new role of hypocrite had taught him to conceal his emotions. 'What miracle?' he asked in his old naïve voice.

'She's going to have a baby,' whispered Margaret. 'Why do you think she hasn't come to this house-warming?' She patted her stomach. 'For the past week or two she has been suffering from nausea and dizziness. Poor old John is so fussy and excited about it he hardly wants her to cross the room.'

'That's splendid news,' said Sidney. 'By God! If it's a son John will give such a banquet of celebration he'll bring down the whole house.'

Within Edward there was a buzzing as of a nest of desperate bees. He sat very still, but there was nothing strained and unnatural in his voice as he murmured: 'I shall be glad for them both.'

All the way home, on the yacht, he kept telling himself: 'But she's barren. It cannot be true.' It was like a refrain that had entered him by enchantment. He began to feel afraid that he would never be able to stop it from running through his mind. It would go on haunting him day after day, week after week until he went out of his mind. . . . 'But she's barren. . . .'

Even the conversation Hubertus tried to make did not make any difference. . . . 'A very neatly planned little cottage, my boy. Your building work is no less talented than your painting of portraits. . . .'

'. . . it cannot be true.'

'They are very good cooks, those Poussins. I understand they supervise their slaves personally in the kitchen.'

'Mrs Houde is the genius,' smiled Rosalind. 'Wouldn't you like to hire her as a housekeeper, Hubertus my dear?'

'I'm sure Edward wouldn't mind,' laughed Luise, adding: 'I'd dig her eyes out before a week has passed – the brazen hussy! Did you see how she kept ogling him when we were in the gallery?'

'I noticed,' said Rosalind, with her acid smile. 'And Edward, quite properly, ignored her. I do wish all men were as proper as our Edward.'

Hubertus, pretending not to hear, smiled at Edward: 'The ladies all become enamoured of you, my boy, though you never lift a finger to attract them. I believe it is your perpetual scowl they must find captivating.'

'. . . but she's barren. . . .'

'No, it's his silence,' said Luise, taking hold of his hand and placing it possessively in her lap. 'The more he sulks and frowns and refuses to reply to their murmured overtures the more it encourages them to persist.'

'He's giving us a good illustration of his silence now,' tittered Rosalind. 'Edward, is there anything dark weighing on your mind?'

Edward fidgeted and grinned. Said nothing.

On the roof of the tent-boat the rain spattered loudly. Rain of early June. The oarsmen sang as they rowed – a low, rather weird African song. A song Edward had heard when a spectator at their *cumfa* dances.

The following morning through a dismal drizzle he set out for Stabroek, arriving at about eleven. The sun was shining by then through a mass of shifty cumulus. The dams were pocked with many a foot-print, but the hucksters sat bravely through the weather and the slush, their heads covered with canvas strips against the drizzle that continued despite the weak sunshine.

Edward made his way to the Brickdam, and had not proceeded thirty yards when he saw Lizzie and her daughter. Lizzie was olive but her daughter could have passed for white. Two baskets of yams and plantains and eddoes were getting low, and even as Edward paused a slave selected half-a-dozen eddoes and a few plantains, put them into his sack, paid for them and departed. Lizzie gave Edward a look of amazement, as did the nearby huckster, a thin fellow with a battered hat on his head. White people did not buy from the hucksters who sat by the dams; white people sent their slaves to buy.

Edward, ignoring the stares, bent and asked: 'Is your name Lizzie?' – his voice low enough to be unheard by the man with the battered hat.

Lizzie did not rise. She smiled, and in her eyes came a light of coquetry. The amazement had gone. Now she knew that Edward had not come to her as a customer. The thin fellow, too, seemed to get this impression, and was smiling to himself, Edward noted out of the corner of an eye.

'Yes, I'm Lizzie,' said Lizzie. 'Lizzie Benjamin. You is Mr Edward van Groenwegel, na so?'

'Yes.' He tried to frown, telling himself that it was a little tiresome the way no female could look at him without that vaguely suggestive gleam; in many it was not vague at all but very obvious. 'There are one or two questions I want to ask you, Lizzie.'

She waited, smiling still. He admired her independent spirit; nothing of the slave in her. The consciousness of her white blood was strong in her.

'You are friendly with Mr Hartfield, aren't you?'

'Yes, Mr Van Groenwegel. Two years now. You good friends wid him, I hear him say. He like you plenty.'

'Thanks.' He shifted his feet about. Hesitated, undecided how to go on. And during this pause Lizzie said: 'I know what you want to ask. You want me to sleep wid you one night, na so? Plenty white gentlemen ask me, but I only for Mr Hartfield. I don't tek other men.'

Edward flushed. 'You're wrong, Lizzie. I haven't come to

ask you to sleep with me. It's something else.'

She giggled – a deep, throaty, fascinating sound. 'You not let me finish talk, Mr Van. I say I don't tek other men dan Mr Hartfield – but you different. If you want me one night I will tek you. I see you plenty time passing here and I like you. You and Mr John only men I could sleep wid.'

'I see. Anyway, Lizzie, tell me this. You say you've been sleeping with Mr John for two years? Regularly?'

'Yes, he come to my logie on North Canal two times a week – one time some weeks. He's a nice man, Mr John. He say one day he might tek my lil' Kate to live wid him as his daughter, but I tell him old man Darke say he want her for hisself. Soon as Mrs Darke dead old man Darke want to tek her to live at de big house. She his child, and he like her.'

'How long have you been free, Lizzie?'

'Four years, Mr Van. Massa Darke proper like me. Only Mrs Darke, she hate me. But she dead soon. She got cancer.' She tapped a full left breast bulging under the calico frock. 'In here. Big cancer. Whole bubby sick. She stink up the whole house.'

Edward winced. 'Just so. But tell me, Lizzie. I'm going to be very personal – and intimate. What do you use to prevent yourself having a child for Mr John? Do you use gulley root?'

'Me? No, no, Mr Van. Nothing like dat. I don't use nothing at all. I glad if I get child for Mr John. I tell Mr John so plenty time.'

'You use nothing at all? Not even ochra?'

'Nothing.'

'Then why haven't you had a child yet for Mr John?'

She shrugged. 'I don't know why, Mr Van. God not will it yet.'

'But you had a child by Mr Darke, your old massa. This little thing here is yours and Mr Darke's, isn't she? You said so.'

'Yes, Mr Van. Mr Darke's child. She can pass for white. My father white, too. Kate got three part white, only one part nigger. She going to be big lady when she grow up.'

'I have no doubt. But, Lizzie, I – you're certain you've told me right? You use nothing to prevent yourself having a child – as – as other women do?' He gulped and added. 'And you've been friendly with Mr John two years?'

'Yes, dat true. I not use not *one* thing but still I not get child. In God's good time it will happen.' She giggled. 'You want come to see me tonight, Mr Van? My logie paint green on North Canal – '

'No, Lizzie. No. Thanks, all the same. I – ' He broke off and laughed. A dry, hacking laugh. 'Only I can see the humour in that, Lizzie.' He put his hand into his pocket and brought out two guilders. 'These are for Kate, Lizzie. Save them up for her. They'll help her to become a big lady.'

'Thank you, Mr Van. But you must come and see me whenever you want. You and Mr John only men I can sleep wid.'

He had already moved off. Within him the buzzing sounded again. The desperate bees preparing more bitter honey for him. . . . The last doubt had gone. Clara was not barren; the fault was with John. And now Clara was pregnant. . . . 'Events have such a way of repeating themselves. . . . I felt afraid – afraid that one day in the far future she might be a threat. . . . '

On the *stelling* it was not the yacht he stared at but at the brown, muddy water. . . .

'Massa Edward, you ready to start home?'

Edward started. 'Yes, Josiah. Quite ready.'

What moved him most of all was the startled look on her face. It reminded him of the occasions when he used to pinch and kick her. Every sentence he uttered might have been another pinch or kick. Frequently he would lean forward and touch her wrist to reassure her that he did not really mean to be cruel. He much preferred fondling her to pincing or kicking her.

Rosalind happened to come out on to the portico, and he glanced up quickly and said: 'Cousin Rosalind, would you please find Cousin Hubertus and come back here with him in a few minutes?'

His mother-in-law seemed to know immediately that something serious was afoot. Her gaze flicked sharply from him to Luise, then she nodded. 'I shall look for him, Edward,' she said, and returned into the house.

'I've been a beast, Luise – not telling you, I mean. That has burned me up more than anything else. I can't stand being a hypocrite, but I felt I couldn't tell you. I was too much of a coward. And now – now I only want to drown myself. John is such a fine fellow – and – and I've done this to him. And you – I've deceived you. That is worse, worse – '

'Edward, control yourself.' There was nothing hysterical in her voice. Nothing accusing. 'What I want to know is this. Did you tell this girl Lizzie not to mention to John that you had questioned her?'

He stared. 'Did I tell her – what do you mean? Why, no. Do you think I should have? Do you think she will . . . ' He broke off, and the buzzing began inside him. He rose. Sat down again.

Luise smiled, leaned toward him and patted his cheek. 'What Clara said was right. You haven't grown up, Edward darling. You're still my sweet green boy with the remote look. And you're still as blundering and unthinking. Stop feeling you must drown yourself because of what has happened. Let me feel that way.' She laughed. 'And yet I don't. I love you more than ever. I couldn't stop loving you if you were to betray me with all the women in Stabroek. And I know you don't love Clara, so why should I be angry with you?' She paused, that slightly mysterious look on her face; it had always fascinated him. She glanced at him and smiled. 'Yet I'm not a fool, Edward, I know danger when I see it.' She spoke calmly, almost with calculation, her eyes slightly narrowed. The richness of her personality swamped him, so that he was afraid to ask what she meant. She sat there looking reflective, mature, lovable yet somehow untouchable; it would be an act of profanity, he felt, to touch her now.

'I won't make the mistake Mother made,' she murmured.

He still could say nothing.

After a silence they heard the footsteps of her parents. Rosalind and Hubertus appeared, Hubertus tense and with an anxious light in his eyes. It was obvious Rosalind must have told him something that had alarmed him.

'My children,' he said, his hands clasped together as he clasped them at morning prayers, 'what is the trouble? What has happened to upset you?'

Edward evaded his gaze, frowning out at the weak sunshine. The drizzle had stopped. The earth was damp and steamy, and the wet, leafy smell of rainy weather saturated the air. There was no breeze, and at any instant the drizzle would commence again.

Nothing was said by any of them for a long interval. Then Luise looked at her father and began to speak. Very calmly. With maturity. With such confidence that Edward thought: She might have planned this carefully a long time ago. Years ago.

Hubertus made no attempt to interrupt. He was like a man hearing sentence passed on him. He seemed to grow more and more haggard as the words issued from Luise.

PART SEVEN

1

THE whole length of the house he would walk – and then the whole breadth. From empty room to empty room.

Sometimes he would pause in a room and stand at a window. Watch the trees – the sandboxes from the northern side, or the fruit-trees from the southern. And let his mind throw lassos back toward the Essequibo. Or nearer. Good Heart, Rylands.

Eventually he would chide himself for being idle and boyish. There was work to be done. The affairs of the plantation must be seen after. Inspections had to be made. Records written up. Consultations held with Groud and the new young assistant Barker. A slave sale in Stabroek to attend. . . .

Yet I have a right to be on my guard, for no matter how occupied I keep myself I can perceive loneliness – not mere solitude, but loneliness – tracking me down.

Still, the past would not be denied. The southernmost room of the three in the south wing drew him most often. Several times he had wondered whether he should not send the furniture to their new house on their new plantation on the East Coast – New Good Heart. . . . He had always decided against . . . Let it remain here to haunt me deliciously. Let the easel and the rubbish, too, in the adjoining room remain as it is. Some hauntings carry delight . . . My talented Edward – talented but ingenuous. My capable, beautiful Luise. . . . 'It may not happen, Father. He may not see her again. But Stabroek is near – much nearer than Good Heart was to Rylands. That's why I feel we must leave. We can get a concession on the East Coast, and Edward, I'm certain, will make as good a planter as he is a painter and house builder. . . . ' That speech on the portico had been a fine one. He had been proud of her – even while he had known she was condemning him to misery and solitude. Her decision had been wise. From all reports, Edward had made a good planter. They were prospering. If only he would have visited them more often, but canal transportation was difficult and involved.

The northernmost of the three rooms in the north wing was the one he dreaded most – yet he visited it twice a day: in the morning after coffee and in the evening after dinner.... 'You're certainly very good at doing your duty, Hubertus. No, I need nothing, thanks.... No, I feel no weaker than I did yesterday. ... I'm sure I'm keeping you from one of your tempting morsels. Does she keep her logie clean?' And the acid titter sharpened by illness.... 'Oh it won't be long now. At any minute of the day or night you may be free of me. Such a relief for you, my dear.... Did you remember me in your earnest prayers this morning, Hubertus? Please don't forget me, for I'm sure that God must pay most close attention to every word you utter, you sweet pious soul!' ... A rustle of the bed clothes and the tittering.... 'Shut the door carefully, and tell Sarah to come to me. Quite an attractive girl, isn't she? How superfluous of me to mention it – to you!'

Later in the evening came a much more pleasant visit. Fine or rainy, he made his way to the little cottage he had had built on the river front for Overgaar. Old like himself, Overgaar lived in retirement with his Indian housekeeper – who had once been his mistress.... Though, unlike me, poor fellow, his vigour has failed, and his liver gives him trouble.... One of the few people who have been very patient with me. He didn't mind my being a hypocrite.

Overgaar could always give him news of people and events up or down the river. The slaves loved him, and brought him eggs and vegetables – and gossip.

He was with Overgaar on this evening in July, 1794, when Jacob came up the steps and asked if he could come in. Jacob had brought news – but not gossip for Overgaar. This was a message for Hubertus from Rylands. 'Massa Clackson sent to say Missy Faustina dead early this morning, Massa.'

On the way to the house, Hubertus kept glancing at the sky. The sky was cloudless and star-dotted. In the west a few saffron wisps of cloud lingered where the sun had gone down an hour ago.... It's all wrong. There should be rain this evening. Why isn't there rain, my beloved! ... He stopped and watched the candle-flies. There were no fire-flies on the coast. Only these small pale specks of light, leisurely in flight. He listened, but no hoo-yoo cry came. Goat-suckers, too, were rare.... Men have defeated the jungle here. If only there could be some rain.... 'You are very wet. You must have been a long time in the rain. . . . ' The drops coming down. On their heads. On their shoulders. . . . 'I would grow old feeling that God had cheated me of the best and most treasured thing I needed. Only once, Hubertus. Here – under this tree. . . . We'll never rest if we don't, Hubertus. We'll grow old itching and in pain. We'll . . .' No soppy carpet of leaves here, my beloved. . . . This is the coast, and the year is 1794. The West India Company is dead. It died three years ago, and now we are a state-owned colony. This is Plantation Kaywana – not Good Heart. Borsselen is jungle. One day we shall wander there – when death has come for me, too.

If only there could be a soft drizzle.

2

YET when there should have been bright sunshine it was raining. Steadily and heavily it rained from a grey sky on the day in April, the following year, when Sarah's voice arrested him. He was walking along the path that led from the factory to the Head Carpenter's cottage.

'Massa! Massa Hubertus!'

It was from the direction of the factory she came. She must have gone there to look for him. She was out of breath when she caught up with him, her calico smock soaking wet, stuck to her skin.

'Massa, I come from the house! Missy – Missy Rosalind – her head – it fall back and she's not breathing. Come and see, Massa. I think she dead.'

On this rainy day in April. She who had loved the bright, clear weather of human relations. She who had rigidly turned away from all that seemed cloudy and sin-shaded. . . . Pulling down the eye-lids, he murmured: 'My dear, you were of the sunshine. Pure and upright. The shade of trees and the drip of rain were not made for you, Rosalind.'

It rained the following afternoon when they lowered her into her grave. The young cabbage-palms that lined the plantation cemetery seemed to Hubertus fitting witnesses to the ceremony. . . . Straight and upright, smooth-trunked, full of dignity, these cabbage-palms would understand such a nature as hers.

'Your mother and I, my boy,' he told Edward, who, with Luise, had barely arrived in time for the funeral, 'are company for sandboxes.' He sighed. 'It's good to see you two. Do you still paint, Edward, or have you given it up?'

'No, I haven't given it up, Cousin Hubertus.' The sensitive frown was still there. And the slightly worried glint. 'I do mostly landscape scenes now – when I can find the time, of course.'

'We have twenty-six fields planted, Father,' said Luise. Still the slim, shapely Luise with the mischievous, dare-devil twinkle. . . . That morning by the water-tanks at Good Heart. Half-naked and carrying two muskets. . . . Probably saved my life, too.

'Twenty-six fields. Excellent, my girl. Excellent. I cannot see Edward as a planter, nevertheless. Simply cannot see – ah, John my boy! Clara! Thank you. Thank you for your sympathy. She was a good woman, my Rosalind. I don't have to be told that, young man. I'm only too aware of how inadequate a husband I have been. And how is that fine son of yours?'

'Doing splendidly, thank you, sir,' John smiled, a look of pleasure on his square, pink face with its faintly tired expression. There could be no doubt, Hubertus thought. He believed it was his son. Lizzie had either held her tongue about that conversation with Edward or what she had told him had failed to rouse any suspicions. More likely she had held her tongue. Women were all alike, white, mulatto or black. They knew when not to talk, especially when men were involved.

Edward had grown silent, but Clara and Luise were chatting amiably.

'What did you name him, John? My memory is getting very bad. Was it Hilary or Henry? You did mention it – '

'Harvey,' said John. 'After my father. I think he resembles Father a great deal. The same brow, and he has the same quiet manner.'

'Undoubtedly, my boy. Undoubtedly.' To himself: Edward's brow. And Edward was a quiet, aloof little fellow, but John wouldn't know that. He didn't grow up with Edward as Clara did. I believe Clara is happy that it has turned out like this. The mother of Edward's child.

A great pity Cranley could not have been here. Too long a trip in too short a time. In this hot climate the human body must be put underground within twenty-four hours of death. Just as well, he supposed. A corpse was no pleasant thing to keep around the house – especially the corpse of one well beloved. . . . They would think me a crank if I told them, but I should have preferred not to have seen Rosalind in death. I would have been content if her corpse had been quietly smuggled away and buried before I could set gaze upon it. . . . I am so happy that I was unable to make the trip to Rylands to see my other beloved in death. I remember her only as the living Faustina. . . .

He started.

It was Mary who had touched him on the shoulder. She had not kept as well as Luise. Her face was lined, and she was prematurely grey. Beside her stood her son, thick-set, powerful lad of seventeen. . . . Not unlike what I looked at his age. Yes, I do believe he has taken after me in physique.

Mary's eyes were very red, her whole mien one of complete misery. It was probably no conventional pose. She had been very attached to her mother. And like her mother, self-righteous, rigid in morals.

'You're going to be very lonely here, Father,' she murmured.

'Me? Lonely, Mary? No. Oh, no, my child. Too many pleasant memories to live on. The past should always be a rich storehouse, Mary, from which, in our senility, we should draw sustenance.'

He heard the sniff she gave, though he knew she tried to disguise it. A sniff of reproach. 'You must know better, of course,' she mumbled. Poor creature. An old lady at forty-three.

Raphael suddenly came striding across to join her, tall, handsome, bewigged, dressed as though for a function in honour of some visiting potentate. There was grace in his every movement, and his smile was certainly charming. Not gushingly so, but just correct for the occasion. 'I know you are a philosopher, Cousin Hubertus,' he said, his voice soft, cultivated, 'and you won't let this upset you too much. I've always admired your courage, and I'm sure you'll successfully recover from the shock

305

of this terrible bereavement.' He exuded a distinct perfume – like a woman. Such a pity about his effeminacy. He lacked sincerity, but he had charm – oh, give him credit there. He had a manner that many of these crude specimens just coming to the colony could imitate. He was well-bred, Raphael – a gentleman – and more English than Dutch. He would prosper.

Two weeks later, a letter came from Berbice in the course of which Wilfred wrote that he knew how devoted Hubertus had been to his sister. 'I have never condemned you for that other friendship, Hubert. Faustina was a splendid woman, and any man could well have been tempted to become involved with her. I respect her memory as much as you must.' Later in the letter Wilfred said: 'We are very happy here, and prospering beyond expectations. And make no mistake, my friend, your old Wilfred has realised his wish. He is the grandfather of two of the loveliest grandchildren imaginable. Graham, the elder, actually resembles me – no exaggeration. Everyone confirms this the moment they set eyes upon him. And Hermine has a slight look of Luise – you know what I mean by that; a wicked, mischievous, recalcitrant child, most uncertain in disposition, but delightful beyond belief. At this moment we are expecting the third which may arrive even before you read this. Both Elizabeth and Storm are in the best of health. They are very popular in our community here, and frequently attend Governor van Batenburg's lavish and distinguished salons at Government House. I fear I am not sophisticated enough for these very fashionable functions, but the young people must have their amusement and I never raise any objections. . . . John is twenty this year, and I am seriously considering sending him to England to take up studies as a doctor of medicine. . . . '

A satisfying letter. . . . The first time Wilfred has ever mentioned what he felt about Faustina. I have often wondered. A big heart, Wilfred. No self-righteousness there. No priggish morality.

It was only a few days after receiving this letter that Groud came to him with an exciting story. Had he heard the latest developments in the war in Europe? No? 'Well, Mynheer, the French have overrun the Netherlands. Holland is no more. The king has fled to England, and the French have declared Holland a republic – the Batavian Republic.'

'They would do such a thing, Groud. Remember what happened in '89 in France. Everything now is modelled on *liberté, egalité, fraternité*. A republic, indeed! But why should I worry, Groud. I'm getting old –'

'But you haven't heard all yet, Mynheer. It appears that the Stadtholder wrote a letter to this colony in February commanding us to admit the armed forces of the English king –'

'But aren't the English already our allies?'

'Yes, yes, that is so, Mynheer, but the position is this: The new Batavian Republic claims to be the true government of Holland, and Their High Mightinesses the States-General sent another letter saying that we must now consider ourselves the friends of France – and this letter reached here a few days ago, *before* the one sent by the Stadtholder. Governor van Grovestins issued orders that only French and Dutch ships should be admitted. But what happens, Mynheer! Yesterday an English frigate called the *Zebra* came bringing the letter from the Stadtholder written in February – the letter written in England by authority of the Prince of Orange! You see the problem that faces us now, Mynheer!' Groud clapped his hands together in his excitement. He was a tall, thin, sallow-faced fellow with hardly any hair on his head, and a long, thin nose that matched his torso. 'You see the dilemma that has come upon us! To whom must we be loyal now? The Prince of Orange, a fugitive in England, or the new Batavian Republic? Oh, we're about to see some interesting events, Mynheer, take my word for it! I hear Governor van Grovestins is preparing to leave the colony for Martinique.'

Hubertus smiled. Groud reminded him of Overgaar as a younger man. So excitable, and so prone to derive pleasure out of crises and troublous events. Yes, Groud and Overgaar were very similar in temperament.

'My dear Groud,' said Hubertus, 'political affairs do not disturb me. I'm past the age when wars and disturbances can mean anything. So long as I am left in peace to finish my years on this plantation, it matters not to me who is in power in this colony. I'm sixty-eight this year. The squabbles of nations no longer interest me.'

All the same, he encouraged Groud to bring him news of

what was happening. It provided diversion, helped to keep loneliness well behind him.

Indeed, in some respects, he enjoyed the next two or three years. He and Groud would meet most evenings in Overgaar's cottage to discuss events. While he and Overgaar remained seated with their pipes, Groud would pace about, wave his arms and shout and laugh.

'Yes, we are a republic now!' shouted Groud one evening early in May, that same year, 1795. 'Our noble citizens declare that they consider the former government overthrown because of the departure of the Governor, and now the Council of Policy has taken full control. Yes, Mynheer! And believe me, we have not one president but *two*! Plettner and De Mellet have both been elected presidents, and when they have served their term Hall and Meertens will be the next two. . . .'

And in July: 'Now, happily, gentlemen, all has been peacefully and satisfactorily settled. Our republic is no more. The Batavian government has had its way, and our new Governor is to be one Mynheer Antony Beaujon.'

'My good friend Mr Bentley won't like that,' smiled Hubertus. 'He was hoping that the Orange Party would have won the day.'

'The English gentlemen are furious, Mynheer. They are ready to explode if only pricked by a pin. Especially so because the Republic refused the offer of the British forces who came some weeks ago and tried to "protect" us. Remember? The English gentlemen feel the government should have permitted the English squadron to land and take charge of affairs. They all shake their heads and say: "What a pity the squadron was not ordered to use force but merely to make friendly overtures!" Oh, they are very grieved, the poor English gentlemen. . . .'

And on the evening of the twentieth of April, the following year, 1796: 'Now the English gentlemen have no need to be grieved, Mynheer. The colony is theirs again. There are ten English ships of war in the river there now, and Governor Beaujon and the Council are pretending to hold a meeting to decide what action should be taken. Haw, haw! As if they can do anything else but surrender! England is at war with the Batavian government, and since we are on the side of the Batavian government – well, the English have a right to come and capture us. And so they have!'

'Never mind, Groud,' murmured Hubertus. 'One day we shall settle down finally to being either Dutch or English – and I have a deep premonition that it will be English. We Dutch are too easy-going. The English are a fighting people – great gentlemen when at peace, but very thorough in their aggressiveness at the first note of the battle-trumpet, which, I feel, is just as it should be. When it is time to fight, fight with all your might, say I.' He nodded and added: 'Half-measures and complacency never won anything in this world.'

One afternoon, a year later, Hubertus told Bentley, who had come on one of his rare visits, for gout and maladies of various kinds made it difficult for him to move from his home: 'I'm beginning to feel, Bentley, that in my old age I have gone over entirely to the side of your English.'

Bentley nodded and returned: 'You have always been on our side, Van Groenwegel, I have sensed it before – years and years before.'

'Yet do not get a wrong impression, Bentley. I still feel, as I have said many times, that this principle of patriotic loyalty is absurd. Look at the number of changes we here have suffered since 1781. From Dutch to English then to French then back to Dutch. Now English again. What do nations matter, Bentley! Why can't we be loyal to each other as members of the human species! I suppose I am an old crank, but that is the way I see it. To me every king is a ridiculous fool who ought long ago to have been dethroned. Our ancestors did not know better, but we claim to be enlightened, rational men of the eighteenth century.'

Bentley, accustomed to his unorthodox views, merely chuckled. 'Yes, yes. There may be something in what you say, Van Groenwegel, but alas – we have not yet come to that day. I doubt whether we English will ever feel differently about our kings. We shall never see a king as a figure of absurdity.' He sighed and changed the subject. 'Anyway, you must admit that our people have done quite a lot for this colony – and are still doing. Just take a look at what has happened in the past year alone. We have a post-office – and a newspaper.' He reached down beside his chair and brought up the two sheets that lay on the floor. '*The Royal Essequibo and Demerary Gazette.* Not, I suppose, anything we would care to compare with *The Tatler* of London, but it is a beginning. Yes, certainly it is a beginning.'

'I agree. We are progressing very rapidly under English management. What pleases me particularly as a planter is the great improvement that has taken place in the slave trade. It's flourishing now as it has never done before, Bentley.'

'Exactly. And all due to English enterprise. Those two new firms in Stabroek are doing a splendid business. MacInroy, Sandbach and what's the other? Pitman, Ashley. That's it. Hardly an issue of the *Gazette* that doesn't contain an advertisement of theirs announcing a sale of slaves.'

Hubertus shook with a low chuckle. 'Yes. "Prime Gold Coast negroes." Or "a parcel of choice Angola slaves just received". I read their advertisements with great care. I do business with MacInroy, Sandbach.'

Outside, the trees were growing dark-green with dusk, and a cicada shrieked at intervals in the hot October air. The scent of starved grass and dry-weather earth drifted through the portico on a breeze from the north-east. . . . How many more dry-seasons will I see? Perhaps Bentley is asking himself the same question. . . . Two old planters complacently talking of times past and time present. The future we dare not speculate about too loudly. For old men there is no future. . . . He tilted his head and sat forward, lowering his pipe. . . . Bentley gave him a look of enquiry.

'Heard it, Bentley?'

'What's that?'

'Listen! A goatsucker. Such a long time I haven't heard one.'

. . . hoo-yoo!

They listened, and it came again. Far away amidst the trees. Hoo-yoo!

3

' . . . YES, seventy, Overgaar. Tomorrow. On the Essequibo, in the year 1727, my mother gave birth to me. She was not a good woman – but I've told you all about that before.'

'Never mind, Mynheer. You yourself are a good man. No one can ever dispute that.'

'How old are you exactly, Overgaar?'

'Seventy-four in November, Mynheer, and because of your great kindness in providing for me, a contented and happy old man. It is not every old man who can claim to be both contented and happy.'

'I agree. Myself, for instance. Contented but not happy.'

'Why would you say you are not happy, Mynheer?'

'The companionship of a woman, Overgaar — it is a lack that, for me, nothing can compensate.'

For a long interval they sat in silence, smoking and listening to the occasional thump of drums. A breeze came through the dusk, and a branch of the mango tree that stood near the cottage brushed the eaves, making a sound between a whisper and a sigh.

Letters, delivered by the new post-office, arrived from Cranley, and from Jacqueline and her family, from Gert Lieker, and from Wilfred and family in Berbice. From Susan in Antigua. And from Raphael and Mary on the West Coast. Ten pounds of his favourite tobacco were sent by John and Clara.

Luise and Edward came in person to congratulate him. They spent the whole day with him. Edward, who had brought as a birthday gift a landscape in oils, already framed, spent over an hour having it hung in the drawing room. It depicted the mill at Good Heart.

'I spent a week up there on purpose to do it,' he said. 'It's exactly as it was. They haven't troubled a brick.'

'So I see, my boy. Only . . . ' Hubertus brushed quickly at his eyes. 'Only I don't recognise those bushes . . . those vines. . . . '

Edward said nothing.

Hubertus began to chuckle — quietly to himself. Suddenly he glanced at Luise. 'You see how gloomy your old father has become since you left him, Luise?'

'Since I left you? Then there has been a time when you were *not* gloomy, Father?'

He shook. 'Just as arch! Just as impudent!' He stopped laughing abruptly. 'I've bequeathed Kaywana to you and Edward, my girl, but you mustn't consider yourselves obliged

311

to come back here. Dispose of it if you wish – or get Raphael to come and run it. Don't be governed by sentiment. Don't think of me. This place means little to me. My heart was left up there. Up-river.'

'We won't discuss that now,' said Luise. 'I'm sure you're going to live to ninety. I'll probably die and leave you.'

'I look as if I'll live to ninety, don't I?' He began to shake again. He nodded. 'I think I will, too. My body is in fine condition. Yet . . . ' He wagged his head.

'Yet what?'

'My spirit, Luise. Always provided that my spirit suffers no major shock, I think I could live to a hundred. My spirit is so vulnerable. . . . '

. . . so vulnerable. . . .

' . . . just what I was telling Miss Luise some time ago. It was on my seventieth birthday, I remember. Three years ago.'

'But Mynheer, why should you worry over such an event? You are by no means singular. Indeed, you should be proud of yourself,' smiled Overgaar.

Hubertus nodded, rubbing slowly at his beard. Stroking and pulling. 'Proud – ummm. Yes, I ought to be proud, Overgaar. At seventy-three it is very flattering. And as you rightly say, I am not the only planter who has brought a mulatto bastard into the world. Yet – well, as I told Miss Luise on the occasion of my seventieth birthday, my spirit is vulnerable. Yes, vulnerable. I'm not any planter, Overgaar. I happen to be myself. I have my own code.' He stirred in his chair, breathing heavily. 'It is not merely a matter of conscience. I don't feel I have done anything morally wrong. Don't mistake me. The longer I live the greater a contempt I acquire for the morals men have created. Men are fools, Overgaar, who deliberately destroy their own happiness by encasing themselves in the rigid cell of their morality. Their asinine consciences turn everything pleasurable into sin. I am in no way ashamed of this child Sarah has brought into the world. I see it as no sin, Overgaar, though the church would deem it that, I know. Why should God frown upon the birth of a child? It is a natural act, cohabiting with a woman. A child is the natural result of such an act. No, don't mistake me, Overgaar. What troubles me is not the moral or ecclesias-

312

tical aspect of the matter – but myself. My own personal code. My spirit is vulnerable in that it is wounded when my personal code – the special, particular philosophy I have shaped for myself – seems to me to have been contravened.

'A strict principle of mine is that I must not cause unhappiness to others. And this child – this little girl who has just come into the world – may be unhappy because of me. Because of my fleshly indulgence. She will grow up in a hostile world – a world that will sniff at her and call her bastard. It is not comforting to me, Overgaar, to know that such a future lies ahead for the little creature. That is what depresses me. That is what brings me closer to the grave. Every time I contravene my personal code some part of me crumbles and Death takes two paces toward me.'

They listened to the crickets cheeping. Tonight there were tree-frogs, too, for it was very wet. Now and then the croak of a bullfrog came dismally from the canal beyond the mango trees in the west. . . . Overgaar looked grey in the lamplight. Wrinkled, lost in a trance of senility. Like the century, he had not much longer to go. . . . He was mumbling something.

'What's that, Overgaar?'

Overgaar started. 'No, I was saying, Mynheer. You should not worry. You should be proud. Proud. You will give them their freedom?'

'Yes. I have already applied for manumission papers.'

Overgaar uttered an old-man groan, nodding over and over. He started again and said: 'A good man, Mynheer. A good man. You will provide for them as you did for me. Ummmm. I have no fear for them.'

The bull-frog. . . . A damp drift of air moved through the room. . . .

. . . so vulnerable.

4

'You won't die in a hurry, Mynheer. The same thing I keep telling Mynheer Overgaar, too,' laughed Groud. 'Every day he thinks is his last, but the next day comes and he is still with us. Look what you've lived to see! Haw, haw! Isn't it comical,

313

Mynheers! Who would have thought that we would find ourselves under the Batavian Republic again! But there it is. I heard it on good authority in Stabroek today. This treaty was signed in March at Amiens, and England has agreed to return all the colonies taken from the Batavian Republic during the war. . . . '

Yes, Groud still kept their spirits up. In December of that same year, 1802, he told them: 'Mynheer Antony Meertens is our new governor. He arrived yesterday. The Orange Party detest him as much as the English gentlemen. And the biggest piece of news that will amuse you, gentlemen, is this: Our first lady of the land is a mulatto.'

'A mulatto?' Overgaar started out of his trance.

Hubertus frowned, then nodded. 'Yes, of course I had forgotten. Meertens did marry a coloured woman.'

'The English ladies won't like it, Mynheers. They won't like it one little whit. The Governor's wife a mulatto! It is unheard of!'

Hubertus shifted in his chair. . . . One never knew. She may make a good marriage. Sarah would be a hindrance, of course. I must see that they are well provided for after my death. . . The least I can do. . . .

' . . . but why should we worry, Mynheers! Next week I may have to report that we are in the hands of the French. Or it may be the Spanish, for a change. . . . '

It was not quite as early as the following week, however, but on the evening of the seventh of September, the next year, 1803, that Groud informed them that a squadron of English ships of war were in the river.

'It is comic, Mynheers! Comic! I am beginning to lose count of the number of times we have changed government – and nationality.'

The two old men nodded – and groaned. Overgaar's chin rested on his chest. Hubertus stared at the floor over a pipe that had gone out.

'Mynheers, did you hear what I said? Tomorrow we shall be English again. The Council of Policy is in session, considering the terms of capitulation submitted by Admiral Hood.'

There was a knock on the door. The two older men raised their heads. Groud opened the door.

The slave had come from the house.

'Massa Hubertus, message just come from Rylands. Mister Graeme send to say that his father, Mister Cranley, dead midday today.'

The premonition had lurked with him for the whole fortnight after receiving that message, and now that he saw Graeme coming up the steps to the portico he felt that it had been no mere fancy of his. . . . *What it is I fear I don't know, but I am afraid nevertheless. . . . At thirty-six, he has my air of calm – the calm I had at thirty-six.*

'Sit down, my boy. Sit down. I received your message yesterday – about your coming this morning. It is no inconvenience. I am delighted to see you. Have been expecting you to call since the news about your father's death. Cranley would have wanted you to come.'

Too voluble. He must see that I am not myself. . . .

'Yes, I told him I would come and see you. He died very peacefully, sir.' Graeme seated himself, shook his head to the slave who had appeared.

'Not even some coffee, my boy? You must have something.'

'No thank you, Cousin Hubertus. Nothing whatever. I had some wine before setting out.'

'Stabroek still in a ferment, I suppose?'

'Conditions are rather upset at the moment, yes. But the general feeling is one of relief. I do hope the English are here to stay this time.'

He seems as uneasy as I, poor lad. . . .

There came upon them a silence. The sun made tiny diamonds on the floor. . . . Edward's lattice-work. . . . They could hear the factory. . . .

Hubertus shifted. 'Have you secured someone to manage Rylands for you, my boy?'

'Yes, Michael Rolfson.'

'Why, of course! I never thought of him. Mathilde's husband. I heard she was married. Any children?'

'A daughter – last year. Very pretty little thing.'

'Excellent! They must come and see me one day.'

'They're coming to Stabroek next month. I'm sure they'll be delighted to pay you a visit.'

315

Silence again. . . . Smell of mangoes in the air. . . . Edward's Willem that morning throwing stones into the mango trees. Incredible to think of Willem a grown-up young man. Came to see me last week. . . .

'Have you seen Luise and Edward recently?'

'Not for some time. I see Willem now and then. He comes to Stabroek to buy supplies for the plantation.'

'Business flourishing – I hear you've gone into partnership with John. Very wise of you.'

'Yes. The new building is being erected. Edward designed it.'

'He did? And doesn't he superintend the building himself?'

'The plantation keeps him too busy. He has promised to come in a week or two. The builder in charge is a reliable fellow.'

'Hartfield and Clarkson. Ummm. Sounds quite respectable.'

Graeme smiled – and fidgeted. Flushed a trifle.

'You're looking very hale, my boy.'

'Yes. I feel hale.' He frowned. Smiled and asked: 'And you? Are you perfectly fit?'

'Fairly, Graeme. I won't say perfectly. A little dizziness now and then. But that is to be expected at my age.'

'Certainly. You shouldn't exert yourself too much.'

'I try not to – but I do.'

Silence again. . . . I wonder if Cranley told him anything. . . .

'Cousin Hubertus?'

'Yes, my boy?' . . . It is coming now.

'Before Father died I was able to exchange a few words with him.' He was staring at the floor, his hands clasped together tight in his lap.

Hubertus waited.

'I'm sure you must have heard the rumours that have circulated about – about my parentage.'

'Rumours?'

'Yes. I – this is extremely embarrassing, I know, but I thought I ought to have it settled for once and all.'

'What is that, Graeme my boy?'

He frowned, then said: 'I asked Father, but he tried – he seemed to think it foolish of me. He more or less evaded my question and left me just where I was before. It – it really is so upsetting.'

316

The premonition had not been false. . . . A dizziness. . . . He put a hand to his head. . . .

'I thought – are you unwell, Cousin Hubertus?'

'No, no. Just a slight dizziness, my boy. Comes on at the oddest moments.' He tried to chuckle. 'Old age, Graeme. Old age. You were saying something about your father evading a question.'

'Yes. You must have heard it said that I was your son and not – you know what I mean!' He was very red in the face – almost angry. 'I can't stand the uncertainty any longer, Cousin Hubertus. These whispers everywhere, I've never had the courage to ask Mother outright. I regret now that I didn't ask her. And Father was so vague I can't be sure if it was merely his illness or – or his deliberate intention to leave me in doubt. I can only – I had to come to you as a last resort. If you don't tell me, then I shall have to remain in doubt for the rest of my life – but it's not a pleasant prospect, I can assure you. It's been weighing on my mind for years, this thing. I want to get married, but somehow I keep postponing it until I discover the truth.'

The factory . . . a soothingly monotonous sound. . . .

'Rumours, Graeme. This is a colony of rumours, my boy. Let me put your mind at rest forever. You are Cranley's son.'

The factory. . . . Mangoes in the air. . . .

'You say this – you say this in all honesty, sir?'

. . . and the smell of cane-juice. . . . What is integrity? . . . Honesty?

'Yes, Graeme. In all honesty.'

'Thank you. Cousin Hubertus. Thank you.' His voice was a whisper.

. . . the final harrowing. . . .

'I shall always be grateful to you for this.'

' . . . I cannot see why you should be so worried, Mynheer. It was for his good. You have made him happy.'

'I argue that way, too, but it is no use, Overgaar. My integrity is gone. To me that is important. According to my own code – my own code – I have done something shameful. I have evaded the truth. I have made him happy on a falsehood.'

317

'A falsehood that was necessary. All lies are not wicked, Mynheer.'

'I know that. But, in my way of seeing it, this lie was wicked. It was a betrayal of his mother. . . . ' He glanced up. 'It's raining.'

They sat still, listening to the rain on the roof. Early November rain.

'All these weeks,' murmured Overgaar, breaking the silence. 'Worrying yourself over this matter. It is affecting your health, Mynheer.'

Hope it will last all night. Soothing. My kind of weather. Not very likely, though. November. If it had been December, perhaps . . . two days before Christmas, 1766. . . . 'You are very wet. You must have been a long time in the rain. . . . '

'Mynheer, is something – ?'

'My head. A little dizzy. I thought . . . '

. . . no sound of rain. Uncertain month, November. Isn't that the factory? . . . Sunshine coming in at a window. . . .

'Overgaar?'

'Would you like me to send for him, Cousin Hubertus?'

'Edward? You . . . '

'Yes. Luise and I – we came yesterday.'

'I . . . a little dizziness at Overgaar's cottage. Where is he?'

'Jackie, go and bring Overgaar. At once.'

'Luise?'

'Yes, Father.'

'I'm glad, my girl. Glad you're here. My hand – hold it.'

Soothing sound, the factory. Designed by Edward. Superior to the old mill at Good Heart. . . . Cloud going over the sun. . . .

'Edward.'

'Yes, Cousin Hubertus?'

'What I spoke to you about – some time ago. That girl Sarah – and the child – you'll see they don't want for anything.'

'Certainly.'

'Good. Can depend upon you – and Luise. Good children.'

'Mynheer.'

'Overgaar. Good. Glad you're here. Forestalled you.'

'Yes, Mynheer.'

318

'I'm not laughing at you. At myself. Your liver – I've beaten it. Going before you.'

Sunshine. Bothers my eyes a good deal . . . wish I could see Overgaar.

'Edward.'

'Yes?'

'Any questions to ask me? Profound questions?'

Silence. . . .

'Ask me anything you wish. I can be honest now.'

A sniffling. Overgaar. Poor old man. Dejected because I've won the race.

'Now I *am* laughing at you, Overgaar.'

'Cousin Hubertus?'

Sunshine. Keeps bothering my eyes. I must answer Edward. . . . It must be a question. He wants to ask me something profound. . . .

'Yes, Edward?'

'A question – just curiosity, but as you want me to ask you . . . do you still believe in God?'

God? . . . He was asking about God. . . . This sunshine. Leaves, too . . . brush them away . . . I must surmount them. To the end I must struggle.

'God?'

'Yes. A Supreme Being – do you believe. . . ?'

'God. A Supreme Being. . . . Yes. Yes, Edward – I believe – have always believed – in myself.'

NEL BESTSELLERS

Crime

T012 484	FIVE RED HERRINGS	*Dorothy L. Sayers*	40p
T015 556	MURDER MUST ADVERTISE	*Dorothy L. Sayers*	40p
T014 398	STRIDING FOLLY	*Dorothy L. Sayers*	30p

Fiction

T015 386	THE NORTHERN LIGHT	*A. J. Cronin*	50p
T016 544	THE CITADEL	*A. J. Cronin*	75p
T015 130	THE MONEY MAKER	*John J. McNamara Jr.*	50p
T013 820	THE DREAM MERCHANTS	*Harold Robbins*	75p
T018 105	THE CARPETBAGGERS	*Harold Robbins*	95p
T016 560	WHERE LOVE HAS GONE	*Harold Robbins*	75p
T013 707	THE ADVENTURERS	*Harold Robbins*	80p
T006 743	THE INHERITORS	*Harold Robbins*	60p
T009 467	STILETTO	*Harold Robbins*	30p
T015 289	NEVER LEAVE ME	*Harold Robbins*	40p
T016 579	NEVER LOVE A STRANGER	*Harold Robbins*	75p
T011 798	A STONE FOR DANNY FISHER	*Harold Robbins*	60p
T015 874	79 PARK AVENUE	*Harold Robbins*	60p
T011 461	THE BETSY	*Harold Robbins*	75p
T013 340	SUMMER OF THE RED WOLF	*Morris West*	50p

Historical

T013 758	THE LADY FOR RANSOM	*Alfred Duggan*	40p
T015 297	COUNT BOHEMOND	*Alfred Duggan*	50p
T010 279	MASK OF APOLLO	*Mary Renault*	50p
T014 045	TREASURE OF PLEASANT VALLEY	*Frank Yerby*	35p
T015 602	GILLIAN	*Frank Yerby*	50p

Science Fiction

T015 017	EQUATOR	*Brian Aldiss*	30p
T014 347	SPACE RANGER	*Isaac Asimov*	30p
T015 491	PIRATES OF THE ASTEROIDS	*Isaac Asimov*	30p
T016 331	THE CHESSMEN OF MARS	*Edgar Rice Burroughs*	40p
T013 537	WIZARD OF VENUS	*Edgar Rice Burroughs*	30p
T009 696	GLORY ROAD	*Robert Heinlein*	40p
T016 900	STRANGER IN A STRANGE LAND	*Robert Heinlein*	75p
T011 844	DUNE	*Frank Herbert*	75p
T012 298	DUNE MESSIAH	*Frank Herbert*	40p
T015 211	THE GREEN BRAIN	*Frank Herbert*	30p

War

T013 367	DEVIL'S GUARD	*Robert Elford*	50p
T015 505	THE LAST VOYAGE OF GRAF SPEE	*Michael Powell*	30p
T015 661	JACKALS OF THE REICH	*Ronald Seth*	30p
T012 263	FLEET WITHOUT A FRIEND	*John Vader*	30p

Western

T016 994	No. 1 EDGE – THE LONER	*George G. Gilman*	30p
T016 536	No. 5 EDGE – BLOOD ON SILVER	*George G. Gilman*	30p
T017 621	No. 6 EDGE – THE BLUE, THE GREY AND THE RED		
		George G. Gilman	30p
T014 479	No. 7 EDGE – CALIFORNIA KILLING	*George G. Gilman*	30p
T015 254	No. 8 EDGE – SEVEN OUT OF HELL	*George G. Gilman*	30p
T015 475	No. 9 EDGE – BLOODY SUMMER	*George G. Gilman*	30p

General

T011 763	SEX MANNERS FOR MEN	*Robert Chartham*	30p
W002 531	SEX MANNERS FOR ADVANCED LOVERS	*Robert Chartham*	25p
W002 835	SEX AND THE OVER FORTIES	*Robert Chartham*	30p
T010 732	THE SENSUOUS COUPLE	*Dr. 'C'*	25p

NEL P.O. BOX 11, FALMOUTH, TR10 9EN, CORNWALL
  Please send cheque or postal order. Allow 10p to cover postage and packing on one book plus 4p for each additional book.

Name ....

Address..

....

Title ....
(SEPTEMBER)

116 01